Burn the Diaries and *Run*

Burn the Diaries and *Run*

KATE FLORA

Encircle Publications
Farmington, Maine, U.S.A.

Encircle editor: Cynthia Brackett-Vincent

Cover design by Deirdre Wait
Cover photographs © Shutterstock

Published by:

Encircle Publications, LLC
PO Box 187
Farmington, ME 04938

info@encirclepub.com
http://encirclepub.com

THE GOVERNOR'S OFFICE

ALBANY, NEW YORK

The aide, who looked like a blond Michael J. Fox, barely stopped to knock before barging into the room, papers fluttering in his agitated hand. Governor Lucius Alfonso, who was a stickler for protocol, glared over the tops of his half-glasses. His campaign manager, Michael O'Malley, was less restrained. "This isn't a college dormitory, Dobbs. You can't barge in here whenever you get a neat idea. We're not mommy and daddy, who think everything you do is cute." He leaned back in his chair, tented his thick fingers over a barrel chest, and smiled maliciously. "So, to what do we owe this interruption?" O'Malley was pale skinned and rusty-haired, with a pugnacious jaw and spirit.

Kevin Dobbs hesitated, his face mottled pink with embarrassment. He'd been so eager to deliver this stunning news that he'd forgotten to bring copies. Now he didn't know whether to hand the papers to his boss or to the Governor. O'Malley settled the question by holding out an impatient hand. "Come on, Dobbs. Shit or get off the pot, eh?"

Dobbs gave up the papers and stepped backward, but he didn't leave the room. He waited while O'Malley scanned the papers, dancing slightly from foot to foot. O'Malley's language had deepened the flush on his skin.

O'Malley finished the letter, smiled triumphantly, and passed it to the Governor. It was written in pencil on white lined paper. Primitive, illiterate, and potentially dynamite. The Governor read it and smiled broadly. "Interruption forgiven, Dobbs," he said. "Sometimes I think the good guy is on our side. Where did you get this?"

"From one of the volunteers at campaign headquarters who was handling mail."

"Do you have his name?" O'Malley interrupted.

"Her name, sir. Of course."

"Who else has seen it?"

"Only two other people, sir. She took it to her supervisor, who brought it to Viktor. Viktor told me I'd better bring it to you right away."

"Viktor was right, Dobbs. Did you read it?"

Dobbs nodded.

"You have the envelope?"

"The envelope?" Dobbs looked blank.

"Envelope," O'Malley said sharply. "Those things letters come in? With the address and the postmark and maybe a return address?"

The Governor, ignoring this exchange, was rereading the letter.

Dobbs swayed on his feet like he was dodging a blow. "Sorry, sir. I never thought…"

"Gotta start thinking, Dobbs, you wanna get anywhere in this business. Where'd you go to law school, anyway? Manatee State? Thought you were one of those Harvard boys, supposed to be so bright?"

"Oh, leave the boy alone, Mike. He'll go back and search through the trash until he finds it. In fact, Kevin, maybe you should do that right now, before someone dumps their coffee or the dregs of a salad?" He waved the letter at Dobbs. "Better take a copy of this so you can spot the handwriting… we don't want to take a chance on losing it, do we?"

Dobbs wanted to stay and be part of the excitement but he hadn't gone to Manatee State and was smart enough to know he'd worn out his welcome. He ducked his head and left. As soon as his curious ears were out of range, O'Malley picked up the phone and called Viktor and Captain Van Allen, the Governor's state police liaison. Then the candidate and his campaign manager exchanged smiles. "So," the Governor said, "looks like Senator Jim Lily White Buxton has a skeleton in his closet after all. Now all we have to do is find this woman."

O'Malley reread the letter.

> Dear Governor Alfonso,
>   I am very pleased that you are run for President.
> Years ago I werked for that Jim Buxton and he was not
> a nice man. He didn't paid me fare wages or anything
> akshully it was his wife who didn't want to pay and I was
> cleaning there house which was a real mess because she

was pig and so were there kids. She is if you will excuse
me for saying this a bitch with a capitol Bee. I wud not
like a woman like that for being the first lady of this grate
country of ours.

To get to the point of my letter. Back when that Jim
Buxton was the torney general up here in Maine, there
was a woman werked for him that he was having an
affair with even though he was married. I know this from
my sister who lived in the same place and she would see
them going to this guy's trailer who was a cop who werked
for Buxton. They wud stay there for a couple hours and
then come out and drive away. I don't think that they
were only working or maybe playing cards because my
sister said she went over and listend and the bed was
squeaking. I guess on acount of there having a good time.
I am telling you this not to get the woman in trubble
because she is a good woman and does a lot of good stuf
for poor people like me, but I can't stand that Buxton is
talking about family values and how we have to werk
on stronger families when he is like a pot calling a kettle
black, isn't he? Plus I'm sick of supporting those people on
welfare when I am agood werking woman myself. And I
don't hold with cheating. If my husband cheated I wud
shoot him.

Next time when you guys do a debate, ask that Jim
Buxton what about this woman and see what he says.
And good luck. I'm going to vote for you.

—Anonymus

The Governor laughed. "Our correspondent isn't the brightest bulb, is she?"

"Her heart's in the right place, though."

By the end of the afternoon, Kevin Dobbs and a couple of New York state police detectives were on their way to Maine, assigned to dig up all the dirt they could on Senator Jim Buxton. On penalty of death, or at least dishonor, they were not to return until they'd learned the identity of Buxton's mystery woman.

THE RESIDENCE OF
SENATOR JAMES BUXTON

WASHINGTON, D.C.

The balding man with the red suspenders continued his stalking pace around the room, stopping by the table to nibble some grapes, to grab a piece of cheese, to throw ice in a glass and pour some diet soda. Grazing like a nervous animal, his movements quick and sharp. The suit pants, belted below a burgeoning paunch, spoke of too many trips to the food table and not enough diet drinks, but the fabric had the soft drape of cashmere and the pinstripe was faint as old memory.

"All right." He tilted the glass and drained it. "This campaign is for real now, Senator. You want it. We want it. The primary voters say they want it. So I've gotta know what's going to come along and bite me in the ass, okay?" He slammed his glass down for emphasis.

He had a high, domed forehead, shiny in the overhead light, fair, receding hair, small, greedy eyes, and a loose, rubbery mouth. Not an attractive man but, despite his reputation as a user and abuser of female companions, women found his aura of power and control appealing. "I don't like surprises," he said. "Everyone has things to be embarrassed about. We know they're coming, we can have a strategy. We don't know they're coming, we're up shit creek. Getting sandbagged by the press or some loose-lipped bimbo isn't my idea of a good time, so take a breath, look deep into your personal closet, and let's have all of those skeletons out where I can take a hard look."

He turned his back on the handsome man on the sofa and stared into the fire. His stance, splayed feet and hands clasped behind his back, suggested a stint in the military.

The Senator frowned. "Come on, Frank. I already told you. I've been married to the same woman for thirty years. I've never screwed a senate page, male or female. Never made an improper advance toward a member of my staff. I don't take bribes. Collect child pornography. Beat my wife or kids. Wear women's underwear. I've never drowned a staffer, fucked a stewardess, or admired a lobbyist's boobs out loud. Never asked some big-haired honey manning a conference table to kiss my dick or give me a blow job."

"Drugs or alcohol?"

"Alcohol in moderation. No drugs."

From the doorway came the slow, mocking sound of clapping hands. The senator's wife went directly to the bar and poured herself a generous scotch. She was a handsome, stocky woman in a soft green suit. Her hair was well-cut, well-colored and well styled, her jewelry classic, understated, and real. She sat down in an off-white chair across from the Senator and lit a cigarette. "Go on with your litany of non-sins, Jim," she said. "Don't let me stop you."

The man at the fireplace turned. "Oh, Margaret. Glad you could join us. I thought you were off cutting ribbons somewhere."

"Hoped I was, you mean."

He gave her a bland smile. "I was just asking about—"

"Peccadilloes, scandals, and skeletons in the family closet. Bimbos, bribes, and bloopers. I heard. Sounds like Jim's a candidate for sainthood, doesn't it?"

The Senator twitched impatiently. "Maggie, please. We're trying to work."

She drained off a numbing portion of Scotch. "And I'm trying to help, dear. Did you tell Frank about your meeting with the Chinese businessmen, after which that envelope full of cash mysteriously appeared in your desk? What about when that S&L guy flew us all to Hawaii on a private plane, and later he didn't get indicted?" She arched her eyebrows coyly and batted her eyelashes. "Frank is looking very confused."

Then her face grew hard. "I don't give a damn about the money stuff," she said. "This is Washington. Everybody does it. No politician would have a pot to piss in if he followed the rules. I just want to know, like Frank does, whether any extra-marital affairs are going to crop up while we're preaching about family values, the virtue of old fashioned ethics, and the revival of personal responsibility to a nation reveling in its victimhood. I want to know…"

She shoved the cigarette between her lips, sucked until the tip glowed scarlet, and then stubbed it out in an ashtray. "I want to know if I'm going to have to start wearing pink suits and dowdy hats and stare up at you adoringly when you speak. If we're going to have to exchange passionate kisses on national television. I want to know if some fuckin' bimbo is going to come crawling out of the woodwork and start describing your dick or your ass or your precious Marine corps tattoo on the national news." She finished her drink and poured herself another.

"You ought to go easy on that stuff, Maggie," her husband said. "You know you're an unpleasant drunk."

"I'm unpleasant sober," she said. "I'm an unhappy, vindictive woman who has realized, too late, she should have had a career of her own; who has sacrificed a large measure of personal freedom to support her husband's ambitions. Whose ambitious husband is now running for President, and who will, if he wins, be condemned to four years of smiling and nodding and worrying about what to wear. Of press scrutiny and disapproval. Much to my chagrin, Jim, I'm not willing to come this far and not go for the gold. I want to be First Lady. It's a lot better than being Mrs. Senator Buxton. A whole lot better."

She tasted her drink, made a face, and set it down with a thump. Amber liquid splashed onto the polished wood.

The Senator grimaced.

"Not that you've ever asked, but what I'd really like," she said, some of the hardness and sarcasm draining from her voice, "is to return to Maine and open a little antique shop. Hire someone to work a few days a week so I could scout around at yard sales and auctions, poke through little towns and dusty shops and talk to people who do something real for a living. Buy submarine sandwiches teeming with oil and onions at small grocery stores. I want to sit in people's kitchens and listen to gossip. Who is screwing who… and believe me, Frank," she had caught the campaign manager's twitch. "…none of those people say whom."

The Senator grabbed a napkin and wiped up his wife's spill. "Can you think of anything else I should tell Frank? Are there any skeletons in your closet?"

"My closet is full of proper suits cleverly cut to give me a waist, innocuous blouses that cover my flabby upper arms and soften the wattles in my neck, garden party hats like the Queen Mum, and the dust of crumbled expectations. As for affairs, it's been so long since I've raised a cock... any cock... even yours, I'm not sure I'd recognize one."

"Maggie, that's not fair. You chose..."

She seemed about to say something, then cast a wary glance at Frank, and grabbed her Camels instead. She stuck another cigarette in her mouth and fumbled with the lighter. Her husband took it from her and lit the cigarette. "Thanks," she said. "It's probably not going to come up, since the press tends to go for fresh meat and not beef jerky, but what about that girl who used to work in your office. Back when you were Attorney General? That starry-eyed brunette? What was her name? Lana? Lily?"

The Senator didn't have to look to know this had piqued Frank's interest. He could feel the man's eyes. Frank had pale, prying eyes the eerie blue of a Husky. He always felt like they saw too much. If he hadn't needed the man, he wouldn't have Frank around. All his other people were loyal and committed to the campaign. Frank was a hired gun who took his cool head and Machiavellian soul wherever the pay was best and the exposure would do him the most good, wherever his keen nose scented success. But Frank was the best. Frank could deliver a crippling blow without leaving a mark and charm birds out of trees. Frank was a chameleon. The Senator tried to remember that meant he belonged to the reptile family.

"So, Jim," Frank asked, tired of the silence, "was there such a girl? And is there anything there to embarrass us?"

What do you mean, us? The Senator shook his head. "Nothing there, Frank. She worked for me. She had a little crush. She was a bright little thing. Dedicated. Idealistic. Workaholic. Everything you could ask for in an employee. But that's all she was. An employee."

"Maybe that's all she was to you, Jim," his wife said, "but you were a hell of a lot more to her. When you were around, she lit up. I've never been blind, however much you might have wished it."

"Jim?" Frank's eyebrows were up. He leaned forward like a pointer, the hand at his waist curled like a paw, as he waited for a response.

The Senator shook his head. "Lila," he said. "Lila Friedman. She was a hell of an attorney. I know there was talk at the time. We worked together. She was young and pretty. She was also one of the smartest and most uncomplicated women I've ever met. She wanted to practice law to help people. As far as I know, she still does. I admired her, liked working with her. I never slept with her."

He walked across the room and put some ice in a glass. He needed to face away from those two vultures for a minute. To shut his mind against the memories. God forgive him for such a lie. He'd never loved a woman the way he'd loved Lila. He slowly poured bourbon over the crackling ice, then returned to his seat.

His wife stifled a yawn, blinking as if being tired surprised her. "I give up," she said. "Fascinating as this discussion is, I can't keep my eyes open. I'm going to bed. Good night, Frank. Good luck cleaning the closets." Her walk was more than a little unsteady.

Frank shut the door behind her and leaned against it. "She's got to get that drinking under control, Jim, or she'll be a real liability."

"She'll be fine," the Senator assured him. "Maggie's a pro. She only lets herself do this when she knows it's perfectly safe. She wasn't joking when she said she wants this."

Frank nodded. "Well, you know her and I don't, so I'll take your word for it." He grazed the food table again, shoving a fruit tart into his mouth, following it with a brownie, before coming back to the couch. An aide came in, handed him a sheaf of papers, and retreated. He scanned them and handed a sheet to the Senator. "Plane leaves at five a.m. I'll have the car here by four." He sat down across from his candidate and crossed his legs. "Tell me about your affair with this Lila woman."

"I didn't have an affair with—"

"Save your denials for the press. You caress her name when you say it. You savor it like expensive caviar."

"Bull. It was over twenty years ago, Frank."

"You were a married man, Jim. Who knew about it?"

The Senator shrugged. "I didn't think anybody knew. We were very discreet."

"What does that mean? You didn't screw her on your office floor during working hours, or you only went to motels out-of-state run by blind men who spoke no English?"

"I never screwed Lila Friedman anywhere. I made love to her a few times at her apartment and in Kenny Bass's trailer."

"She had neighbors?"

The Senator nodded.

"Who weren't blind?"

Another nod.

"So someone probably saw you. You said there were rumors?"

He didn't want to talk about this. He'd always kept Lila separate in his mind from the world of politics. He loved the life, the power and glory, the chance to make big things happen, but she belonged in some sweet, sacred, innocent place where his professional life couldn't intrude. Lila Friedman had possessed a special quality that even after two decades could lift his spirits. "I wanted to marry Lila. I was going to leave Maggie. Then Senator Fuller died. The party tapped me to fill the slot. I chose ambition over love. She married someone else, had a family. She's made a good life, I hear. I haven't seen her since I left Maine."

"And if the press gets wind of this and asks you about it, what are you going to say?"

"Whatever you and my press secretary advise me to say. I will deny her three times before the cock crows, even without thirty pieces of silver, or I will admit to a brief mistake during a troubled time in my marriage. Whatever you want. I would prefer, however, that nothing hurt Lila, if that's possible."

"Deep as first love, and wild with all regret."
—Tennyson, "The Princess"

CHAPTER ONE

She'd been driving too long. After fourteen hours on the road, her eyes ached from staring into the tunnel of the headlights, trying to see the lines through the downpour. She viewed the luminous needles of rain through a haze the defroster couldn't dispel. The heat and the rhythmic *thunk* of the wipers were lulling her to sleep. Out on the rim of exhaustion, she felt dense and slow. Disconnected. The car might have been a rocket, hurtling through space, for all the contact she felt with earth and other people.

The sudden sharp blast of a car horn startled her awake. She jerked the car back into her lane, the sharp prick of adrenaline sending her heart racing as her face flushed an embarrassed red there was no one to see. Time to pull over and rest her eyes. Jenny flipped on her signal and eased off the road. As she braked to a stop, she heard her father's cautions about wet brakes. Were those parental voices there forever?

She jammed the car into park and closed her stinging eyes, jumping as a gust of wind slapped a sudden burst of cold March rain against the car. Jenny squeezed her eyes tighter, shutting out the angry menace of the night. The drive was almost over. She was almost home. Home floated on the horizon of her mind, bright and warm and welcoming, like a beacon to guide her in. Why did her body fail her now?

As soon as she closed her eyes, the image she was fleeing came rushing back. Over the past twenty-four hours, she'd watched this ugly scene repeatedly, wishing the mind had a delete button, the capacity to blot out things she didn't want to remember. But her mind was fixed on the image of her boyfriend Drew in their bed with her best friend.

She should have suspected something when she said she had to do research for the paper she wanted to write over vacation and Drew hadn't complained. In Drew's world, Friday night was party night, no matter how much work was waiting, but he hadn't objected. He'd been understanding. He'd watch a movie with his friend Ahmed and when she returned at ten, they'd go out for a drink to enjoy their last night before she left for vacation. What had she read somewhere? When something seems too obvious, it bears examination. She'd had hours on the road to examine it.

In the library, she'd just written down her title when the fire alarm went off. A librarian, moving through the stacks, said, "Better take your stuff. It's a bomb scare. There's no telling when they'll reopen." Everyone waited on the steps, their breaths forming steamy clouds in the crisp March air, until an official announced the library wouldn't reopen until morning. She'd slung her pack over her shoulder and gone home.

The car in front of their apartment was her friend Betty's. Betty often hung around and watched movies. Betty still lived in a dorm and had the world's worst roommate—the messy kind with stinky feet who ate potato chips at three a.m. and hummed while she worked—so Betty spent as little time there as possible. *The more the merrier,* Jenny thought. Drew liked a crowd.

She let herself in the back door, catching it so it wouldn't slam and annoy the fussies upstairs, dropped her pack on the counter, and grabbed a beer from the fridge. She didn't bother with a light. Here the dark felt warm and cozy. The room still smelled of the stir-fried onions and peppers she'd made for dinner, the dishes still in the sink. She resisted the temptation to clean up. That was Drew's job, though training him to do his share gave her at least as much training in patience as he got in sharing responsibility.

She flipped off the cap and carried her beer into the living room. The lights and TV were on, but the room was empty. Maybe they'd gone somewhere in Ahmed's car. She hoped they wouldn't be long. The bomb scare felt like a reprieve, giving her more time with Drew before she headed home. She picked up the remote and looked for something to watch.

Somewhere in the building, a giggle. It couldn't be the people upstairs. They were the most humorless couple she'd ever encountered. She turned down the sound and listened. It was somewhere in the apartment. She checked the tiny second bedroom they used as a study. Sometimes Drew and Ahmed played video games on the computer. The room was empty.

She heard a thumping noise, like bed knocking against the wall, accompanied by a woman's voice. "Yes, yes, yes, oh yes." She'd never heard Betty in the throes of lovemaking, but that was Betty's voice. Maybe Drew thought he was being kind, lending their bed to Betty and Ahmed, but Jenny didn't like it. Their bed was private. He probably hadn't even changed the sheets.

It was only eight-thirty and they weren't expecting her until ten. She could make a quick trip to the drugstore and they'd never even know she'd been here. She went to the kitchen and unzipped her pack to get her wallet.

She heard footsteps behind her, and the two of them, stark naked, came dashing into the kitchen. She backed into the corner where it was darkest. Ahmed went straight to the refrigerator. When the light spilled out, the man illuminated was Drew.

Her pain was as sudden and sharp as a punch. The keys dropped from her hand with a clink. Drew shut the refrigerator and snapped on the light.

"Who's there?" he demanded, clenching the beer bottle menacingly. "Jenny? Shit! What are you doing here? You're supposed to be at the library."

She stood with her back against the door, wallet in one frozen hand, the other reaching for the dropped keys. The little nail that held the calendar dug into her head, the sharp little pain confirmation this was really happening. When she tried to speak, all that came out was a keening sound that reminded her of Betty's moans.

Frozen into his own place, Drew stood brandishing his beer bottle. She couldn't face that nakedness. Drew's body was—had been—important to her. She felt the hot surge of tears. A painful tightening in her throat. She dropped her eyes so he wouldn't see her cry. There was a spot on her toe. Something green.

Betty broke the silence. "I've got to go," she declared in a strangled voice, and rushed from the room.

Her departure freed Drew from his spell. "Look," he said, setting the beer down, "I know this looks bad... I know how you feel about fidelity and all that shit... but this doesn't mean anything about you and me. It's just something that happened. It's just sex, you know. No big deal. It's not like I care about Betty or anything. She's just like... you know... one of the guys."

He seemed to be expecting agreement that sex with her best friend was no cause for concern. Jenny studied the spot on her shoe. Quite an unusual shade of green. Where had it come from? It was March. Not much green stuff around. Not that anything in nature was quite that color.

"Jenny?" he said. "Hey, Jen, come on baby, talk to me. It's not the end of the world." He reached out but she batted his hand away.

"Stay away from me, Drew."

He took a step closer, his penis bobbing, and reached for her again. Did he believe the crap he was saying? She wanted to grab a knife and gut him like a fresh-shot deer. Did he seriously expect she wouldn't be mad? She could taste the salt of her tears. "Don't come any closer."

"Come on, baby. Relax. Set your things down. Come in the living room. I'll fix you a drink. We'll talk about this. There now, give me that."

He plucked the wallet from her hand. Set it on the counter. Picked up the keys. "Okay, baby, that's good, now—"

Betty's quick steps rushed through the living room. The door opened. Slammed shut. A car engine started.

"You should get dressed," Jenny said.

He did a foolish dance from foot to foot, as if suddenly discovering he was naked. "You're right. I should. Be right back." He opened his beer and took it with him.

As soon as he was gone, she put on her jacket and put her the wallet and keys into the pockets. Her bags were already in the car. She went into the bathroom, dumped toothbrush and toothpaste into her cosmetic bag, and stuffed it into her backpack. She picked up the day's mail from the counter, shoved that in, too, and left.

o   o   o   o   o

Someone banged on the car window. When she opened her eyes, the car was bathed in swaths of swirling blue light. A tall state trooper loomed beside the car, tapping on her window with an enormous flashlight. She took a deep breath and rolled down the window. Water poured in. "Excuse me, ma'am," he said, "are you all right? Do you need assistance?"

He loomed like something from a horror movie, his pale face washed with eerie colors from his headlights and flashing blue bubbles. Rainwater poured off the brim of his wide hat. His dark coat glistened. "Ma'am?"

The water running onto her leg was startlingly cold. "I'm all right," she said, furious at the tears in her voice. "I just… I've been driving since dawn. I pulled over to rest my eyes."

"There's a service area just a few miles ahead," he said. "Maybe you should stop and get yourself some coffee. Walk around a little. Wake yourself up. Where you headed?"

"Hallowell."

"Spring break?" he asked.

Sometimes she felt like she had "kid" tattooed on her forehead. Both men and women called her "dear" and "honey" and patted her. Sometimes, when she was out walking, deep in thought, people would ask if she was lost. She half expected them to take her by the hand and try to lead her back to her mother. Hard when you're in Ohio and your mother's in Maine.

Jenny nodded, not trusting her voice. When she'd planned this trip, she'd envisioned long talks with her mom about her future with Drew. Her mother was the wisest, and probably the best person she knew, her father a close second. Now there was no future with Drew. Even if she wasn't going to talk about marriage, that wonderful institution she'd seen so solidly exemplified in her parents' relationship, at least she'd have understanding shoulders to cry on.

The cop bent lower. "You eaten anything today?"

She shook her head. She hadn't been able to.

"Well, you'd better stop and get something. It's a nasty night to be driving when you're not a hundred percent."

"Thank you, officer. I will." Was that tiny little voice really hers? Had Drew's betrayal not only battered her spirit but stolen her voice? The trooper squelched away through the rain. She rolled up her window, put on her signal, and pulled out into the traffic. Behind her, the blue lights went out, and the police car disappeared.

A big green sign appeared out of the dark. Food and Fuel. Two miles. She didn't want to expose her swollen, blotchy face to bright lights and staring eyes, but the trooper was right. It wasn't responsible to drive in her present condition. She poked along in the slow lane, feeling logy and dense, until the exit. Then she parked and stepped out into the rain.

Inside it was all bustle and hubbub. Laughing packs of teens and scampering children. Big bellied men in faded sweatshirts, women in leggings who shouldn't be wearing them. People clutching phones like lifelines. Intent type A men in suits, notebooks spread, negotiating their way through life. She felt a kinship with none of them. She visited the ladies' room, following her mother's rule that a sensible person goes when the opportunity presents itself, and then emerged to stare at the food counters. Italian. Burgers and fries. Ice cream. Maybe she could choke down a bagel. She ordered cinnamon-raisin with cream cheese, and a coffee.

The woman behind the counter was kind, asking patiently if Jenny wanted it toasted, and serving the coffee in a double cup to protect her from the heat. She counted out Jenny's change carefully into her hand and folded her fingers around it, as if she could read the dislocation in Jenny's brain. Jenny staggered away from the counter, bagel in hand, looking at the milling people, racks of T-shirts and bagged candy, machines selling lottery tickets and cash cow machines giving money. No place to sit. She was about to dump the bagel in the trash when a hand seized her elbow.

"Over here." With the hand went a commanding voice. She looked up. A long way up. The man was tall, even for a trooper, even without the hat. He steered her across the room into a booth. He set down his tray, tossed his hat and coat onto the bench, and slid in across from her. He opened the bag, pulled out the bagel, unwrapped it, and set it in front of her. Then he pried the lid off her coffee. "You want anything in that? Cream? Sugar?"

She hadn't been this helpless when she was five, but tonight she was grateful. "Yes. I mean both. Please."

He seized her cup, and strode away. People were staring at him. People always stared at state troopers in uniform. There's something both reassuring and repelling about those we've hired to serve and protect. We want to know them, yet we like them to remain a mystery. But this guy was also big, and people stare at big people, and he had an interesting face. All craggy angles and unusual, over-sized features, like Van Gogh turned loose with an identikit.

He brought the coffee back, unwrapped his first burger, and inhaled it in three bites. He gave her an embarrassed smile. "You aren't the only one who hasn't eaten," he said. "It's been a long day. Weather like this, people lose their common sense, start acting like idiots. Do that behind the wheel of a two thousand pound hunk of metal, you can do a lot of damage."

"You do look tired," she said.

He picked up half of the bagel and put it in her hand. "Eat," he commanded.

Obediently, she took a bite, chewed, and swallowed. It might as well have been sawdust.

"You want to talk about it?" he said. "I'm a good listener."

"I don't know if I'm a good talker."

"Give it a whirl. Can't be worse than keeping it inside." He was steadily demolishing a supersized order of fries, one of two on his tray. "Take another bite. Have some coffee, and tell Uncle Roland."

Dutifully, she took another bite. Sawdust with raisins. Drank some coffee and raised her eyes. His second burger was gone. "How many calories a day?" she asked. "Five, six thousand?"

The wide mouth spread in a grin that made him look like a gigantic twelve-year old. "My momma says a boy's gotta eat if he wants to grow."

She thrust a hand across the table. "I'm Jenny," she said. "Jenny Cates."

He engulfed it. "Roland Profit. So, what is it? Family? Money? Romance?"

"That about covers the bases, doesn't it? Romance," she said. "Last night I… I found my boyfriend…" She swallowed hard to force down the lump. Drew was not going to silence her with sorry lumps so she couldn't talk. Someday she'd stop seeing Betty's big breasts, her ineffectual efforts to cover blonde pubic hair with plump, wide-spread hands, the sullen, guilty look on her face. "And my best friend. You know. It's an old story."

"Not for you." He kept her hand in his. "It hurts. So you left where?"

"Ohio."

"And headed home. And you've been driving pretty much steadily since you left?"

She nodded.

He released her hand. "Keep eating," he said. "Home. Will it be a good place for you?"

She swallowed another bite of bagel. Drank some more coffee. "The best."

"Good." He collected his wrappings and piled them on his tray. Crossed the room and dumped it in the trash, coming back for his hat and coat. He smiled down at her, the hopeful smile of a big brother whose little sister has been wounded by love. "Good luck, Jenny Cates. Thanks for the company. I hope life starts treating you better. You drive carefully out there." He pulled on his coat, set his hat on his head, and left.

Jenny finished half of the bagel. Not because she was hungry but to appease the spirit of the kind man who'd briefly taken her under his wing. Her wound still felt open and raw, but a state trooper named Roland Profit had stuck on the first Band-Aid, fulfilling his mission to serve and protect.

"But the tender grace of a day that is dead
Will never come back to me."
—Tennyson, "Break, Break, Break"

CHAPTER TWO

As she came onto the porch, she saw her dad sitting in his favorite chair. He had papers spread around him, his black-rimmed reading glasses perched on his nose and a pencil over his ear, frowning at something. The same ratty floor lamp with the masking tape patches that she'd used to read her favorite books shone over his shoulder, bathing him in a cone of yellow light. He had on his test correcting music. Even over the rain, she could hear the stirring Beethoven.

She paused there, watching, as he plucked the pencil from his ear, made a notation on a paper, scratched his head with the eraser, and parked it again. She was weary and her eyes ached, but viewing this familiar scene, she felt a lightening of her gloom. So comforting to know that however screwed up some parts of life might be, things here were normal and predictable.

A jagged bolt of lightning raced like a strobe light through the black sky, washing everything in stark white light. From habit, she counted the seconds. Steam engine one. Steam engine two. Steam engine three. *Kablaam*! A crash of thunder rattled the windows. Her father raised his head, looked around, and came over to peer out. Jenny considered teasing him by staying where she was and peering in, but all he would see was a dark shape. She hurried to the door and turned the knob. It was locked. They never locked the door. She knocked.

Instead of unlocking it, he asked, "Who is it?"

"It's me. Jenny."

Locks were undone and the door flew wide. Her father scooped her off her feet, and carried her into the hall, setting her down with a thump.

He snapped on the overhead light and studied her the way he always did when she'd been gone more than a few days. She knew what was coming. The inventory. "Let's see. Four limbs. One head. Two eyes. Nose. Mouth. Two ears. Still got all your teeth? No visible body piercing. No canes or crutches or other signs of disability. I guess we'll keep you." He would have kept her with canes, crutches and multiple body-piercing. Still, she found the ritual comforting.

He reached past her, pushed the door shut and turned the dead bolt. "Come in the kitchen," he said. "I'll make some tea. We weren't expecting you until tomorrow."

She hung her coat on a peg and followed him into the kitchen, noticing he gave the room a quick scrutiny before entering. "What's with the locks and bolts, and knock-knock, who's there?"

He grabbed the kettle off the stove and filled it. Waited for the burner to burst into flame. "Somebody tried to break in yesterday while we were at work. Luckily, Mrs. Mason saw them and called the police."

Home was supposed to be inviolable. Jenny's stomach knotted. She'd come here for sanctuary. "They catch 'em?"

He shook his head. "Gone by the time the police got here. Seems that after Mrs. Mason called 911, she got out Hugh's shotgun and came over to make sure nothing happened before the police arrived. She found two of 'em using a crowbar on the back door, called out, 'Yoohoo!' and when they turned, she put the first barrel into the ground by their feet. Says she didn't mean to do it, that thing always had a hair-trigger. She says they lit out for their car like the devil was chasin' 'em. Much as it bothers me to think of someone trying to break in, I wish I'd seen it."

Jenny nodded. Adele Mason was bean-pole skinny, seventy-seven years old, and about 4' 10". The biggest thing about her was her voice. She was one of the women her mother had used as a role model when Jenny was growing up. She never let size, age, sex or any other damned thing stand in her way. She had married her sweetheart, borne him a son, then seen him go off to Vietnam, and gotten back a changed and shaken soul, a man too timid to drive or hold a job, barely able to leave the house. Other women might have crumbled under such a burden, or wallowed in self-pity at the bad hand fate had dealt. Adele Mason had taken tender, loving care of her husband for forty years without a word of complaint. Along the way, she'd borne two more sons, the last when she was in her forties, and afterwards, started a trucking business. The business grew along with the sons. When Adele retired at seventy, she'd passed along a rock-solid work ethic and a thriving business.

She could have moved to a bigger house, bought fancy clothes, a nicer car, but Adele was a make-do Yankee. She'd taught Jenny how to knit, crochet, make a quilt, and how to make jam and jelly, things Jenny's mother had lacked the skills to teach. She'd served as Jenny's surrogate grandmother, coming to Jenny's concerts, her plays, her high school graduation. She had taught Jenny to take pride in her accomplishments and chided her when she was afraid to be good in school because the boys made fun.

Her sons, Hugh, Tom, and Andy had been Jenny's uncles. Hugh taught her the constellations, sitting outside with her on summer nights, showing her the sky through his telescope. Tom taught her to shoot cans off the fence. Andy, the youngest, had been her favorite. He'd let her ride with him on the tractor, letting her steer while he worked the pedals. She'd called him 'Dandy' even since she'd first toddled over to him on chubby legs and held out her arms, demanding, "Pick me up, Dandy." She hadn't even realized it wasn't his name until she was about eight. He'd called her 'Spitfire,' 'Spit' for short and still did. Dandy had taught her to hit a softball and drive a truck. How to say 'no' to a guy and mean it. When Dandy got married, she'd felt betrayed. Recently, Dandy's wife had left him, taken their kid out of state, and broken his heart.

"Jenny, you want anything in this? Milk, sugar, lemon?" He had to repeat the question twice before he got her attention.

"Sorry. I was thinking about Adele and the boys. Got honey?"

"Have I got honey?" He opened the pantry closet and called back over his shoulder, "Rosemary, clover, or Old Stroudwater?"

"Old Stroudwater? What the heck? Sounds like vodka, or something Tom and Huck had to take to the cemetery."

"Al and Carole Howard, gentleperson farmers, being pretentious."

"I'll have clover. Rosemary doesn't sound right for tea. Where's Mom?"

He tipped his head sideways as though considering. "Well, let's see. It's Saturday night, so where would she be? Country western line dancing? Down at The Brewery, slurping suds? Baked bean supper? Give me your best guess."

"At the office."

"Bingo," he said. "Give the woman a prize. Let's see what we've got. Rubber chicken? Whoopee cushion?" He took something from the top of the refrigerator. "How about a stuffed rabbit that eats a carrot if you wind it up?" He wound it and set it in front of her. Its buck-teeth chattered as it raised its paw and stuck a mangy-looking felt carrot into its mouth. After the tenth time, she wanted to shoot it.

"I am certainly lucky to receive such a prize. Where'd it come from?"

"Physics class. It was competing with me for attention, so it was forfeited in the interests of science." He sat down across from her. "Pleasantries being dispensed with, tell me why you've been crying, kiddo."

Her tears flooded back. "Oh, Daddy. That rat Drew… he…" Her father offered a handkerchief smelling of Ivory Snow and hot irons. God, it was good to be home! Through high school and college she'd listened to people complain about their families. How had she gotten so lucky? This big calm man with the ugly name, Elmer, had always been there to pass her handkerchiefs and to listen when she needed that.

She blinked back tears. "I came home early from the library last night and caught Drew in bed with my friend Betty. He said it was no big deal. That Betty didn't matter to him so sleeping with her shouldn't matter to me. I don't see how having sex with someone you don't care about is less of a betrayal." She stared at the floor. Decades of busy feet had worn the pattern off the linoleum. Her parents, more into ideas than decor, hadn't bothered to replace it.

"I was shocked. It was as if he'd stabbed me, and he stands there, stark naked, smiling and trying to make conversation. I couldn't stay to talk about it. I told him to get dressed, then grabbed my stuff, got in the car, and started driving."

She shrugged. "And here I am. My lover. My best friend. I just don't understand."

"You want to talk about it?"

"Think I need to brood first."

"You know where to find me."

"Right. In your workshop. In your chair. At the high school."

"I have a new interest," he said. His gray eyes twinkled.

"You know I don't like change," she said warily.

"Jennifer Cates, you're only twenty-one. You should embrace change."

"Sorry. Too many generations of Maine stick-in-the-muds, I guess."

"Stick-in-the-muds? They were adventurous, Jen. Think of it. Leaving their settled homes and lives and coming to a wild, harsh place like Maine. Bears and Indians. French trappers. No law and order. No near neighbors. On my side of the family, you've got pioneers, not stick-in-the-muds, and on your mother's side? Well, if anything, they were more adventurous. Fleeing Cossacks and pogroms. Traveling across Europe by night, frightened, hungry, hunted, hoping to get someplace where they could take a ship to America."

"You make it sound so dramatic."

"It was dramatic, kiddo. It was nature red in tooth and claw, as Tennyson said." She drank her tea. Tea always tasted better here. Maybe it was well water. The water in her apartment always smelled like chlorine. The clock on the wall said ten. "Shouldn't Mom be back by now?"

He looked at the clock and then his watch, as if he doubted the number. "She should. She just ran down to pick up a few files, said she'd be back by nine-thirty. There was a program she wanted to watch at ten. But you know how she is. Maybe there was something in the mail or a phone call to return, even if it is Saturday night. If she's immersed in her work, a tornado could carry the building away, and she'd just brace herself with a foot and keep working. That's where you get your passion for work from."

"I got a double dose." She smiled at him. "You weren't eating bon bons and reading the latest Tom Clancy, were you?"

"Were you spying on me?"

"Watching. Indulging in a moment of nostalgia."

"Nostalgia. Haven't they got some new medicine for that? Clears your sinuses and relieves nostalgia in minutes?"

"You should talk. You still have the little metal soldiers you played with as a boy."

"Probably worth a fortune by now. I'm saving them for my retirement."

"To sell?"

"To play with." He checked his watch again. "Let's call your mother, tell her you're home."

Jenny looked around the kitchen, so comfortably familiar. The same pictures and cartoons and invitations stuck to the refrigerator by a motley assortment of magnets. The same canisters and appliances on the counters. The African violets by the sink, plants her mother disliked but tended out of duty. Gifts over the years from Adele. Sensing they weren't loved, they would not thrive, but neither would they die. Except one, which bloomed lavishly, obscenely, a mass of pale pink flowers. This was the one her mother had dashed to the floor at Christmas, yelling, "Three leaves. Seven years this plant has camped out here with three miserable leaves, not doing a damned thing! A wart would be more satisfying." Crash went the pot. Smash went the plant. In a moment of weakness, her mother had repotted it and put it back on the shelf. It had bloomed ever since.

She laughed.

"What's this?" he said. "I thought you were in the depths."

"That stupid plant."

"Your mother is thinking of changing professions. Abusive plant therapy. She thinks it would be fun to have a greenhouse where she tossed plants around, beat them up, and generally mistreated them. No more judges, opposing attorneys, desperate clients or paperwork."

He crossed to the phone. Beside it was a message board. One message said, "Call Drew." Like there was anything he could say that would make things okay. She erased it.

Her father dialed a number, waited, hung up. "She's not answering. Must be on her way." This time they both checked their watches. The office was five minutes away. Her father wandered over to stare out the window. "Lotta rain," he said.

She murmured an assent. She was watching the second hand on the clock make its rounds. A violent crack as jagged lightning shot through the darkness. A ball of blue fire shot out of the telephone, crackling in the air. Jenny counted. Steam engine one. Steam engine. This time the roar was so loud she jumped and cried out. Her father put an arm around her shoulders. "Some storm," he said. The lights flickered and went out.

Automatically, she opened a kitchen drawer, took out a flashlight, and opened the pantry door to look for candles. The power went out often enough that her mother kept a supply of candles, batteries, and a propane lantern on the top shelf. She got down the lantern and handed it to her father. There was a hiss, the scratch of a match, and then the kitchen was filled with glaring light. "Ugly," she said.

"Useful." He checked his watch. "Been fifteen minutes."

"We should go check."

"I can go. You've driven enough. You're tired."

"No, Daddy. You can't leave me alone in this scary house. Besides, my car is behind yours."

"Wouldn't be the first time I've maneuvered around your car, kiddo." He turned the lantern down low and found a second flashlight. "Get your coat, then."

Her coat smelled like fast food and bad coffee. She wrinkled her nose as she grabbed a baseball cap off a peg. A red one with Mason Brothers Trucking on it, stolen from Dandy at Christmas. Her father undid the locks, waited for her, then patiently redid them. She slid behind the wheel, waited until he'd fastened his seatbelt, and backed smoothly out of the driveway. Around them the night roared and crackled. All the lights on the street were out.

They crawled down the street, the car plowing through giant puddles like a sturdy little tug. Stopped at the corner and turned right, flowing with the streaming water down the big hill to Main Street and turned right again. She pulled in and stopped behind her mother's battered old Saab, then squeezed her father's hand. They didn't speak. They opened and closed their doors in unison, and ran to her mother's building. The door opened with a squeal, admitting them to a staircase. The power here was on but the lighting was dim—a single bulb trying to illuminate a brownish yellow stairwell and the worn wooden stairs. Her mother was a poverty lawyer. Her clients couldn't pay for plush carpeting and fancy digs.

Their feet echoed hollowly on the uncarpeted stairs. At the top, they turned left. The office door, a half-glassed number with Lila Friedman, Attorney-at-Law, in chipped gold letters, stood open. The room beyond was dark. Jenny reached for the light switch, snapped it on, and put her hand to her mouth, muffling a scream. The room had been ransacked. Files had been dumped, drawers pulled open, books knocked off the shelf. The flowers Lila always had lay on the rug. Side-by-side they stepped into the big room where her paralegal and the secretary worked, trying not to step on the papers. The office beyond was dark and the door was shut.

"Maybe she went to get the police," he said. "We should check."

"Wait!" Jenny stepped across the room like someone crossing a stream on slippery rocks, and opened her mother's office door. She flicked the light switch. Nothing. Light coming in through the low, crescent windows, wasn't bright enough. She pulled out her flashlight, sliding the beam nervously around the big dark room. Like the outer office, this room had been trashed. Papers lay in drifts on the threadbare carpet. She explored the room with the beam of light, finding nothing.

"Over there." Her father pointed with his flashlight. "What's that?" Something white was sticking out from behind the desk.

Jenny started walking, keeping the beam on it as they crossed the room. They moved slowly, avoiding the strewn papers, until they could see a slender woman's hand, unadorned except for a slim gold band.

"Lila!" Her father rushed forward and threw himself down beside the still figure.

Jenny followed quickly, bringing the light. The yellow circle fell like a spotlight on the woman on the floor. She lay face down in a pool of blood, her long, dark hair hiding her face.

"Lila!" he said again as his fingers burrowed through the hair, seeking a pulse. "Oh. Lila. No!" He pulled his hand back and buried his face in both hands, then sprawled across the woman's body, sobbing.

Jenny gripped her mother's wrist with gentle fingers, searching for a pulse. She felt as if the world had come loose from its moorings. Nothing that was supposed to be, was. Not back in Ohio, not here. "Come on," she whispered. "Please. Be alive."

Outside the window, lightning slammed into a transformer. A spectacular shower of sparks cascaded toward the ground like fireworks. The dim light in the other room went out.

She shifted her fingers and tried again.

"It's no use, Jenny," he said. "She's gone."

Then she felt it. A thin, faint pulsing under her fingers. "No, Daddy. No. She's alive."

Her mother lay in a pool of her own blood, a heavy cut-glass vase in pieces around her head. Her father was draped across the body, his crying sharp as knives in the cold, dark room. He hadn't heard what she'd just said. She grabbed the phone on her mother's desk. The line was dead. She fumbled her cell phone out of her pocket and called 911.

"Daddy, there's an ambulance coming," she said. He hadn't heard. He was muttering to his wife, telling her how much he loved her. Jenny hurried across the office, heedless of the papers this time, rushed downstairs, and into the street. The rain had turned to snow. Fat flakes slapped her face and clung to her hair. She stood at the edge of the street and waited for help to arrive.

"Tears from the depths of some divine despair
Rise in the heart, and gather to the eyes..."
—Tennyson, "The Princess"

CHAPTER THREE

The very young local cop who was first to respond followed Jenny up the stairs and charged in, flashlight waving wildly, spotlighting each of them in turn, then brought the beam back to rest on her mother. "Jesus Christ, what happened here? What happened here?" His words burst out in an unprofessional wail, real pain in his voice, like a child stunned by a first taste of harsh reality. If she hadn't her hands full trying to cover her mother and keep her warm while calming her shattered father, Jenny would have tried to comfort him, too. He was probably one of the people her mother had rescued. Lila collected wounded souls.

He was followed by two EMTs with a stretcher who asked Jenny, her father, and the distraught officer to light the area with their flashlights and then went calmly and efficiently to work. Jenny concentrated on steadying her light, trying not to watch their manipulations of that pale, bloody head. The hushed darkness and the men toiling in beams of light created a scene so unreal it felt like a bad high school play. She desperately wished someone would yell, "Curtain," the lights would come back on, and her mother would rise up, smiling, and brush the dirt off her jeans. Instead she lay still and white while strangers ministered to her.

Her mother was never still.

While the men treated her mother, the room filled up around them. Police came with flashlights, cursing the storm, muttering and stomping and bumping each other in the half-dark like a herd of nervous animals. They dripped all over the papers on the floor, crushed the flower stems, filling the air with an herbal scent, and ground bits of glass into the floor.

Jenny's chest hurt from holding her breath, Her arm shook from steadying the light. Finally, with no warning or explanation, they loaded her mother onto the stretcher and began to wheel her out.

"Wait!" Jenny said. "Wait! Where are you taking her?"

"KVMC," the nearer man said, using the initials of the local hospital, "but with head injuries like this, likely they'll send her on to Portland." He left the rest of his sentence, "if she lives that long," unspoken.

For a moment, Jenny was paralyzed by that 'if,' then shook it off. She took her father's arm, tugging him gently toward the door. "Come on, Daddy," she said. "We've got to follow them to the hospital."

The policeman in charge stopped her with a question. Intent on her desperate need to get to the hospital, she couldn't make sense out of his question. It was only a jumble of tones. She tried to brush him aside but he was twice her size and between her and the door. She heard herself responding, with no idea what she said, and he let them go.

Her father, not a small man, was leaning on her so heavily she was afraid they wouldn't make it down the stairs, but the young policeman detached himself from the group and lent a strong shoulder to get them to the car. Once her father was belted in, the policeman carefully shut the door. Then he held out his hand to her. "Miss Cates, I can't begin to say how sorry I am. Your mother is one of the finest women, finest people, I've ever known. I hope she'll be all right. If there's anything I can do…"

The ache in her throat made response impossible. Jenny shook his hand and jumped behind the wheel. She headed up along the Kennebec River to the hospital, creeping through the darkened streets and past rows of snow-covered cars like ranks of white coffins lining the road. It was snowing heavily now, nature's frozen tears driving at her like a million silver swords.

Beside her, her father cried gut-wrenching sobs. Lila was the tough one. He'd always been more tender. When life had dealt Jenny a bad hand, the middle-school girls had been mean, or Jenny lost an academic competition, her mother's counsel was buck up, get on, get even. Her father had given her a shoulder to cry on and a handkerchief to dry her tears.

Her heart raced as she crossed the high bridge over the river. She couldn't speed. The road was slick. A gust of wind shoved her car into the other lane and she struggled to hold it on the road. Snow tossed up by the tires beat against the underside of the car, hissed under the tires, flew in arcs around them.

She turned into the hospital lot and braked to a stop. Snow was piling up fast. Spring never really came in Maine, it flirted and tempted, like a teasing girl, denying winter-weary people its favors.

She slumped over the wheel, gathering strength to face the lights, the people, the questions, her mother's voice in her head. "Jenny, we do what we have to do in life—tired is no excuse." Lila had never understood tired. Jenny, who'd just driven from Ohio, was a basket case.

Swirls of ice scratched the window. The wind moaned and shrieked, things she felt like doing herself. Suppose they hadn't worried? Hadn't gone down? Please let them have been in time. Let her live. Let her fine, cool, analytical brain and her warm, generous soul be intact. Let her be there to be Mom, dishing out wisdom and advice, criticism and humor, funny little nose twitches and unexpected confidences. Jenny still needed that small, strong hand to guide her.

This was no time for self-pity. She got her flashlight and went around the car to get her father. The wind whipped her hair into her face and icy needles stung her eyes and cheeks. She opened his door and leaned in. "Come on, Daddy," she said. "Undo your seatbelt. We're at the hospital."

He followed her instructions like a stupefied child, stumbling along beside her, his disorientation and helplessness frightening. When they reached the door, she realized this side of the river had power. Feeling foolish, she clicked her flashlight off and led her father up to the receptionist, a thin, sharp-faced woman who closed her Harlequin romance and looked at them warily.

"They just brought my mother in. Lila Friedman?" Jenny said. "I'm Jenny Cates and this is my father, Bud."

Looming over her shoulder, her father echoed, "Lila Friedman. My wife."

The woman nodded. "They just brought her in." She pointed down the hall. "The waiting room is just there. Someone will be out to talk to you as soon as they've assessed the situation." When they hesitated, she said, "I know this is hard but you have to give the doctors time. They're very good about keeping the families informed."

Jenny would have gone to the waiting room, but her father looked hopefully at the woman. "Can we see her?"

The woman shook her head. "You have to stay out of their way and let the doctors work, Mr. Cates."

"Not even for a minute?"

She shook her head. "I'm sorry, but no. Not yet."

"But they will come and let us know as soon as… as soon as they can?"

The woman nodded. "They will." Then she thawed a bit. "Everyone loves your wife, Mr. Cates. You know we'll do everything we can."

"Daddy, come on." Jenny tugged at his arm and led him to the waiting room. Despite the storm and the late hour, they weren't alone. A disheveled couple who looked much too young for parenthood struggled to calm a wailing toddler. A gaunt old man with blood down his shirt held a bloody towel to his pale gray face while the skinny young woman next to him masticated her gum, ignoring him in favor of a magazine. In another corner, a morbidly obese woman in bulging pink leggings sat with two fat children, all of them staring glassy-eyed at a television set. Occasionally the woman grabbed her abdomen and moaned.

Jenny tried talking to her father but he was in his own world. She tried to stay calm. But she'd never been able to sit and do nothing. Too much Lila Friedman in her. "I'm getting my pack from the car," she said. "I'll be right back." If nothing else, she could make lists of people to call. Even though her mother worked all the time, she had dozens of friends, something Jenny, essentially a loner, had always envied.

When she got back, she found her father talking to a man in a white coat. "Oh good, you're back," he said. "Dr. Greene says we can see her for a minute before they move her to Portland."

They followed the doctor through a set of swinging doors and into a room that was all harsh light and gleaming instruments. Her mother lay on a stretcher, her head swathed in bandages, hooked up to an alarming array of tubes and bottles. She smiled faintly at her husband and breathed a faint, "Bud," as he rushed forward and seized her hand. Then her eyes shifted to Jenny. "Oh. Jen." Her voice was so faint Jenny had to bend down to hear. Her mother reached for her as she whispered, "Run, Jen. Run. Burn diary and run." Her eyes closed and she was still.

"We'd better get her moving," Dr. Greene said. "Normally we'd send her by helicopter, but they can't fly in this wind. One of you can ride with her if you'd like, as long as you don't get in the way." The stretcher was already moving, steady, efficient, inexorable, the people surrounding it moving with it, her father among them, back into the stormy night.

Jenny watched, trying to comprehend what she'd just heard. She was supposed to run? From what? From whom? Where was she supposed to go? She wanted to go in the ambulance. Something primitive in her believed if she let her mother out of her sight, her mother would disappear forever. But her father was clinging to the hand of the woman he loved. She was still alive, still with them. Nothing else mattered. He seemed to have forgotten Jenny was there.

She was confused by what her mother had said. Wanted to grab her father and demand to know what it meant, but he was out of reach. Grabbing him would do no good. Numbly she watched her parents moving away, leaving her behind.

Dr. Greene saw her and took a step in her direction. "Did she say anything about her attackers?" Jenny asked.

He shook his head. "You've seen her most lucid moment. She only said there were men in suits." He put a fatherly hand on her shoulder, looking down with tired eyes. "You should be prepared for the worst," he said. "Her head injuries are very serious. I'm sorry." He withdrew the hand and followed her mother out through the swinging doors.

She stared after them, the breath knocked out of her. His words, well meant and so gently delivered, had left her reeling. Then she headed off through the snowy darkness.

Staring with aching eyes at the clusters of white meteors rushing at the windshield, she wondered what her mother's words meant. What diary was she supposed to burn? From whom was she supposed to run? She wished she understood what was going on. She wished she could close her eyes and wake up to find that the last few days had been a bad dream. But Jenny was no dreamer. This was bad reality.

"How dreadful knowledge of the truth can be
when there's no help in truth!"
—Sophocles

CHAPTER FOUR

Through the grimy hospital window, Jenny watched the golden glow of dawn emerge from the retreating fog. Sunshine seemed impertinent today. Last night's wild storm had been more fitting. She identified with the trees bowed down by the snow. Hiding here at the end of a corridor, she felt swamped with adult responsibilities she wasn't ready for.

After two nights without sleep, two days without food except what the kindly trooper had made her eat, and disaster piled upon disaster, she was running on will power. Luckily, she had lots of that. Her parents had both modeled "grit your teeth and do what has to be done." She was a poster girl for the "tough it out" school of life.

Once she went back to the waiting room, she'd be surrounded by people and questions. Despite the storm, her mother's friends were arriving, and more would come. They'd check in with the kindly salmon-smocked volunteer at the Special Care desk and join others keeping vigil in Waiting Room 2. Their worried eyes and anxious questions would just put more pressure on her. They'd look to her for information she didn't have while she tried to hide her own terror and tears.

The doctors weren't offering much hope for a happy ending. During the night, her mother had lapsed into a coma. Now she lay in the ICU, still and white, monitored by a wall of machines. Phrases like 'don't get your hopes up,' 'you must be realistic' and 'cases like these rarely resolve in a positive way,' had been the message.

Down in the street, a power company truck had its bucket up, a man in a yellow rain suit and hard hat working on one of the poles. The storm had left the rapidly brightening world a mess of broken branches and bent trees, as if a giant egg beater had slashed over the landscape. The sharp split-ends of softwoods, scraped off the street by plows, protruded from the snow banks like yellow rat's teeth. Outside, the air would have the sweet and pungent scent of fresh-cut wood.

She went in the bathroom and splashed cold water on her face, steeling herself for what she had to do. There was an iPad in her backpack. She wished there were clean clothes there, too. She'd been wearing this stuff since Friday morning. There were clean clothes in her car, but it was at the other end of the hospital, buried under a mountain of snow. She bundled her dirty hair into a crude braid and used some mouthwash, but her teeth felt like they were wearing little coats. Her eyes were gritty. Her skin oily.

Something crackled in the pocket of her jeans. She pulled out a crumpled slip of paper, smoothed it, and read two words in her mother's hasty scrawl: *Buxton tape.* What was that doing in her pocket? Then she remembered. Last night, when she'd lifted her mother's hand searching for a pulse, the paper had fallen out and she'd tucked it in her pocket. It meant nothing to her. She should give it to the police. Maybe they could make sense of it.

But these were her mother's last written words. She ran her fingers lightly over the paper, then pocketed it and returned to the waiting room.

This place had a far greater air of desperation than the one in Augusta. This room had the biting, old-sweat odor of fear. Red-eyed family groups, sealed in their own circles of anxiety, moved in small orbits. Pretending to read. Filling in new arrivals in hushed whispers. Whenever someone in a white coat entered, all the eyes in the room turned. The eyes turned away when someone on a phone delivered news to another who wasn't there.

When she unzipped her pack, the mail she'd tossed in as she was leaving tumbled out. On top was a letter from her mother. She opened it with nervous hands. It would be strange enough to get a letter on an ordinary day. Her mother didn't write letters. She texted, e-mailed, or called, more efficient for a woman always pressed for time. Her mother had quickly mastered the hit and run quality of texting. Sometimes, when Jenny had been particularly bad at communicating, she'd get one liners like, "Did you die out?" or "You been kidnapped?" or the query, "Whatever happened to Jenny Cates? America wants to know."

Her mother wrote to enclose checks or return official forms, but none were due. She also wrote to convey important information, like the passing of relatives, but no relatives had passed. Jenny shivered, afraid to read the letter, then set it aside and started her lists. But her rumbling stomach reminded her how long it had been since she'd eaten. No wonder she felt weak. She wasn't hungry but, knowing the day would be full of ringing phones, cops, friends, the press, and busybodies, she should eat. But getting food, like getting clean clothes, meant leaving this area and possibly missing some news.

She returned to her list, but the letter hovered in her consciousness. She sighed and opened it.

It was hand-written on rich cream stationery.

> *My Darling Jenny,*
>
> *I'm deeply ashamed of myself for communicating something so important in this cowardly way. You know I've always believed in facing life's truths, but though I've considered this seriously, searching for a better way, I believe it's necessary to put this in writing in case something happens to me. Although what I am about to tell you will be painful, for you and for us all, this is a situation where, due to circumstances beyond all our control, what you don't know may hurt you.*
>
> *Twenty-two years ago, when I was a beginning lawyer working my first job in the Attorney General's office, there were some important cases where I got to work directly with the Attorney General. The Attorney General at that time was James Buxton. You'll recognize the name, since he has long been the ranking Senator from Maine, and is at present campaigning for the presidency. Although Jim Buxton was a married man, he and I felt an enormous attraction for each other. I am ashamed to say that, being young and headstrong (Jenny, I was only a little older than you are now), I yielded to my impulses and we had an affair. At the time I believed, and I think he did, that when the moment was right, he'd leave his wife, and the two of us would be together. I think you know, Jenny, that I do not treat relationships casually.*

They say that politics make strange bedfellows. In any case, just when Jim had resolved to leave Maggie, Senator Fuller, one of the two senators from Maine, died suddenly, and the party asked Jim to fill the seat. Twenty-two years ago, Maine was a lot more conservative. A man who left his wife and children for one of his employees could expect to kiss his political career good-bye, and Jim loved politics more than he loved me. So it was me he kissed good-bye and he and Maggie went off to Washington. I stayed on in the Attorney General's office, married Elmer, and had you.

I tell you all this now because, as the political campaign heats up, I fear that Jim's opponents will be digging for any dirt that they can find. Even though it is ancient history, my affair with him is exactly the kind of thing that might be dug up. There was some gossip at the time, state offices being a whole lot like small towns, but we were very discreet and, to the best of my knowledge, no one knows for sure. I just wanted you to be prepared in case this ever comes up. If I am ever asked about it, I intend to deny that anything ever happened. Lord knows, I've tried to live my life as an honest woman, but this is one case where I cannot see how any good will come from the truth. It would hurt Jim, who has been a good and effective Senator for this state, it would hurt his wife, and it would hurt your father and you.

We can talk more about this when you get home.

Your cowardly mother

p.s. Burn this after you've read it. Please.

Jenny stuffed the letter in her pocket. All this melodrama about something that had happen so long ago. What was the big deal? Did anybody seriously care about an affair more than twenty years old? Surely Senator Buxton's opponents required better ammunition than that? And why had her mother put it in a letter, rather than waiting and telling her in person? But, as her mother had said, she was writing in case anything happened to her. Ominous words, and quite unlike her mother. Lila expected to live forever and would still be catching up on work the day she died.

Was it possible the attack on her mother was related to this long-ago affair? Their part of Maine was hardly a hot bed of thugs in suits, unless you counted the Legislature. But surely an attempt to embarrass Senator Buxton would be more effective with a live person? What would they gain by hurting her mother?

Unfortunately, she could answer that question. Buxton's opponent might want her mother alive in order to use her to embarrass the candidate, but what about Buxton himself? It was hard to imagine how anyone who had loved her mother could conceive of harming her. But what if politics had corrupted him as it had so many people? He'd walked out on her mother's love because he was ambitious. Who knew what such ambition might countenance?

Jenny looked around a room filled with regular Maine people. Men in overalls with bushy beards and beer guts. Overweight women in stretchy pants and sweatshirts. Tattooed teen-age girls in jeans and short tops and eye-makeup streaked from crying. Young men in John Deere caps and work boots. White-haired women in neat polyester dresses clutching vinyl purses on their laps. It was sickening to imagine the sprawling taint of national politics, with its 'end justified the means' philosophy, and its belief that every lie and misstep just needed the right "spin," reaching into a peaceful Maine town and striking down a good woman, just so a philanderer might not be embarrassed.

She pulled the scrap of paper out and read the words again. Buxton tape. What on earth could it mean? Maybe her father knew. She put the scrap of paper away with the letter.

Her father came in, looking stunned and broken, dropped into the chair beside her and sat staring at his clenched hands. "They said I had to leave. They need to do some procedures."

"Any change?" she asked. He didn't seem to have heard. She touched his arm. "Daddy, we should call people and let them know. Who should I call? The Masons? Uncle Clyde and Aunt Bonnie? What about Uncle Billy?"

"Don't you dare call him." Suddenly her father was back.

"He's her only living relative."

"Yes, and this is probably all his fault."

"What are earth are you talking about? Uncle Billy acts like a spoiled baby and jerk sometimes, but he'd never hurt mom. She's the only one in the whole world he cares about besides himself."

"He cares about himself too much."

His bitter tone was so out of character. "Explain this to me," she said, touching the outline of the letter in her pocket. "Something strange is going on."

"What do you mean, strange?"

"I'm talking about this." She handed him the letter. "And this paper, which was in her hand. I'm talking about why, last night, she said, 'Run, Jen, run. Burn the diary and run.' Run from whom? What diary? What was she talking about?"

He stared fixedly at the wall. "She was just babbling, honey. She didn't know what she was saying." He wouldn't look at her or the letter in his hand.

"Read the letter," she insisted. "Look at this paper. Then tell me, honestly, how you can believe she was just babbling. Someone tried to break into our house. Someone did get into her office."

With terrible reluctance, he pulled out his glasses and unfolded the letter. He read it slowly, running his finger under the words like a beginning reader. Then he returned it to the envelope, put the small paper in with it, and handed it back without comment. There was reverence in the way he handled it which she knew was respect for her mother's writing, for paper she'd recently touched with the hand that now lay so still.

Jenny bit her lip. It wasn't kind to pressure him but this felt urgent. Something awful was going on. "Daddy. Please. Tell me what this is about."

Her father shook his head as if he were trying to dislodge words that were stuck, then buried it in his hands. He looked old suddenly, and fragile, his silence a tangible thing between them. With an effort, she squelched her impatience. Across the room, a woman in a group clustered around a doctor covered her face and wailed.

"Oh, God, Jenny. The sins of the fathers." He pushed himself up and left.

She didn't follow, though she was exploding with frustration. She knew how he worked. He'd gone off to think. When he had things clear, he'd return and explain it to her. Her father was an amiable man, but he had to come to things at his own pace, even at times like this. Besides, one of them had to stay and wait for news.

Sighing, she got out her phone and started making calls. About half the people she reached had read about it in the paper or online or gotten a phone call. While she was on the phone, her mother's two best friends, Rose and Charlie, short for Charlotte, came in and sat down. Settling in for the long haul, Rose pulled out her needlework, Charlie some papers.

She saved the hardest calls, the Masons and Uncle Billy, until last. When she finally did call the Masons, Andy answered. "Dandy, it's Jenny," she said. "Did you hear?"

"I heard," he said grimly. "How's she doin'?"

"Not good, Dandy. At least, that's what they say."

"Adele's been squinting at her shotgun all morning, wishing she'd gone ahead and killed those two fellas when she had the chance. She's sure it's the same ones. Look, we're heading down there in a few minutes. Need anything?"

"Food," Jenny said. "I don't dare leave in case something... well, just in case, Dandy."

"You know Adele. I don't believe my mother's ever set foot outside the door without a basket of food, unless she's going grocery shopping. Don't worry. We'll bring food. Anything else? People I should call?"

"Look in on the house, would you? We went out in such a hurry last night, I don't know what state we left it in. We only meant to be gone a few minutes. There's probably still a propane lantern burning somewhere, unless it ran out of fuel. Is the power still out?"

"Came back on an hour ago, Spit. Don't you worry about anything here. I'll check it out. And we'll see you 'bout an hour, okay."

"Dandy. It's locked. The house."

"No problem." Of course not. Even if they'd installed new locks, her parents would have given the Masons a key.

She didn't want to let him go. She liked listening to his comforting voice. But there was nothing else to say. Dandy's own personal life might be a shambles, but like it is with good people you've always known, he had a way of making the world seem better. Right now, she needed that.

Growing up, he'd been the perfect big brother. Once, when her date had gotten drunk and refused to drive her home because he had intentions involving her that she wasn't interested in, Jenny had gotten out of the car and called Dandy. He'd come right away to get her. She could have called her parents, but she wanted someone who'd understand how betrayed and vulnerable she felt. Her mother would have told her she should have had more sense than to date one of the Jones boys; her father would have been sympathetic and made her tea. What she'd needed was someone to be outraged on her behalf, not understanding. She'd needed to rant and rave and weep. Dandy had let her do that.

It was time to call Uncle Billy, her mother's younger brother. She couldn't put it off any longer. Uncle Billy was a good time guy, lazy, amoral, self-centered, charming. Kind of like Drew. He never lived in the same place long, because of his habit of not paying rent. He always had two devoted girlfriends to keep the chaos in his life at a high level. He couldn't hold a job because the bosses treated him unfairly, had unrealistic expectations, played favorites, and expected him to work more than a few days in succession. He was the bane of her mother's life, regularly appearing for bail-outs until a couple years ago, when Lila abruptly stopped speaking to him.

Not that that stopped Billy. He still dropped in when her mother's car was gone, to cadge meals and cash from her father, and occasionally from Jenny herself. He was the fun uncle who let her do unsafe things like riding in the back of his pickup truck with her feet hanging off the end, jumping off bridge railings into swimming holes, and shooting beer bottles and street signs with a .22. Once she shot out a street light, but only once. The guilt had been too great.

She dialed the latest number she had for him and waited while the rings piled up. Billy didn't have an answering machine. Most of the people trying to reach him were looking to collect on bad debts. Finally, on the thirteenth ring, a tearful woman's voice answered.

"Billy Friedman, please," Jenny said. "This is his niece."

The woman started crying harder. "Oh, God, it's so awful," she wailed. "And poor Billy was just startin' to get himself on the straight and narrow, too."

Jenny felt a premonitory chill. "Has something happened to him?"

"Oh, gosh, honey, I'm sorry. I thought you knew about poor Billy's accident."

"What accident?" She could hardly bring up the words.

"Why, last night, in that awful storm, you know. Billy went down to the store to pick me up some cigarettes, and he never come home. Not that Billy ain't done that before, only not since he reformed and all. Then this morning I got my sister to come over and drive me, you know that I don't drive."

Jenny didn't even know who she was talking to.

"And when we went past the lake, I looked and there, stickin' outta the water was this antenna with a limp little raccoon's tail on it, just like Billy had on his truck. You know that part of the lake, where the river comes in, that don't freeze? I just gave the biggest scream, like, you know, that's him out there. Then the cops come and towed it out and poor Billy's still sittin' there in the truck, like he'd tried to drive it outta that lake. I never saw nothin' like it. Who'd you say you were?"

"His niece, Jenny."

"Oh. Billy always said you were a great kid. He liked you a lot. I'm sorry to have to be the one to tell you and all. Guess you'll take care of tellin' his family then?"

"Sure," Jenny said, head bobbing like a turkey gobbler. "I'm sorry. You must be very upset."

"I am," the woman said with a sob. "We were going to have a baby. Now the poor thing's gonna be born with no daddy, just like me. And let me tell you, that's the pits."

"I'm sorry," Jenny repeated.

"Maybe your mom, being a lawyer and all, can get me some money for the baby, on account of its daddy being drowned. Maybe there's some insurance or social security or something. You go ahead and ask her, all right? Tell her to call back Miss Jasmine Smith at this number, okay?"

"Okay." She would have agreed to anything to get off the phone.

But Miss Jasmine Smith had one more piece of information to impart. "You tell your mom Billy said she don't have to worry no more about that tape that had her mad as a wet hen. He wasn't never gonna sell it. He says it's somewhere nobody's gonna find it. He said it was on ice. Or, uh, he'd iced it or aced it or some such thing. You know how he talked. All that movie slang. Anyways, you ask her about the money, okay?" And poor pregnant, sobbing Jasmine was gone.

Jenny buried her head in her hands. Her mother on life support. Uncle Billy dead. Uncle Billy was a feckless loser but he'd led a charmed life, bouncing, like his checks, from one thing to another. Jobs. Women.

Schemes. People like Billy didn't drive their pickups into ponds. They drove them into the sunset, leaving fans and critics reading their bumper stickers. NUKE THE WHALES. NO, BUT I'VE HUGGED YOURS. BADASS BEER: HELPING UGLY PEOPLE HAVE SEX SINCE 1846.

What the hell was going on?

THE GOVERNOR'S OFFICE

ALBANY, NEW YORK

The Honorable Lucius Alfonso didn't read Maine papers. He read New York and Washington papers. He read *U.S. News & World Report*. He read the memos his aides prepared to brief him on national issues. He knew more about welfare and health care, Medicare and Medicaid and military spending and education than he'd ever cared to know. Occasionally, when he was alone, he read Hustler and dreamed of ramming those plump, inviting asses. More often, he dreamed of watching the good Senator from Maine, James Buxton, fall face first in the mud. If necessary, he'd carry the water and make the mud.

He raised his head and met O'Malley's dancing eyes. "I don't see how it does us any good to have her dead, Mike. We need a living, breathing woman. From the pictures, she was a nice little piece, too."

The woman across the table cleared her throat. Keris Carlyle hid her neat body and lovely long legs beneath high-necked blouses and boxy suits. Her only feminine indulgence was her hair, gorgeous, breast-length, Marilyn Monroe platinum hair. The governor couldn't keep himself from imagining it on his pillow.

Now Keris tossed that hair and said a single word, "Pig."

The governor flushed and fumbled with some papers on his desk. O'Malley had brought her in to help him improve his image with women voters, to raise his consciousness about his unconscious sexism. At least ten times a day, she made him feel like a horny little boy.

"She's still living and breathing, Lou."

"In a coma. On life support. That's your idea of a good time?"

Keris cleared her throat again.

"Did we do this?"

O'Malley's face was perfectly blank. "Not to my knowledge," he said. "But our operatives in the field report rumors that there's a video tape somewhere of the good Senator and Ms. Lila Friedman bumping uglies."

Keris cleared her throat a third time

"Shit, Keris, you're supposed to be keeping track of him, not me."

"You speak for him," she said quietly. "You are his public representative. He will be judged by what you do and say as well as by what he does and says. You can't go around sounding like a paternalistic, red-neck wildebeest, Michael, whether you like it or not. In here, you can do it if you want, so long as you're aware of what you're doing. Out there..." she pointed at the closed door, "you can't do it at all."

She switched her focus to the governor. "Look, Lou." She tapped her pencil on the table. "You've already got an image problem. Angela has been a brick, but your daughter Gina has publicly accused you of hitting your wife. We're working on bringing Gina into the fold, giving her a role in the campaign, but that's your one bite of the apple. You can probably diffuse being a wife-beater if you show up enough places with Gina and Angela at your side. But not..."

She paused for effect. "Not if your eyes pop every time a nice set of tits walks by. Not if you drool every time a big, round ass rolls past. Not if you see women as a collection of body parts you'd like to back up against the wall and fuck instead of intelligent people who vote."

Damn, Alfonso thought. She's read my mind. He tapped the article again. "So, Mikey, we've got total deniability on this?"

O'Malley nodded.

"What about the tape?"

"We're working on it. Unfortunately, the only person who seems to have known where it is took a permanent wrong turn and ended up at the bottom of a lake."

"That's all we've got? No gossipy best friends, confidants, nosy neighbors? Jealous other women? There has to be something."

"May be hard for you to believe this, Lou, but the woman is a saint. Brave, dedicated, hard-working poverty lawyer, willing to give her all for her clients. Happily married. A mother. No lovers. No scandals. People up there are more likely to point at you with a shotgun than tell you something bad about her."

"There must be something, Mike. Nobody's perfect."

"Other than Buxton, she comes close. Maybe the daughter knows something. Rumor is they're tight. Maybe Friedman confided the details of this past love to her daughter as a cautionary tale."

"How would we use anything we got from the daughter?" the governor asked.

"Like something from the *National Enquirer*," Keris suggested. "Get close to the kid. She's bound to be upset. Get her talking. A few drinks, a sympathetic ear, get her to spill her guts. Especially since her boyfriend just cheated on her with her best friend."

"How do you people learn this stuff?"

Keris and Mike exchanged smiles. "Tearful daughter reveals mother's death-bed confession of affair with Senator Buxton."

He slapped the table with glee. "You two are soulless fiends."

Keris lowered her eyes modestly. "Thank you, Governor," she said. "We do our best."

"Get Dobbs on the phone and have him find the daughter. Keris, I want you to fly up there and make the contact personally. You'll know how to get her talking. Be sure you record every word she says. O'Malley, you keep working on that tape. Someone must know where it is."

The governor watched them walk out of his office. O'Malley was getting fat. His ass jiggled when he walked. Oughta send him to the gym. But then poor Mikey might have a heart attack, and he couldn't do the campaign without him. Carlyle, on the other hand, had a perfect ass. The governor grinned his wolfish grin. With their help, Buxton's mud was on the way. He could hardly wait to see old holier than thou wallowing in it.

THE BUXTON CAMPAIGN

WASHINGTON, D.C.

He considered it his duty, as a Senator from Maine, to read the daily papers from Portland, Bangor and Augusta. Most mornings, he ate breakfast absently as his fingers grew black with ink. Today was no different. On Saturdays, unless they had an early appearance, Maggie slept late. It was one of her few indulgences, and he preferred eating breakfast alone. Over the years, he'd trained himself to be "on" and gregarious at all hours, but he loved solitude.

So Maggie wasn't there to see his face, and ply her bitter tongue, when he read that a popular local lawyer was in intensive care after a vicious attack in her office. There was a picture of Lila, another of her husband and daughter. He lingered over Lila's and felt a stabbing pain in his heart. Probably not signs of a heart attack, but maybe signs of an attack of heart. She'd changed so little! She still wore her dark hair long, still had that great, warm smile and those little crinkly lines between her eyebrows when she smiled. Her daughter looked just like her.

There was that twinge again. Not surprising. He'd spent a lifetime controlling himself and others, becoming the perfect political creature. But a woman like Lila Friedman was rare. He might not think of her for a decade, but let her into his consciousness and she was back 100%. Lila had been a unique experience for him. A woman of extraordinary passion. Physically small but emotionally large. Her beauty came from warmth and vitality that gave her an inner glow. He was not being fanciful. Everyone who knew her felt it. He had basked in that heat. Loved her, used her, depended on her and shared his deepest secrets. He had walked away, knowing she'd keep his secrets, and never looked back.

He was known for his empathy with regular people—for being able to connect with their suffering and offer comfort. This morning that was nothing but a burden. He sat in his comfortable Washington home imagining Lila's family and friends huddled in a sterile waiting room, suffering. His eggs grew cold, the toast hard, the coffee cool before he folded the paper and went to the phone. "Frank," he said, "we need to talk."

"Got a tight schedule today, Jim. I could swing by around two?"

"Now, Frank. As soon as you can get here."

"What's this about?"

"I'll tell you when you get here." Then he called his long-time press secretary, Linwood Bean. "Woody? Jim. Can you give me a few minutes?" He called the state trooper, Ken Bass, who had come from Maine with him to be in charge of security, with the same request. Ken and Woody didn't just work for him; they were his two best friends.

Ken and Woody came promptly. Buxton showed them the pictures of Lila, and had them read the story. Woody made fresh coffee. Ken opened the box of doughnuts he'd brought. They ate and drank and waited for Frank. Half an hour later, he showed up, irritable and impatient.

The Senator spread the newspaper out on the table and pointed to the article. "You seen this yet?"

Frank shook his head, not really looking. "What's the point, Jim? I've got a million things to do."

"Read it, Frank."

His campaign manager scanned the article. "So she had an accident, Jim. These things happen. Violent crime's increasing in rural areas. What's the big deal?"

"You see this?" the Senator asked, opening the paper to another story, the one about Billy's unfortunate drowning.

Frank scanned again, his cruel bright face giving nothing away. "Any relation?" he asked.

"Her brother," the Senator said.

"Weird coincidence," Frank said.

"A little too weird, Frank. I need to ask you one simple question."

Frank straightened his tie and looked out at the blooming day. "What's that, Jim?"

"Did we have anything to do with this?"

Frank's laugh resembled nothing so much as the bark of a seal. "Why on earth would you ask that? Why would we have something to do with it, Jim?"

"There are people whose way of dealing with a potentially embarrassing situation is to silence the potential embarrassers permanently."

"But that," Frank smoothed the collar of his shirt, "would not be consistent with our campaign values, would it? So it can't have been us. Even though we want desperately to be President and recognize that ambition must sometimes be ruthless." He took a few steps toward the door. "There were rumors Lila Friedman kept a diary. Also that the two of you were memorialized on video. I don't recall you telling me about those things." His face was as bland as applesauce. "Maybe that's what they were looking for. With her brother gone and Ms. Friedman comatose, I guess we'll never know. Unless Alfonso calls a press conference for a little show and tell, in which case, your lines are: It was a long time ago, during a rough patch in your marriage, Maggie has long since forgiven you, etc. Was there anything else?"

This was the person who was going to get him elected. A man he hated more every day. He couldn't fire a man who knew so much. It was like discovering your priest was screwing altar boys when the man knew all your sins.

As soon as the door had closed behind Frank, he turned to his friends. "Keep an eye on him," he said. "I want to know what he's up to. And Ken, ask your buddies back home to keep us informed, okay? I want to know who visits the hospital. I want updates on her condition. Tell them to keep a close eye on the rest of the family. Got it? And see what you can learn about any diaries or video. I thought that tape had been destroyed years ago."

"In a moment, in the twinkling of an eye…
we shall be changed…"
1 Corinthians 15:52

CHAPTER FIVE

Jenny returned to her chair, moving with the stunned mechanics of an accident victim. She stared at the pad in her hand, numbed by one too many pieces of bad news. Gradually, she realized someone was talking.

"Jenny? Honey, are you all right? Is there anything I can do?" Rose Hawthorne stood there, her kind face knotted with worry. Rose was a soft, billowy woman with natural pink cheeks and irrepressible blonde curls skewered into a knot from which they always escaped. She had quick, bright eyes and always smelled faintly of flowers. She had been Jenny's kindergarten teacher.

Jenny felt the tears start. Rose was another person it was safe to cry with. "Uncle Billy is dead."

Rose dropped down beside her, pulling Jenny's head against her gardenia-scented shoulder. "There, darling, there now. It's all right to cry." Rose handed her a soft pink tissue. "Have you eaten anything?"

Jenny shook her head. "I didn't want to leave. In case…"

"Of course. Well, Charlie and I brought muffins and orange juice. Would you like that?" Rose signaled for Charlie to join them. How thoughtful these women were.

When she'd wolfed down a muffin, Charlie said, "So, what's the story?"

"She's in a coma. There's been no change for hours. They warn us not to expect too much, but how can we not? She's spent her whole life being a tough, won't back down woman." Her voice faltered. "Why would she be different now?"

Charlie squeezed her hand. "That's what I think, too. Can we see her?"

Jenny shook her head. "Immediate family only. And we're only allowed in on alternate Thursdays between 2:00 and 2:05. a.m." At Rose's shocked look, she explained, "We're only supposed to be there a few minutes at a time. Seems like as soon as we go in, they need to do a procedure and send us out again."

"Jenny, I—" Charlie bit her lip, trying to make up her mind about something. Then she reached into the canvas work bag and pulled out a book-shaped package wrapped in brown paper. She balanced it on her knees, tapping it with busy fingers. "Maybe I'm jumping the gun," she said.

Jenny'd exhausted her capacity to handle complications. She wanted to snatch the package and tear it open. With difficulty, she sat on her hands.

"Your mother came to my house one night last week on her way home from work, carrying this package," Charlie said. "She was behaving strangely. Nervous. Distracted." She lapsed into another nerve-wracking silence. "If she wasn't the world's bravest person, I'd say she was scared. She asked if I'd keep it for her. Of course I said yes. When a friend asks for a favor, what else do you say? She said if anything happened to her, I was to give it to you. I thought it was silly, you know, but she was asking. I never imagined anything would happen, and I don't know if this…" A tear streaked its way down her cheek.

In the harsh light, Charlie looked washed-out and old. Jenny felt guilty for her impatience. This was Charlie's tragedy, too.

"I don't know if this is what she meant by something happening," Charlie said. She pulled out a tissue and dabbed at her eyes. "And I can't ask her. So here." She held out the package. "I'm giving it to you."

"What is it?" Jenny asked.

Charlie shook her head. "I have no idea. Maybe there's a note inside."

A small man in blue hospital garb with a dry, supercilious face came through the door carrying a clipboard. The room fell silent, all the eyes fixing on him. "Mr. Cates?" he said. "Mr. Elmer Cates."

Jenny went over to him. "I'm Jenny Cates," she said. "His daughter. Your patient is my mother."

"I'm afraid I need your father, honey," he said. "I need an adult to sign this form."

"I am an adult," she said, trying not to sound huffy. "What's this all about?"

He signaled for her to follow him back through the doors into the blank, airless hallway where other groups with red eyes and strained faces had gathered around tired men and women in printed blue scrubs that looked like toddler's playwear. "Your mother needs an operation," he said. "There's been swelling, putting pressure on the brain. We need to relieve that pressure to prevent further damage."

"I thought you took care of that last night," she said.

He shoved the clipboard at her, angrily clicking the pen to life. "Look, you can sign it or not," he said. "She needs the operation."

"What's the operation supposed to do?" she asked. "What are the risks? Do we have any choice? Is there a 'wait and see' alternative?"

He shrugged. "I'll make it simple for you, sweetheart. She has it, and maybe she survives. She doesn't, she dies." He waggled the clipboard and the pen.

Jenny took them. "This is informed consent?"

He didn't answer.

She looked at her watch. Six hours since they'd had any information, and repeated, "This is what you call keeping the family informed?"

"Look, dear, either sign it or don't. Your choice. I haven't got time for this. I've got people in serious conditions waiting."

She signed the form, holding back tears as she forced words around the lump in her throat. "What can you tell me about her condition, other than that she needs the surgery?" *Anything,* she thought. *Just give me something hopeful to cling to.*

He shrugged. "Besides the swelling? Nothing new."

She lost it then. Just sign it, Dear. Honey. Sweetheart. Hadn't anyone ever taught him about dealing with women? With people? Her mother would have eaten this guy alive. The thought of someone so insensitive working on her mother sickened her. She hoped for an inverse relationship between skills and bedside manner. She squinted at his name tag. "Actually, the person in serious condition is you, Dr. Feeney. You've lost your humanity." She rushed back through the swinging doors.

A nurse. She should find a nurse. They were the ones who'd tell families what was happening. But not while her voice was shaking and she couldn't hold back tears. She walked out and down corridor after corridor. Walking blindly, the passing scene nothing but a blur. Where on earth had her father gone? She reached the far end of the hospital and stared out the window. A glorious day with clear blue sky and golden sun.

She was a college student on spring break. Shouldn't she be sitting on a beach somewhere?

She retraced her steps to the L.L.Bean Special Care unit. L.L.Bean. Such irony. She knew it simply reflected philanthropy, but the idea of a well-known supplier of outerwear and sporting gear appending its name to a wing serving helpless people wired to banks of machines struck her as absurd. Her mother wasn't snazzily dressed in a velvety-soft microfleece night shirt, clutching a moose mug as she gazed out at the snowy landscape. She was wearing a faded blue and white johnny, tugged down to accommodate all the electronic leads glued to her chest. Her feet weren't cozy in slippers, but in elastic stockings to keep her circulation going.

Her eyes blurred, vision obscured like a downpour on a windshield. She passed the volunteer behind the desk with a nod, grabbing a handful of tissues from the tiny box on the desk. Why, in a place so full of tears, did they have such tiny boxes?

Her father was outside the waiting room, talking with Adele and Andy Mason. "Daddy," she said, "where have you been? They were looking for you to sign a consent form. They need to do another operation. I signed it, but you should see if you can get more information about what's going on."

He rushed off without a word, leaving her with the Masons.

Adele hefted a basket. "Got enough food in here to keep us all for days," she said. "Andy said you were hungry."

Jenny reached around the basket and gave the old lady a hug. "Thanks for coming," she said.

"Hey, where's my hug?" Andy complained.

"Hug an old thing like you, Dandy? Why would I do that?"

He picked her up in bear hug, swung her around, and set her back on her feet. "Because I'm your friend," he said. "What's the news?"

"She's in a coma. Now they say she needs surgery—something about relieving pressure on the brain. That's all they've told us. Except to expect the worst."

"Not from Lila," Adele interrupted. "They're seeing what they see, not knowing what we know. Your mother is tough."

Jenny agreed.

The pale, limp Lila who was plugged into all those machines looked awfully vulnerable. Every time she stood near her mother, watching the multi-colored rows of blips on the monitor, hearing the mechanical breathing, she had a powerful wish to transfuse some of her own life. She would have given it all to save her mother. Her father would have, too. Any of her friends would have. How odd to go through conversational rituals when every one of them wanted to beat on the ground, holler, storm through the doors and demand action. When even gentle Rose would have gladly dismembered Lila's attackers.

"Everything okay at the house?"

Dandy nodded. "Lights off. Doors locked. I've asked the police to keep an eye on the place. Oh, while I was in the kitchen, your boyfriend, Drew, called. He wants you to call. Says it's important."

"Drew thinks everything he wants is important."

Dandy made a defensive gesture. "Up to you, Jen. He said he knows you don't want to talk to him but to ask you to please call anyway. Something about the apartment. He sounded frantic."

She was sure she knew what this would be about. Something bad had happened. Another bad thing. She wasn't up for more bad news.

"Here's the number." Dandy handed her a piece of paper. "Has your dad eaten?"

"I don't think so."

"We'll go see," he said, opening the door and holding it for his mother and the basket to pass through. "You call that guy. He sounded upset."

"He should be."

Dandy just gave her his "don't go being an uppity woman with me" look. He'd been giving it to her since she was thirteen, when she first became an uppity woman.

Obediently, she went to the end of the corridor and got out her phone. It wasn't the apartment number. He must already be at home. When he answered, she said, "It's Jenny."

"Oh, Jen. Thank goodness. I must have called a thousand times. Listen, don't hang up on me, please. I'm at home. I guess you know that, since you called me here. Betty called me. Yeah. Guess I know how you feel about that, too."

"Like hell you do."

"Look, just let me say this, okay, then you can call me every name in the book. Someone broke into the apartment last night and completely trashed it. They tried to set it on fire, but I guess the couple upstairs smelled smoke and called the fire department, so things aren't bad. Just messy. I wanted you to know, in case, you know, you came back or something. I didn't want you to think I did it. I'll clean it up when I get back but like, right now, I can't face it. Sorry. You've got the number here, right, in case you need me?"

"I've got it."

She pictured their neat little apartment a shambles like her mother's office. It was the first place besides Hallowell she'd thought of as 'home.' What on earth was going on? She wanted to take refuge in some internal place like her father could. But she had a photographic memory. She'd always be able to recall her mother's limp, white hand. The crumpled form. The vivid red of the blood contrasting with the dark, dark hair. The vulnerability of her mother's white neck when her father pushed the hair aside looking for a pulse.

"Jen? You still there?"

"Yes." She was going to cry again.

"I'm sorry about your mother. I know how much you love her. And I may be a no good shit, but if you ever need me for anything, I'm here."

"I've got to go." She closed the phone, stumbled back to the waiting room, and collapsed against Dandy's chest. "Poor Dandy. You get all the hard jobs, don't you?"

"Sit down and eat," he said gruffly. Dandy was a taciturn Mainer, like his mother. Being thanked made him uncomfortable. He poured out strong black coffee from a thermos. "You take sugar and cream in yours, right?"

She took the coffee and the thick turkey sandwich on homemade bread, but after one huge bite, she wasn't hungry. Hollow and empty but not hungry. Carefully, she folded the sandwich back into its wrapper. "Sorry," she said. "I can't eat right now. I just found out..."

She took a few slow breaths, willing her throat to relax. She needed to get these words out. "I just found out Uncle Billy's dead. Drove his truck into a lake last night in the snowstorm. But I don't think it was an accident."

Adele was watching her with intent, bright eyes. When Jenny said this, she nodded. "Ever since I saw those two trying to break into your folks' place, I've thought something mighty strange was goin' on."

"Now mother, you can't go building a federal case out of a couple of housebreakers," Dandy said.

"Andy Mason, you don't know what you're talking about," his mother said. "When's the last time you heard of a couple rural Maine housebreakers in business suits with polished shoes?"

Andy stared down at his own muddy Bean boots.

"You got any more of those sandwiches?" her father asked, dropping heavily into a chair.

"Enough for the Russian army."

"Daddy, did you learn anything?"

He shook his head in exasperation. "I've worked with autistic kids more communicative than that damned Feeney. They're taking her to surgery now."

"Why now? Why didn't they do it last night? What does it mean?"

Her father sighed. "Honey, I wish I knew. I called Dr. Hadley and explained the situation. He's going to make some calls and see what he can find out. You know how doctors are. They'll tell each other things they won't tell us." He seized the sandwich Adele offered and wolfed it down. "Good," he muttered around the last bite. "Great. Got another?"

She held out her own sandwich. "Here, you can have mine."

"No, Jen," he said. "You need to eat."

"I can't." She unwrapped the sandwich and pressed it into his hand. When her father had finished the second sandwich and some coffee, she stood. "Daddy, can I talk to you for a minute. Alone?"

For a moment, she thought he'd refuse. Then he said, "Excuse us a moment," to Dandy and Adele, and led her into the hall. "Jenny," he said, looking out the window instead of her, "this is a lot more complicated than you think. I'm not ready to explain it. I know you have a right to understand what's going on. Just give me some time, okay? I'm too worried about your mother right now to think clearly."

She'd brought him out here to tell him about Billy, not press him about the letter, but she wasn't letting that subject slip away. "I don't see what the big mystery is. So what if Mom had an affair before she married you. It's no one's business but theirs. If she wants to deny it and he denies it, that's the end of it. What's the big deal?"

He ran a hand through his graying hair and returned to staring out the window. "It's more complicated than that. More embarrassing. There may be a..."

"Tape," she finished.

"A tape," he echoed.

"Which Uncle Billy had. Why would Uncle Billy have a tape of Mom and Senator Buxton?"

"Because Billy is a shit," her father said.

"Was," she corrected. "Billy is dead."

Her father stared at her. "Billy's what? What are you talking about?"

A roar in her brain threatened to drown everything out. Something very bad was going on here. Her mother attacked and unconscious. Uncle Billy dead. Now her father acting like a stranger. Why didn't her father want to explain? They'd always been honest with each other.

"I called to tell him what had happened. Uncle Billy. I know you're mad at him, but he had to be told. The woman who answered said he was dead. Went out last night for cigarettes and drove his truck into a lake. She said to tell Mom you guys don't need to worry about the tape. He's... what did she say? Put it on ice? I don't know what she meant. I don't think she did, either. I know you know what's on that tape, Daddy. What the hell is going on?"

She gripped his arm. "I'm not a baby. The people who are being hurt I love and care about, too. My apartment's been trashed and burned. My mother's in a coma. My uncle is dead. My mother once had an affair with her boss she thought was important enough to write me about. Before this happened, she was worried about a tape. And you know why."

Very slowly, he turned toward her, his face the color of ashes. "You have your mother's diary?"

"What diary? What are you talking about?"

The roar was getting louder. Driving home from Ohio, a lifetime ago that was only yesterday, she'd felt alien, detached from her connections with the rest of the species. Everything she'd believed about herself and Drew was false. She'd been fleeing to home, to love and good sense, order and security. Now she felt more isolated than ever.

"Your mother's diary. She was worried about having it. I thought she'd sent it to you."

Was the package from Charlie her mother's diary? Jenny said, "Charlie gave me a package."

"Billy's really dead?"

"That's what his pregnant girlfriend says."

Her father started walking away. All her frustration with the things she couldn't control and the answers she couldn't get exploded. She went after him and grabbed his arm. "Daddy! Come on. You can't walk away. You've got to tell me what's going on."

He turned, his mouth moving, though at first no words came out. "Jennifer... I wish I didn't have to."

He hesitated. "You might as well know..."

Looking like he was in acute pain, he cut her loose from everything she'd taken as a given. "Senator Buxton is your biological father."

"…but what am I?
An infant crying in the night:
An infant crying for the light:
And with no language but a cry."
—Tennyson, "In Memoriam"

CHAPTER SIX

The motel was somewhere in western Massachusetts. Jenny couldn't have given any better information. She'd seen the sign just as her eyes threatened to close and no amount of cold air, will-power, or loud music could revive her. The room was plain. Brown carpet. Brown upholstery. Brown and yellow bedspread. Ugly painting of unnatural ducks on an unnatural pond. It smelled of cigarettes, stale air, and sweet air-freshener. She'd never stayed in a motel by herself.

Not that decor mattered. Since she'd left Portland, imaginary bad guys had lurked in her back seat, in other cars, and all the roadside stops. Fear had driven her on, refusing to let her stop except for a dash to the bathroom and a snatched cup of coffee, until she could go no farther. She was bone weary. Her body ached. Her heart ached. All she cared about was a shower and a bed. Her face in the mirror looked like one of those magazine ads: All she has ever known is poverty and sorrow. For just pennies a day, you can help little Jenny.

Damn! She was going to cry again. She'd cried her way home from Ohio to Maine, and found disaster rather than refuge, and cried back through Maine, New Hampshire and most of Massachusetts while she tried to keep Dandy's puke-green Plymouth Fury on the road. After her own little car, it was like piloting the Queen Mary. Her mother had said, "Run, Jenny, run. Burn diary and run." Someone had tried to kill her mother. Someone *had* killed Uncle Billy. So she was running. But she wouldn't burn the diary until she read it and understood what this was about.

Her escape had been plotted by a bunch of amateurs while she had huddled in stunned silence, processing her father's shattering news. She still hadn't. It sat in her brain like a sharp pebble. She couldn't coat it with soothing layers and turn it into a pearl. The ugly bit of information about Senator Buxton shook loose a piece of her life.

On Friday, she'd been a happy college student, in love, coming home to discuss her future with her parents. Now so much had been torn away. Her lover had betrayed her. Her mother had gone into a place where she couldn't be reached. Her apartment was trashed. Her Uncle Billy was dead. Her father had revealed she was someone else's child. She was used to defining herself in relation to others. Lila Friedman's daughter. Drew's girlfriend. Dr. Horner's best student. It had been easy to be strong and competent in the relative safety of a college campus, her parents only a phone call away.

Now she felt a profound sense of dislocation, walking a tightrope for the first time without a net.

In her wallet, and, because she was cautious, in the key pocket of her bra and in her shoe, were wads of cash gathered from her father, Dandy, Adele, Rose, and Charlie, with a supplement from her father's ATM. She also had Dandy's bank card, along with the information that his password was "Skunk." She was on her way to a farm near Elmira, New York, to stay with one of Rose's cousins. Their hastily concocted story was she'd had a fight with her father, borrowed Andy's car keys, and disappeared.

Buying into their panic, she'd left before her mother got back from surgery, letting them make plans for her without reflection. Bundled out, still in a daze, the package from Charlie in her pack. She let Dandy walk her to her car so she could get her suitcase and give him her keys. It was only when she was on the road that she'd begun to be afraid. Someone was killing her family, one by one.

She shook her head at the drawn, tired woman in the mirror who'd stolen her face and wasn't taking care of it. "We are something from a bad novel."

She got clean clothes from her suitcase and went into the bathroom, pulling off the clothes she'd worn so long. They smelled. She smelled. Her hair was greasy. Undressed, she looked skinnier than ever. The original ninety-eight-pound weakling, or, in her case, the 108-pound weakling. Maybe less after all the meals she'd missed.

She stepped in the shower, scrubbing as though she could wash the last few days away. Then she closed her eyes, giving herself up to the soothing heat. She loved her mother. She loved her father who was not her father. She wanted to be home in her old room, eating buttery cinnamon toast and reading in bed.

Thinking of home dragged her back to her reality, to a self awash with scary, out-of-control feelings. Drying with a towel big enough for a small dwarf on a dry day, she started getting angry. She'd been a good person. A loving girlfriend to Drew, a loving daughter to her parents. She didn't deserve this. Eventually, her anger focused on those it was hardest for her to be mad at: her parents. She felt betrayed. Why wait twenty-one years to tell her this? Or, since for twenty-one years it hadn't been something they wanted to share, why tell her now?

Of course, she knew why. Because she might become a pawn in a nasty political game. Because whoever wanted Lila Friedman silenced might want Jenny silenced, too.

She hated being so scared and anxious, which got her mad at the real culprits here—the candidates. Mad at people who put ambition above humanity, who had deemed her mother, her uncle, perhaps herself, expendable. Who else wanted to hurt any of them? Something bad happening to her mother and her uncle the same night was no coincidence.

Anger was energizing. Alfonso beat his wife. Buxton had had an extramarital affair. Neither man was decent enough to be president.

Cursing Buxton for his fateful infidelity provided the energy to get dressed and plan her next steps. She put on a shapeless T-shirt, a big black sweatshirt she'd appropriated from her father, and baggy black sweatpants from the Salvation Army. A small label in the pants declared she was Jon Blakely. It was six o'clock. In half an hour, she'd call the hospital for news. There was a public phone near the motel office she could use—a dinosaur in this cell phone era. But Jenny'd been educated by movies and TV—use a pay phone if you don't want to be caught, and keep it short. Then she'd eat something. An army marches on its stomach, even an army of one.

She turned on the news for company and was rewarded with a couple of fires, a murder, and two accidents, one involving a fiery crash at a toll booth, cheering fare under the circumstances, then commercials for fast food and antacids to combat the effects of fast food, followed by the national news. The lead story featured Presidential candidate James

Buxton, shown racing from one primary to another, as the commentators announced he'd made a major speech decrying tax cuts when the country still had a huge deficit, when there wasn't enough money for health care, when there was a desperate shortage of affordable housing. When DACA hadn't been renewed.

Despite growing up near the capital, and her parents' sometimes heated political debates, she'd ignored the campaign. Tonight she couldn't take her eyes off the screen, viewing Buxton not as a presidential candidate but as a parental candidate. She peered at the face on the screen not for sincerity but resemblance. She watched the way he spoke, the way he moved, studied the details of his face. In the end, it was his eyes. Intense blue eyes with thick brows and ample lashes. She turned off the TV, went and stared in the mirror. Jenny thought she saw Buxton's blue eyes staring back from her own face.

How dare he leave his mark on her, this hit and run man who'd loved her mother and abandoned them both? She kicked the tub in fury. Her eyes, her very own eyes, eyes she lined in blue and widened with mascara, suddenly felt like a taint she couldn't scrub away.

At 6:25, she grabbed her purse, put on her coat, and headed out. At the door she paused and got the package Charlie had given her, which she assumed was the diary. Something important enough to burn, maybe important enough to kill for, shouldn't be left unguarded.

The night was brisk and windy, the outside phone just a small Plexiglas shell on a post. She pulled her jacket tight, readied a handful of change and dialed the number. Her father answered on the first ring, breathless with anxiety. "Jenny? Honey? Are you all right?"

"Just tired, Daddy. I'm going to eat and go right to sleep. How's Mom?"

An ominous silence.

"Daddy?" Even to her own ears, her voice seemed frantic.

"The surgery seems to have relieved the pressure on her brain, but then her heart stopped... what do they call it? Cardiac arrest. They've revived her twice. She seems stable now but they're urging us to be realistic."

She searched for encouraging words. "They don't know her like we do. They look at her and see a delicate, middle-aged woman. We see a fighter. Next time they let you in, you bend down and whisper that she'd better not wimp out. Tell her we're counting on her."

"You bet, honey." He was crying, muffled sobs traveling like piercing arrows down the wire. She stretched a hand into the darkness, longing to touch him. Damn! She'd meant to buck him up. The phone was a crappy medium for transmitting the nuances of communication. A blunt instrument.

"I'll call in the morning, okay? Around six?"

He made an affirmative sound.

"Get some rest if you can, Daddy. I love you."

She was alone with a cold black receiver in her hand, standing in the March wind in a place she didn't want to be. Bits of trash scuttled by like windblown crabs. On the highway, cars and trucks passed in a blaze of sound and light. Life going busily on while they were all frozen in a tableau of waiting. Numbly, she walked to the coffee shop, picturing her mother's still body, the wall of machines and monitors, life measured in multicolored charts and graphs.

The hostess glanced at her incuriously. "One?" she said.

Jenny nodded and followed the woman to a table by the window. She slid onto the red plastic bench and opened her menu. The place was quiet.

"Can I bring you something from the bar while you're deciding?"

Jenny looked up, startled. A drink. Did she want a drink? She thought she did. She couldn't get more muddled and it might help her sleep. "A glass of white wine," she said.

The waitress nodded. "May I see your license, please?"

Jenny handed it over, not used to being carded. At school, she mostly drank at parties and at home. At the restaurants they went to, the waitresses knew her. Most were younger than she was. The waitress read it and handed it back. "Sorry," she said. "Rules, you know."

"I know." When she brought the wine, Jenny ordered chicken potpie and salad. Potpie sounded homey and comforting, and salad nutritious. She couldn't recall the last time she'd eaten anything green. The word green reminded her of the spot on her toe, the one she'd stared at while trying not to look at Drew. She checked her shoe. It was still there.

Everyone else was eating in groups of twos, threes, and fours. She'd never eaten alone in a real restaurant before, just in fast-food places. She stared at the tablecloth and out the window, concentrating on her wine, wishing she'd brought a book—she wasn't about to open the diaries in public—and feeling her aloneness. Pretending everything didn't seem more threatening as it grew dark.

A few minutes later, the hostess seated another single woman at a table across from her. She looked like she might be a young mother or an aerobics instructor—blonde pony-tail clipped back with a flowered barrette, tight jeans and a baggy U-Mass sweatshirt under a barn jacket. She took off the jacket and studied the menu. When the waitress came, she ordered a glass of wine and got carded just like Jenny had. She smiled over at Jenny. "I suppose when we're forty, we'll find this flattering, right?"

Jenny nodded. "I know they have to but it makes me feel foolish," she said. "Are you alone?"

The woman nodded. "I had to make a delivery. I make stained-glass windows and they said they needed the window today. I ran late, rushing to get it done. You know how things always go wrong when you rush. Then they were late showing up at the house. I'm sitting there in the van cooling my heels and thinking some pretty ugly thoughts. You know how it goes, hurry up and wait. And then they haggled about price. I hate that. Next time I'm getting the money up front. I always ask for half, but it's a lot of work and..." She paused as the hostess walked between them to seat a couple. "...and then a lot of times they hem and haw about paying." The waitress hurried past again.

"Look, what if I move over there," the woman said. "So we can talk. Except, I wouldn't want to be a nuisance or anything," she hesitated, "if you wanted to be alone."

"No. I mean, come ahead," Jenny said. "I've been driving all day and it would be fun to talk to someone besides the radio."

The woman slid onto the bench across from her. "Jeannina Barnes," she said, "Nina for short. I'm going home to Becket, you ever heard of it?"

Jenny shook her head.

"Cute little place, out in the middle of nowhere, just the way I like it. But we've got dance and rolling hills and interesting people. I teach at a school there. I was delivering the window to Newton. Someone's big mansion. Nouveau mansion. Bad taste nouveau mansion. Normally I'd go straight home, it's not so much farther, but when I'm working, I forget to eat, and I was so hungry my stomach was rattling. Where are you coming from that's had you driving all day?" Her wine came and she sipped it eagerly.

"Maine," Jenny said, adding, "I'm Jenny."

The waitress came to take Nina's order. "What are you having, Jenny?" she asked.

"Potpie and salad."

Nina folded her menu. "I'll have the same," she said. "And bring us each another glass of wine."

When the waitress was gone, she said, "And where are you headed?"

Jenny was a bad liar, so she fell back on advice she'd read in books—stay as close to the truth as possible. "Ohio. Back to school."

"End of spring break, huh? Yours was early." She finished her wine and set the glass on the table with a satisfied thump. "You were at home?"

Jenny nodded.

"How was that? I used to avoid going home. My folks were always on my case about something. How I dressed or whether I had a boyfriend and was I keeping up my grades because I had to think about my future, and was I looking for a summer job. All that stuff. I'm so glad to be grown-up and on my own. But not everyone feels that way."

"I guess I'm lucky," Jenny said. "I like being at home." Her dinner arrived, the potpie steaming hot and smelling like home-cooked food.

"That looks great," Nina said. "Good choice. I always think of stuff like that as comfort food."

"Me, too," Jenny said. She poked tentatively at the crust with her fork, wondering, since they weren't really together, whether it was rude to go ahead and eat.

"Go ahead," Nina urged. "Don't wait for me." Jenny broke the crust to let it cool. "You must be a senior, if you're old enough to drink?"

"That's right. Almost done. Now I have to figure out what to do with my life. How did you ever get into stained glass?"

Nina laughed. "It was the furthest thing from the law I could think of. My parents are lawyers and they wanted me to be one, too. Guess I took the teenage rebellion thing too seriously, because I deliberately went looking for something creative, something that would keep me in abject poverty all my life. What about you? Following in your parents' footsteps?"

"Maybe." Jenny had just shoved a forkful of salad in her mouth. She finished chewing. "Mom's a lawyer and Dad's a teacher. I'm an English major... one of those useless things... so I'm getting my teacher certification, too. I've been doing practice teaching with seventh graders. I thought it would be awful but I love it."

The waitress brought Nina's food and two more glasses of wine. Nina broke the crust on her potpie, just like Jenny had, smiled at the rising steam, and started on her salad. "What kind of law does your mom practice? Mine's a litigator. All business and tough as nails."

"A little of everything."

Jenny didn't want to talk about her mother. She stared out at the parking lot, searching for a new subject. Small talk was not her thing. Drew teased her about it. She'd even read books on how to improve her social skills. That was Jenny in a nutshell—when in doubt, ask a book. Generally the advice was get people talking about themselves. She was about to ask Nina about stained glass when a movement in the lot caught her eye. Someone standing by her car. As she watched, he tried the doors.

"Excuse me." She dropped her fork. "I think someone's trying to break into my car."

She hurried into the parking lot, rushing straight toward the man who was using some kind of tool to unlock her car. She passed a man getting out of his car. "Go to the office," she yelled. "Tell them to call the police. There's a man breaking into my car!"

She rushed at the man by her car. "Hey, you! Get away from my car." It wasn't her car. It was Dandy's, and ugly as it was, he loved it. From the corner of her eye, she saw the guy hurrying toward the office. The car thief raised the bar he'd been using to try and charged toward her.

Behind her, Nina screamed. "No! Stop! Don't hurt her!"

The man shoved roughly past Jenny, knocking her to the ground, and ran off into the darkness. Jenny got up slowly, using the hand Nina held out. Her hip was bruised from the fall, her clean pants were smeared with mud, her hands crusty with gravel. So much for clean clothes. Figuring the harm was already done, she wiped her hands on her pants and picked up her fallen purse. "What a crazy thing to do," she said. "It's not like this is a deserted lot or the car's worth stealing."

"I don't know." Nina studied the puke-green car. "Maybe it's a classic. Or he has a passion for ugly green cars." She tucked a hand under Jenny's elbow. "I doubt he'll be back. He's probably still running. Let's finish dinner."

The man who'd gone to the office arrived with the manager, who looked around and said, querulously, "Where's this so-called car thief?"

"We saw him through the window, while we were eating," Jenny said, "and we ran out and…"

"We scared him away," Nina interrupted. "He had a pry bar. He was trying to open her car."

"Is that right?" the manager asked the man.

The man nodded.

"Shoot, that's the third time this month. I keep askin' the police to keep an eye on things but do they? You bet they don't. Well, I'm sorry, girls. I'll call this in, ask the cops to drive through a few times tonight, but I doubt he'll be back. Most of 'em are just kids. More looking to make mischief than anything else."

He considered Jenny, standing small, subdued and muddy beside the more glamorous Nina. "Tell you what, girls. To apologize for the inconvenience, your dinners are on the house. All right?"

He patted her shoulder, like a child or a pet. Jenny wanted to bite the pudgy, condescending hand even though he was trying to be kind. "Thanks," she said. "And thanks to you, too," she said to the man who'd gone for help. "Most people wouldn't have bothered." That raised a smile and a polite bob of the head. Jenny was afraid he was going to pat her, too. She was grateful when he didn't.

"Let's go," Nina said. "Our food's getting cold. If he comes back, you'll see him through the window."

Jenny wanted to stay and guard the car, but it was cold without her coat. Too bad she didn't have Adele's shotgun. A few encouraging blasts and that car thief would be running 'til dawn. Reluctantly, she let herself be led back inside, checking for her car keys in her coat pocket. The potpie was still warm.

Nina picked up her glass. "Here's to quick thinking and happy endings," she said.

Jenny touched glasses and drank. Her hand was shaking. She didn't want to think about endings. "Tell me about stained glass. What was it like, this window you just delivered?"

"It was a fixed panel to go above the stairs in a two-story entranceway," Nina said. "About four feet wide by about three feet high. A family portrait, if you can believe it, of this guy and his wife and their two dogs. A six-bedroom house and no kids." She signaled for the waitress and pointed at their glasses.

Jenny shook her head and the waitress hurried away. "So when they have kids, you'll get another commission," Jenny said. Nina seemed nice but how was she going to drive home on back roads after three quick glasses of wine? "That's a pretty big window. How much does something like that weigh?"

"A lot," Nina said. "Look, it's sweet of you to be interested, but after the day I've had, I'm sick of glass. Could we talk about something else? Tell me about your family. Got any brothers or sisters?"

Nina didn't want to talk glass and Jenny didn't want to talk family. "Nope," she said. "Just me."

The waitress brought Nina's drink and asked if she could clear. "You ladies interested in any coffee or dessert?"

Nina tapped the wine glass with a finger. "This will be my dessert," she said. "Aren't you going to drink yours?"

"I'm not much of a drinker." Jenny studied the menu. There was apple crisp, her favorite dessert. More comfort food. "Can you serve the apple crisp warm with vanilla ice cream?"

"Of course," the waitress said. "Is that what you want?"

Jenny's dessert came just as Nina finished her wine. "Guess I'll call it a night," Nina said. "Maybe you'd like to come back to my…" Her words were lost in a sudden spasm of coughs, her eyes watering, her face blotched red. "I think," she gasped, "I'm the only person in the world who can choke on air." She patted her heaving chest. Her nails were long and neatly polished. "Time to hit the road." She opened her wallet and pulled out a five. "Might as well tip the woman, I suppose, even if the meal is on the house."

"Oh, right," Jenny agreed. "I'm glad you reminded me."

Nina shrugged on her coat. "Nice having dinner with you. Have a safe trip back to Ohio."

Jenny waved as Nina walked away, a tall woman taking big strides with those nice long legs. Jenny could easily lose herself in a crowd but Nina would have a hard time. Jenny hoped she'd drive carefully the rest of the way home. She watched the blonde head pass all the motel rooms to the far end of the parking lot. An odd place for someone to park who'd only stopped to eat. Maybe she needed more space for a van. As she watched, she saw someone step out of the darkness. Nina paused, as if she was speaking to the stranger, then they both disappeared from view.

She left her own five beside her plate and returned to her room, feeling better after warm food and friendly conversation. She wasn't two steps into the room when she stopped, fear tightening her scalp. Her suitcase, which she had left open, was closed. Her hairbrush, which she always left face down, was face up. And the bathroom door, which she knew she had left open, was half-closed. Someone must have followed her. Even now, they were either waiting for her in the bathroom, or outside watching. A wave of fear went through her. She held her breath and listened.

"But when to mischief mortals bend their will,
How soon they find fit instruments of ill!"
—Pope, "Rape of the Lock," Canto Third

CHAPTER SEVEN

The room was empty. Whoever it was was gone, leaving traces of their search everywhere. Most people wouldn't have noticed but Jenny was blessed—or cursed—with an almost photographic memory. She'd had this ability to remember the details of places and things she'd seen only once even before she could talk. She could walk in the dark through rooms she'd seen in daylight because she knew where the furniture was. She could help people find lost things. Tonight it meant everywhere she looked, she saw where things had been moved, saw unknown hands touching her possessions.

She leaned against the door, fighting a rising panic. She wasn't fleeing because of other people's unrealistic worries. This was real. Someone was after her. She slid slowly down to the floor, pulling herself into a tight, defensive ball. Nothing in life had prepared her for this. Where do you go when you can't go home, when your apartment's been trashed, and all your friends there are gone? What do you do when the only people you can trust have told you to run?

She heard her mother's voice. "Jennifer Cates, you get up. You can't sit there on the floor in a hopeless muddle. You've got to take charge. Straighten those shoulders. Lift your head. And think."

She stood up. In case someone was watching, she turned off the lights and sat in the dark, running her mind around the parking lot. Were there any cars she remembered seeing during the day? The white Ford Taurus with Massachusetts plates and two large men in it. She'd noticed it behind her two or three times, figuring someone was taking the same route from Portland to New York. It happened all the time on long trips, seeing the same car over and over. The Taurus had stopped when she'd stopped. Bought gas when she'd bought gas. She'd found it rather friendly. Now it didn't seem friendly at all.

So two men were watching her, ready to grab the diary and heaven knew what else. She couldn't stay here, but how could she leave without being followed? Was there anything else she'd seen? Another car? Another person? No. The absence of a car, or, more specifically, a van. Nina said she was driving a van. When she left the cafe, she'd walked to the far end of the parking lot. But there'd been no van there. And instead of driving away, she'd met someone and they'd stepped out of sight. Nina, who had ducked Jenny's questions about stained glass. Who'd repeatedly tried to get her talk about her family. Who'd tried to get her drunk. Nina, claiming to be an artisan rushing to meet a deadline, who had perfectly manicured nails.

Jenny changed out of her muddy pants, put her jacket back on, picked up her purse, and walked to the office. As she'd hoped, the man behind the desk was the same one who had offered the complimentary dinner. She gave him her best smile. "Thanks for the dinner. It was great."

"You're welcome," he said. "Hope your car's all right."

"It seems fine. Actually, it's my brother's car and he'll kill me if anything happens to it."

The man nodded. He probably understood about guys and their cars.

"I was hoping you could help me," she said. "You know the woman I was in the parking lot with? The tall blonde. I met her at dinner in the cafe, and since we were both alone, we decided to eat together. Anyway, she invited me back to her room for a drink. I said I had to make some calls and I'd be over, but I've forgotten her room number."

"Hold on a sec." He thumbed through some cards. "Here it is. Keris Carlyle. 22. If you're interested in cars, that little BMW roadster is a real beauty."

"Thanks," Jenny said. "Maybe someday we'll all be driving BMWs."

"I'm still waiting for my first new car," he said.

She checked the parking lot before moving carefully up to number 22 where there was the usual motel Peeping Tom gap. She could see Nina, or rather, a woman named Keris Carlyle, sitting on the bed facing the men from the white Taurus. If she moved fast, she'd be out of here before they finished their conversation.

She knelt beside the fancy BMW and let the air out of one front tire, a trick she'd learned from Uncle Billy. The way things were going, it looked like Uncle Billy would be a valuable resource. Her mother had encouraged character, reasoning, and initiative, her father generosity and compassion. Uncle Billy had taught her law-breaking, derring-do, recklessness, and the importance of covering your ass. With luck, this odd assortment of mentors had provided the tools she'd need.

Back in her room, she threw her stuff into the suitcase, snapped it shut, and carried it out to the car. She left the television on, the key on the dresser. One more chore and she was out of here. She walked to the white Taurus, took out her Swiss Army knife, and punctured all four tires. *Good thing*, she thought with the heady glee that comes from performing wicked acts, *that the police didn't follow through on their promise to patrol the parking lot frequently, or she'd be on her way to jail.*

Fifty miles down the road, the high had worn off and she deeply regretted the wine. Dandy's car was just as hard to steer, her body just as tired, the number of hours she'd gone without sleep even greater. She needed a major coffee infusion. She needed sleep. She stopped at a rest area, bought a large coffee and a map, and forced herself to think. What you do when you can't reach your destination because you've physically run out of gas is call your friends. Brittany Carnevale, Britt to her friends, lived in Saratoga Springs. North of Albany. Jenny thought she could make it that far. If only Britt was home and not in Florida or skiing in Idaho with her boyfriend.

She dug out her address book and pulled out her phone. No cell phones, she'd been warned. Too easy to trace. But there was no pay phone here. By the time Britt said, "Hey, Jenny, what's up?" she was almost crying with relief.

"Friday night I found Drew in bed with Betty," she said. "I've been going around in a muddle ever since. I started driving home but I can't face that right now. All the questions they're going to ask. I was wondering. Could I stay with you for a few days?"

"What a bummer," Britt said. "I can't believe Betty would do that. Of course you can stay here. I've only asked you like a thousand times, right? Where are you?"

"I'm not sure. Maybe an hour from Albany. I've been driving blind, trying not to think. It's going to be pretty late but if you don't mind, I'll just keep driving."

"Get here when you get here," Britt said. "We're a pretty easy going bunch. You need directions?"

"Hold on." She dug out a pen and wrote down directions.

"You'll love it here," Britt said. "Absolutely nothing ever happens except reading junk books and watching junk movies; the bathtub is big enough to stretch out in and there's always food."

"Sounds like heaven."

"Oh, and my mom just baked a chocolate cake with frosting an inch thick. Which you will need, chocolate being the universal panacea."

"I'm on my way."

"Drive carefully, Jen. I'll leave the porch light on."

She finished her coffee and hit the road. She turned the radio up loud and opened the window so cold air blew in her face. She was still achy and had to work to keep her eyes open, but having a destination helped. Funny what Britt had said—that she couldn't believe Betty would do that. Did that mean she believed Drew would, or was it just the instinctive reaction of sisterhood where one of the rules of the game was you didn't steal your friend's guy?

She hadn't thought much about Betty, though the image of Betty's aggressively female nakedness haunted her. Why would a friend, someone she'd helped write papers, someone she'd shared so many hours and cups of coffee and confidences with, do that? Maybe what Drew had said was true for Betty, too. Maybe they both thought sex was okay if they didn't care about each other and Jenny was totally out of sync with the times.

Jenny couldn't imagine being that intimate and exposed with someone you didn't know and love, someone you could trust with your moods and your secrets, but she knew so little. The sum of her sexual experience, other than some strong-arm struggling in high school, and dates that hadn't gone much beyond kissing, had been with Drew. She'd believed she was making a serious commitment; he'd said he felt the same. Had he been lying? Just been having some fun with her, too? Had all the things he'd said been lies?

Suddenly, she felt surrounded by lies. She'd spent a lifetime finding similarities between herself and her father. He'd always said, "You can trust me. You can tell me anything because I'm your father and I love you more than anyone else in the world." Now she knew part of that wasn't true. Her real father was not the good and gentle man she'd always known, but a slick politician. She had believed in parental invulnerability and now her mother was in a coma. The first man she'd ever loved and trusted had screwed her best friend for fun.

They might not be physically here to counsel her, but their voices were in her head. Her mother's especially, gently but firmly inquiring how she planned to handle this. Her mother had always been direct. When things didn't go well and Jenny would fall into a funk, her mother's question would be, "Well, what are you going to do about it?' while her father would say, "Oh, Lila, she's just a kid. Give her a chance to brood a bit." Right now, their competing voices, one urging her to face it and plan, the other to rest and regroup, overwhelmed her.

"Stop!" she said aloud, scaring herself and veering over the line. She gripped the wheel firmly and pushed the questions away.

Those headlights behind her had been there too long. The road was deserted, and in deference to her tired state, she was traveling at a law-abiding pace. No one else should have been going so slowly. But the car stayed there, always maintaining the same safe following distance, like someone stuck in Driver's Ed forever. As a test, she moved into the right lane and slowed down. The headlights moved with her and stayed there, imprinted like a baby duck.

She felt a gut-tightening surge of fear, followed by anger. How many of them were there? Had a whole platoon been sent to keep an eye on one small woman? She longed for Adele's shotgun again. If these people didn't stop following her, she'd find a handy local gun dealer and buy herself one. She sped up. Her escort did the same, but she didn't have time to watch them closely. She was coming to a whole bunch of signs and needed to follow Siri's directions for 87 North.

She took the exit too fast. The Fury lurched wildly. She hauled it back onto the road, wondering why Dandy was so fond of this damned car. It handled like a truck; the rear-end was too light, and it spun its wheels like crazy whenever she accelerated from a dead stop. It did have a big engine. Maybe that was what he liked. Maybe the rich, throaty roar when he accelerated made him feel like a kid again. He'd bought it when his wife left. That was when men bought impractical vehicles.

She raced up the entrance ramp, put her foot down, and headed north. The Fury took off. "All right, assholes," she muttered. "Let's see what your car can do." She leveled off when she got to ninety, watching the mirror. No sign of those stupid little lights, too close together like eyes in a narrow face, that had been boring into her for miles. She kept her foot down, amazed at how much better the car seemed now that she was breaking the law. Maybe it was just a badass car.

They always get you when you let down your guard. Hadn't her mother told her that a thousand times? Hadn't she been raised by a wily trial lawyer? Taught to be cautious, suspicious, to watch her back? She remembered too late. They *must* have had a whole goddamned platoon because the vehicle that slammed into her, sending the Fury into a wild, fishtailing plunge across the lanes, was not the narrow-eyed bastard, but a squatty, bull-like Toyota Landcruiser.

She wrestled the Fury back under control but the vehicle came roaring back, gave her another whopping slam in the side and sent the poor puke mobile careening right off the road, across the breakdown lane, and ass-over-teakettle down a steep bank. It was like the Octopus, the Tilt-a-Whirl, and a dozen other carnival rides rolled into one, except it wasn't fun. She was caught on the ropes, hung up by her seatbelt, upside down, right side up, the belt scoring her in a dozen places, arms, legs and head flailing helplessly, slamming into things, until finally she landed with a truly bone-jarring crash, upside down, at the bottom of the hill.

Dazed with pain, she tested her arms and legs to see if they still worked. Running on instinct now, figuring that bad guys determined enough to do this would be efficient enough to check and see if they'd finished the job, she fumbled the seatbelt loose, dropping into a mass of broken glass, found her purse, kicked out the rest of the window, and crawled through. When she was away, lost in the night, she could experience the pain that was making her breathless and take stock of her injuries.

She slung her bag over her shoulder and started walking.

Her body wasn't with the program. She had to force her legs to move. Left, right, left, right, forward, march. She might have been wading through sludge. One foot. Two feet. Black and blue foot. How could anyone's life change so much in two short days? Left, right, left, right. Blood running down her face, blinding one eye. Not that it made any difference. It was black as pitch.

She knew she was going slowly up hill. The ground was becoming shrubby, making her stumble more often. Behind her there was a pop, like a small explosion, and then another. Something on the car was exploding. She didn't look around. If the car was on fire, it would light up the night. The last thing she should do was turn around and let her white face be illuminated. Otherwise, she was just another shadow. Dark clothes, dark coat, dark hair. Everything except her shoes was dark. She shoved her hands in her pockets and kept walking.

She walked until she ran headfirst into a tree trunk, uttering a dazed "excuse me," as she staggered around it and fell to her knees. On hands and knees she kept going until she found a tree with low spreading branches. Like a child playing house, she crept forward until she was inside an evergreen tent. The ground was thick with needles, and dry. She curled up in a ball, wrapped her arms around her knees, and cried herself to sleep.

GOVERNOR'S OFFICE

ALBANY, NEW YORK

The call came in on the line reserved for very special calls. Alfonso winked at O'Malley. It was two in the morning, but Alfonso, blessed with the need for little sleep, was disgustingly lively. "This will be Keris, reporting in. You think she's landed our fish?"

O'Malley, who needed more sleep but believed in humoring his boss, shrugged wearily. "She's a smart one, Lou. And very capable. I'll be surprised if she doesn't have good news." He yawned. "I hope she's got good news. I've got to get some sleep."

Alfonso picked up the phone. "So?"

Keris Carlyle's voice, soured with frustration, burst in his ear. "So this pitiful little girl who looks like a helpless twelve-year-old managed to disable both cars and take off."

"Is that the good news or the bad news?"

"That's the good news. The bad news is that a car which fits the description of the one she was driving crashed and burned north of Albany a little while ago. The police... your police... still haven't established whether anyone was in the car."

"So we've got no tape, no tearful statement, no nothing?"

"Not yet, but it's not over 'til the fat lady sings, Governor. That kid is a survivor if I ever saw one. Until we get a confirm that she's been killed, I'd get your guys out there combing the woods. I'd send your biggest, kindest, most fatherly troopers out to look for her and I'd treat her like she was my own. Private hospital room, TLC, and a personal visit from you. But you'd better move fast, because what happened was no accident."

"The hell you say. What's going on?"

"State police had a report from someone claiming they'd seen a car being driven off the road. Driver didn't want to get involved, of course, so we've got no name and address, but you can bet your ambitious little boots it means our friend Buxton's as keen to find this kid as we are."

"So where the hell are you, Carlyle?"

"On the scene, Gov. Standing by the roadside, freezing my buns off, getting dizzy from all these blue lights. But I can't go after her, even if I did relish tromping through the woods in the dark of night. She's made me. What do you want to do?"

"Morrissey there?" he asked.

"Just got here," she said. "Big as life. Your poster boy state trooper has arrived."

"Put him on. Then get your ass back here. And Carlyle?" He paused for effect. "It's a very nice ass."

"We're on a cell phone, Governor," she said coldly, and was gone.

O'Malley blinked his eyes sleepily. "No go?" he mumbled.

Alfonso shrugged. "Either she's toast or she's hiding. Hi, Tom? Lou Alfonso, look, we've got a situation."

THE RESIDENCE OF
SENATOR JAMES BUXTON

WASHINGTON, D.C.

Maggie Buxton claimed she hadn't had a full night's sleep in twenty years. She slept lightly. She slept badly. She had bad dreams. On this particular Sunday night, she wasn't even trying to sleep. Her husband, Jim, was sleeping soundly. She'd always resented that he could sleep so easily. She sat in the living room, an unopened book on her knees, waiting for the phone to ring. The signal was turned off in the bedroom. The candidate needed his beauty sleep. He was having brunch with a bunch of rich businesswomen in the morning and he needed to be fresh and bright to charm the dollars out of their purses before he left for more primary stumping.

She got it on the first ring. "Maggie?"

She murmured an affirmative.

"I think your worries are over. Friedman's brother went for a swim; Friedman is on life support and even if she pulls through, which is highly unlikely, they expect she'll be a vegetable—and just to be sure, in case she knew anything, the daughter just burned up in a car wreck somewhere north of Albany, New York. You happy now?"

"You're a sick man, Frank."

"Realistic, ambitious, and a good contingency planner, Maggie. That's all. Anything else you'd like me to worry about? You sure Jim doesn't have a few more Lila Friedmans in his past?"

"It might surprise you, Frank, but when Jim says that except for Lila he's been a faithful husband, I think he's telling the truth."

"Good. I'd hate to have to do this again."

Maggie's fingers plucked nervously at the cording on her robe, the diamonds in her rings sparkling as she moved. "I hope she didn't suffer. I hope it was quick."

"Maggie, she rolled over five or six times and then the car burned up. Either she was tossed around, smashed and battered until she died, or she burned alive."

"God, Frank. I wish you hadn't told me." She felt like she was going to be sick.

"You're the one who wanted the problem solved once and for all, remember?"

"I didn't ask you to do this."

"Oh, yes, you did. I believe your exact words were, 'take care of it Frank. I don't care what you have to do, but take care of it. I will not be embarrassed by some little tramp Jim took a fancy to twenty years ago, and Lou Alfonso would go to town with something like this.' Do I remember that correctly, Maggie?"

"I meant... never mind what I meant. I didn't... don't... want to know the details."

"Of course not. You just want it taken care of. But it's good you know the details. It's called shared complicity, Maggie." He cleared his throat and she braced herself for his words. "You know what they say. If you can't stand the heat, get out of the kitchen. You want to be first lady so badly you can taste it, so don't get all righteous with me. Pull yourself together. You wanted it done; I did it. Good night."

"Wait! What about the tape, Frank? Did you find the goddamned tape?" Too late. Frank was gone. She was swearing at an empty line. She started to slam down the phone and caught herself. A loud noise might wake Jim.

She sat in her lovely living room, plucking at her robe, the cording smooth and hard under her fingers, staring out at nothing. Behind her unseeing eyes, flames danced and a woman jumped and screamed. Maggie had three daughters. Three lovely, cherished daughters. What if someone did something like this one of them?

She expelled an angry breath and sat up straighter. It would never happen. Unlike Lila Friedman, she'd never done anything reckless enough to put them in danger.

"Man is the hunter; woman is his game."
—Tennyson, from "The Princess"

CHAPTER EIGHT

She woke suddenly, not knowing where she was or what had woken her, until the prickly needles scratching her face and neck and the evergreen scent reminded her. She was so battered even breathing hurt. Welts of pain across her chest and stomach felt like she'd been whipped. Her left wrist throbbed like pain had a heartbeat. Something had woken her. She forced herself to be still and listen.

Leaves crunched. A stick broke. A man's voice said, "Well, someone has been through here. See?"

"Probably just a deer trail."

"Not unless the deer around here wear shoes. Look." A light swept back and forth, sifting through the branches in broken yellow streaks, like car lights through venetian blinds. "…starting here she was crawling. See those rounded indentations? Knees. And bleeding, too. See those drops?"

The other man gave a snort of laughter. "Tom, you're a veritable Chingatchgook, you know that?"

"A veritable what?"

But the other man was still talking. "Poor kid. After what happened, who can blame her for running? I'd run, too."

"Yeah. Our girl's got guts, getting herself as far away as she could, even if she had to crawl. But where the hell is she?"

"You don't suppose they found her, do you? Followed her here and…"

"I didn't see any other tracks, did you?"

Jenny liked inventing people from their voices. Conversations overheard in dressing rooms, talk drifting over restaurant partitions, people on the street and in lobbies. Right now it was better than thinking about pain. The deep, rumbly voice, she decided, was a very big man. Older. Probably graying. Comfortable with command but instinctively given to teaching. Not arrogant about position. The other man was younger, smaller, his voice lighter and more gentle. More impatient and impulsive, too, but empathic. And educated. Possibly too sensitive for his job. She also knew they were cops looking for her.

She wanted to be found and taken someplace warm and safe. Somewhere she could wash her face and kill this pain, could close her eyes and rest. But she didn't know if she could trust anyone. Not anymore. The woman who'd called herself Nina had pretended to be nice and then someone had followed her and run her off the road. She didn't know who "they" were, so she didn't know how to protect herself. Even if these men were cops, and cops are supposed to be your friends, cops worked for the government, and she was sure government, at least politicians, were behind this.

Maybe she'd watched too many of Drew's chase movies. The normal accident victim doesn't refuse help from the cops. But the normal accident victim is usually the victim of an accident. She was not. She was living a chase movie, running from strangers who had already killed, or tried to kill, two members of her family. However enticing rescue was, however desperate she was to stop this pain, she'd stay put. When she could, she'd walk out of here, or crawl, if necessary, find out where she was, and call Britt. Britt would come, no matter what, just for the adventure of the thing.

Eventually she'd have to call Dandy, too, and give him the sad news about his car. Dandy was a generous man. Maybe it would be enough for him that she was safe. And she was supposed to report the accident to the police and Dandy's insurance company, too. It wouldn't sound so benign if she said, "I'm calling to report an attempted murder."

Tonight someone had tried to kill her.

"I'd better get some more guys up here searching," the second voice said. A radio crackled. She heard the indistinct mumble of his voice, and then, more clearly, "Looks like it's going to rain again."

She had a cramp in her leg, the kind that goes from clenched fist painful to code red agony unless it's dealt with. Slowly she tried to unbend it, her mouth buried in her sleeve in case she made noise. Just that slight movement and her body came alive with shooting pains. She groaned. The flashlight turned her way like a pain-seeking missile.

"You hear that?" the rumbly voice asked.

She closed her eyes, trying to stay still as their feet crashed through the brush around her. *Don't come any closer,* she thought childishly. *Go away and leave me alone.*

The branches above her crackled and snapped as hands pulled them apart. A flashlight beam stabbed through her clenched lids. "Here she is! Over here! Tom! I've got her." The younger guy, eager and excited. She sensed him bending down until he was close enough to touch her. Felt his cold hand on her neck, looking for a pulse. She flinched and opened her eyes, another involuntary groan drawn out of her. How could she possibly run from them when every move hurt?

He settled back on his heels. "Oh, hey, I'm sorry," he said. "I didn't mean to hurt you. Don't be scared. I'm Joe. Joe Trask. I'm here to help you. I'm a cop."

Doesn't he know that's one of the common lies? Trust me, I'm a cop. "Do you have…" God. It even hurt to talk. "…identification?"

He looked surprised but pulled out a badge.

"Closer," she whispered. "Where I can see it please." He trained the light on it. It looked real enough. "Thanks." She closed her eyes again.

"She's conscious?" The one he'd called Tom came crashing up to them now, bending down with his own light to confirm her existence.

Joe mumbled an affirmative.

"Can she talk?"

"A little. She seems pretty weak, though. Weak or hurting badly. Can you believe it? She asked to see my badge."

Tom bent closer now, close enough so his breath ruffled her hair and she could smell aftershave. Close enough so she could feel his body heat. She wanted to wrap it around herself. "What's your name?" he asked.

"Jenny."

"I'm Tom. Where are you hurt, Jenny?"

She could tell he was itching to get her out where he could do a more thorough inspection. "Everywhere," she said. "Please don't touch me."

"We want to get you out of these woods before it rains. Get you to a hospital where they can take care of you. Do you remember what happened?"

Cold raindrops splashed her face. "Yes."

"Damn!" the one called Joe muttered. "And my raincoat's in the car."

"What happened to you?" The big man sounded like he had all the time in the world.

"I was forced off the road by a car. Rammed." She put her arm over her face to keep off the rain. There was more but it was too hard. Talking meant breathing. Breathing meant pain. She was no stranger to pain. She'd played field hockey and soccer, gone through the rigorous sports conditioning programs that, thanks to Title IX, were available to girls as well as boys. Been kicked in the back of the knee, whacked with sticks, shouldered, elbowed, knocked heads trying to reach the ball. She was no fragile blossom, but this was bad.

Branches crackled as he knelt beside her, his hands working their way under her body. "Now I'm going to pick you up."

"No!"

"I'll try not to hurt you."

"But you can't help it," she whispered, pleading, trying to roll away from his hands. "Everything hurts." It wouldn't make any difference. They were certain they knew what was right. It would be wrong to leave her lying here in the rain. Their job was carrying her to safety. Maybe, if she was lucky, she'd die when he picked her up and she wouldn't have to know about the rest. "Watch my wrist, please. I think it's broken."

He slid an arm under her shoulders and another under her knees and lifted. Her scream startled him so much he almost dropped her. She felt the hesitation in his arms, the sudden forward motion of his body. "There now, Jenny," he murmured. "There now. Be brave. It won't be long before we get you back where people can help you."

"Shouldn't we wait for a stretcher?" Joe asked.

"Leave her out in this rain another forty minutes? It'll take at least that long. You walk beside me and light the way. She's just a little bit of a thing. Light as a feather. And don't forget her purse." Laughter rumbled in his chest. "Isn't that just like a woman? Rolls over five or six times, crawls out of a burning car, blood pouring down her face, and she remembers to bring her purse."

She wanted to hit him but she was too busy trying not to scream. Setting her jaw and biting her lip, her swinging arm a pendulum of pain. "Please," she said. "My arm."

The man named Joe carefully folded her swinging arm onto her chest and the one named Tom tilted her so it wouldn't roll loose.

After a while she got used to it, burying her face in his chest to stifle her moans. He was very gentle, holding his arms like a cradle to soften the jarring, when it would have been easier to carry her tight against his body. He was a very big man, just as Joe was the smaller, slender one, and he strode along so rapidly, even with his extra burden, that Joe was panting.

Eventually they reached the highway and a milling crowd, flashing lights, a fire truck, and an ambulance. A chaos of voices assaulted her ears. The bright lights hurt her eyes. She closed them and buried her face in his chest again. "Okay, Jenny, we're going to put you in the ambulance now. I know it's going to hurt. I'll do my best."

He handed her over to the ambulance attendants, got her purse from Joe, and climbed in beside her. She heard the two of them conferring. Then Joe left, the doors were shut and they were rolling through the night. The attendants began by asking her name and if she knew what had happened.

"The bad guys didn't win," she said. She could tell they didn't get it.

They moved on to pulse and blood pressure and shining little lights in her eyes, running prying fingers over her body, tugging her clothes this way and that as they assessed the extent of the damage. It was intrusive and painful and not at all comforting. As they dealt with her body, doing embarrassing things and exposing her to cold air and the watching cop's eyes, she moved away from things she couldn't control and on to things she might—like what to do when she got to the hospital. She needed a bed, some quiet, and something to kill the pain. What she'd get was more of what she was getting. She'd be poked, prodded, punctured, questioned and exposed. Almost certainly separated from her purse and clothes.

So far, all the big trooper had done with her purse was set it on the floor, but the time would come when they'd go through her things and find her mother's diary. Protecting that diary was critical. If she clung to her purse and made a fuss, it would focus their attention exactly where she didn't want it focused. So what was she going to do?

"Ouch!" Her scream startled the man who was manipulating her wrist. She felt like throwing up. "Please," she begged. "I don't know what you just did, but don't do it again."

She waited for the sickness to pass, forcing herself to plan. When she got to the hospital, the first thing she'd do was ask for the chaplain. She couldn't think of anyone else who might not be in league with the bad guys. It wasn't unreasonable for someone who'd nearly been murdered to need spiritual reassurance. She could only hope the chaplain believed in confidentiality. They were supposed to, but she looked young, and people were less likely to honor the rules when it came to kids.

If that happened, she'd move on to plan B, as yet unmade.

The EMT did something to her wrist again that really hurt. The intensity of the pain scared her. Could someone hurt this much and not be seriously injured? Everything inside her felt scrambled and broken. She held her good hand out toward the cop. "It hurts so much," she said. "I'm scared."

"You're okay now," he said, taking her small cold hand in his big warm one. "We're going to take care of you. No one's going to hurt you. Now, can you tell me anything about the car that hit you?"

She tried to remember. She'd been watching those headlights in her rearview mirror. Concentrating on them so hard she'd barely noticed the other vehicle coming up on her so fast. "There was a car following me. I was watching it so I didn't see the second one. It came up so fast. It was big, like a Suburban, and dark. Wait. It was a Toyota. Landcruiser. He hit me hard. Twice. First time, I did okay. The second, I couldn't keep the car on the road and then I was rolling over and over and over. I was afraid I was going to die."

She took a long, shuddering breath. Sometimes having a vivid memory wasn't a blessing. She was back in the car, being thrown around, seeing through the cracking windshield as the car rolled and headlights illuminated the topsy-turvy landscape. She felt her head banging against the window, her wrist coming loose from the wheel and slamming against everything, her shins and ankles knocking against things. Her body repeatedly thrown against the seatbelt, jerked and wrenched in all directions. The final crash, metal groaning as the car hit bottom and came to rest upside down. The sound of metal twisting. The clatter of broken glass. Disoriented, terrified, fumbling herself free, dropping onto the roof and crawling out the window through a sea of glass.

"I was afraid they'd come after me. I was afraid the car would burn. I tried to get away. Far enough so no one could find me."

"Poor Jenny," he said. "No wonder you were scared. But we couldn't leave you out there in the rain and cold."

She gripped his hand more tightly. "Everything hurts."

"I'm sure it does. Seat belts and airbags save lives but they can leave nasty bruises. You won't believe this, but you're a very lucky girl."

Because she wasn't badly hurt? How did they know? And taken in the larger context, it was laughable.

"The car you were driving wasn't yours," he said. "Where did you get it?"

She'd meant to be cooperative and sweet and vulnerable, so he'd be inclined to indulge her when they got to the hospital and she asked for a chaplain. "I b... borrow... borrowed... f... from..." she began. She couldn't get the words out. When she took a breath to speak, pain surged everywhere. "S... s... s... sorry. I can't."

Self-control fluttered away like bits of confetti. Killed her uncle. Tried to kill her mother. Tried to kill her. Tried to KILL her. One deep, quavering breath and the sobs came bursting out, wave after wrenching, shuddering wave. Just what she wanted to do before an audience of strangers, flat on her back in the glare of lights, helpless as a bug on a pin. This was what she'd planned to release when she was finally safe and alone. Not here. Not like this.

"Someone... tried to... k... k... kill... kill me... and I... I... I'm so... scared." She turned her head sideways, trying to hide her face.

The big cop stopped trying to gather information, slid one thigh onto the edge of the stretcher, and pulled her gently against his chest. Ignoring the attendants' protests, he folded his arms around her, chanting a rumbling mantra of "it's okay," into her hair. It was a long time before her tears were spent, and when the sobs subsided, she was more exhausted than she'd ever known.

When he released her, his movements so tender and careful, she slipped into a daze. Neither unconscious nor conscious. Falling into a deep, quiet place. Maybe they'd given her some drug, something to relieve the pain. Something that was stealing her wits, her consciousness, her will. It was too soon. Later, when she'd taken care of business, it would be fine. But she needed her mind a little longer.

Like a peasant gleaning for bits of grain, she searched through her body for bits of energy, gathering them for the task ahead. It was desperately hard work. She wanted to give up. But not yet. She gritted her teeth, forcing herself to stay awake as the ambulance door burst open and she was carried inside.

"And oftentimes, to win us to our harm,
The instruments of darkness tell us truths,
Win us with honest trifles, to betray 's
In deepest consequence."
—Shakespeare, "Macbeth"

CHAPTER NINE

It was easier than she'd expected, perhaps because she wasn't in such dire straits they didn't immediately start doing procedures. She was triaged off to a curtained cubicle to wait while more urgent cases were dealt with. Seeing how quiescent she was, Tom went off to get himself a nice, warming cup of coffee, leaving Jenny alone, and a kindly nurse agreed to fetch her a chaplain.

The chaplain was young and easily prevailed upon, with her sad story of her boyfriend's brutal betrayal followed by an anonymous highway assault, to carry off her diary, detailing her love and heartbreak, and keep it from others' prying eyes. She was too desperate for the guilt she normally would have felt at lying. Desperation was making her ruthless.

They'd given her pain killers so every movement and touch wasn't agony. When the curtain closed behind him, she gave herself up to mindless lassitude, too tired to fight any longer. She was poked and prodded, wheeled about, twisted and turned, X-rayed and cat-scanned, stitched and bandaged and wrapped in plaster, lying limp and unresponsive as they discussed her like she wasn't there.

How pleased they were that being thrown against the seatbelt and smacked with the airbag hadn't left her with a ruptured spleen or a dangerously bruised heart or lung or liver. She wondered how they'd feel about being so hurt as the result of a deliberate attack. How they'd process the knowledge they'd been targeted by killers? She sure didn't know how to process it.

They shined lights in her eyes and waggled fingers in front of her, asked the same questions over and over and declared themselves pleased that her concussion was so mild. Would they have found it pleasing to be black and blue and swollen from head to toe? Did they believe the sickening throb in her wrist was a bagatelle? The seven stitches in her head minor irritants? She would gladly have given any of them her bruised ribs. Even doped to the gills, she couldn't move without agony, and pain killers wear off.

She so effectively convinced them she wasn't there that two nurses gossiped openly about their sex lives while they picked out pieces of glass and slapped on another dozen bandages. Finally, when she was certain that every pair of hands in the hospital had been run over her body at least once, when her meager little hospital johnny had been raised and lowered yet one more time to show someone the livid bruises, when she felt so violated it was as if she had been emotionally raped, she was wheeled into a dark, quiet room, tucked into bed, and ordered to swallow pills.

Grateful to finally be alone, like an exhausted fox having reached its den without being torn to pieces by the pursuing dogs, she curled tightly within the cave of her body, desperately weary yet afraid of what might happen while she slept. Finally, she dozed off. When she woke, shivering with cold, her body one enormous ache, it was still dark. The lights in the room were dim. A man in a uniform snoozed beside her bed. The smaller trooper. Joe.

Time to get out of here. As quietly as she could, she peeled the tape off her hand, disconnected the IV, and slipped out of bed. Beyond the curtains, the other half of the room was empty. Her watch was gone, in its place a bulky plaster cast. She crept to the phone beside the other bed and called Britt's number. When Britt answered, she said quickly, "It's Jenny. This is going to sound completely fantastic but it's true. Someone tried to drive me off the road and kill me tonight. I'm in the hospital in Albany." She found the hospital's name on a plastic tag on her other wrist. "Can you bring your red wig and a great big coat and get me out of here?"

Among Jenny's friends, Britt was the perfect choice. She didn't ask questions. "It will take me at least an hour but I'll get there as soon as I can. What room are you in?"

Jenny read off the number.

"Fine. I'll look in and pretend it's the wrong room. We'll take it from there, okay? Do you think you're being watched?"

"I've got a cop right beside my bed."

"Ah. A challenge," Britt said. "Are you okay?"

"I rolled the car six times. Broke my wrist. I've got stitches in my head and I'm a mosaic of blacks and blues. You'll see. It's not pretty."

"I'm on the case." Britt hung up.

Gritting her teeth, Jenny performed essential functions. They'd had plenty of time and energy to gossip, but none to clean her up, so she washed the blood off. The girl in the mirror had a pale, pinched face, one side bruised and swollen, dotted with cuts and scratches, with wide, desperate blue eyes. "You poor thing," she said, reaching out to her reflection. The extended hand dripped blood onto the stainless steel sink. She stared a moment, fascinated by the vividness of the red when everything else was pale and dark, then closed her eyes against the dizzy feeling, clinging to the sink for support. She didn't like blood.

A woman knocked on the door, asked, "Are you all right?" and opened it without waiting for an answer, assaulting her with a barrage of questions. "What are you doing out of bed, Jennifer? Why didn't you call? What's happened to your IV?"

The questions felt like an assault and every nerve in her body went taut. She clung to the sink while harsh words poured out of a pursed and lipsticked mouth. "You're in no shape to be out of bed. Come along now."

Jenny opened her eyes, becoming that fox again, crouching in her den as intruding paws tried to unearth her. She could hear the panting breath, almost see the saliva dripping from yellow teeth.

The nurse reached for her arm. "Come along now," she insisted, "back to bed."

"Please don't touch me."

A hand locked onto her arm, pulling her toward the door, making fingerprints on her bruises, while an arm around her shoulders pushed her. Impersonal brutality in the name of TLC.

"I said don't touch me," Jenny repeated. "Are you deaf?"

"What?" The woman stared at her blankly. "Come along now young lady, don't be silly. You must go back to bed." The nurse was literally propelling her across the room.

Jenny stiffened her legs and stopped, putting some authority into her voice. "Take your hands off me."

"Come along now and stop this nonsense. You need to be in bed."

"What I need is to be left alone!" Jenny said. "I need you to take your hands off me. I am twenty-one years old and competent to make my own decisions."

"You're in no condition to…" the nurse said. "You're a hospital patient who needs to follow medical orders."

"Great," Jenny said, knowing she sounded hysterical and utterly unconvincing. "You go get 'em and read 'em to me, okay? Then I'll decide if I want to follow them."

"Is there a problem here?" Joe Trask asked quietly.

"I can't understand it," the nurse announced in an aggrieved voice, releasing Jenny's arm. "She won't go back to bed."

"She's had kind of a hard night," he said. "Maybe we should give her a few minutes."

"She's taken out her IV," the nurse said testily. "She needs those fluids."

Jenny turned her back on them, their voices only background noise as she watched the slow drip of blood down her hand.

"Hey," Trask said. "Anything I can do?"

She felt hollow and depleted. Nothing left for dealing with this cop. "You'd better go," she said. "I'm going to be sick."

"And I've never seen that before."

"I'd just like some privacy."

"Sure," he agreed. "Call if you need me." He left her in peace.

Throwing up when your body is crisscrossed with seatbelt contusions, when your ribs may be cracked, you're so bruised your skin doesn't look like skin, and your head is as fragile as an unhatched egg is a miserable experience. Jenny wouldn't have wished it on anyone. Except on whoever drove her off the road, Drew, or the men who'd attacked her mother.

Her mother. That pale, still figure filled her mind, reminding her she couldn't let them win. She cleaned herself up, then opened the bathroom door to the welcome support of Joe Trask's arm. "I don't know what came over me," she said. "I didn't mean to fight with that nurse."

He offered a steadying arm. "Feeling helpless," he said. "Being pushed around. I'd be the same way. You want me to call her?"

"Not yet. If you could find me another blanket and a cup of tea? And my phone. My purse. There are calls I should make. About the accident. The car."

"Your purse is right here," he said, opening a cupboard in the bedside stand and giving it to her.

Jenny liked his face. He had nice brown eyes. She liked that he hadn't immediately bonded with the nurse who was trying to tell her what to do. He might be one of the bad guys, but right now she felt better having him around.

"I'll see what I can do about tea." He smiled. A cute smile, and she wished she didn't look like something the cat had dragged in. "But you've got to promise you'll stay in bed until I get back." He patted the handcuffs on his belt. "I wouldn't want to have to use these."

Her trapped feeling flooded back, with a surge of anger that he could find her situation amusing. She tried not to let it show. "Don't worry. I'll be good." Being good by being compliant. She was too much Lila Friedman's daughter not to find this infuriation. They might think she was a helpless girl, but they were wrong. She would not make this easy.

She closed her eyes. She was exhausted almost beyond comprehension, her body desperate for rest, but so wound up she had to work at being relaxed.

"That's good, Jenny," he said. "Get some rest. I'll be right back."

The door opened and closed. He was gone. All the air in the room was hers. She sucked it in greedily as though, when others had been present, there hadn't been quite enough. Until Britt arrived, she had no way to escape. She had to stay here, rest, and be 'Good Jenny.' Practical Jenny. She'd need her strength. She looked inside her purse. Her wallet was missing. Probably locked up somewhere? She had no money, no credit cards, but she had mascara, lip gloss, and pens.

She pretended to sleep, listening to life around her. Joe came back with tea, put a blanket over her, then sat in his chair. Tom came to check on her. Even pitched low, his big voice filled the room. "How's our girl?" he asked.

"Asleep. Worn out."

"You talk to her?"

"Had to break up a fight between her and a nurse."

"You're kidding. She hardly looks like the fighting type."

"Don't let appearances deceive you." Joe's laugh was lighter. "This kid's a fighter. She's scared and hurting, but she's no marshmallow. She knows someone's after her, doesn't know who to trust. It won't be easy to get on her good side and chat her up. She's not spilling her guts at the first kind word."

"That's why they picked a handsome, sensitive fellow like yourself," Tom said. "Just bat those big brown cow eyes of yours and treat her like a little princess. Remind her there are bad guys out there, and you're here to protect her. She'll talk to you."

"Let's talk outside," Joe said. "She drifts in and out. They haven't sedated her."

"Well, they should—" Tom began. The door shut, cutting off the rest.

So they *were* bad guys, though from what they said, and what she knew, there were other, badder guys out there as well. Better to know than not, she supposed, though it was scary to think how right she'd been. It troubled her that she'd responded to Joe's niceness when it was only play-acting. Men were turning out to be pretty unreliable. But then, Keris Carlyle was a woman.

She fell into deep sleep, almost waking when someone took her hand. A comforting gesture, she thought, until a swipe of alcohol and a fierce jab said it was her IV line being reinserted. She'd get the benefits of modern medicine whether she wanted them or not. "Wake up, Jenny." A hand rocked her shoulder. Her bruised, aching shoulder. "Time for your pills." The rattle of pills in a little paper cup.

She opened her eyes. "What are they?"

The cup rattled again. "Painkiller. Sleeping pill."

"You woke me up to give me a sleeping pill?"

"You aren't my only patient," the nurse said. "I bring what the doctor orders. Just take your medicine so I can get on to sicker people."

Jenny held out her hand for the cup. Peered into it. There were three pills in the cup. Red and gray, bright yellow, and white. The red and gray was pain, she knew. She popped it in her mouth, and swallowed, palming the other two, then handed back the cup.

"Where's my cop?"

"Downstairs getting breakfast."

There was a sharp knock on the door and a punk young woman with short jet-black hair, dead-white skin and black lipstick opened it and marched in. "Grandma?" she said. "Mom's downstairs parking the car. I brought you those things you wanted." She leaned an overstuffed brown shopping bag against the wall and approached the bed, carrying a large floral-wrapped package. She stopped at the foot of the bed, glaring at Jenny and the nurse through narrowed eyes. "What the fu... you aren't grandma? Where the hell's grandma at? They told me downstairs she was in 314. Ain't this 314?"

"This is 341," the nurse rolled her eyes. "Please go. You're disturbing my patient."

The young woman clutched the package to her chest, looking, for all the bizarreness of her appearance, surprisingly chagrined. "It's my dyslexia," she said softly. "I'm sorry." She backed nervously out of the room.

"I don't know what she's even doing here," the nurse said. "It's not visiting hours." She charted Jenny's stats and left.

As soon as the door closed behind her, Jenny was out of bed, moving with the alacrity of a Galapagos tortoise. She detached the IV needle for the second time, then carried the bag into the bathroom. Britt's idea of an escape outfit was strange, but it might work. Blue workman's coverall with Rice Brothers Plumbing on the back and Sal over the pocket, a pair of ancient, scuffed work boots, a wig with long, curly red hair, and a baseball hat. There was also an enormous pink bathrobe. Jenny put on the clothes, slowed by the cast and the bruises.

A knock on the door. Her heart stopped. "Who is it?" she called.

"I've come to take you to the lab," a familiar voice said.

Jenny opened the door. Britt, pert, blonde and looking about sixteen in a candy striper's jumper, stood beside a wheelchair. "Maybe you'd like to put your robe on for the trip downstairs?" she said, scooping up Jenny's purse and tucking into the pocket behind the seat.

"Only if you help me."

"That's what I'm here for. To assist the feeble." Britt's tone was light, but her face reflected her shock at Jenny's state. Britt bundled her quickly, but gently, into the robe, helped her into the chair, and zipped out the door. "You look like shit," she whispered as they waited for the elevator.

"Feel like it, too," she whispered back. When they got out in the lobby, she caught a glimpse of Tom and Joe, deep in conversation. "Quick, stand beside me."

Britt placed herself between Jenny and the cops, waited until they'd passed, then wheeled her passenger around the corner, and immediately through the door of a handicapped toilet, locking the door behind them. "Your watchdogs?" she asked.

Jenny nodded.

"Then we haven't got much time. Let's get you out of that robe."

"I have to see the chaplain first. He has my mother's diary. That's what the bad guys are after."

Britt's breath hissed out impatiently. "Jen, we haven't time for this. In a few minutes, they're going to figure out you're gone and all hell will break loose."

"You think I don't realize that? I have to get the diary or I might as well just stay here. If I run, he'll get suspicious and hand it over, I guarantee. Look, maybe if I give you my driver's license and a note, he'll give them to you." Jenny wrote the note, fished out her license, and gave it to Britt. She never kept her license in her wallet. Part of her "what if I lose my wallet" paranoia. "I'll stay here with the door locked until you get back."

Britt shoved the stuff in her pocket. "Yeah, and what's the secret knock?"

"SOS."

"You bet."

Jenny locked the door and buried her head in her hands. The effort involved in getting this far had left her a wreck. If anything went wrong, she couldn't run, never mind fight. She'd just have to hope nothing went wrong.

Less than five minutes later, there was an SOS on the door. Jenny opened it and Britt waved the manila envelope. "Some days, the good guys win," she said. "Let's roll. You go first. Fourth floor of the parking garage. Out of the elevator, turn right, five cars down, the black Toyota. Sure you can do this?"

"I've got no choice." With her help, Jenny shucked the bathrobe and stuck on the baseball cap. The mirror said between the hair and the cap pulled down low, not even her mother would have recognized her.

Thinking of her mother sent a twinge through her. She'd call to see how things were when she got to Britt's. She put the diary in her nice metal lunch pail and walked out through the lobby and into the parking garage. Her pained, lurching walk was so unlike her she felt like a huge arrow was pointing at her, but no one seemed to notice.

Two minutes later, Britt appeared with her purse, grinning like the Cheshire Cat. "Am I good or what?"

"You're good."

Britt unlocked the car. "In the back. On the floor," she said, "until we're out of town. Sorry, but it's the only safe way to do things, in case they noticed me coming in. I put in some pillows."

She pulled her black wig out of her pocket, tucked her hair up neatly underneath it, got a black shirt from the trunk to cover her cute pink stripes, and smeared her mouth with black lipstick. Not the full makeup she'd done earlier, but close enough for a dark garage. Jenny carefully lowered herself onto the pillows, the pain bringing tears to her eyes, and Britt covered her with a blanket. It was pretty bad—a hump is still a hump, however you pad it—but a small price to pay for freedom.

GOVERNOR ALFONSO

ON THE CAMPAIGN TRAIL

Governor Alfonso was not a happy camper. "What the flaming hell do you mean, you lost her?" he yelled, pounding his desk with a hairy fist. "What are you, a bunch of morons? I thought I made it clear that this was important."

O'Malley, who still hadn't gotten any sleep, stared with weary eyes at his boss, the governor's pale skin blotched red with irritation at the events they were now assessing. "Take it easy, Lou," he soothed, "we'll find her. She can't have gone far. Not in her condition. The kid could barely walk.

"The kid who could barely walk, the kid Keris described as helpless as a twelve-year old, has managed to slip through our fingers twice in less than a day." He opened his hand wide, then clenched it back into a fist.

O'Malley thought it looked like a furry starfish.

"I don't care what you have to do or how many people it takes. I want that girl found. No mistakes, no glitches, no escapes. I don't care if you have to drug her, wrap her in duct tape and stuff her in a laundry bag. I want her here! Got that?"

"She's not going to cooperate if you treat her like that," Keris said.

"She's not going to cooperate if you treat her like that," the Governor mimicked. "Christ! So far, listening to you people has gotten me nowhere. She'll cooperate, one way or another. We'll find a way to persuade her."

Two uniformed men with red faces and hangdog postures appeared in the doorway. Captain Van Allen and Lt. Thomas Morrissey, New York State Police, wishing they were anywhere else on earth. "Get your asses in here and shut the door," O'Malley growled. "You want the whole world to hear?" The two cops took seats as near the back as possible, staring down at their nicely shined shoes. "Where's the boy, Tom?"

"I left him interviewing hospital personnel, sir."

"He'll be lucky if I don't send him off to count antlers in some Adirondack backwater." The Governor tented his fingers and leaned back in his chair. "I don't suppose anybody has any good news, before we get on with this disaster?"

"I might, Sir," Morrissey said.

"Well?" Alfonso leaned forward, his thick eyebrows pulling together over his eyes.

Morrissey was 6' 5", 260 lbs., and a twenty-five year veteran of the state police. Just now, with his bent head and hunched shoulders, he looked like a chastened school boy. "Last night, while she was waiting to be seen in the ER, Jennifer Cates asked to see the chaplain. She gave him a manila envelope which she said contained a personal diary documenting her betrayal by a boyfriend which she was afraid someone might read."

The Governor shot a triumphant look at O'Malley. "So, where the hell is the envelope, Morrissey?"

"This morning a candy striper went to the Chaplain with a note and Jenny Cate's driver's license, and retrieved the package."

Damn! O'Malley thought. This girl is smart.

"I don't understand this at all." The Governor had a deceptively mild way of delivering disapproval. "I thought you understood she was to be isolated, kept dependent, until Trask could make a connection. So you do what? Leave her alone while you two go to breakfast and you leave her her purse, so she has ID, money, credit cards. Anyone would think you did"t have a brain between you."

"The hospital has her wallet. She didn't have clothes. And she'd been given a double dose of sleeping pills," Morrissey said. "If you'd seen the shape she was in, you wouldn't have thought she could walk across a room. She didn't do this alone. Security found a pink robe and a wheelchair in a first floor restroom. And no one on the staff recognizes the description of the candy striper."

"So maybe she called a friend." Keris began.

"Here's what we know," Morrissey said. "While the nurse was checking her vital signs, a young woman barged into the room looking for her grandmother. When told she had the wrong room, she said she was sure it was 314, then said she wanted 341. But 341 is in the maternity wing, and the woman in that room is only twenty-four herself."

O'Malley rose and strode to the window, staring glumly out at the glorious day. Screw sunshine. His mood was black. "You know what this means?"

Captain Van Allen got to his feet. "You think Buxton's people snatched her?"

"We're assuming they tried to run her off the road last night," the Governor said. "When that didn't work, they went to the hospital and took her."

"Poor girl," Keris Carlyle sighed.

"Poor? From all I've heard, it sounds like we're dealing with Superwoman," the Governor said.

Morrissey shook his head. "You ought to see her. She's just a little bit of a thing. Ms. Carlyle's right, she looks about twelve. Biggest thing about her is those eyes. Brave as hell, though. She's no Superwoman, just a scared kid trying to survive."

"I hope they don't hurt her," Keris said.

"Oh, spare the sentimental bullshit," O'Malley said. "Of course they're going to hurt her. They're trying to kill her, remember? Unless…" The whole room hung on his 'unless', which he didn't mind at all. "Unless she got away on her own."

"So, campers," Alfonso said, "what are we going to do about that?"

O'Malley flicked his chin at Morrissey. "You copied her address book, right?"

Morrissey nodded

"Start with her friends. Run the names, beginning with whoever's closest." He checked his watch. "Time to go, Lou."

Alfonso grabbed his briefcase, pausing to glare at the assembly. "No more screw-ups," he said, "understand?" He followed O'Malley out.

WASHINGTON, D.C.

Linwood Bean, Buxton's press secretary, sighed, folded his newspaper, and reached for the phone. Before he could dial, his wife Elnora put a hand over his. "How're you going to tell him, Woody? This is like a good news/bad news joke, except it's for real."

Elnora Bean was lovely. She was good. And she was wise. Because his wife was wise, he held off making the call, waiting to hear what she had to say.

"Do you honestly think he has no idea?" She poured him more coffee, stirred in two teaspoons of sugar, and set the cup in front of him. The cup said, "World's best Dad."

He stirred it again. Passing time. Considering. "I do," he said finally. "I've been with Jim more than twenty years and he's never, in all that time, even hinted at the possibility."

"But how could he not? You think he really loved her. What kind of man abandons a pregnant woman he loves, without a backward glance?"

He shrugged. "You have to understand the relationship they had. It was quite unusual. Lila Friedman was... is... quite unusual."

"It must have been quite unusual, Woody, because I don't understand. I don't see how a man could walk away from something so important." She caught his look. "I wasn't born yesterday. I know guys abandon pregnant women all the time. But this is Jim we're talking about. And even if Jim wanted to walk away from it, what about her? I don't see how a woman could have a child by a man she loved and never tell him."

"It was the politician in him that she loved, I think, the driven, ambitious, looking for a venue to do good kind of politician Jim was when they met. He was sort of a knight in shining armor back then. They both were. They were drawn together by their shared passion to right wrongs. He was the Attorney General. She was an able and eager young lawyer. He was handsome. She was attractive." He stared into his cup. "Beautiful, I mean. She had a kind of personal electricity that crackled around her. She worked with him on a few cases. Cases they were both passionate about winning. Long evenings together, head to head, arguing. Pretty soon they were having dinner together so they could go on talking."

"So far, it sounds as common as cheese," Elnora said, sweeping his dishes into the sink.

"I never said they rewrote the book on romance, but Jim and Maggie had drifted apart. She wasn't interested in what he was doing. She was tied up with the kids and with her status as an 'important wife,' and then along comes Lila. Everything that mattered to him mattered to her. It would have been hard for him not to fall in love. Even then, Maggie was sour and critical, while Lila was smart as a whip, energetic, bursting with enthusiasm, and incredibly warm. People brightened up whenever she was around. She was a magnet for good."

Elnora studied him with narrowed eyes. "You make her sound like a saint. Were you in love with her, too?"

"I was always waiting for you." He saw a smile beginning as she turned away.

"So Jim fell in love with Lila, and?"

"And just when he'd decided to leave Maggie for Lila, he was tapped to fill Fuller's vacant seat."

"And he couldn't expect to succeed as a divorced man, so he rode off into the sunset, leaving Lila behind?"

"Unless she left him behind. The point is, Lila didn't mind."

"How could she not mind? She loved him. She was having his child."

"Because she was as ambitious for Jim as he was for himself, and the least possessive woman I've ever known." He studied the cup some more. 'I'm not saying she wasn't sad, or that she didn't feel pain, Nora. I'm just saying she had the generosity to put his needs, and the needs of her home state, before her own."

Elnora shook her head. "If you say so. Well, Jim's in for a hell of a shock, learning he's got a daughter he never knew about and then learning she's dead."

"This will hurt him a lot," her husband said. "But I have to tell him. The risk it will come out is just too great. If we can see it, other people can, and Jim doesn't like surprises."

"You mean, Frank and Maggie don't like surprises," she said. "Anyway, that's not why we're telling him, is it?" She swiped at her already clean counter with a sponge and set it on the sink.

He reached for the phone. "Hi, Jim. Woody. Look, something's come up. Something we need to discuss right away." He listened. "Yes, I know you're supposed to lunch with the ladies. Stop here on the way. I wouldn't ask if it weren't important." He listened again. "I'm not telling you over the phone. It's sensitive. We could talk on the plane, but there isn't a lot of privacy. Right. See you."

"Well, that was cryptic. Now he won't even be able to tie his tie straight. When's he coming?"

"Fifteen minutes."

"Better rewind that tape then. He won't have much time."

Twenty minutes later, Buxton was sitting in their den, watching a tape of a high school graduation. The young woman giving the valedictory speech was a small, attractive brunette with a heart-shaped face, long hair, strong eyebrows, and startlingly blue eyes. He turned to Woody. "What am I supposed to see here? Who is this girl?"

"Just look at her, Jim. That's Lila Friedman's daughter, Jenny Cates."

The Senator went back to the screen; Woody and Elnora to watching the Senator. Waiting for the camera to zoom in for that close-up, and fill the entire screen with Jenny Cates' face and Jim Buxton's eyes. He couldn't help but see it. It jumped right off the screen. They watched his skin grow pale, saw him shake his head in astonishment. "My God! We have a child. Why didn't she tell me? How could she not tell me?"

Woody shut off the tape. "She's dead, Jim. Run off the road last night. Witnesses say it was intentional. First Lila, then Billy, now the girl. Now, your daughter." He handed the Senator the folded newspaper with the article about Jenny's accident.

"Lila's not dead," Buxton said. "And that bastard Billy. He's the one who taped..." The Senator snapped his mouth shut.

Woody pounced. "The one who what, Jim?"

Buxton looked like he'd jump out the window if he could.

"The one who what?"

The silence lay heavily on all of them. "Made a video of me and Lila," the Senator said in a strangled voice. "He said he'd destroyed it."

"Maybe that's what they were looking for when they tore Lila's office apart. And it would explain this." He handed Buxton a copy of a letter to Governor Alfonso.

Buxton scanned it. "Jesus, Woody! Where the heck did you get this?"

"It just popped out of my fax machine one day, Jim."

"And I was born yesterday." Buxton stared at the newspaper again. "Are you sure the girl... Jenny... is dead?"

Woody shook his head. "I thought so when I read the article but we should send some of our people to check. Late night accident. Early deadline for the paper. Maybe they ran with unsubstantiated facts. It seems undisputed that Jenny Cates was driving the car, and that someone deliberately drove her off the road. Here's what worries me, Jim. Alfonso has no reason to want her dead. He has every reason to want her alive, staring out at the voters with those blue Buxton eyes, while the Buxton campaign..." He trailed off.

Buxton shook his head. "Oh, no. Oh, no, Woody, I don't think so. You're not suggesting that I? That we? No. I swear. Until today, I had no idea that girl even existed."

Woody put a hand on his friend's arm. "Not you, Jim. But sometimes people get overzealous. I'm suggesting we have a little talk with Frank. And I'm suggesting—I hope this won't offend you—that we have Ken do some sniffing around. Maybe make some discreet FBI inquiries."

Buxton slumped in his chair, his handsome face showing its age. "Hell of a way to start the day, Woody. I found a daughter. Maybe I lost a daughter. And the whole package comes with a big load of shit." Then he shook himself. "Get Kenny. Get Whitehead from the FBI. Call Burrage. We'll talk on the way to the airport. See Frank on the plane."

He stopped at the mirror, checked his tie, and left.

Buxton got in his car thinking why had she never told him? He knew the answer. To protect him from an impulsive act that would have ended his career. Because Lila had had more faith in him, and higher expectations, than he'd had for himself. She'd married her devoted school teacher without a backward glance. Did the teacher know? Had he raised the child as his own or kept her at a distance?

He thought about the confidence with which he'd assured Frank that there were no more skeletons in his closet. No more skeletons! This was a full-fledged human. Perhaps she wasn't dead. He wondered what she was like and suddenly he wanted to know the details, the story of this blue-eyed girl's life. Then, with a shudder, he thought about Maggie. Maggie would run down Jenny Cates with a steamroller and not bat an eye. Maggie must never know.

"While my little one, while my pretty one, sleeps"
—Tennyson, "The Princess"

CHAPTER TEN

Britt stopped at a rest area and opened the back door. "I'm going to change out of this silly dress," she said. "You want to move into the front seat where you'll be more comfortable?"

Jenny slowly pushed herself up, moving with the alacrity of a sloth, and met Britt's worried eyes. "It would take a gallon of morphine to make me comfortable."

Britt slapped her forehead mockingly. "Stupid me. How could I forget?" She dug in her purse and pulled out two pill vials. "Which would you prefer, Demerol or codeine?"

Jenny bit her lip, incapable of dealing with the question. "What does the doctor recommend?" She'd forgotten Britt's dad was a doctor, a left-over sixties radical poverty medicine guy, a fanatic speaker at legislative hearings, a fanatic writer of letters, a rabid anti-smoker. According to Britt, the only time in her life he'd ever laid a hand on her was when he caught her smoking in eighth grade. Britt reported him as saying, "I'd rather break every bone in your body than have you dying a slow death with rotting lungs." He was the paternal equivalent of Jenny's mother, another passionate champion of the downtrodden and righter of life's wrongs.

"He says most people think they want Demerol, but codeine lasts longer. So here." She shook out two pills and opened a water bottle.

Jenny crawled out of the car, still bent over, held out her hand, and took the pills. Britt offered an arm and Jenny felt like an old grandmother. She wanted to stand straight and walk normally, but it was impossible. Slowly, she folded herself into the front seat and closed her eyes. Britt went to get changed. When the door opened and the engine roared to life, she didn't even open her eyes.

"I can't believe someone deliberately did this to you," Britt said. "You feel as awful as you look?"

"Much worse. If I looked as awful as I feel, you'd be turned to stone."

"Well, we'll be home soon and the doctor can look at you."

Reality sliced through Jenny's visions of warm baths, tender hands, soft beds. Under normal circumstances, going home with Britt would be the most natural thing in the world, but these circumstances weren't normal. "Oh, God, Britt. I wasn't thinking. We can't go to your house. It's the first place they'll look."

"Why? I mean, how will they find us?"

"My address book."

"You're kidding. You think they copied your address book?" Like it was a crazy idea.

"I'm sure they did. Look at me. This is not a normal situation. In normal situations, people aren't deliberately run off the road. They don't have cops trying to befriend them so they'll spill their guts."

She realized she hadn't told Britt anything. Not about her mother, or her uncle, or even about herself. She wasn't up to lengthy story-telling, but she couldn't drag her friend into this without an explanation. "It's a long story, but we're on our way to Elmira, so we've got time." A sudden panic seized her. "But maybe you don't want to go that far, or get mixed up in this. Only I don't know what else to do."

"Hey!" Britt's hand was on her arm, a firm, pay-attention grasp.

Jenny winced and the grip relented.

"Sorry. Look, you didn't drag me. I volunteered, okay. Now I'm in this up to my eyeballs, aren't I? Aiding and abetting a fleeing felon, or some such thing?"

"Felon? I'm the victim here. All I've done is check myself out of a hospital against doctor's orders. That's no crime, is it?"

"Then why is all this happening? Do you have some secret life I don't know about?"

"Worse. I have a secret life I didn't know about." Woozy with exhaustion and the effects of the pill, she gave the briefest explanation she could. Any minute, she expected to hear sirens, see police cars. "Look, can we get going? I'm having a heart attack here, thinking cops will appear any minute."

Britt didn't move. "If you really think they've got your addresses, then they'll probably show up at the house pretty soon, right? I must be your closest friend, geographically speaking. I haven't got time to drive you to Elmira, because by the time I get home they'll be there." She stared out the window, considering. "Okay," she said, with a decisive nod of her head. "I know what to do. I can't take you to Elmira, but I know someone who will, while I am home reading Proust and eating madeleines. The picture of innocence and uninvolvement. I picked you up at the hospital and dropped you at the bus station. I asked no questions. The perfect friend, right?"

She gave a delighted wiggle, then noticed Jenny's expression. "Oh, Jen. Honey. I didn't mean to make light of this. I'm not abandoning you. Honest. I'm just trying to make you safe."

She rested her hand, very gently this time, on Jenny's. "Listen. I am not like that bitch Betty. I am not like that woman you met in the restaurant. I am not like that deceptively charming trooper Joe Trask. I am your true friend and my only goal here is to keep you safe. Believe me?"

"I believe you."

"Then fasten your seatbelt, pal. This flight is ready for departure."

"Can't do it," Jenny said. "You'll just have to be careful."

Britt took her hand off the gearshift. "Look, I've spent too many years with my father. I can't drive unless everyone in the car is wearing a seatbelt."

"Let me show you something." Jenny unzipped her coverall and held it open so Britt could see her bruises. "That's what seat belts do."

"Jesus, that's ugly!" Britt reached over the seat and grabbed the blanket. "Here. Put this over you. Now tell me where you're going in Elmira and then you can close your eyes and go sleepy-bye."

Jenny was too tired to object. She winced as Britt fastened the seat belt, gritted her teeth as they pulled out onto the highway, then took a deep breath and repeated the directions to Rose's cousin's house.

Britt listened attentively and said, "Okay. I've got it."

Jenny was only dimly aware of being moved from one car to another, of voices, Britt's and another, of instructions and commotion, of Britt's farewell kiss and whispered good wishes. She dreamed that she was back in the car and it was rolling over and over and over, and with each roll, the jarring sent waves of pain through her. She opened her eyes. Better awake than asleep with dreams like this. The pain didn't stop. She was going up a stairway, carried by a handsome Black man with a gentle smile.

"Sorry," he said in a voice that had a touch of the islands. "I know it hurts. Give me one more minute and we'll have you in a nice, comfy bed." They went through the door into a bright bedroom. Still daylight. She'd lost all sense of time. Efficient hands stripped off her jumpsuit and work boots and pulled up soft sheets that smelled fresh from the laundry. She wasn't Sal the plumber any more. It was the bed she'd dreamed of, so warm, so soft. She thought she could sink down into it and keep sinking forever. But the man who had brought her was still standing beside the bed.

"My name is Etienne Sampler," he said. "I'm a doctor. I work with Brittany's father, and Brittany, she says I must take good care of you, so I must check some things before I go."

She felt the sheet being drawn down and stiffened in anticipation of pain and invasion.

"Ah, I see that already you are worried, so I will not lie. This may hurt some. I will do my best. I think you have been hurt enough." There was anger in his voice, as there had been in Britt's.

She wanted to reassure him, and thank him. All she managed was a sigh.

His hands moved lightly over her body, checking her pulse, listening to her heart, taking her temperature, and, finally, smoothing her hair away from her face. She heard him cross the room and the mumble of voices as he spoke with Rose's cousin.

Then he returned and bent over her. "Go back to sleep, Jenny Cates. That's a good girl," he said. "You're safe now. Safe. You can sleep as long as you want and this good woman, Pansy, will take care of you."

She sensed shades being pulled and an extra blanket being spread over her. Then the door closed with a click.

From time to time, she was vaguely aware of someone in the room, coming and going, murmuring things in a soft voice, but she never completely woke up. She didn't even wake fully when the woman fed her pills or walked her to the bathroom. For days, her nerves had been as tight as piano strings and her body had run without food or sleep, so she was grateful for the rest. This peace couldn't last. The time would come when she had to wake, confront the reality of her situation, and plan. But for now, she could let her body rest.

THE GOVERNOR'S OFFICE
ALBANY, NEW YORK

"This is beginning to sound like a good news, bad news joke, Mikey," Alfonso said, setting down his pen and flexing his hairy hand. The bright morning sun caressed the shiny bald spot on his head. Though it was still winter, the bald spot had a perfect tan. "First you locate a school friend in Saratoga Springs. Good news. The friend's family owns a car like the one the security camera captured leaving the parking garage being driven by a young woman with black hair. Good news. We search the premises and the kid's not there. Bad news. Girl says she dropped her friend Jenny Cates at the bus station. More bad news. Bus station personnel say they have no memory of having seen Cates. Has she disappeared from the face of the earth?"

"We'll keep an eye on her friends," O'Malley said. "She'll turn up. No money. No credit cards. What's she gonna do? A little ingenuity, a little bravado. She can't keep this up much longer." Neither could he. He was running on too little sleep and the sunshine annoyed him. There were a million things to worry about besides the whereabouts of a slippery twenty-one-year old. Like running a political campaign. All they had to do was wait until spring break was over and she'd go back to school. They could get her then. Unless Buxton's people got her first. That was the only thing that worried him, losing her before they got the stuff. He didn't even care about the girl. He wanted the tape, if there was a tape, or whatever it was she'd given to the chaplain. The man admitted he'd peeked in the envelope and it looked like a diary, like the girl had said.

The governor's wolfish grin came and went. "We keeping an eye on her friends?" O'Malley nodded.

There was a knock, and the governor's brusque "In," brought Keris

Carlyle, rested and smiling, looking like she'd just won the Kentucky Derby.

"What the hell are you so cheerful about?" O'Malley grunted. At this point, he resented anyone who didn't look like they'd been through the wringer. He'd seen his own face. The genial Irishman after a two-week bender. "Didn't anybody tell you this is doom and gloom day. Unless you've come to tell us you've found her."

"No such luck," she said. "But maybe I've found something better."

"The video tape?" O'Malley said hopefully.

"Not yet. But take a look at this." Keris reached in the envelope and pulled out a large color photograph of Senator James Buxton, laying it on the desk in front of the governor.

Alfonso made a face. "Who's this guy? Someone I'm supposed to know? Looks like some pansy-ass wasp politician."

She pulled out another photograph, this one a color studio portrait of a teenage girl, and laid it down beside the first. "Notice anything?" she asked.

Alfonso and O'Malley bent over the pictures. O'Malley saw it first. "No shit!" he said. "Hot damn and praise the Lord. What a gift!"

"What?" the governor demanded impatiently. "What gift? I see Buxton. I recognize the girl. Nice little piece, but what's the big deal?"

"Look at their eyes, Lou," O'Malley said. "Look at those big blue fuckin' eyes."

Alfonso picked up the photographs and held them out before him, staring silently from one to the other. "Holy Mother," he said softly. "You're right, Mikey. This is a gift. Now all we need is a bit of blood from each of them. See if the hospital still has any of the girl's. And find a way to get Buxton's."

He leaned back in his chair, grinning. "What are you waiting for, people," he said. "Let's get cracking. I'm out for blood."

THE BUXTON CAMPAIGN

SOMEWHERE ON A PLANE

Buxton had a splitting headache. The pills he'd taken weren't making a dent. Since Woody had dropped his bombshell, he'd done lunch with the founders of Emily's List, glad-handed his way through a cocktail party, spoken at a labor union dinner and stopped at a second union event to give a post-dinner address and shake a million hands. Usually such a productive day left him pumped with adrenaline and eager to dissect the events with Frank and Woody and often with Maggie. Today he felt like doing none of that.

Surprisingly, neither Frank nor Maggie seemed eager to make him do it. They were huddled in a corner with their heads together. An increasingly common sight, and one that made him uneasy. He wasn't keen on having Maggie take too big a role in the campaign. If he lost, it would be that much harder on her and consequently on him. Maggie had made it clear how important winning was, equally clear about the sacrifices she'd made for his career and what she was owed. Calm and relaxed, Maggie had excellent judgment. Excited, she lost it. And this campaign was getting her excited.

As the campaign heated up, he worried her ambition was making her too prominent. Sexist or no, the public didn't like a candidate's wife to be more than wifely. It was fine if she kissed babies and stood by his side. She could lunch with the ladies and open daycare centers and talk about the parental role and the working mother, so long as she espoused the party line and wore feminine suits. Much less fine if she began to express opinions of her own.

On the way to the airport, he and Woody and Ken had tried to get a handle on Frank's level of involvement with Lila Friedman and Jennifer

Cates. Frank's "What's the big deal?" had been dismissive. He'd raised his almost invisible eyebrows and tilted his head so he was looking down his nose at them. "Friedman's still in a coma. Her troublesome brother had an accident, and so, alas, did the poor girl. So many potential problems solved so quickly. You should be pleased."

He'd switched topics and then there had been the fuss of getting on the plane.

Now, despite his aching head, Buxton needed to finish the conversation. Frank didn't know Jenny Cates was still alive. His callousness was chilling; his ignorance of the true state of things disturbing. Arrogance, carelessness, and indifference were not desirable qualities in a campaign manager. The campaign manager was supposed to have his fingers in all the pies, his eyes on all the players, and manage to keep all the important balls in the air. If this ball had dropped, and Frank didn't even know it, what other important things had slipped through his grasp?

It's a fact of political life that people one wouldn't ordinarily want to be in the same room with are tolerated, even courted, because of their savvy. Frank was supposed to be the best. Was it just a facade? Buxton felt an unnerving stab of panic. They were in the lead but with nothing like a comfortable margin. This was no time for his campaign manager to stumble. He signaled Frank and Woody to join him, said in a low voice, "We never finished discussing Jennifer Cates. Have we been following the girl?"

Frank's shrug was too casual. "Why would we? It was the mother who posed the threat."

"I think you know why, Frank. You're pretty observant. I'm just hoping that Maggie isn't. In fact, I'd like it to be your job to ensure Maggie doesn't think about the girl."

Frank shrugged. "The girl was never important, and anyway, she's dead. There's no issue."

Frank's response roiled a stomach already made queasy by the headache, and by his rising fear that Frank, this sleaze bag his success depended on, had missed too many vital things lately. But he couldn't deal with it when it felt like his brain was being pressed out his ears. "There's an issue," he said. "Woody will explain."

Shrugging his shoulders wearily, he went in search of better remedies for his pounding head. There was a meeting with state party officials when he landed, and tomorrow he had a eighteen-hour day. The man hadn't winced or flinched, but he was sure Frank had been involved in Jenny Cates' accident. Involved, if not responsible. He hadn't been watching faces thirty years and learned nothing. The tells could be small. Just a slight twitch near the mouth, a slight shifting of the eyes.

Ominously, that shifting had been toward Maggie, who, as much as he, had a stake in keeping the Lila Friedman business under wraps. More than once, Maggie'd sworn she'd kill him if anything embarrassing to her came out during the campaign. Beneath her polished surface and ready charm, his wife was a born hater. Her unyielding stances sometimes astonished him.

He hated to imagine his wife and campaign manager colluding behind his back, but few things surprised him anymore. They had to rein Frank in or go down in flames. A wily politician can weather a lot. People get paid off, with connections, proximity, jobs, contracts. Politicians cheat on their wives and are forgiven. It's all part of the game. Murder, however, is not.

Linwood Bean leaned forward. "The girl's very much alive, Frank."

Frank cast a nervous glance at Maggie. "How the hell do you know?"

"I make it my business to know," Bean said quietly. "You should, too. In particular, you should make it your business to see that nothing happens to the girl. The Senator has a particular attachment to her, if you get my drift. He is concerned for her safety."

Frank pulled a rumpled handkerchief from his pocket and mopped his sweaty brow. "He'd do better to be concerned for his own safety. We'd all be a whole lot better off if that girl was history, Woody. Rumor is she's carrying a steamy videotape of the Senator and her mother."

Linwood Bean wondered about Frank's sources, which seemed to be giving him different information, but he said, "So find the girl. Destroy the tape. Do not destroy the girl. And, Frank..." Frank's head came up like a startled deer. "She's just a kid. Her mother is attacked. Her uncle dies. She's forced off the road, nearly dies, and then she's so scared she runs from the hospital. Find her before Alfonso's people do. They'll make a circus out of this."

"She survived the accident?" Frank said.

"Survived the accident. Then ran from the hospital. You're supposed to know this stuff. Alfonso thinks we snatched her."

Frank's eyebrows rose. "Unless he's got her and this is just disinformation."

"Great word, Frank. Why don't you get on to your spies, see what you can learn. And since you're supposed to be so almighty on top of things and in the know," he set two photographs down, "see if you can figure out why our candidate has a particular interest in the girl."

It didn't take him long. "Holy shit!" He picked them up cautiously and stuffed them in his briefcase. "I gotta go to the can." As soon as the lavatory door shut behind him, he jerked out his phone and started dialing.

"But, for the unquiet heart and brain,
A use in measured language lies;
The sad mechanic exercise,
Like dull narcotics, numbing pain.
—Tennyson, "In Memoriam"

CHAPTER ELEVEN

Safe in Pansy's comfortable bed, Jenny opened the package from her mother. There were two diaries, so she opened the first and started reading.

New diary. New job. New life. I feel like I'm standing in the middle of a great, wide road, rising smoothly upward with nothing but endless possibilities. I don't know why I feel so exuberant. I made a total ass of myself this morning. Maybe some people are just born clumsy? If so, then I'm one of them. First day in the Attorney General's office. My dream job. All the new attorneys are introduced at staff meeting. I stand up when my name is called and spill half a cup of coffee down the front of my new skirt. Lila Friedman. Human klutz. I hope no one noticed. It was a sensible brown skirt. I know better than to wear clothes that show the dirt. But I survived. Got a couple good assignments, thank goodness. I know how to think and I know how to write. I was in the law library until nine p.m., when they threw me out.

Now I'm here at home, trying to figure out how, with exactly $123.47 between me and the poor house, I'll make it through the next three weeks until my first paycheck. Luckily, my first month's rent is paid.

The noontime sun pressed in through every window, as if trying to entice Jenny out of bed. It tried in vain. Propped against pillows in the big sleigh bed, she was oblivious to everything except the volume in her hands. Beside the bed was a blue and white jug filled with daffodils. There was a tentative knock on the door. Reluctantly, she raised her eyes and called, "Come in."

A gray-haired woman with a soft, billowy body came in with a tray. "I brought you some soup," she said, setting it next to the daffodils. "Beef barley. Homemade. I spoke with Rose a while ago. She says to tell you hello and to be sure you know Andy's not mad about the car." She hesitated. "They went to your friend's house. Britt? Searched for you everywhere, even though the family said you weren't there."

Jenny looked up at the kindly face. It was clear Pansy hated being the bearer of bad news. Rose's cousin had taken tender care of her and asked for nothing in return. All Jenny had done was sleep. "I love Rose," she said, drawing a sweet smile from her hostess. "Did she have any news about my mother?"

Pansy shook her head. "Not exactly. She was very cautious, as you can imagine, since none of them have much information, and she didn't want to discourage you. And then, you know Rose. She only likes good news. But she said that while on the surface things appear unchanged, the nurses are smiling more and talking to your mother more, as if they expect she's listening."

"What about my dad? How's he doing?"

Pansy shook her head. "Not so good," she said.

Jenny hugged the diary against her chest. "I wish I could be there." The news made her anxious. Any improvement in her mother's condition put her mother in greater danger. She assumed the doctors knew that and would keep things secret, but with someone like Feeney, who was barely human, they couldn't count on discretion. And from her brief time there, Jenny knew the place was wide open. Anyone could walk in or out, especially if they wore something vaguely medical or slung a stethoscope around their neck.

Pansy—evidently her family went in for flower names, since there had also been a reference to a sister named Daisy—gestured toward the soup. "Better eat before it gets cold, dear. I left a robe and nightgown in the bathroom, in case you want a bath. There's an elastic and a plastic bag to cover your cast." She gestured toward a chair. "Or, if you feel like getting dressed, here are some of my old things. Pretty big on you, I'm afraid. I'm going run out to Walmart and pick you up some clothes."

She pulled an index card from her pocket and waited, pencil poised. "If you could just give me your sizes?"

Jenny rattled off a list of sizes.

Pansy gave some unsettling instructions about escape and flight, if they became necessary—the kitchen door, the ell, the barn—and left.

After her rescue from the hospital, Jenny needed gentleness and peace. She needed sunshine through the windows. She also needed the underwear and socks Pansy was getting. Dr. Sampler's pills and Pansy's tender ministrations had begun to restore her. Now, all she wanted to do was read her mother's diary.

Written when her mother wasn't much old than Jenny was now, they were an intimate look into her mother's past. From the first lines, Jenny's reactions had had an unsettling duality. She'd felt like a voyeur, and she'd been mesmerized, caught up in the story and emotions as if her mother were a friend confiding in her.

As she sat up and rearranged the pillows so she could eat, she caught a glimpse of herself in the mirror, startled by the stranger reflected. She hadn't seen herself since the hospital mirror when she was at the dead end of exhaustion. The person in the mirror was her, yet it was not. She didn't look restored. Her hair was a rat's nest, her face still bruised and swollen, and with deep circles beneath her eyes, she looked old and haunted.

Though the last few days seemed like a dream, she didn't have to pinch herself to know that this was real. Her pain was real, the leaden weariness, and the coil of fear that even in this bright bedroom wouldn't let go. She grimaced at the mirror. Her face had a pinched quality, all eyes and aggressive dark brows and a small, stubborn chin that lifted defiantly as she watched. "To hell with all of 'em," she said. "This time the good guys win."

So far, the good guys had taken quite a beating. She didn't know the rules of the game. Maybe they scored by catching her, she scored by not getting caught. Whatever the rules, it wasn't fun.

She sighed and picked up the bowl. Holding it awkwardly with her left hand, which didn't have much mobility due to the cast, she tasted some soup. Like a stone falling into a well, it went down, down, down, landing with a splash in the bottom of her stomach. The last meal she'd had was that pot pie. She gobbled the soup and looked at the tray, hoping for more. There was a tall glass of milk and a plate of cookies.

She grabbed the milk, the cookies followed, and seconds later, glass, plate and bowl were back on the tray, and Jenny was reading the diary again. She had already followed her mother through the acquisition of her first job. Those first nervous weeks, desperately poor, trying to stay afloat until her first paycheck. Now she was watching her mother learn to be a working woman in a man's world. For Lila Friedman, it hadn't been easy.

I don't know whether to trust my instincts or not. My friend Cassie says I don't know anything about men. Why should I? I've spent the last seven years with my nose buried in books. Cassie thinks I'm a riot. She says she's never seen such a smart woman who is so dumb about men. Tonight, in the office, I was explaining some of the legal points I've been researching, things I'm excited about because I think I've found an argument which will give us a real edge in the case. Well, I got into my excited lecture mode, the one where I'm taken over by ideas, and when I looked up, Jim Buxton was sitting there with the oddest expression on his face. It was almost like he hadn't been listening, only watching me talk for the fun of watching me. He has the most wonderful eyes and I couldn't help it. I felt a blush that must have started at my toes. It didn't help that I said the first thing that came into my head. "But you're married."

He grinned like a teenage boy caught peeking into the girl's locker room. "That doesn't mean I'm blind," he said. "When you're excited about something, like now, you almost glow."

It was about the most romantic thing anyone has ever said to me, so I said, "Oh, pooh, Jim, don't be so silly. People don't glow. Come on, we've got work to do."

He laughed, picked up my outline, and we went back to work. I wondered if he was going to try anything, but he was a perfect gentleman, we got the memo written, and then, both exhausted, we called it a night. I don't know about Jim, but I didn't sleep a wink. I tossed and turned all night, alternating between wondering if I should quit my job before I got into serious trouble, and knowing I couldn't quit when I had the most wonderful job in the world. Am I a traitor to the feminist cause if I think it's unfair for him to make me feel this way? Do I concede too much power to a man if I admit he has the upper hand? Damn him! I just want to be the best lawyer I can and help people. Why does he have to make it so hard?

Jenny stared unseeing at the sunny window. She had trouble with this version of her mother. Lila Friedman had always been so definite and certain, at least the side she'd shown her daughter. Forceful. Deliberate. Sure of herself. The roles she had modeled for Jenny had been strong ones. Know what you want and devise strategies to get it. Know what is right and do what is right. Don't take the easy way out, do the work necessary to do the job well. Remember your obligations to help those weaker or more needy than yourself. Rules Jenny had taken to heart. She'd always held herself to these standards.

Was the mother she knew really the same woman who had blushed from head to toe at a look? Could Lila Friedman ever have struck anyone as so insecure or uncertain a friend accused her of knowing nothing about men? Had the woman who'd coached her since birth to stand up for her rights actually considered quitting a job she loved because the boss had roving eyes? Wouldn't Lila Friedman have rapped him sharply across the knuckles and ordered him to get a grip, act his age, and stop making her uncomfortable? Even though she knew how this story ended, Jenny was fascinated.

I never expected to have my personal morality tested this way. For the past week, Jim was away with his family on a Florida vacation. I didn't expect to miss him. After all, I've always known his place was with them; always told myself this was just a professional relationship, a business acquaintance which has grown into a casual friendship. I told it to Cassie, when she stopped by and found me weeping into my wine, and she just laughed. 'Oh, Lila,' she said, 'you're such a hoot. Do you really not know you're in love with the guy?'

I said 'Of course I'm not in love with him. We just work together. He thinks I'm smart. He likes that. And we agree on a lot of things. That's all. If I'm in love with anyone, it's with Bud Cates.'"

"At that she laughed harder. "Lila, dahlin', men and women can't be just friends." She said that I wasn't in love with Bud, Bud was in love with me. "Stares after you like a love-sick dog," is how she put it. That made me mad. Bud Cates is the nicest man I've ever known. We're so comfortable together it's like we've always known each other. I told her that. She said, "Sure, Lila. It would be like marrying your brother." Then she left and I wasn't sorry to see her go. The problem with Cassie is that she's so darned sure of herself. She says things with such confidence I wonder if she's right even when I don't agree.

And I don't agree. Maybe there aren't any fireworks, but I love Bud Cates and know that I will marry him. I'm just not ready to settle down yet. I want to spend more time at my career first. And I don't see why Jim Buxton and I can't work closely together without anything physical happening. I don't see why I can't admire him for his politics, for his passion to help people, for his determination to preserve his integrity and not fall into a bunch of cheap compromises that won't be good for Maine's citizens in the long run. I don't see why I can't admire these things and share these passions without falling into bed with him.

Cassie's know-it-all face appears before me. "Because passion leads to passion." If she were here, I'd hit her. She's wrong about me and the Attorney General.

So why do I miss him so much? Why did I not sleep well all week? Why did I jump every time the phone rang, hoping it was him? Why was I so hurt when he rushed past me in the hall today and didn't even say hello? Why *did I sit and stare at the same paragraph for an hour this afternoon, when one of the Deputies was waiting for a memo? I know I have to do a good job if I want to get interesting work. I know the few women in this office are held to a higher standard and if I let down, I let everyone down, not just myself. I let down Sarah and Judith and Sheilah and even that self-centered bitch Ellen. I don't know why I worry about her. She'd stab us in the back and walk over our bodies if she thought it would help her get ahead. I always wonder about people like Ellen. Where they come from, what shaped them, where they get that incredibly self-centered drive. I'd want to be more like that if it weren't for the awful selfishness. I'd like to be more certain, confident, driven. Ellen's older, so maybe it comes with time. Live long enough and I, too, can be an Ellen. It's a scary thought.*

Then at five, when I was finally focused and getting work done, he comes in, sits in a chair across from me, and just stares. Just stares at me and sighs and leaves without a word. I could have killed him. Just when I'm getting my concentration back, he comes back, sits down, and says, "Lila, I think I'm falling in love with you." He leaves and this time he doesn't come back.

My heart is dancing, whirling, caught up in a wild dance. My hair flies out in the wind, the music grows louder, my feet are dancing on air. He has gone away with his family and he has come back to me! I don't give a damn if it's wrong. I am ecstatic. I go into the ladies room to splash cold water on my face and see myself in the mirror, flushed and radiant, and I am ashamed.

This cannot be, I remind myself. I must not encourage him. Jim Buxton is a political creature. He has a bright future which getting entangled with me could ruin. But isn't that his problem? He's the married one. I'm free and single and can do whatever I damn please. Why am I worried about my self-control? Why doesn't he worry about his? I'm not the one who announced I'm in love. I don't sit in his office and stare at him. I'm just a humble staff attorney, trying to write a memo. What am I supposed to do, quit? I love this job. I love this job. I love this job.

The last declaration of love for her job trailed off in a blur of smudged ink. *A tear,* Jenny thought. She wanted to reach back into the past, and comfort the confused young woman her mother had been. She wanted to grab Jim Buxton and shake him. Tell him to grow up, be more responsible and stop trifling with the affections of a young and vulnerable female employee. If only there were time travel. If she went back in time, she could protect her mother. And prevent herself.

She closed the book. Fascinated as she was, this was hard going. She needed a break. A bath and some rest. The hands holding the book were trembling and she felt suddenly overcome with weariness. Weariness and sadness for the vulnerabilities of that long ago girl who became her mother.

The sunlight was fading as she poked the two volumes under the mattress and got ready for her bath. She didn't even have clean underwear. Just a hair brush and a toothbrush. She'd never thought of herself as a materialist but this sudden poverty hurt. All her clothes, many of them favorites, burned. All her books and notebooks and papers had gone up in flames with Dandy's car. At least this was a better story than "the dog ate my homework."

If she ever got back to school to tell it.

If anyone would believe her.

Footsteps on the stairs signaled Pansy's return. The kind woman came up the stairs carrying several shopping bags. She set them down on the floor with a smile. "It almost feels like Christmas," she said. "I had fun getting you new things. I hope you'll like them."

"I was about to take that bath," Jenny said. "And thanks for the soup. It was delicious."

"I'm making a pot roast for dinner," Pansy said. She hesitated. "As I was coming back, I saw a police car slowing near the house. He went off again, so I expect it's nothing. But if anyone shows up, don't worry, dear. I'll send them away."

Jenny sorted through the bags, finding underwear, yoga pants, and a sweatshirt. She carried them to the bathroom, filled the tub with water, secured the plastic bag over her cast, and lowered herself slowly down into the stinging heat. Her body was a colorful collage of bruises, everything from deep, livid-purple stripes to patches of egg-yolk yellow and sickly green. She resembled one of her kindergarten finger paintings. She rested her left arm on the edge of the tub and submerged the rest, like a hippo in a river, occasionally coming up for air. Sooner or later, she was going to have to deal with her present. For now, she was visiting her mother in that famous long ago. Soon, as the tale skimmed along, they would do the dirty deed and she would be conceived. She wondered whether Senator Buxton knew he had another daughter. Maybe she'd call him up and ask.

*"So it is more useful to watch a man in times
of peril, and in adversity to discern what kind
of man he is…"*
—Lucretius, from *The Way Things Are*

CHAPTER TWELVE

The second time she almost fell asleep in the tub, Jenny decided to get out before she drowned. Leaving the soothing warmth and hauling herself to her feet would be unpleasant. The lure of the diaries finally got her out. Now that she'd started, she needed to go on.

Stories had always had the power to lure her into another world. This story had special power. Through it, she was connecting to her mother in a way she'd never been before. Given a chance to meet a younger, more vulnerable and open Lila Friedman. Her mother had meant her to know this, meant for them to have this connection, only in the event something happened to her.

Jenny understood. Everyone's past is personal, and her mother had been a very private person. The evolving relationship Lila Friedman was describing, between herself and the Attorney General, and between herself and herself, was important enough to have written down and saved all these years, but too intimate to be shared. It was being shared now only because of the very real prospect her mother might die.

Her mother had wanted Jenny to have this story, to read it, to know it. Recognizing the danger it posed for her daughter, though, she'd dragged herself back from the cusp of death to give a warning. Propped against pillows, Jenny heard her mother's voice. "Run, Jen, run. Burn diaries and run!" Even in her most extreme moments, her mother's thoughts had been of her.

The idea of burning these diaries seemed like sacrilege, but her mother would never want to share them with the world. So Jenny would burn them as soon as she'd read them. It would hurt to let them go because of the connection with her mother. It would hurt far more to read them in a tabloid, hear them fall mockingly from the lips of politicians, see her mother dumped into company with Stormy Daniels or Monica Lewinsky. Her mother was no politician's honey. As much as it was in Jenny's power to prevent it, Lila Friedman wouldn't be a pawn in someone's vicious political game.

I didn't sleep at all last night. After he left, I finished the memo—a frightfully bad job, I'm afraid—and went home. I thought I was hungry, but when I saw the meal I'd fixed, it looked so unappealing I put it away. I tried to watch TV, but there was nothing on. I thought maybe if I had a drink and a bath I might unwind. I'd been rushing around breathlessly for what seemed like hours and I was getting dizzy. I hate this! I hate it that my emotions can overrun me like this, that my mind can dash away, out of control. I believe in control. I believe in the rational mind. I believe in self-discipline. I believe that part of becoming a mature adult is learning to master feelings, learning to take the long view, to stop indulging in instant gratification. I did not work myself to exhaustion getting through college and law school to blow it all now because someone's handsome blue eyes make me breathless. It must be time to look for another job.

And then I think, dammit, I don't want another job. This is the best job in the world. I'm getting paid to wear a white hat. This is what I've always dreamed of. I can't believe the power I have. I can't believe they actually let me make decisions about important things, when I'm barely out of the cradle. It's hard and demanding and every day there's a new challenge, but the highs feel like lifting weights and drinking champagne. And I can get immersed it in. Spend as much of my time as I want, give it all my energy. Early mornings, late nights, weekends. They all belong to me and I can use them any way I want. It's hard to imagine, even though sometimes I'm so afraid of making a mistake I can't breathe, that life could get much better than this.

The DA in Bangor offered me a job. It would get me out of here, and I've always wanted to chase bad guys. Talk about white hats! But I've got opinions to write on the constitutionality of proposed legislation. I've got a case involving discrimination against native Americans by the ironworker's union. I've got a bank that routinely fires women just when their pension rights are about to vest. I've got a lawyer who wants us to sign off on a piece of property, half of which has escheated to the state, for a token payment, while his client walks away with a couple hundred thou. It's not just a cloud on the title, buddy, it's a great big ugly stain! And contrary to popular opinion, we government lawyers are not all morons.

Jenny read on, envying her mother a life in which she could be so completely immersed. It wasn't so different for her. She was very much her mother's daughter in her ability to become completely engaged in what she was doing, and to delight in it. Many people Jenny knew never found delight in anything, were never able to let themselves go, to make their lives and their work become one. Drew had been jealous of it. Her ex-friend Betty had made fun of it. But deep down, even though it made her unlike other people, Jenny had reveled in it.

Now, sitting here reading about her mother doing the same thing, she felt a kinship, a sisterhood that made her want to reach back through the decades and whisper, "I know. I understand. Don't let them drive you away from what you love."

The Attorney General has been out of the office for the past two days, meeting with business people in Portland and Bangor. I saw a glimpse of him as he was heading for his car, but that's all. When he's gone, I can breathe, knowing I won't meet him around the next corner, knowing he won't come into my office and sit there and stare at me. Knowing he's not going to say something that upsets my equilibrium. I have a very fragile rein on my emotions these days. It's like having that funny, infuriating, emotional day before my period starts go on for days.

Last night I had dinner with Bud and I felt so deceptive. I've told him the truth as I know it, that there's this attraction which distracts me but nothing is going on. I can't stand it that he's so nice to me. I can talk to him about absolutely anything and he listens so well. He's like my brother and my best friend and my boyfriend all in one great package. How, with a guy like this, can I look at anyone else? A guy who loves his work, loves the kids he's teaching, and loves me. I mean really loves me. Knows who I am and loves me warts and all. Because the heart isn't rational. After dinner, we went back to his apartment and drank some wine and had some nice, cozy, roly-poly sex. He's pleasing and fun and generous and unquestionably the best man I will ever meet. What the hell is wrong with me?

Jenny had to stop. She wanted to grab her mother and shake her. What the heck *was* wrong with her? Why wasn't Bud Cates enough for her? Sure, she, Jenny, would never have existed, but her mother and father—that is, Lila and Bud—would be pursuing their happily ever after without thugs in suits. Without a bank of bleeping monitors and a staff of specially trained ICU nurses. She wondered why her parents had never had any more children. She hadn't been that bad, had she?

This morning he brought me coffee. Just came waltzing into my office, carrying two cups and two doughnuts from the blind vendor in the basement. He set mine down on the desk, settled into my visitor's chair, and stared at me again. No words beyond "good morning." I didn't have anything to say. I was hung-over from wine and my hair needed washing, which I couldn't do very well at Bud's because I need my special dryer and brush, and I was wearing one of Bud's shirts with yesterday's skirt, and also, as a joke, one of Bud's ties. I'd stuffed my hair back in a ponytail and thought I looked like hell.

I pried the lid off my coffee, trying not to spill. Those eyes made me so nervous. All sexy bright blue and dancing. I picture them on a child. He's got three daughters, I think, but I've never seen any of them. His family doesn't seem to play much of a role in his life. They haven't even moved up from Portland. Cassie says Augusta is too much of a backwater for his wife. He keeps an apartment in Augusta for when he works late. I wonder what it looks like. Probably tiny and messy and very masculine. It probably smells like stale scotch and feet.

"You look about twelve years old today. Same age as my oldest daughter," he said.

"Well, I'm not twelve. I'm twenty-four and I've got work to do." I didn't mean to be snappish; only he makes me so nervous and I did have things to do.

"Have dinner with me tonight," he said. "I want to ask your advice about something."

Dinner was a bad idea. I waved my hand airily. "You can ask right now." Spilled my coffee into my lap and down my leg. Hot, hot coffee. I yelped and grabbed my box of tissues out of the drawer. Next thing I know, he's got a fistful of tissues and he has his hand up under my skirt, trying to keep the stuff from burning my legs, he says. Then, because I'm shaken and it hurts and my clothes are ruined, he tucks me into my coat and tells his trooper to drive me home. Ken Bass is not much older than I am but he's got the rigid posture and inscrutable face that go with the job. So Ken Bass drives me home without a word, and I assume he knows what his boss is up to and strongly disapproves, but when we get to my house, he opens the door for me and insists I take his arm to go upstairs, and then he tells me to get out of my clothes right away and soak in a cold tub. While I'm struggling out of my clothes, he starts the bath and leaves some aspirin on the sink.

Nice guy, Kenny Bass. He waits so patiently while I get dressed again and then drives me back to the office. This time, he talks. He even tells me he didn't talk before because he figured I was coping with the burn, and being drenched with coffee, and my embarrassment at having it happen in front of the Attorney General. It's clear he's a rock solid member of the Jim Buxton fan club. He speaks of the man in awed tones. I know how he feels. When I listen to the AG speak, I feel like I'm hearing something important. And he's such a politician—the AG, not Kenny—he has this way of making everyone feel special. His secretary worships the ground he walks on. His deputies beam when he tells them they've done well. I wonder what he's like when he's mad.

Jenny closed her eyes, which were stinging from reading. Soon she had to plan. Even here, eventually someone would find her. These people had a knack for tracking her down. She'd finish reading them, burn the diaries, and plan.

He stayed away all day and let me work in peace. A good thing, too, because one of his deputies came rushing in almost as soon as I got back and needed some research right away. I spent the day in the law library, frantically researching and writing, hoping what I was turning out was coherent. It was almost seven before I was done. By then, I had such a blinding headache it hurt to move. I'd missed lunch and dinner, which didn't help. My neck ached. My legs were tender from the burn. All I could think of was crawling into bed.

I managed the going home part, but ten minutes after I walked in, the doorbell rang. Jim Buxton was standing there with Chinese take-out. When I get a bad headache, I get all pale and puffy and look like something the cat dragged in and then the dog chewed on, but he took one look at me, and instead of running, he said, "Oh, you poor kid. I know you haven't had anything to eat today, so Kenny and I thought we'd bring you some dinner."

How did he know I hadn't eaten?

He put the food on the table, ordered me to sit, went around behind me, and started massaging my neck and shoulders and the back of my head. I was not born yesterday and I know this is a seduction technique a lot of guys use, but he didn't make any moves on me even though I might have let him. I was so confused! He massaged my neck, he brought me aspirin and a glass of water, he asked if there was anything else he could do, and then he left. Bringing me dinner. No strings attached.

Bastard! He has to know what he's doing. And yet, sometimes I wonder. Am I conceding him too much power? What if he's as confused as I am?

I ate dinner, crawled into bed, and slept right through my alarm in the morning. By the time I got up, I was so late I grabbed the first thing I came to in my closet, and it wasn't until I got to the office I realized I was wearing a dress I'd deemed too short and tight for office wear, at least without a jacket. At lunch, I slunk out and bought a jacket and some dark stockings. This is stupid. Twenty years from now, I'll read this and think I spent my whole time at work worrying about my clothes. I never think about clothes! They're just something to cover my body. It's that damned Jim Buxton again. He's making me self-conscious.

Sure enough. I had a meeting with him and several people from the human rights commission, and he kept staring at the place where the buttons gape. I can't help it. I'm built just like my mother. We're little European peasant women. We look lovely as girls, all skinny arms and legs and big chests, and then the rest of our bodies expand to match our chests until we're built like sturdy little fireplugs. If I have one wish, it will be that my daughter, should I ever have a daughter, not inherit this body. It's nothing but trouble.

But her mother hadn't filled out like a fireplug, though Jenny understood, from the little she'd known of her grandmother and her aunt, a pair of fireplugs, what her mother meant. In her mid-forties, Lila Friedman still had slender arms and legs and a big chest and masses of dark, curly hair. Too busy to eat, always running at high rpms, how could she ever gain weight? Jenny was carrying the body type into the next generation. She might have those damned Buxton eyes, but she had a Friedman body. Right now, the Friedman body was shivering.

She pulled up the blanket, found the painkillers and swallowed two. She picked up the diary again, sure she was about to get to the good part.

Today was another marathon day. I hadn't even gotten my coat off when one of the other attorneys, Jeff Greenwald, rushed into my office, red-faced, and said, "Have you got any spare time?" I looked at the stack of stuff waiting for attention. "I don't know, Jeff. Is it an emergency?"

He waved a paper at me. I snatched it out of his hand so I could read it. It was an order to produce records for discovery in a suit by the state employees union against the state and the board which had revised all the employee classifications. It was signed by the meanest superior court judge in the state. And the materials were to be produced by tomorrow morning. "It's been sitting on Matt's desk for a month," he whined, "and he gives it to me this morning."

I shrugged airily. Not my problem, but it looked like no big deal. "Get the Board's staff to pull it out for you."

"There is no board. It was dissolved about a year ago. So there's no staff. The stuff is in a bunch of boxes in the state library basement, Lila. This is an emergency! No kidding."

No kidding. Jeff and I spent the day in a dusty basement, going through boxes, the later afternoon and dinner hour reading the complaint and other papers and deciding what we had to actually produce, and half the night hunched over copy machines, making the necessary copies. No secretaries, they were strictly nine to five. No paralegals, the office didn't have any. Just good old Lila and Jeff. By the time I got home, I was grimy from head to toe and bent over like the Hunchback of Notre Dame. And this time, when I really needed it, no one brought me dinner. I was too tired to eat anyway. Just showered and fell into bed.

The next morning I discovered the milk was sour by pouring it over the last of the cereal, and arrived at the office starving, achy, and cross as a bear. As penance for snapping at my secretary, who commented that I looked tired, I wrote three letters, revised a memo and returned four phone calls before opening my bag of doughnuts. I was one bite into my first jelly doughnut—the first of three, the minimum number necessary to improve my disposition— when Jeff appeared again, snagged one of the doughnuts, and dropped himself disconsolately into my chair. He was clutching an ominous sheaf of papers and looked like he was on his way to be executed.

I moved the last doughnut out of his reach. "Now what?"

He shoved the papers across the desktop. "Interrogatories," he said. "Matt just found them this morning."

I thumbed through the papers. "These are due today."

He shrugged wearily. "I know."

"So go ask for an extension."

He stared at me with spaniel eyes. "Been there. Done that. Denied. Judge Watson all but nailed my balls to the bench as a warning to other dilettantes."

I refrained from commenting on his balls. One thing I've learned in my limited time at the bar. Male lawyers talk and think about balls almost as much as major league players. "Two days ago I was naively thinking public practice was fun."

"Oh, it is, Lila. It is. But the level of competence varies. When you're playing with the big guys, it feels like heaven. When you're cleaning up after morons, it's more like hell. You'll get used to it." We spent the day driving all over the state, driving and calling and sending state troopers out with stacks of papers. The clerk's office closed at four. At three fifty-nine, we staggered through the door with our answers.

At four-ten we walked into the nearest bar, found ourselves a dark, quiet corner, and ordered drinks. When my bourbon came, I glared at Jeff over the rim and said, "I've helped pull your ass out of the fire twice in two days, so you owe me, right?"

He nodded.

"Good. I'm going to drink until I fall over, and you're going to drive me home."

"Deal," he agreed. We clinked glasses.

I'm not a big drinker but the bar was dark and restful and I was tired and thirsty. We ordered burgers and fries. Nice, thick greasy cheeseburgers with lettuce, tomato and onion and buns so thick I could barely get my hands around them. I was two bourbons in, my nose starting to get numb, when Jeff suddenly checked his watch and jumped up. "Sorry, Lila," he said. "I'm supposed to pick up my daughter ten minutes ago." He dumped money on the table and rushed out.

"Hey!" I called after his disappearing back that he was my ride, but he was out of earshot. I was in no shape to drive and finding a taxi in this town was as likely as finding a New York-style deli. I walked, slowly, carefully, only tripping once or twice, to the phone and called Bud. No answer. It was his softball night. Playing the state police. I'd been a pinch-hitter on the office team when they played the state police. A mean bunch. I should have been there to cheer him on.

Decision time. It was four miles to my apartment and half a mile to my car and my office. I could sleep in the office, drive home in the first blush of dawn, change, and come back. It sure beat getting arrested for OUI. The office frowns on that. I paid the check and went into the ladies room. My eyes and nose were rabbity pink, my eyelids were at half-mast and I looked even more drunk than I felt. I slapped some powder on my nose, which only made it look fuzzy as well as pink, stuffed myself into my jacket, picked up my briefcase, and left. I would have done fine if there hadn't been steps. I was on the third step when my heel caught in a hole and I started to pitch forward. The only thing that saved me from going ass over teakettle was that someone coming up the steps caught me. Jim Buxton.

Here we go, Jenny thought. Now he'll drive her home and take advantage of her. She forced herself to read slowly, though she wanted to skim through the pages until she got them into bed. She was being ridiculous. This wasn't a novel. This was a true story. Her mother's story. Her story. At some point in this, she was going to be conceived.

"…the woman is so hard
Upon the woman."
—Tennyson, "The Princess"

CHAPTER THIRTEEN

Wondering what time of day it was, she glanced out the window and her heart jumped. A police car was turning into the yard. She fumbled on socks and shoes, inept as a toddler, and arranged the covers so the bed was neat. She hung the robe and nightgown inside the closet door. She hated to leave this beautiful, peaceful room. The clean white walls, the shining pine floor, the cheerful blue and yellow bedspread and sunny daffodils. She scanned the room for any other signs she'd been here. The tray. She carried it to Pansy's room and left it beside the bed. Then she hurried to the window and peeked cautiously out. The police car was still there, the driver talking on the phone.

She didn't dare risk that he was here on some innocent mission.

She pulled on Britt's jacket and flew past the bathroom, stuffing toothbrush and hairbrush into her purse. At the top of the stairs, she paused, trying to recall Pansy's directions. Go out through the back door, you'll be in the summer kitchen, go through that into the barn and at the back of the barn there's a path into the woods.

No one should have looked for her here. She was being stalked by bad guys with ESP, unless, while she was in the hospital, they'd implanted a microchip and were tracking her by satellite. A wacko idea that no longer seemed so far fetched.

She inched down the stairs, a watchful eye on the front door. Slunk down the hall, reminding herself of the way her mother's cat, Fido, moved through the house. Pansy was in the kitchen.

"There's a cop in the yard," she said.

Pansy's hands fluttered in the air. "But how…" She shook her head.

"That path leads to a little camp out in the woods. The key is behind a shutter."

Jenny nodded, opened the back door, and entered the chilly junk room beyond. She fumbled through a jumble of coats, looking for a hat and gloves. Found a hat with fold-down ear flaps. The kind her grandfather and uncles had worn for hunting back before blaze orange. Thick red and black wool with a warm quilted lining. One jacket had a pair of gloves in the pocket. Too big, but better than nothing. She wished she had a nice double barrel shotgun as well.

One hand half-way into a glove, she stopped. If her father wasn't her father, then her uncles weren't her uncles, her cousins not her cousins. She stood frozen, feeling the rift like a tear in her soul.

But there was no time to waste on wondering and regret. Tolstoy and Dostoevsky might have allowed their characters hundreds of pages of agonized introspection and political philosophizing, but though her situation had all the drama of a novel, she didn't have time for a paragraph. She crossed to the next door and went through into the barn.

It was colder there and smelled of old hay. The flyspecked windows were festooned with cobwebs. In the fading light, she saw half the space was occupied by a vintage pickup truck on blocks, the rest with miscellaneous bits of furniture. On a shelf by the door was a flashlight. She checked to see that it worked, then stuck it in her pocket.

She wove her way through the flotsam to the back of the barn, scanning the stacks of junk for a door. There were several old doors leaning against the wall. None that seemed operational. She heard a the slam of a car door.

In the back corner farthest from the house, she found a door, but when she turned the knob, nothing happened. She put her shoulder against it and leaned, pushing harder. Still nothing. Gasping, she reared back and slammed it as hard as she could. With a scream of rusty protest, the door burst open. She fell through, tumbling toward the ground, automatically putting out a hand to break her fall. Then, remembering her broken wrist, she twisted, taking the impact on her shoulder and hip, smothering a stream of expletives in the sleeve of her jacket.

Where the hell was Superman when you needed him? Breaking down doors would give her bruises on her bruises. Cautiously, she raised herself up and looked around. If she inched forward, she could see around the corner of the barn to where Pansy and the policeman stood in the farmyard, talking. The cop was staring curiously in her direction. On hands and knees, her bag slung over her shoulder, she crept behind the shelter of the barn, got to her feet, and headed into the woods.

She'd lost her watch, but thought it must be after five. Another cold day. As she tramped along the soggy path, she thought if this cloud had any silver lining, it was that it wasn't mosquito season. Darkness was almost complete, her feet were cold and wet, and it felt like she'd walked miles before the rough track ended in an overgrown clearing where a ramshackle little building perched at the edge of a pond so overgrown with vegetation she would have called a swamp.

She found the hidden key and unlocked the door. She was so cold. Hoping no one would see the smoke in the dark, she lit the woodstove. Then, almost at the end of the first diary, she curled up in a musty chair, wrapped herself in a scratchy gray blanket she found, and clicked on the flashlight. How many people are handed the story of their own illicit conceptions? Get to hear stories that make them want to go whack their mothers upside the head? She buried her head in her hands. Oh no. She didn't mean that. Someone *had* done that. Tears trickled down her face. Tears she had no time for.

How many people want to push their way into books and warn their fathers that their mothers are about the betray them? Can you betray someone when you're not married? Dumb question. Wasn't that what Drew had just done to her? She was filled with the desire to go back in time and warn Bud Cates—her father by nurture, love, and example, the things that real fathers are—that a seed was about to be planted by her biological father. She saw her father's face, plain, kindly and serious, with his dorky glasses and his generous smile, and missed him intensely.

The AG set me back on my feet and stared down at me, smiling. "I hear you've been working too hard again."

"Just doing what has to be done," I said, forcing my tongue to form coherent words.

"You know why they always come to you?" I shook my head, not trusting my voice. "Because you're the best."

I raised my eyes to his, looking for mirth or mocking. He looked completely serious. I didn't know what to say.

I can't handle praise. It throws me off balance. Makes me blush and stammer. "I have to go now. I'm afraid I've been drinking and my ride home just ran out on me. And I..."

Buxton was laughing. "Drinking? In a bar? Goodness me. Why don't you come back in and have another? Kenny and I were about to."

Drink has always been like truth serum to me. I gave him my best smile. Sort of loose and gooey and filled with delight at being a little drunk and seeing him and getting a compliment about my work. "My nose is numb and I can't walk straight, sir. Maybe you could call me a cab."

"Sir? You make me feel a thousand years old." He put am arm around my waist and turned me around. "Okay, Lila. You're a cab," he said, and led me back into the bar. "And please, when we're not in the office, call me Jim."

We all had a drink and then they drove me home. That is, Jim drove me home, and Kenny brought my car. Jim was a perfect gentleman. He helped me up the stairs, opened the door for me, put my purse on the counter, and walked me to the bedroom. There he took me by the shoulders and sat me down on the foot of the bed, sitting down beside me and taking my hand.

"This would be the perfect moment to take advantage of you. You'd have the excuse of being drunk and helpless, and I'd be a cad unable to resist an opportunity to sleep with a beautiful young woman. I'm not going to, Lila. If and when we sleep together, something that shouldn't happen, something maybe we won't be able to resist, I want you 100% there and a willing, knowing participant. I don't want a quick and dirty screw we'll both try to forget."

He took my chin in his hands and studied my face. "Oh, Lila. You aren't the only one who's confused. You make my heart race. You make me breathless. You make me crazy. I want you like I have never wanted another woman. But if I ever do make love to you, make love with you, that's what it's going to be: making love. So it will have to be something we talk about seriously, not just fall into.

"I've tried staying out of the office. Meetings all over the state. Tried not coming near your office. But how can I? Even if I didn't need to look at you, I need your advice."

He dropped his hands. "I want you to know... I've never been unfaithful to my wife. But when I'm near you, my resolution is like confetti. It flies away in a million directions and all I can see is your face. All I can think of is you. Your voice. Your smile. That funny tough way you hold up your hand and say, 'Wait a minute' when you think we're not listening. That tender way you have of reaching out and touching someone when you think they need caring for. You're becoming the soul of the office. Where you are, the air seems to glow. Goddammit, listen to me. I've never said things like this to anyone. If I stay here longer, I'll do something I'll... we'll both regret."

He pulled me to my feet and took off my jacket. Then he knelt down and took off my shoes. He looked up at me with those mesmerizing blue eyes. I wanted to pull him into my arms. Grab him and pull him down on top of me. I forced my arms to stay at my side.

"You're worn out, Lila. Go to sleep." Then he walked out without looking back. The entire time he was in my apartment, I never said a single word.

It was the last entry in the first diary. Precious words, especially if she never spoke with her mother again. Jenny bit her lip, tears rolling down her face, as she opened the stove and shoved it in.

THE ALFONSO CAMPAIGN

A HOTEL ROOM ON THE CAMPAIGN TRAIL

O'Malley gave a satisfied grunt and put down the phone, grinning. The governor, high from the cheers of a supportive crowd, pumped from the hand-shaking, back-slapping, feeling like he'd really connected, was savoring the bouquet of a nice red wine. He set his glass carefully on the table and raised his eyebrows. "Don't tell me we finally got a piece of good news?"

"They've got her cornered," O'Malley said.

"It's not good news until they've got their hands on her. Hope they brought an army this time, Mikey. We know the girl's a weasel."

"They're bringing an army, Lou. Don't worry. She's not getting away this time."

"What the hell are they waiting for?"

"Enough troops. Too easy to lose her in the dark if they spook her and she runs. They'll surround the place. A little shack out in the woods, few miles outside Elmira. As soon as they're assembled, they'll move in."

The governor wasn't satisfied.

"I could tell them to move in now, Lou. It's riskier, though."

"Not if they surround the place in a nice, tight little circle." Alfonso smacked his lips. "I can't wait to get my hands on her. Tell 'em to move in."

Keris Carlyle looked up from some papers. "I hope you didn't mean that literally."

"Mean what?" he asked irritably. He was sick of her dogging his words, clinging like a leech, whispering in his ear about when he should acknowledge various important women, when he should touch his wife's shoulder, take her hand, give her a look. Pretty women shouldn't be too smart. It spoiled things.

"That you can't wait to get your hands on her."

"Oh, get a life, will you, Keris," O'Malley snapped. "When it's just us, we're supposed to be able to relax, remember?"

"Just doing my job, Mikey." She made a face at him and returned to her papers.

"I'll call 'em back and tell 'em to move in now," O'Malley said.

The Governor, happy as a fox in a chicken house, nodded.

O'Malley gave the order, listened to opposition on the other end, and said, "Alfonso says now."

The governor drained the glass, then poured himself another. By the time they got back to Albany tomorrow, they'd have the girl and, hopefully, the tape. His heart rate sped up with excitement. He could hardly wait.

THE BUXTON CAMPAIGN

ON THE CAMPAIGN TRAIL

Frank Follet combed his thinning fair hair back over his bald spot and frowned into the mirror. He was sweating and he hated it, the ugly beads on his face, the way his shirt went limp, the clammy feel of his skin. A few hours earlier, he'd called Mr. Smith and Mr. Lopes, two of the gentlemen helping him locate Jenny Cates, and gotten a shitload of bad news. The sweet young girl who ought to have been no contest for them continued to be elusive as smoke.

Meanwhile, Maggie was sharpening her teeth, getting ready to gnaw on his balls. Another day like this and he'd sick Smith and Lopes on her. They didn't care what they had to do so long as they got paid. Nice, simple men, these thugs for hire, and in the past, quite effective. This time it was like they were spinning their wheels while O'Malley and his governor ran circles around them. For Frank, although it was a political no-no, things got very personal. Letting O'Malley get an edge on him made him furious. And O'Malley had just trumped him twice.

Might as well get it over with. He opened his phone and dialed. Lopes answered, curt and impatient, as always.

"It's Follet. Talk to me."

"We're gonna need an army, boss. Kid's holed up in a camp outside Elmira, 'bout a million state cops goin' in to get her. Since we haven't got a million troops of our own, and it would be impolitic to try to outgun the staties in their own state, I suggest we wait until they nab her, and then do a deft little snatch of our own."

"So where the hell are you two?"

"We be four, boss. Elmira, naturally. And we be watchin'."

Lopes liked playing around with his persona. Tonight Frank found it irritating. "Why the hell do they keep getting the jump on us?"

"They be smarter, maybe? At least there be more of them. You want to authorize more recruits, we could have us a little war?" Lopes sounded like he'd enjoy that. Man liked scaring people. Hurting people. Killing people. So how come he couldn't control one timid young woman?

"Your orders were simple," Frank said. "Eliminate the lady and get the video tape. Now we've had a wild goose chase, the lady's still alive, and we haven't got the tape."

"Haven't got the diaries, either," Lopes said.

Frank felt a rush of frustration. He continued to be one step behind and didn't like it. "What diaries?"

"What that little girl be carrying, according to our sources. That's what O'Malley and The Guv be seeking."

"Oh shit! And she's about to fall into their hands? With the diaries?"

"Remains to be seen," Lopes said. "So far, they haven't done any better than we have, so I figure, a cabin in the woods, surrounded by burly, hard-assed state cops, what are the chances the girl gets away? I give it fifty-fifty. Maybe give the girl better odds, looking at her record. How 'bout you?"

"Jesus H. Christ, Lopes. This isn't a game. An election may be at stake."

"Cool your jets, man. I know that. Just sayin' all I can do right now is wait and see how this thing goes down. Maybe get a chance to grab her myself."

Frank sighed. "Look, stay in touch, okay? And if you do get the girl, don't smoke her before we get a chance to talk to her. Even if she doesn't have the tape, maybe she knows where it is. So stash her and call me. And Lopes? Try not to hurt her so bad she won't talk to me."

"Maybe the only chance we get is to shoot her, eh? You want us to sit on our hands... uh... guns... and let her get away again?"

"I'd rather have her alive."

"Know what you mean. I like 'em alive myself."

He hung up on the man's obscene laughter. Frank was a realist. Sometimes politics got ugly. If you had big dreams, you needed a tough mind, a tough hide, and a tough heart. It was a hard man's game. But the highs made it all worth it. Frank loved to win. Whether he liked it or not, Buxton was going to be delivered to the White House on election day, the darling of the American people, the champion of old-fashioned values, and no little chippie he spent a night with twenty years ago was going to stop that. No chippie and no spawn. Frank didn't believe in love.

"Some are Born to sweet Delight
Some are Born to Endless night…"
—Blake, "Auguries of Innocence"

CHAPTER FOURTEEN

She wanted to read the second thin volume that lay unopened in her bag. She was totally hooked on the story. She liked the young Lila Friedman, nervous, dedicated, already too hard working, precociously bright and genuinely unaware of the response she stirred in people. And for now, at least, she liked Jim Buxton, who for all his teasing and disconcerting ways seemed genuinely to value her mother and was unwilling to take advantage of her. Despite her protective feeling for the hopeful and devoted Bud Cates, hovering in the wings, part of her couldn't wait to get them into bed. But like the work-weary Lila Friedman she'd been reading about, she was worn out and needed to sleep.

She turned off the flashlight and sat in the darkness, listing to the wind sighing through the trees, looking out the window to see if she could see any stars. That's when she saw the light. She peered out into the darkness. Nothing. She moved to the next window. All she saw were different shades of black.

Another time, another place, she would have dismissed her worries, but experience had made her cautious. She huddled a long time in the dark, listening. No voices, no lights, no nothing. Just deep, silent black. But that little flash of light had sent her adrenaline soaring. Thinking about the possibility of a quick escape, she slung her purse over her shoulder and stuck the flashlight in her pocket.

All seemed still and quiet, but she didn't trust it, not after the ease with which people were able to track her down. They were out there. It was only a matter of time. She couldn't know whether these were killers or captors, whether they planned to quietly dispose of her or noisily display her, whether they planned to destroy the diary or blaze her mother's private words all over the papers. She only knew her goal was to avoid them.

She reviewed the lay of the land. Beside the woodstove, there was a cupboard where wood was stored—a cupboard that opened to the outside so the wood would be stacked there, just like the one in her grandmother's camp. Between the camp and the pond was a thick clump of bushes. There was a similar clump on one side. On that side, the woods were closer to the clearing, and, from what she remembered seeing in the fading light, there were more coniferous trees as well, with more low-hanging branches for shelter. It was also the side where she'd seen the light.

Still, she thought that was the way to go. No one would expect her to slip out through the woodbox. A woodbox only half full. Room for a small woman to crawl out. Dragging the blanket behind her, she inched her way past the wood. There wasn't a lot of space. A nail grazed her forehead and she felt anxiously for blood. Pausing often to listen, she worked her way forward until her head was outside, emerging just beside the clump of bushes.

Holding her breath, she listened. To her right, a branch snapped. To her left, a muffled cough. She froze. There were people here and they were close. She waited for her eyes to adjust, for the black to take on shades and shapes. It was a clear night. Chilly. Her breath made a faint cloud. Beyond her sheltering bushes, across maybe eight feet of open ground, the branches of an overgrown ornamental evergreen, a yew, perhaps, swept so low they almost touched the ground. Still staying low, she crept toward it, the rough gray blanket clutched against her body by her useless hand. Fighting the almost overpowering urge to rush, she crossed the open space and slipped under its drooping branches.

She huddled on the damp ground, fighting the fear that made her want to break cover and run, feeling a sympathy for hunted animals that, growing up in a hunting culture, she'd never had before. Not far away, a foot shifted, sending a rock rolling in her direction. She muffled her shocked intake of breath as she watched a shadow in the darkness become a man moving slowly forward toward the camp. If she could see him, why hadn't he seen her?

Because she'd spent her childhood in the Bud Cates school of animal spotting, all those late nights coming home in the car when he'd point and say, "see" and she'd concentrate until she could pick deer out of the darkness. She'd gotten to the point where she was showing him things. Foxes and raccoons lurking by the roadside. Herds of deer grazing. Once a big bear at the edge of the woods. Her mother, who never saw anything, complained that they were making things up. But they just had Maine hunter's eyes. Something for the nature versus nurture folks to ponder.

She heard someone pass her bush on the other side, and took advantage of the noise to make some progress herself in the opposite direction. When you're making noise yourself, it's hard to hear anyone else's. It reminded her, in a perverse way, of a gigantic night-time game of kick-the-can and the heady, scary excitement that comes from rushing out of the darkness, trying to free the captives and not get caught. That's exactly what she was trying to do.

All around her, she sensed, rather than saw, people moving out of the woods and creeping slowly toward the camp. As they went forward, she went back. First on all fours, then in a cautious crouch, and finally almost erect as she hurried away from the camp, trying to put as much distance as she could between herself and them before they discovered she wasn't asleep inside. Several times she stumbled and almost fell. More than once, she stepped in a stream or a puddle. Her legs were soaked with icy water to well above her knees, the soggy cloth chafing her thighs, the seams rubbing raw patches, her toes numb with cold as she slogged on.

Once, pausing to catch her breath, she'd smelled smoke and seen the red glow of a cigarette coming toward her. Panic flaring, she huddled down, pulling the blanket over herself so she was no more than a lumpy gray rock in the darkness. Then she was back on her feet again, tripping, stumbling, and now sometimes falling, as she made her weary progress away from people who did not have her best interests at heart with no idea where she was going.

Eventually that steady, stumbling progress brought her to a highway. She heard the faraway hiss of tires, caught glimpses of fleeting lights, first white then red, through the trees. Her legs ached. Her heaving chest was desperate to slow down and breathe more easily. Her eyes felt raw from staring through the darkness. But she couldn't stop. As soon as they'd figured out she wasn't in the camp, they'd fan out and start searching for her. She had to get out of here, far from here, and the quickest way was to hitch a ride.

An eternity later, she stumbled out of the woods onto the roadside, and bent over to catch her breath. Then, fearful of being in the open, she retreated to the cover of the trees, watching cars come and go. Once or twice a police car passed, moving slowly, trolling. Then she saw it. A big truck approaching. She scrambled up the bank and ran into the road, waving her arms frantically. *Please*, she thought, *please stop. Please!*

It didn't seem to be slowing. It came steadily at her, a terrifying leviathan piercing her with powerful lights. He'd just have to run her down. She didn't have the energy to move. Like a possum in the road, the lights transfixed her. Not even the ear-shattering blast of its horn shifted her. Okay, so she was dead. At least she could stop running. At the last minute, as she braced herself for the impact, preparing to bid farewell to a soulless, heartless world, it slowed, gears grunting and whining, and came to a hissing, screeching halt.

"Like one, that on a lonesome road
Doth walk in fear and dread…"
—Coleridge, "The Rime of the Ancient Mariner"

CHAPTER FIFTEEN

She meant to haul herself up and open the door, to show the driver she was cool about trucks, but by the time the truck had rumbled to a shuddering stop, she was a spastic mass of nerves with jelly knees, her heart banging against her chest. He got out, came around, and fixed a flashlight beam on her. "You almost got yourself killed, little girl," he growled. "What the hell did you think you were doing?"

"Trying to get you to stop," she said. Her voice no more than a whisper. "Running away."

"Who you running from?" Curiosity and suspicion mingled in the few loud words.

She tried to see his face to gauge who she was talking to but the light shining into her face was blinding. She had an impression of middle-aged, pleasant-faced, and huge. The hand holding the flashlight nearly swallowed it up. The motor of the truck looming above her rumbled like a snoring giant. Beyond the cone of light cast by the headlamps, the night seemed vast and evil. Any minute, she expected cops to swarm out of the woods or come roaring down the street. "Let me get in the truck and I'll tell you."

She died a thousand deaths waiting for his response, swiveling her head to check the woods for lights and the road for cars. If he didn't take her in, she didn't know what to do. She'd already lost precious minutes. They were bound to come soon and she didn't have the stamina to run.

He expelled an exasperated silvery cloud of breath and offered a grudging capitulation. "All right. Get in. But this better be good. I got no patience with liars and damned fools."

He watched as she hauled herself into the cab, making no move to help, then went around and got in on his side. "Well?" It was as much a grunt as a question as he settled back into his seat.

She cradled her aching wrist against her chest, shaking uncontrollably in her wet, clothes, too scared to think up a story. "I've got a bunch of New York state cops looking for me, but I swear I didn't do anything wrong. I know it sounds preposterous, but if you don't help, I'm afraid someone's going to kill me." Her chattering teeth made it hard to talk. "Look, can we please go? Please?"

"There a good story behind this?" he asked. He was about the biggest man she'd ever seen. An easy 6' 5" and bulky, with forearms like hams, a swooping mustache and graying curly hair, layer-cut, cascading to his shoulders with one long tail down the back. There were tattoos on the arm she could see below the sleeve of his black Harley T-shirt.

"Yes." People were trying to kill her and he wanted a good story? She stared at the road, squirming with impatience. The truck didn't move. *Please go or it will be too late*, she thought. Her entire body felt breathless. Another few seconds and she'd have to jump out and start running.

He dropped a hand on the gearshift, then hesitated. "You sure you ain't a hooker?"

The sound that burst out was between a laugh and a sob. "You're kidding, right? You get a lot of hookers running out of the woods in the middle of the night, soaked and freezing and covered with mud, flagging down your truck?"

He made a noise in his throat. "Nope. Get women who're pretty creative about tryin' to get in my truck, though."

"That wasn't creative, that was desperate," she said. "And no, I'm not a hooker. I've slept with one guy in my life. Thought I was going to marry him until Friday night, when I found him in bed with my best friend. Now can we please go?"

Any second now, she'd explode with frustration and this suspicious, laconic stranger'd have to scrape her off his truck.

The truck stayed put. "That why you're running around in the woods like a crazy woman?"

"Never mind," she said, opening the door. "I don't have time for this. I'm sorry I bothered you, but someone really is trying to kill me and if you won't help, I haven't got time for a game of twenty questions. Too bad you didn't just run over me." Blinded by frustrated tears, she swung sideways, feeling with her foot for the step.

He made another noise between a growl and a hiss—the sort a person who spends a lot of time alone might get in the habit of making—then grabbed her arm and hauled her back. "Make sure that door's shut and put on your seatbelt," he said.

He put the behemoth in gear and moved off down the road. "My name's Jerry. With a J."

It felt like she'd been holding her breath the whole time she was in the truck. Now she sucked in air the way a thirsty person drinks. Shivering so hard her bones hurt. He seemed to be waiting for her to introduce herself but she was temporarily beyond speech. She meant to say, "Nice to meet you, Jerry. I'm Jenny." What came out, from a dry mouth, through chattering teeth, was a small, strangled, "Jenny."

"Ginny?"

"Jennifer. Jenny."

"Oh. You want some more heat, Jenny?"

She made a noise she hoped sounded affirmative, watching in awe as he worked through the gears. Truck drivers always amazed her. When she was little, she'd beg rides from Andy's big brothers, and they'd take her down to the ice cream store in the cab once it was detached from those huge trailers. Jenny would perch on the front seat feeling like Alice in Wonderland at her smallest, her feet not coming near the floor, high above the street and the rest of the traffic. It was scary and wonderful and felt a little bit like playing God.

Now that she could breathe, now that they were moving, she felt a little of her terror slip away. Just enough so her throat relaxed. Maybe she could use her voice. "Where you from?" she asked.

He took so long to answer she wondered if it was an impermissible question. Finally he said, "No place you've ever heard of. Warren, Maine."

"I'm from Hallowell," she said. "You know any of the Masons? Hugh, Tom or Andy?"

"I know Tom and Anday."

When he said 'Anday,' she heard the Maine in his voice. Maybe before her ears had been too scared. Or she'd been afraid to trust it. After the last few days, she was reluctant to trust anything. "Adele Mason's my next door neighbor," she said. "I just wrecked Dandy... Andy's car two days ago."

"That part of the story?"

"Oh, no!" She stared into the darkness, every muscle tensed, as a police car with flashing lights came toward them and went shrieking past. When it was past, she realized he was still waiting for an answer. "Yes. Dandy's car is part of the story." Her teeth were chattering. From cold, from fear. From the unbearable tension of the last few days. She didn't want to talk. She wanted to curl up in a tight little ball, close her eyes, and whimper. But he was waiting for her story.

"You think that cop's looking for you?"

"Probably."

"You kill someone? Your boyfriend maybe, or that girl he was in bed with?"

The thought astonished her. "What? You think I could?"

"Honey, I don't know you from Adam." The massive shoulders rose and fell. "It happens. Don't you read the papers? Watch TV?"

"I don't believe in killing, Jerry."

He sighed. "So why you runnin'? You musta done something to get all these cops after you."

"Watch out!" she interrupted. "There's a deer up there on the right."

He avoided the deer that plunged into the road in front of them, moving down through his gears and back up in a deft mechanical ballet. "Good spotting. I didn't even see it."

Jenny knew just how the deer felt. Not long ago, she'd been chased out into the path of the truck. "Guess I'm lucky you saw me," she said, adding, "My daddy taught me."

"Your daddy's a hunter?"

She made an affirmative noise—this noise making was contagious—and thought about the word "daddy." She felt an actual pain using it, like she'd been stabbed. Bud Cates had always been her daddy. Still was. But there was the ugly "fact" that someone else was her daddy. Someone who might be trying to kill her. They rode in silence for a while, Jenny waiting nervously for him to demand her story again. She was terribly thirsty and she needed a bathroom but she didn't want to ask any more favors.

When he did speak, he said, "That your teeth chattering?"

"Yes."

"Hungry?"

"Yeah."

"There's a blanket back there if you want it. I've gotta make a pit stop soon. Get you some food and coffee, you'll feel better."

She got the blanket. "Jerry, I can't go where anyone can see me."

"Mosta these guys, they're so tired and hungry, they wouldn't notice if Godzilla walked through the room, 'less it had tits and low-cut top. All they notice is whether they got the two scoops of mashed potatoes they asked for."

"I'd better tell you what's going on."

"That might be a good idea."

She kept it short and sweet. She told him about finding her mother, about Uncle Billy, about how her mother told her to run. About the woman at the motel. She did embellish that part enough to include disabling the cars. She thought he'd like that, and she was right.

His noise was a genuine chuckle. "Guess they underestimated you," he said. "I can see why. You look like a kid."

"I feel old as Methuselah."

"Oh, shit!" he said. "Pardon my French." He flipped on his signal and began moving slowly off the road. "Looks like we've got company. There's a nice little space back there under the bunk. Think you can squeeze yourself into it, quick as a bunny?"

Despite the urgency of the situation and the chill that went through her, when her brain said "jump," nothing happened. He put out a hand, scooped her up, and shoved her in, blanket and all. A tight fit, barely room to turn her head. He stuck a hand in and felt around. "Maybe you wanna move a little farther back?""

She did wanna. She wiggled as far back as she could and lay there, waiting. What did you do over spring break, Jen? I took an Outward Bound survival course. How had Anne Frank and her family ever stood it? Because the alternatives were worse. Considering what other people had gone through put it in perspective, but this was America. A democracy. She was a free citizen being terrorized by two presidential candidates. It was ludicrous. It was happening.

She heard him brush dirt and debris off the seat, muttering string of obscenities uncomplimentary to the constabulary. Otherwise laconic, here his vocabulary was rich. She heard the window open, felt the inrush of cool air, smelled exhaust. "Evenin', Officer."

"Where you coming from?"

"Corning."

"We're looking for a girl. Small, dark-haired, early twenties, maybe looks younger. Wearing dark clothes. Motorist reported seeing her standing by a stopped truck."

Mesmerized by his lights, she'd never seen the car. Jenny thought her heart had stopped. She could feel the skip, the hesitation, dizziness rolling over her. When she finally had to breathe, it sounded like the roaring of a wind-tunnel. She couldn't get her arm up to muffle it. She hoped this wouldn't take long. She could feel the bed above and the floor below closing in on her, like in one of those nightmares where the walls are moving.

"What'd she do, this girl?"

"Breaking and entering. Theft. Malicious destruction of property. Resisting arrest." She had to strain to hear over the roar of her own fear. "You seen her?"

There was silence, then Jerry said, in his slow, careful way. "I don't pick people up when I'm drivin' my truck."

"Why's the seat over there wet, then?" the cop asked.

"Put my foot up to tie my shoe."

"Only been raining about half an hour. How'd your foot get wet?"

"Thought I hit a deer," Jerry said. "Got out to see. Look all the hell over the place. Didn't see nothin'."

"You always stop when you think you've hit something?"

"Something big," Jerry said. "Don't you?"

His interrogator ignored the question. "Mind if we take a look inside your truck?"

Jerry grunted. "Do me any good if I did? 'Course, we could go all around Robin Hood's barn 'bout whether you got a warrant, but then you could keep me here all night while you got one, and I ain't got all night." She heard the grind of the door handle. "Watch yourself," he said. The springs creaked and groaned as he swung the door open and moved his bulk out of the seat.

They'd done a heck of a job drumming up charges against her. She couldn't figure out where they'd gotten any of them, except malicious destruction of property. She'd happily done that. But not in New York. Resisting arrest? By what, running away? Theft? And what had she broken and entered? She closed her eyes and waited to be spotted, seized, dragged out. And then what? If she survived this, her nervous system would never be the same.

The cab seemed full, with two men talking, moving around, and shining their lights everywhere. She'd turned her head so her face was away from them, and tucked her hand under her body so that she'd be nothing but darkness to someone peering in, pressed herself against the wall, trying to become smaller. A hand, feeling around under the bunk, grazed her shoulder. She willed herself still. Waited for it to travel away from the rough blanket that might feel like carpet and find her hair. Waited for the shout of triumph and hands grabbing her and dragging her out. Panic was building. This was impossible. Insane. Something was tickling her nose, making her want to sneeze. She pressed her face against the wall.

One of the policemen swore and snapped off his light. Jenny thought she could feel the weight of their shadows lift as they backed out of the cab. The air felt lighter, freer, more mobile. There was a brief mumble of voices, then she heard Jerry climb into his seat and slam the door. With a hiss and a roar, the truck lurched into motion as he muttered, "Blow it out your asses, fuck heads."

Jenny stayed put, waiting for word that it was safe to emerge. In her tight little space, she felt like she was a part of the engine.

She sneezed and Jerry murmured, "Bless you." Eons later he said through the roar, "Guess it's safe to come out now." Slowly she levered her way out and climbed over the seat, collapsing against the door. "Scare you?" he asked.

"Took twenty years off my life," she said.

"I had it to do over, I don't guess I'd stop."

"I don't blame you, but I'm glad you did."

He made a growling noise followed by a hiss of frustration. "I dunno. Soon as we're outta New York, I'm finding a motel and leaving you there. Every minute you're in the truck, I can feel those cops got their eyes on me. Messes up my concentration. So you're outta here, see."

She stared at the ribbon of gray highway rushing at them. They were in the middle of nowhere. No houses, no billboards, no lights through the trees. "You can drop me here if you like, Jerry. I never wanted to give you any trouble. I'm just scared. All that stuff they said about what I've done? It's bullshit."

"Some folks might call a knife in the tire malicious destruction," he said.

Her temper flared. "What about the malicious destruction of my whole life?"

A snort of laughter. "You got a point there." He waved a hand toward the bunk. "Got a ways to go, yet, you wanna get some sleep. I ain't leaving you by the roadside. It ever got back to Adele Mason I did something like that…" He didn't need to say more. Even a tough giant like Jerry wasn't about to cross Adele Mason.

"I'll just keep the blanket." She wrapped it tighter, curled up against the door, and fell asleep.

THE BUXTON CAMPAIGN

SOMEWHERE IN A HOTEL

The Senator's suite was still crowded, even though it was well after midnight, every available surface littered with empty cups, plates, soda cans and fast food containers. The Senator sat on the couch, conferring with Frank and Woody. He was tired and kept rubbing his forehead. Frank was snappish and impatient, Woody trying to keep the peace. Maggie was in another corner of the room, conferring with her own press secretary. Kenny Bass was in the bedroom, hunched over the phone, his creased and solemn face growing more solemn as he listened.

"Mmm-hmm. So the paint scratches on the bumper make you think it was no accident?" He listened again. "Billy always was a jerk but I don't think anyone deserves that." Nodded, though he was alone in the room. "What about Lila?"

As he listened, he looked increasingly sad. 'Two men in suits, that's all you've got? Oh, city fellahs, huh? Mr. Nondescript and someone big and mean-looking? Yes, well, at this point, she's not the only one sorry she didn't take a shotgun to them, is she? Look, Dick, is someone on watch at the hospital? All the time?"

He listened, made some notes, listened again, and suddenly sat up straight, his sallow face reddening. "What? You think we're doing this? There are people up there who actually think so? That's total bullshit. Jim's not like that. What's the basis?"

He cocked his head and listened again. "Guys in suits at the hospital, shoving ID in people's faces, talkin' national security and asking for access to the phone circuits? Oh, they didn't ask? Yeah. Yeah. Demanded. Right. And nobody at the hospital can describe any of them? Was it Nondescript and the big guy again?" He listened and sighed. 'Yeah. Yeah, I hear you.

They wore suits and they carried badges and so the whole world opened to 'em. Anybody look at the badges, Dick? I mean, it could have been something from a cop goods store, or won at a carnival."

This time the man he called Dick spoke longer, and Kenny Bass's face got grimmer. "FBI? No shit. I got one or two of those in my drawer, Dick. Any idea what they were doing with the phone circuits? No one asked? Not even your people? No!" His "no" thundered in the empty room. Ken Bass was a calm guy who rarely lost his temper, but this conversation was getting to him.

"Look, Dick, this is giving me a major headache Even if God himself shows up to do a wiretap, you ask for the court order, right?"

He listened to the gravel voice of Dick "Tricky Dicky" McPartland, head of the homicide unit, sitting in his office up the in Maine Department of Public Safety, take a few minutes to curse out people's lack of curiosity, with a few jabs at Washington thrown in. Then McPartland said, "So we threw our own tap on the phone. Legal, mind you, just to see what these guys might be looking for. Got one at Friedman's house, too, just in case. Only phones they tapped were the Special Care nurse's station and the pay phone in the waiting room."

"Yeah, real odd," Bass said. "They tapped the phones the daughter might call in on to see how her mother's doing."

McPartland missed the irony. "Yeah. Funny how the daughter just vanished into thin air like that, isn't it? You don't suppose she had something to do with this, do you""

Kenny Bass snorted. "Dick, someone kills your uncle and tries to kill your mother, you might get a little spooked, too."

"The dad didn't run, while the kid borrowed a car and crashed it, ran away from the hospital, and hasn't been seen since. Looks suspicious to me."

Ken Bass had known McPartland a long time. The guy had risen more from seniority than brains. In Bass's opinion, there was as much gravel in the man's brain as in his voice. "Sounds like you aren't talking to your own people, if you think the girl's involved in this."

"What the hell's that mean?"

"You find a trooper named Roland Profit and ask him about the night Lila Friedman was attacked."

"Profit's on traffic. What's he got to do with this?"

But Ken Bass was annoyed. He didn't like slipshod police work. He didn't like suspicion falling on the kid, with all she'd been through. In particular, because it came painfully close to his own fears, he didn't like suspicion falling on the Buxton campaign. "Ask Profit. And while you're at it, ask the cop who was in the emergency room at Kennebec Valley what Lila Friedman said to her daughter. Or you could ask one of the nurses. It's right there in your police report, if you care to read it. She said, 'Run, Jenny, run.' She said something else, too, but that's all the listeners could catch. So maybe, just maybe…"

His voice dropped into a lower register, a rumble to rival McPartland's. "Maybe the poor kid is running because her mother told her to. It might be amazing in this day and age for a kid to do something because a parent told her to, but I hear Jenny Cates is a real good kid who adores her mother."

He waited for McPartland's response.

"I'll follow up," McPartland growled, "but you'd better hope I don't find your candidate tied into this. I'm not covering up nothing for nobody, not even some hot-shot US Senator. Understood?"

Ken Bass had worked hard to maintain his contacts with the state police, and McPartland's attitude troubled him. Mostly people were cooperative, happy to help out Senator Buxton and his staff. But he knew McPartland would love to finish his career on the high of busting a US Senator. "Understood, Dick," he said. "Keep me informed, will you?"

Silence, then grudging acquiescence. "One more thing," Bass said. "I don't think you ever answered. Has anyone tried anything at the hospital?"

Another silence, then McPartland said, "Hell, yes. Twice. First time the husband spotted it; second time it was a nurse. We're worried as hell about third time lucky, and that's with a cop on the door at all times. Woman's got such a following, you'd think she was a saint instead of a lawyer."

So even though it was his case, McPartland had no idea who Lila Friedman was. How could he solve an attempted murder if he didn't even know his victim?

"Dick?" Kenny Bass said. "You know what? She is a saint." He hung up but made no move to leave the bedroom. The Senator would want to know about the call, and the man was already exhausted from the long campaign day. He didn't need more bad news right now.

"I must become a borrower of the night
For a dark hour or twain"
—Shakespeare, "Macbeth"

CHAPTER SIXTEEN

When Jerry nudged her awake, she was completely disoriented. It was dark. She didn't know where she was. She slumped against the door, clinging to the blanket, and stared at him blankly. She wanted to slip back into sleep. Lately, night and day jumbled like a tossed salad. "Come on," he urged impatiently. "I've got you a motel room. You can sleep there. You'll be perfectly safe. It's prepaid and in my name, but it's taken a chunk of my time, and I've got a delivery to make."

She stared at the gigantic man, with his fleshy body and dandy's hair, stared at the interior of the truck's cab, and it all came back. The cabin, the flight, the cold. Her rescue, the cops, the fear. A lot to process, but she didn't need to do it on Jerry's time. Time was money to truck drivers. Slowly, she unwrapped herself from the blanket and opened her door. As she slid down the side of the truck, his hand followed her, dangling a key. "You'll need this," he said. "Room 37. Four doors down on the right."

She took the key. "Thanks for everything, Jerry. I'll pay you back."

"No need," he said. "It's for Mrs. Mason." The truck was rolling as soon as her feet had touched the ground.

She was so stupefied it felt like she was swimming through soup as she made her way to the door of number 37. Stunned or not, an instinctive distrust of everything, born of her experience these past few days, made her examine the room carefully. Except for some dust balls, stranger's hair, and a few fingernail parings, she seemed to be alone in a room so carefully prepared for her arrival that it even had a paper strip on the toilet and real glass glasses encased in little paper bags.

Despite the sanitized strip, the bathroom had the faint acrid scent of urine. She wondered if Jerry had checked out the room before handing her the key, and thought of Drew, all 5' 9" of him, standing at a public urinal next to Jerry. Jerry's flow would have been disconcertingly close to shoulder level. She shook her head in disgust and bent down, breaking the paper seal. Losing her mind, or at least the disciplined part of it that should have made such thoughts impermissibly crude.

Charming, cocky, happy-go-lucky Drew, with his tight runner's body and crazy eyes, who liked to come up behind her and cup her breasts in his hands, an act that always shocked her and yet was very sexy. Those happy days in their apartment seemed ages ago. Funny how a few days of violence can change your life.

She brushed her teeth and washed her face, staring for a moment at the image in the mirror. Every day she looked more pathetic, more desperately in need of adoption, or at least a foster home. Little Jenny has been the victim of political violence in her own country. Driven from her home, her family members killed and injured, she has been on the run from factions who want to destroy her as part of their bid to rule the country. For only pennies a day, you can help little Jenny and others like her who seek to flee from tyranny and lawlessness and find asylum.

"Dream on," she snorted at the big-eyed waif in the mirror. "Asylum where?"

Her mother's diary was burning a hole in her mind. She stripped off her filthy pants, washed them and wrung them as dry as she could, and hung them, and her sodden socks, near the heat. Then, though visions of sleep danced in her brain, she switched on the bedside light and opened the book.

"Hello, new book. Are these pristine pages ready to absorb the sordid matters I intend to confide to them? I wonder sometimes about diary factories, about those women... I always think of them as women, though they might be men, or even machines... who stand all day performing the functions that convert a bunch of paper and cardboard into diaries. I even wonder about people who keep diaries at all. In fiction, diaries are always being used to advance the plots, or reveal deep, dark secrets, and yet, in real life,

I'm the only person I know who keeps one. But I need this book!

The problem with growing up determined and ambitious in a world that expects girls and women to be soft and passive and grateful is that I've always been a misfit. It's better now. A million times better. College was better than high school and law school better than college. I've gradually moved into a world where the women I meet are more like me, but it wasn't that way growing up. I was smart and I was Jewish. The only thing that could have made it worse would have been if I was tall. I wanted to be tall, too, but with four small grandparents and two small parents, that wasn't in the cards. I guess I should be grateful. There's only so much gumption given each of us, and I used most of it surviving my teens.

I like being an adult. I like being a professional. I've never given much thought, despite my feminist strivings, to whether I like being a woman, but I guess I wouldn't want to be a man, despite their advantages, because I like being me. And, an admission I can safely make here, where the only audience is myself, I'm glad I don't have a penis.

"Mom!" Jenny laughed out loud, and leaned in toward the book, eager to learn her mother's thoughts on the subject.

Maybe I'll publish this some day, when I'm old. Lila Friedman's eccentric thoughts on penises, A Midnight Discourse on the Male Member. I wouldn't even be writing this now if it weren't that alcohol always knocks me flat on my ass and puts me to sleep for a few hours, and then I wake up hot and headachy and miserable and can't get back to sleep. So here I am at two a.m., knowing I need my beauty sleep, which ought, more properly, to be called brain sleep, to function in the morning. After all, I don't go to the office to be decorative, no matter what Deputy Attorney General Josh Riteman may think. I go to do good work.

So I'll sit here, in the dead of night, and that's what this feels like—dead, because the noisies downstairs have finally subsided, their drunken caterwauling swallowed up in drugged sleep—and write about penises because it keeps me from thinking about Jim Buxton's hands, and Jim Buxton's smile, and Jim Buxton's honorable departure, and about how little I wanted him to go and how grateful I am that he did.

Penises. Why I wouldn't want one. Why not? They really are a rather magical creation with their ability to be small and vulnerable or big and menacing. And surprisingly silky and smooth. I suppose that makes functional sense, doesn't it? But that vulnerability would bother me. That exposed, right out there, quality. Necessary, but I'd worry about something happening to it. About it getting stuck in zippers and stuff. Not that breasts are much better, sticking out there in the wind, bobbling when I walk, getting in the way and getting stared at. Now, that's one thing that doesn't happen with penises. People don't get to stare at them. It's a lot easier to tell if a woman has a small chest than if a man has... Oh, hell, Lila Friedman, you drop this subject!

Jenny was sorry her mother stopped. She'd enjoyed this diversion from what she knew was a rocky but certain path toward an illicit affair and an unwed conception. She wrapped her arms around her knees, pulling herself into a ball, wondering what had Attorney General, then Senator Buxton done when he learned he'd made her mother pregnant? Suggested an abortion? Offered her money? Done a quick fade into the world of Washington and stopped taking phone calls? And how had her mother felt? She wondered if the answers were here. She resisted the temptation to read the end first.

Another day at the salt mines. Sometimes I wonder whether I'm a lawyer or a baby-sitter. Other times I wonder why I even try to get taken seriously in a world that sees my sex, my age, my chest and makes judgments that have nothing to do with who I am or what I know or can do. I'd be better off if I were fat, but I'm too vain, I guess, to gain weight just to be loved for my mind. I haven't entirely escaped social conditioning.

Okay, dear diary, why am I blathering so? Well, it started this morning with me being sent, totally unprepared, to assist the Board of Registration that oversees hairdressers, who were trying to draft a new set of regulations. With the help, I might add, of some numbskull in this office who had given them an incomprehensible draft to work from. They spent the first hour whining about how incomprehensible the regulations were, and the second hour, after I told them they could use common sense and plain language, arguing about whether people had to wear uniforms or whether they could wear their own clothes, and only half an hour on training and experience requirements, and supervision of apprentices. It was scary. I had to remind myself that hairdressing is not physics. Luckily, there is no Board of Registration in physics. That would not be my strong suit. And all the while, I was itching to get back to my real work, and they were so happy to have a real lawyer, even a girl lawyer, they wanted as much of my time as they could get.

Then, in the afternoon, that same deputy who thinks I'm brainless because I'm a dame, suddenly calls me into his office when I'm in mid-memo and balancing a dozen thoughts very precariously on the tip of my brain, and says he's forgotten to assign anyone to a Medical Board hearing and I need to drop everything and rush over there. Sometimes I wonder who has advised these people in the past. It was, not surprisingly, an all-boys club, and they were disconcerted to find themselves handed a woman attorney. There they were, ready to hold a hearing on someone's license, on someone's ability to continue to earn a living, and they had no procedures, formal or informal, and absolutely no notion of due process or what constituted evidence.

I'm just a baby lawyer, but I could see this was a recipe

for disaster, so I excused myself—they probably thought I was going to powder my nose—and called the other Deputy, the one who can find his ass in the dark, and asked him what to do. His stellar advice? Wing it. Do the best I can. Be sure the evidence gets in in such a way as to support a revocation if they vote for one. He promised they'd be very next on the list to overhaul of their regulations. Yeah, I'll probably get assigned that pleasant task, too. Be careful what you wish for, Lila. Some days I wonder what ever made me want to practice law.

I felt like I walking a tightrope in stiletto heels while the good old boys were having a bachelor party at which I was what had jumped out of the cake. The Chairman, to whom I was directing most of my sound, serious, useful advice, said aloud, in the middle of the hearing, apropos of nothing that was happening, "I'm not scared of you. I sleep with a lawyer every night." I didn't reply that I'd rather sleep with a gorilla than an asshole like him, and only said, "I hope you don't think you're bragging." That brought down the house, but it wasn't a contest I wanted to win, and the whole hearing, concerning a doctor who'd prescribed so many drugs for his neurotic wife she'd become addicted, was sad and sordid and generally a bad scene, though I gathered from the Boards' reactions that it was a fairly common story. The doctor left with a probationary license, required to work under supervision and to get counseling, forbidden to write any prescriptions for his wife. I left feeling like I needed a shower.

Wow. Her mother had never talked about any of this and it was so interesting! It was hard to imagine having such a complicated and demanding work life, and no one to confide in about it so she had to write it in a book. Then she reconsidered. She didn't share much with people, either. She liked keeping it to herself, believing it was her job to puzzle it out, wrestle with it, master it and come to an understanding of how to make her life work. Where had she learned that? At her mother's knee.

Still. Her mother had had her father as a sounding board. And a rock.

Her mother had been able to throw herself into her career, and give so much to her clients, because she had Bud Cates there to help manage the home front and provide a stable, loving, anchor. Coming home from school, Jenny's first act, most days, had been to go and look at her father. That's what it had been—a look. He'd have his nose in a book or be immersed in some project. All Jenny needed to do was peek around the door and see him there and then, no matter how the day had gone, she'd felt better. Her mother often did the same thing.

"I'm an icon," he'd once said. "All you guys want to do is touch me and then go about your business. Why don't you stop and talk to me some time. I make pretty good conversation."

"We don't like to disturb you," her mother had said.

"Oh, go ahead. Disturb me. You might make amazing discoveries."

Sometimes they had disturbed him. Jenny had always gone to him with her puzzles, her troubles, for comfort when the world was mean. Sometimes her mother had, too.

A noise outside. The swish of tires through the parking lot, slowing down. She closed the diary and snapped off the light. Clutching it to her chest, she crept to the window and peeked out. The bright taillights of a police car flashed red and then disappeared as the car eased out into the street. Shaken, she turned the light back on, searching through her bag until she found matches. She was going to finish reading the diary and then burn it.

Thanks to that idiot Riteman I missed lunch. By the time I got back to my office from the Medical Board hearing, even the blind coffee vendor was closed and my stomach rumbling like a summer storm. The unfinished memo sat in the middle of my desk like an accusation. It needed to get finished and that was going to take several more hours. Since I was already feeling victimized and cranky, I decided not to be a martyr, so I got my coat and my car keys and drove down the street to the market, where they agreeably made me a tuna sub and threw in a bag of chips. That plus a Coke and a brownie—dry but still chocolate— and I was ready to take on the world.

The world left me completely, disappointingly alone.

I'd even forsworn onions on my sandwich, much as I love them, because of the secret—is it a secret once one writes it down?—hope Jim might drop by. Around me, the building grew quiet. No one burst in with any emergencies. No one cared if I lived or died. In my lonely state—oh, Lila what a self-pitying twit you are sometimes—I wrote eloquently. Passionately. I told the legislature that in the Attorney General's opinion, certain language in the proposed bill was unconstitutional and I explained, carefully, point-by-point, why. When I cite Supreme Court cases, I still feel vestiges of the awe I felt the first day I walked into Constitutional Law. As I wrote, my self-pity dropped away and I felt mighty and wise and on top of the world. I was the shadow legal voice, the ventriloquist who would speak through Jim Buxton for the State of Maine. For the people about their law. Is it any wonder that I love this job?

Jenny knew her mother was a good writer. She'd had that guiding hand on many a paper. The calm, correcting voice suggesting changes which would make the point more clearly or more forcefully, the tactful suggestion that the point Jenny thought she was making had not yet, in fact, been made. Sometimes resented. Sometimes painful. Always making her better. But this was moving. She loved this feisty, vulnerable young woman. Burning this diary seemed like a sin. Yet she had no choice. Jenny reading these words was one thing. Having them broadcast in the press quite another.

But don't I have a stake in this, she wondered? What do I want? She lowered her eyes and read on.

I left the memo on my secretary's desk. She's begun complaining she hates to come to work in the morning because she knows I'm going to have some huge project waiting, but I don't feel guilty. The secretaries in this office don't work that hard but to listen to them talk, you'd think they were galley slaves. Outside it was velvety black and still and I was glad, after going to law school in Boston where sometimes, at night, the air had an electric ping of danger, to live where I could walk through a parking lot late at night and not feel the slightest twinge of fear. When I got home, feeling more dead than alive, there were Jim Buxton and Ken Bass sitting in a car outside my place.

My reaction surprised even me. I marched over and tapped on his window, and when he rolled it down I said, "This is just not smart for either of us." He looked surprised, like no one had ever yelled at him before. I could see it in his face, the look that said, "Hey, I'm the Attorney General. People don't talk to me like this."

And then I said something equally surprising. I said, "Rein in your ego for minute and listen. You aren't the most invisible person on the planet. You sit outside my house at night with your pet bodyguard, someone's going to notice. And once they notice, they'll talk. And once they start talking, we aren't even going to be able to exchange good mornings without the gossips glancing and giggling. You'll be embarrassed, which you can probably live down pretty easily, but I'll have to quit my job, Jim, and I love my job. So go away. Please."

I wanted him to go away like I wanted my toes amputated without anesthesia, but I was worried for him. He was a grown man and one I, along with a lot of other people, had high hopes for, but there was something sweet and boyish about him, too. He would have to lose that side, or where he was going, the sharks would eat him alive. Then the thought hits me, why would I want to send a nice person to a job that would require him to become a not-so-nice person? Because someone has to have the job. And the job needs good people like Jim Buxton and not sleaze-bags who belong to big corporations. Jim knows what it's like to be poor, to be rural, and to feel helpless. He knows about being embarrassed by government surplus food and tattered clothes. He knows about the black hole of fear that shutting down a shoe factory creates. And then there was another side of Jim Buxton: the orderly, planning mind, the schemer who was naturally charming and thrived on taking risks.

Maybe these are the types who are drawn to politics.

While I'm standing there, immersed in my personal musing about his future, he gets out of the car, takes me by the elbow, opens the back door, and pushes me into the back seat. Then he gets in beside me and says, "Drive around, Kenny." So we drive around.

"I can talk in front of Kenny," he says. "I hope you don't mind."

I don't know whether I mind or not, so I say the first thing that comes into my head. "It's the middle of the night and I have to work tomorrow."

"So come in late," he says. "Or call in sick."

"I can't. I've got work to do."

"You are something else," he says. "Something special."

I am completely tongue-tied. The surge of feelings, now that I'm this close to him, makes it hard for me to breathe, let alone talk. I just knot my hands together and struggle for control, not daring to look at him, knowing I'll melt, I'll blather, I'll make a complete fool of myself. I'll throw myself into his arms, I'll kiss that mouth I've been picturing all day.

Kenny drives and the only sound is the hiss of tires. Then we both speak at once. I say, "I had a nightmare of a hearing today."

He says, "I don't know what to do, Lila. I can't get you out of my mind."

We both stop. Laugh. Start over.

I say, "You have to…"

He says, "The Board of Registration in Medicine is…"

In the front seat, Kenny laughs.

He says, "Shut up and drive, Kenny." Takes me in his arms. Mutters, "I'm sorry, but I can't—" Kisses me.

Oh. Hell fire and damnation. I am not a romantic soul, but this?

"The hell you aren't," Jenny said aloud, startling herself, thinking, this incredibly romantic man falls in love with you. You marry the nicest, kindest, most loving man on the face of the earth. I think I'm in love and he turns out to be a 24-karat rat. How did you get to be so lucky?

And then a shiver ran through her. Her mother was so lucky, wasn't she? So lucky someone tried to smash her head. So lucky a man she adored made her pregnant and left. So lucky she had to live with a dark secret the rest of her life.

Jenny stared up at the room. God, she hated motel rooms. The dull, oppressive decor. The lingering smells people left behind—sweat, smoke, perfume and alcohol. The knowledge that dozens, if not hundreds, of bodies had lain in the bed, bathed in the tub, spat in the sink.

Outside, a car door slammed and she felt that current of fear again. She snapped off the light again and peered out. Watched a policeman get out of a car and go into the office.

She didn't wait around to see if it was an innocent visit. Heart pounding, she flew across the room, tugged on the wet sweats, wiggled her feet into her shoes, stuffed her toothbrush and the diary into her purse, grabbed her coat and the room key, and left.

GOVERNOR ALFONSO

ON THE CAMPAIGN TRAIL

O'Malley's pounding head felt like if he didn't hold it firmly with both hands, it would split open and spill his brain onto the floor. A floor at the moment littered with the detritus of a political evening—food wrappers, cups and cans, spilled food, discarded campaign materials, drafted and printed with such high hopes. They might as well hand out Kleenex, or comic books. Comic books. Maybe that was the answer. Alfonso comic books written at a fourth grade level. A cynical smile lifted his thin lips and fell away again. Against his sallow skin, his freckles stood out like rust spots.

Everything was going to hell, and if Lou didn't stop yelling and let him get some sleep pretty soon, this campaign was going to be without a manager, because of the sad fate of O'Malley's brain. O'Malley's brain sounded like a modern Irish short story. Finnegan's Wake. O'Malley's Brain. He pressed harder with his hands.

"Jesus, Mikey, are you even listening? The way you squeeze your head, looks like you're trying to pop a giant zit."

Keris Carlyle, who had just come in, made a gagging sound. O'Malley didn't even look around. Sudden movements made him nauseous. "Sorry, Lou. I've got to get some sleep. I'm worse than useless right now."

"Far as I can tell, all of you are worse than useless. You go out there with an entire goddamned army, and that little girl just walks away again. What is she, Keris? Some kind of magician? How the heck does she do it? You'd think we were dealing with a Navy SEAL here, and not some bookish college girl."

"Woman," Keris muttered.

"Shut the fuck up!" Alfonso snapped, glaring at O'Malley. "Tell me what we do now?"

O'Malley resisted the urge to tell the Governor they couldn't shut up and speak at the same time. Alfonso wasn't known for his sense of humor. He wasn't known for his smarts, either. What he had in endless measure was ambition, and the willingness to do whatever it took to realize that ambition. Something O'Malley could respect. He worshipped ambition.

"Van says they're sure she got into a truck. They stopped all the trucks that could possibly be the one, and didn't find her, but she's so small she's probably pretty easy to hide. So we're following up. I'm pretty sure we'll find her again soon."

"Find her again soon! Shit's sake, Mikey, what if they find her first?"

"We just have to hope they don't. And if they do, then we'll have to steal her back."

"You think they'll leave her alive that long?"

O'Malley shrugged.

"We got people on their team?"

"Does the Pope…"

O'Malley got slowly to his feet, still holding his head, and lumbered toward the door. "Gonna go lie down. I'm not back in two hours, send someone to wake me."

His bulky frame was halfway through the door when the Governor shifted his angry red eyes to Keris. "You got any clever suggestions?"

"I do," she said. "Let's all get some sleep and reconvene in a few hours, when we can behave like civilized human beings."

"When I'm President, I'm finding the factory that made you and blowing it up."

"Right," she said, getting to her feet. "If you were rested, you'd know better than to talk like that. Some day you'll do it to the wrong person, she'll trash you, and the whole house of cards is going to tumble. It's too bad, too, because you've got talent." She looked almost as bad as O'Malley felt.

Alfonso, who never got tired, wasn't listening. "Dammit. I want that girl. Call Van Allen and Morrissey. Tell them to put more people on it. Then get some sleep."

"Thanks, Lou." She followed the miserable O'Malley out the door, pitying him. Mikey could be crude and blustery, but he was a good guy, and a hell of a campaign manager. She'd taken this job because she wanted to work with him. She was halfway through the door when the phone rang. She hoped it was something to boot Alfonso out of his piss-poor mood. She had five older brothers and spoiled sullen moodiness didn't cut any ice with her. Some days, she wanted to send the whole male population to boot camp.

He snatched up the phone, the ugly lines in his face smoothing out, something more malicious than a smile spreading across the olive countenance until it was the grin of a wolf spotting an inattentive bunny. "Okay," he said. "Just grab her. Do what you have to do. Call me the minute you have news."

He looked over at Keris. "Morrissey. They've found her at a motel in Western Massachusetts. They're going in now. You've got a place to stash her, right?"

Keris nodded. "They'll take her to Morrissey's place. It'll be easy to secure."

"Good, because in a few hours, we're going to need it." He rubbed his hands together with such glee that for a moment, remembering her meeting with Jenny Cates, Keris felt sorry for the girl. Then she remembered her slashed tire, and how much she hated coming in second. She shrugged and closed the door.

"...the breath,
Of the night wind down the vast edges drear
And naked shingles of the world."
—Matthew Arnold, "Dover Beach"

CHAPTER SEVENTEEN

She didn't know where she was. What city, what town, what state. Well, she knew what state she was in. The state of confusion. Abject fear. The state of utter, beaten-down exhaustion. Her wet pants flapped against her calves and her frozen toes clenched inside her squashing shoes. She clutched the jacket tightly around her as cold wind pushed its way between buildings and jabbed at her with icy fingers. *Personification*, she thought. *The attribution of human characteristics to inanimate things or to nature.* Not that this wind was in any way inanimate. It would take her clothes, her purse, her very self, if it grew much stronger.

Her ears stinging with cold, she turned the jacket collar up, hunched her shoulders, and went on, wet feet freezing, her calves numb, tingling fingers shoved deep in her pockets. Somewhere she'd lost the hat and gloves. The wind whipped up tears in her eyes, then tore them away before they could run down her cheeks. She stumbled more often as her body grew less able to obey the commands of her frightened mind. Every dirty cup skittering along the sidewalk seemed out to get her, every flapping sign, rattling window, and slow-moving car was the enemy.

At last, seeking respite and a shelter, she stumbled into a phone booth and closed the door. It felt good to be out of the wind, but a brightly lit phone booth in an otherwise dark landscape was no kind of hiding place. She lingered as long as she dared, resting her legs, trying to get warm, but the damp had permeated her clothes. They hung on her, heavy and chilled. The leather jacket wasn't warm enough. All alone in the stark blue-white light, she smiled ironically, a child of the TV generation, and emitted a sound bite. "If she'd only worn polypro, it would have wicked away the moisture and left her dry and comfortable."

Finally, she forced herself back onto the street, moving with a monotonous trudge. It was foggy and the occasional streetlight had a luminous, crystal ball quality. Ahead, the gaudy pink and orange of a Dunkin' Donuts was softened like a melting ice cream cake. She moved toward it, seeking heat and coffee. She wrestled the door open against the opposition of the wind and dumped herself at the counter, a soggy maiden in distress.

She ordered soup and a sandwich and coffee, knowing, with her muddy wet clothes and stringy hair, that she looked like a street person. Oh well. Even street people had to eat. She fought the desire to rest her head on the counter and sleep. Across from her, a frail old man with tufts of white hair and few teeth was clutching his suspender straps with both hands and talking to his coffee cup. Down the counter, two hard-looking young women with heavily mascara-ed eyes and blood-red mouths masticated gum almost in unison, their red-nailed hands holding thin raincoats closed over skimpy dresses. One wore dark stockings. The other was bare-legged, with a line of bluish bruises from hem to ankle.

The food came fast and she ate it even faster, aware her wolfish behavior screamed out desperation. She felt like the server and the hookers and the old man were all watching and wondering. But when she looked around, the others seemed indifferent. The room had that cold otherworldliness places get when they're open past people's bedtimes.

Thinking maybe more coffee might warm her, she ordered another, then sat staring at the dark, steaming liquid in her cup. She wanted to stick her hands into it. They seemed no warmer for having been wrapped around the cup, her fingers still stiff, the tips a dead-looking purplish white. She drank the coffee, then went to the ladies room. The woman with the bruised legs came after her, stopping her outside the door.

"Hey!" she said.

Jenny stopped. Was there space to rush past the woman or would she have to be pushed out of the way?

"Hey," the woman said. "Don't be scared." Jenny flattened herself against the wall, ready to flee. "Look," the woman said. "You just, like, looked like you might be in trouble or something, you know? I don't want to butt in or anything, it's your business." She hesitated, as if waiting for some sign, some response.

"Thanks, but I'm fine," Jenny said.

"Yeah. And I'm the Easter Bunny. Think I never seen that rabbit-faced, chased by a pimp or an abusive boyfriend look before? Think you're the only person in the world ever had troubles?" She turned away, raising her arms in an elaborate, contemptuous shrug, as the other woman wandered over to join her. "Didja hear that, Dawna? Girl's fuckin' fine." She laughed and tossed her hair. "Fuckin' fine. Dawna? I ever tell you what fine means?"

The other woman shrugged. Her dark eyes had a glazed, drugged look. The jaw working her chewing gum was the only animated thing about her. "Dunno."

"Fine. Fucked-up. Insecure. Neurotic. Emotional. That's like me, huh? I'm fine. Very fine." She turned back to face Jenny. "Just like you, honey." She held out a hand. In it was a dog-eared, grayish business card. "Here. Take it. If you don't need help, no problem. If you do, maybe this lady can help."

Jenny took the card. It had a street address on it, a phone number, and the words, "For Help." No city. No name.

"What's this?"

The woman shrugged. "Some crazy left-over hippie lady. Likes to help street people. Goes around giving out these cards."

Jenny pointed to the address. "Where is this place?"

The woman shrugged again. "Dawna?"

Dawna bent down and squinted at the card, then motioned Jenny to the window. Pointed. "Down this street. 5, 6 blocks. Fire station. That's Mabry." She hesitated, pondering, then said uncertainly, "Left, 'nother 5-6 blocks."

"She takes people in?" Jenny asked.

The nameless woman nodded. Dawna just blinked and stared. Her stare was unnerving.

"Thanks," Jenny said.

The bruised woman put an arm around Dawna's shoulders and gave her a squeeze. "Dawna's great, isn't she? Just great."

The bruised woman ought to be a teacher. She had an instinct for building self-esteem. A way of finding the best in people. Maybe a blank slate like Dawna made it easy. Jenny nodded, said thanks again, and used the rest room. Then, because she had no more reason to stay here, she went out, leaving the anonymous stranger, her arm still draped over the catatonic Dawna's shoulder, staring after her.

The wind welcomed her back with a vengeance, quickly snatching away the little warmth she'd built up. She shifted back to her trudge mode, remembering simpler days, remembering the sports field, where she'd relished the challenge of keeping going when her body wanted to quit. "We're not quitters," her mother always said.

Okay. She wasn't a quitter. Just scared shitless and frozen stiff. When the going gets tough, the tough just keep putting one foot in front of the other, until they get there or die trying. She wasn't about to die. People didn't die from being a tired and cold. Yeah, Cates, keep on telling yourself that. She crossed a river. Something Dawna had failed to mention. The wind came shrieking down the open water like a train building up steam before a climb, shoving her off the sidewalk and into the street. She fought her way back and used the guard rail to finish crossing.

One foot, two foot, red foot, blue foot. She stumbled. Went down on one knee, and when she looked up, realized she was beside the fire station. Time to turn left. She checked the street name against the card, the wind nearly snatching it out of her grasp. Mabry. And she was on Wintergreen. How sweet.

Help me. I'm broken down on the corner of Wintergreen and Mabry. Crying now, the wind stealing her tears before they could warm her cheeks. An enormous gust of wind, roaring like an angry giant, whipped around the corner and slammed her into the wall.

A door opened and a man stuck his head out. He spotted her. Came over and helped her to her feet. "You okay?" he asked. A fireman, she thought. Waiting for something to happen.

"I'm fine," she said, thinking how right the woman in the donut shop had been. "Thanks. I'm fine."

"Little late for you to be out," he said, giving her a professional up and down.

"I'm not a kid," she said quickly, afraid he might decide to take her under his care, or, worse, call the cops. She held out the card. "I'm trying to go here." Tight, scared little voice through chattering teeth.

He peered at the card and grinned. "Another of Araby's lost souls? Hold on a sec. I'll get my coat and walk you there."

"You don't need to. I'm fine, really," she said.

"Kind of a bad part of town to be walking around alone," he said. "Wouldn't want anything to happen to you, you've come this far."

He didn't know the half of it, did he?

He turned away, then turned back. "You wait." This time it was a command and not a request. He was back almost immediately, shrugging his way into a heavy raincoat. "This way." He turned and headed across the street. Not in the direction Dawna had told her.

"Wait." She pointed the other way. "Don't we go there?"

"Not if you value your life much," he said. "Not if you want to find Araby."

She couldn't see a reason why he'd try and trick her, so, keeping a distance from him in case she had to run, she followed him down the street. He marched along without saying anything. Just walked, turning his head occasionally to be sure she was still with him. "I'm not going to bite, you know," he said.

She felt nostalgic for the girl she'd been not long ago, who wouldn't have been suspicious, and wanted to explain. She found herself using Dawna's shorthand way of talking. "Things have been a little rough lately. Makes me cautious."

"Yeah," he said. "Kinda looks it. Araby'll straighten things out." He lapsed back into silence and they trudged on.

She was curious about this Araby, the left-over hippie woman who would straighten things out. All she wanted was a hot bath and a bed. Would the price of those be conversation? Probably. She ought to have a story ready, but when she tried to compose a plausible fiction, she got the jangled sizzle of tired circuits and slow Frankenstein speech. "I'm Jenny. Nice to meet you. I fall over now. Bye."

"Watch out!" He seized her arm and dragged her away from a gaping hole in the sidewalk. "You want to break your neck?" Like a father whose kids are still pretty young and inattentive, though he looked more like a grandfather.

"Sorry," she said.

"Here we are," he said, turning up the walk of a looming gray Victorian. A hanging light, shaped like a star, burned over the front door. He marched up to the door and banged on it loudly. Waited a few seconds and banged again.

Suddenly, the inside door flew open and a woman gazed out at them from the blackest eyes Jenny had ever seen. Large, hooded eyes that seemed both wise and sad. She had dark hair with dramatic streaks of gray in a long braid down her back. A generous mouth under a slightly hooked nose. She wore an elaborate paisley dressing gown of purples and reds and golds and greens. Definitely a dressing gown, not bathrobe. The garment spoke of dressing, and gowns, and not of baths or robes. Despite the lateness of the hour, Araby had been up. It was not something thrown on in the dark.

Araby smiled at the fireman. "So, Tony, you brought me another one?"

"Found her in the street," he said, shuffling his feet like a schoolboy.

The woman shifted her eyes to Jenny, who swayed on her feet, clinging to the door post. "Come in, dear. Come in. You're probably wet and cold, and it's cozy inside."

Jenny stepped into the room, unhappily aware of her wet shoes on the shiny hardwood floor. Stumbling like a sailor first setting foot on land. The floor seemed to rock and sway. "I should take off my shoes."

The woman exchanged glances with Tony. "Nonsense, dear. Just come in the kitchen. You can leave them by the stove. You have time for coffee, Tony, or do you have to get right back?"

"I've got time."

Jenny followed, willing her reluctant synapses to keep her feet moving. The rolling motion of the floor was getting worse. She was passing an immense, carved sideboard, and reached toward it for support, but it was moving away, slipping through her fingers, ephemeral as mist. Odd, because it looked so solid.

"Help her, Tony," Araby said. "You might as well bring her right to the bedroom."

She was swung up into the air, felt the wet rubber of his raincoat against her cheek. The coat carried the slightly bitter smell of ashes. His arms were strong. Spending her spring break in strange men's arms. A positive orgy of intimate contacts with strangers.

Swooping down through the air again, onto a wide pink surface. A mattress? Araby's face bent over her, uttering requests for cooperation as the wet shoes and socks were tugged off. "Right arm," Araby ordered, and Jenny stuck out her right arm. "Left arm." The weight of her coat went away, dropped with a soggy thud onto the floor. "Arms up." Identical to her mother's command when Jenny was three. Up went her arms, the wrist with the cast resisting, and her sweatshirt was swept off. There was the sharp intake of breath, and then Araby said, "What on earth happened to you?"

"What hasn't?" she giggled.

"Tell me," Araby said, dropping a nightgown over her head and then seizing the waistband of her pants. "Bottom up." Jenny lifted her bottom and Araby deftly peeled off the pants and dumped them on the floor with the rest. Covers smelling like Ivory Snow were pulled up around her, and Araby, bending low, soothed the hair away from her face. "You're safe now. Tell me what happened."

Delicious lassitude beckoned her in with black velvet arms. Jenny fought its clutches, forced her eyes wide. "My purse?"

Araby held it up where Jenny could see it. "It will be right here by the bed. It's not going anywhere. I promise. I won't touch it. What happened to you?"

Jenny closed her eyes. "Someone killed my uncle," she said. "Then they tried to kill my mother, so I ran away. They followed me and ran me off the road. The car accident, that's where I got all these bruises." She giggled again. "I look like an abstract painting, don't I? A bad abstract painting. They keep following me. Keep trying to catch me. I just have to keep running and running, and I'm so tired."

"Who's chasing you? Who's doing all these things to you?"

Jenny giggled again. She couldn't get a handle on it. "I don't know if it's Senator James Buxton, you know, the presidential candidate. You see, he's actually my father."

Sleep tugged at her, but Araby was being so nice, she wanted to explain. She wanted Araby to understand, so she wouldn't think Jenny was just some runaway kid or street crazy or something. She knew she wasn't doing a good job. "But I don't know. See, there were these two New York state cops who said they were my friends and trying to help me so the other guys wouldn't get me, the ones who really are trying to kill me. And the New York cops, they work for Governor Alfonso. See, I'm a victim of political oppression. Right here in America. Hard to believe. Guess I'm not making much sense, am I?"

The words were flowing now, rushing to get out, a confused babble of words and thoughts and stories, but she supposed Araby was used to this. "See, there are two different sets of people looking for me. One that wants to use me and one that wants to kill me, because of something that happened over twenty years ago, but I have no way of telling them apart. I have to keep running so neither of them finds me."

It felt like she was falling right down through the mattress, through a sky full of clouds, through an endless soft darkness. "I spotted them at the motel. See, I got away from the car crash," she said, "but they found me and made me go to the hospital, but then I got away from the hospital, and I went to stay with Pansy, but they found me there, too, so I went and hid in the camp by the swamp, but they found me there, too. I had to escape through the woodbox and run for miles through the woods, and then I flagged down the truck driver, and I hid in the truck, and he took me to a motel, but then the cops showed up there."

Her voice rose. "No matter where I go. No matter what I do. They find me. They find me. There's no way to escape! I run and run, and every time, they find me."

"It sounds like you've had a terrible time. You need to get some sleep," Araby said. "We can talk in the morning, when you're feeling better."

Her hands moved over Jenny's face again, soothing back the last sticky bits of hair. "Close your eyes," she said in the mesmerizing voice of a hypnotist. "You're safe now. Close your eyes and sleep."

Obediently, Jenny closed her eyes and slept.

"Alone, alone, all, all alone,
Alone on a wide, wide sea!"
—Coleridge, The Rime of the Ancient Mariner

CHAPTER EIGHTEEN

Once again she woke in a strange, dark place, not knowing where she was. She fumbled in the darkness for the light. Her latest place of refuge was a small, rectangular room with one big window, basic furniture, a cheerful rug on the floor and pink curtains and bedspread. The lower shelf of the bedside table held a few books, some Nancy Drew and young adult novels and *Anne of Green Gables*. In the single chair sat a big black and white stuffed panda with a red bandanna around its neck. Two identical doors which, upon examination, led not to a lady and a tiger, but to a closet and tiny bathroom.

She woke from a dream in which she was being chased down wet, dark streets, through endless stretches of black forest. She had to cross a busy eight-lane highway, dodging the cars and trucks which raced at her without pausing, to get to her mother, waiting on the other side with outstretched arms. She had managed to cross and ran toward the figure, only to have it vanish. She had woken crying, her arms stretched out.

She was still exhausted and her body ached terribly, but the dream left her reluctant to return to sleep. Darn Araby, with her gentle hands and soothing voice, for stirring up this longing. Those tender ministrations had kindled a need for her mother's arms, her soothing touch.

The clock beside the bed said four-thirty in glowing, green numerals. No wonder she'd dreamed of her mother. That was her mother's usual hour to get up. She liked to do her thinking while the rest of the world slept. While, as she put it, the waves from other people's brains didn't impinge. Jenny flashed on the last thing she'd seen—that still white hand against the crisp white sheet. She didn't know what the picture was now, didn't even know if her mother was alive. It had been days since she'd checked. But if she called from here, just a quick call, and called the ICU nursing station and not the pay phone, she didn't see how she'd give herself away. She didn't see how Araby could mind. She'd pay for the call.

She crept down the stairs, acutely aware of the nocturnal creakings of the unfamiliar house, of her sense of disconnection, an alien in other people's familiar worlds. She remembered seeing a phone on a stand at the bottom of the stairs. Quietly, she knelt on the hardwood floor and lifted the receiver. There was enough light in the front hall, from a street light outside, for her to dial. She punched in the numbers, and waited.

"Maine Medical Center," a voice twanged at last.

"Special care," she said.

"Please hold while I connect you."

"Special care."

Jenny crossed her fingers and said, "This is Jenny Cates. I'm hoping you can tell me how my mother is doing. Lila Friedman? She's one of your patients?"

There was a silence, then the woman said, "Can you hold, please?"

Jenny counted to fifty, took three deep breaths, and counted to fifty again. Fears of the worst filling the void. A different voice came on the line. "Who is this, please?"

"Jenny Cates. Her daughter."

There was a silence, then the voice said, regretfully, "I'm sorry, but we're unable to release any information about that patient."

She's dead, Jenny thought. *She's dead and they don't want to tell me over the phone.* Panic and grief closed her throat. Numbly, she cradled the phone and stared out at the street light, gleaming through its halo of fog. She tried calling her father at home, but all she got was the machine. She didn't leave a message. Then, because she had to know, she shed her caution and tried the waiting room pay phone.

It rang several times before anyone answered. "Is there a man named Bud Cates in the waiting room?" she asked.

"Hold on." She heard the voice, it sounded like a teenage boy, asking, "Anyone here named Bud Cates?" Then the boy was back to her. "Hold on," he said again. "They've gone to find him."

She should hang up. Staying on the line was too dangerous. But she had to know. It wasn't enough to assume that because he was still there, her mother was alive. She'd been too long without news, without any kind of contact. She had to hear his voice.

Finally, she heard his voice. The minute he said, "Jenny, is that you?" she burst into tears.

"Oh, Daddy. Everything has been so awful. I've been so scared. So worried."

"Jenny, sweetheart, where are you?"

"I don't know." She couldn't keep him on the phone long enough to explain. "It's a long, horrible story. We don't have time for that now. Tell me about Mom. When I called the nursing station, they wouldn't tell me anything. And I was sure that meant—" She couldn't finish.

"We've asked them not to. To protect her. I guess you realized that. She's..." He took a deep breath, and her imagination filled the silence with a thousand awful things.

"She's much better. I'm almost afraid to say it, for fear it will set her back, but the coma seems to be lifting. I know that's not the right term, but that's how it looks. Like she's slowly coming out back to us."

"Oh, God, Daddy. Oh, God. I feel like I've spent these last days with my fists clenched, waiting for news. Tell her I love her, please. When you bend down and kiss her, whisper that Jenny says hi. Tell her that I'm fine."

"Are you fine?" he interrupted.

"Not even close," she said. "But a very kind woman has taken me in, so maybe I can stop running and get some rest. I'm so tired."

"You sound tired. Get some sleep, sweetheart. Call again when you can. And Jen."

"Yes?"

"Don't worry about your mother. There's a policeman outside her door twenty-four hours a day."

"Just keep checking their ID, okay? These people are so evil."

"I know," he said grimly. "You bet your ass I do."

"Bye, Daddy."

"Bye, Jen." His hesitation over her name told her the dozens of questions he was holding back, his reluctance to let her go as great as hers. She could have stayed on the line all night while they breathed together, and felt closer and safer. "Jenny? I'm so sorry for all this." And he was gone.

Slowly, sadly, she replaced the receiver and sat in the dark hall, longing for familiar places and familiar people. Even cradled and silent, the phone felt like a tangible link between herself and the people she loved. Her family. Her tiny little family. Eyes closed, she reached out her arms and imagined she was gathering them in. An imagining so vivid she could almost feel them, almost smell their special, individual scents, almost hear them breathing. Her mother, cool and soft, never quite still; her father, large and lean and warm. The brush of their lips on her face. She would have given anything to travel back in time just one short week.

"What are you doing, sitting down here in the dark?" Araby's voice sent her parents scattering.

"Oh!" Jenny's hands fluttered toward the phone. "I hope you don't mind. I used your phone to call the hospital and check on my mother. She was attacked by…"

"You told me," Araby said, "by some politicians, right?"

It sounded odd when she said it like that, but Jenny nodded. That was what had happened. "Right. I was just imagining I was back home with them, with my parents, and everything was fine. I'm sorry about your phone bill. I'll be happy to pay."

"Don't worry about it." Araby felt her hand. "You're freezing," she said. "You'd better get back in bed, where it's warm. We'll talk in the morning."

Jenny followed her back upstairs, let herself be tucked in again, and waited until Araby's footsteps had faded away. Then she took out the diary and started to read.

> *Oh, hell fire and damnation. I am not a romantic soul, but this was the most romantic thing that ever happened to me. It was, to get all trite and clichéd, the kiss I'd always dreamed about and was absolutely sure never existed except in fiction. The kind that made me tingle right down to my toes. The kind that made me want to cast discretion to the wind and have sex with him right there in the back seat, Kenny behind the wheel be damned! The kind that made me melting and compliant and hungry.*
>
> *Maybe I should give up the law and become a romance writer. Another night like tonight and I"m not going to have any career left anyway. How can I be around him*

and not blush like a goddamned traffic light? How can I not advertise to the world what's running through my head when I think of him?

He was the one who finally pulled away. "Oh, Lord, Lila, what are we going to do?" But that was after he'd unbuttoned my blouse and kissed the tops of my breasts, and the side of my neck. After my lips were bruised and swollen. After he had whispered that he wanted me so badly that he ached. And I, for once, hadn't been able to summon the outrage to give him my blue-balls lecture. Because I felt the same way. Blue ovaries?

But I'd had a proper, old-fashioned up-bringing, and I knew better. So when he did pull away and ask what we were going to do, I said, "I've had a job offer in Bangor."

The silence was long, and then he said, "You'd do that?"

"I don't want to. I love my job, but—"

"But what, Lila? But what?" He sounded impatient and angry. Hurt, like I was brushing him off. Running away, when it was the last thing I wanted to do. I tried to explain.

"This is going to sound stupid and preachy, Jim. I'm not stupid and I"m not preachy, but I believe in you. I mean, I believe that you can make a difference in the world. Getting involved with someone in your office, when you're married, could keep that from happening. We need to look at the bigger picture." It did sound preachy but I couldn't find a better way to put it. He's the politician, not me. I'm only eloquent on paper.

"How can I see the bigger picture, when all I can see is you, Lila? You fill my whole horizon."

It went on like that, with me talking about how he was a married man with a family and a brilliant future, how he had a bigger duty than just to do what pleased him, he had a calling to do good for all the people of Maine, and him talking about how all he cared about was me and how he hadn't heard a word from me about what I wanted, until Kenny cleared his throat and announced that if we wanted to talk any longer, he'd have to get gas.

So they brought me home, but he made me promise I'd see him again tomorrow night.

Now I don't know what to do. When I'm with him, I feel like I've been transformed from the edgy and competitive smart girl that the guys shied away from to some kind of wise and sensual goddess. Again, it sounds like a basketful of clichés, but I do feel transformed. I feel beautiful and desirable and special, even if I can't flaunt it like Yeah, Yeah, look at me, girls, I've got the biggest and best prize anyone ever caught! At the same time, I know he admires me for my mind. I know he values my work. I know that the praise he's given me, and the encouragement and advice, have been because he thinks I'm already a good lawyer and will become a much better one. Loved for my mind and loved for my body? Loved for my looks and also for my passion and my politics? Is it any wonder I'm having trouble getting a handle on this?

Tomorrow I'm going to call the DA's office in Bangor and arrange an interview.

Don't do it, Jenny thought. *Don't let him drive you out of this job.* She knew that wasn't fair. Jim Buxton hadn't asked her mother to change jobs. He'd asked her not to. This was her mother's attempt to protect both of them from a scandal that could ruin their careers. The impression she'd gotten was people might have had suspicions, but no one knew the affair was going on. How had they managed it? And what about the video tape? She felt such love, such empathy for her mother's struggle, seeing, at the same time, her mother in the hospital, the pale, inert form gradually reanimating. She read on.

I shall draw a little tombstone on this page, and write upon it, "Here Lies Lila's Virtue." After last night, that certainly is the case. I'm not talking about virginity. That was left behind some time ago. I'm talking about the right to cast the first stone. I'm talking about violating my personal code of ethics. I can never condemn anyone again for the follies of sex with the wrong person, because I have transgressed.

Transgressed. I love it! The word has such a high falutin'
sound. I'm dancing on air. I confess to having no regrets.
None. Not a shred. If it weren't a deep, dark secret, I would
proclaim to the world at large that my expectations have
been met and exceeded.

I am Helen Reddy, strutting, singing, "I am Woman."
The other woman. Woman in love. A Man and a Woman.
I am overjoyed and full of regret. But for this one day,
before I drift back down and touch earth and run smack
up against cold reality, I will not think of Bud Cates, or
my mother, or Jim's wife, and what they all might think
of me. I will not think about the Democratic Party, nor
the possibility that even though I believe him and adore
him, I might yet turn out to be one in a long line of secret
conquests. I will think about how sore I am, and how good
it feels. I am taking a sick day, because I need twenty-four
hours to think. To think, among other things, of how a
woman who has spent her life being cautious and avoiding
risks, could have gone on making love long after we'd
run out of condoms. Of how poor Kenny Bass will have
to throw out those sheets, perhaps even that mattress. Of
excess. Indulgence. The sheer delicious madness of having
been utterly swept away.

No, Jenny thought, this was not something she'd like to see in the
national press, topped with lurid headlines, in every supermarket
checkout line:

She didn't want a penis of her own, but she sure wanted Buxton's.
Buxton's Babe Bares All.
Legal Days and Illegal Nights.

Why on earth had her mother kept these? Why hadn't she burned
them herself? Her mother had never been a sentimental woman. But
that wasn't entirely true. On her mother's desk was a picture of Jenny
winning the state spelling bee. Bangs too long and a loopy, toothy grin.
A picture of Bud Cates being named Teacher of the Year, looking young

and abashed and a bit like a physics wonk. A picture of Billy graduating from high school, waving his diploma, and itching to go out and make trouble. Those she loved retained a cherished place in her heart. She had loved Jim Buxton.

The diary entries grew more sporadic, more brief. No longer pages, but little hasty paragraphs.

> *Billy knows something is going on. I've never been any good at hiding things from him. He sees right through me. So last night, when he showed up to tell me about his latest job venture and I was trying to get him out of the apartment because I was supposed to go and meet Jim, he just sat back on the sofa and grinned at me and said, "Whatsa madda, Lil, got ants in your pants? Think I can't tell that you're trying to get rid of me? What's so special about this new guy that you can't introduce him to your brother?" We had a fight about that, me saying I had a right to my privacy, and Billy, the perceptive little bastard, announcing that if he couldn't meet the guy, there must be something I needed to hide. Finally he stopped asking and left.*
>
> *I raced over to Kenny's, found Jim in a state, sweating and clammy and pacing like a panther. He grabbed my hand and held on so tightly it hurt and he asked in a desperate way, "Lila, have you got any of those painkillers left?" But when I opened my purse and took out the Tylenol, he gave a bitter laugh and looked at me like I was stupid "Not that stuff. The real stuff. Prescription stuff."*
>
> *I had something the dentist had given me when I had my wisdom teeth out. A whole big bottle. I said yes. Jim looked like he was having a seizure or something, all pale and jittery. He said, "Give your keys to Kenny and tell him where to find it. I need you to stay here with me."*
>
> *He looked so bad and was acting so odd I followed Kenny into the kitchen and demanded to know what was going on. Well, Kenny Bass is 100% Jim Buxton's man. He would have stonewalled, but I'm not always sweet,*

agreeable Lila. If there's one thing this job is teaching me, it's how to get answers. I put my foot down and said no keys and no drugs unless he told me, and reminded him that we were in this together, whatever "this" was, and I'd stand by Jim just like he would.

He hemmed and hawed and I stood my ground and then Jim was in the doorway looking gray as death. He said, "For God's sake, Kenny, tell her what she wants to know and go get those damned pills."

And then Ken didn't have to tell me anything. I just knew. Knew why he was sometimes so unpredictably moody and irritable. Why he was always taking pills. Why, once or twice when he was at my place, I'd heard the medicine cabinet open and shut. I hadn't thought twice about it, or assumed he was being curious about me. Foolish female vanity. I'd been secretly flattered by his nosiness when he was stealing my pills.

I felt a strange combination of betrayal and anger as I held out my keys to Ken. "In the medicine cabinet. Second shelf." And I turned my back on him because I didn't want him to see my face. "It's not his fault, Lila." I ignored him. "Really. It was the back pain and then recovering from surgery. He was too busy to slow down and rest so it could heal, so he just kept popping pills. Now he's hooked."

"Hadn't you better be going, Kenny?" I said it snottily because I was feeling betrayed. It's a shock when your heroes fall off their pedestals. But Ken didn't go. He stayed there in the kitchen—we were in the trailer and it was an ugly, dark room, too small for big feelings. "Look, Lila," he said. "He's the same man you knew yesterday and the day before. A great man who happens to have a problem. Maybe instead of getting all righteous and huffy, you could think of some way to help."

That bastard Billy. If I could get my hands on him, I'd kill him. His idea of joke. Taping me and Jim. Probably thought he was getting some hot, steamy sex, which means he hasn't seen the tape yet. I don't know when he set it up,

*or how, but this is a thousand times worse. Kenny and I
had talked it over and decided the only way to help Jim
was to walk him through a cold turkey withdrawal. We
figured we'd use my place and just take turns sitting with
him until it was over. God, it was awful. A hundred times,
Jim begged me for relief and it took all my willpower to
say no. And keep saying no, as he got sicker and shakier
and more pathetic and desperate. Kenny was no better. He
loved Jim too much to watch him suffer. Friday was bad
and Saturday was worse, and it was Saturday night, with
Jim green-faced, vomiting, and wildly out-of-control, and
me dirty and exhausted, that Billy got on tape.*

*Billy dropped by acting so weird, with this big, impish
smile that always means he's got a joke going on someone,
I had to ask, and he had to tell me. When I demanded
the tape, he said no, said he wanted to watch it first, and
then I really lost it, and I literally went for his throat,
all the while telling him what kind of harm he might be
doing. He did have the grace to look abashed, but he won't
give me the tape, and now, because he knows how mad I
am, he's gone into hiding. I mean, you never know where
Billy is living. Usually it's with the woman of the moment,
and they change more often than his underwear. Jim sent
Kenny and some of the other state cops looking for Billy,
and when they found him, they beat the crap out of him
but they didn't find the tape, and now I don't know what
we're going to do.*

She wondered if the men who were chasing her thought she had the
tape, and then wondered whether they knew what was on it. Not likely.
Probably, like Billy, they were looking for steamy sex. It would be so
much more damning to find sweaty drug addiction. Outside, the sky
was beginning to get light. Another night without enough sleep. But she
couldn't stop reading.

*Jim said he had some bad news for me. That as I must have
known, the senior senator from Maine had had a heart*

attack, but what I didn't know, because they were keeping it under wraps, was he wasn't expected to recover. I asked the question I knew I was supposed to ask. "What does this mean for you?"

"They've approached me... it's still very premature, of course... about filling the seat."

I felt like someone had knocked the breath right out of me. Sat there in Kenny's stark trailer, staring at the false wood paneling and the utilitarian greenish-brown carpeting, and let the impact of Jim's words sink in. Feeling like I was dying right there, my incredible joy packed away for eternity. We had talked about where things would go between us. He'd described his marriage as bleak and loveless. Described his wife Margaret as an attractive and competent person he admired very much, but as someone who had lost interest in him and, for the most part, in his political career. He'd said he didn't think she'd be that opposed to a divorce, assuming the terms were favorable.

I had allowed myself to believe him when he talked about our future, when he spoke of leaving Margaret, even though I knew he had children and hated the idea of hurting them. I had entertained visions of the day when Jim and I would work, side-by-side, to change the world the way he planned to change it. I had imagined a cozy little home where I cooked while he practiced politics, and, because I'm a feminist, where we cooked while we practiced politics. I had even, shame, shame be my name, envisioned a child. A sturdy little boy with Jim's eyes and my hair, coming to us for help with his homework, bringing his tales from school, walking between us as we strolled down the road of life, holding our hands.

When Jim said he was being considered for the Senate seat, I literally felt sick. I felt like someone had taken all my hopes and dreams and ripped them out by the roots, like a tooth extracted without anesthesia. And the space where they had been filled with blood, a hot, surging river of it, so that I felt like I could open my mouth and it would pour out. I excused myself and locked myself in the bathroom. Knowing that once again I was being a cliché, the woman who says she doesn't care, who says, "no strings," who therefore shouldn't be devastated. I was devastated.

I knew I had to send him away. Tell him good-bye. Let him go without wavering, without hesitation, without laying a guilt trip on him or trying to hold him back and without letting him change my mind. I was devastated because I was pretty sure that I was pregnant with Jim's child, and knew I could never tell him.

Jenny blinked away tears and closed the book. There was a little more, but she couldn't face it. Not with the image of the young Lila Friedman sitting in a dingy trailer, desperately in love with a man she was preparing to send away. Pregnant with the child of a man she loved, willing to let him go because she believed he had a destiny. Because her hopes for him were, if anything, larger than his hopes for himself.

A thought hit her. Why did she call her mother's sacrifice crazy? Why was it crazy to believe in someone? What was so crazy about putting someone else's interest above one's own? Jenny's mother hadn't been crazy, she'd been noble, in an antiquated way the me-first world didn't value. Except for one thing—there had been Jenny. And didn't she have a stake in things, too?

But her mother had provided a father so wonderful, so completely paternal, that Jenny had never wanted for anything in the father department. She had believed the lie of her paternity, never had any reason to doubt it. And her father, her actual father, the man who had raised her, had never wavered in his love, steadfastness, and devotion.

It made Jenny jealous for a minute. Her mother had been cherished and desired and adored by two fine men, while she herself had loved one who had betrayed her. She shook it off. Down that path lay nothing but misery. She liked feeling close to the young Lila Friedman. From her mother's own words she knew that at the same age, her mother had been much like her. Slightly too self-consciously smart, the outcast, the one who had waited on the sidelines to be chosen for the love team. Until she'd met Bud Cates and Jim Buxton, and had her embarrassment of riches. And then her mother had discovered, as one so often discovers, that when you get what you wish for, it often takes a form that makes you regret having wished at all.

> *I am going to push Jim Buxton out of my life and close the door. It's the only thing I can do. If I give him any hope, he'll try to find a way for us to stay together, and blow this wonderful opportunity. It would be even worse if he knew about the baby. But all that can wait. Tomorrow I'll invite him to my place, cook him dinner, and have a night to remember. And I hope it will be good. It has to last a long, long time. Forever.*

She closed her eyes and saw her mother's sad, young face staring ahead into the future. Then she opened her eyes and started reading faster. Suddenly she wanted to know how it ended, how her mother had concluded this book. She was filled with an ominous sense that when the sun came up, some new hell would break loose. No matter what the day brought, it was time for this diary to come to an end—a physical end—eliminating the chance that anyone else would ever see it. It was too personal. Too precious. In the vicious world of political campaigns, there was no respect for feelings, only for agenda and advantage. It would give Governor Alfonso a hell of an advantage if he could show his opponent in the jittery, vomiting throes of kicking a drug addiction.

With her lower lip caught between her teeth, she read the last page.

> *Last night my baby, our baby, was born. Jennifer. She is lying beside me now, quiet and curious, studying the world with her restless blue eyes. Every mother must feel this, but she seems to me the most beautiful creature the world has ever seen. Her perfect fingers. Her perfect tiny toes, pink and precious and with those amazing little toenails, not much bigger than pinheads. Bud has been wonderful. I think he already adores her and I know, because of the uniquely good man that he is, that he will never treat her differently because she's not his biological child. He will make her his child. Already, watching his big hands encircle her tiny body, I see the affinity between them. They*

will love each other. Deeply. Profoundly. Her life will be cushioned by his goodness.

I am wicked, when this has ended so well, to dwell on might have beens, but in a corner of my heart, I still feel a sharp sorrow that her father will never know this child. Never know she exists. It's a hard secret to keep, but no one ever said that life would be easy. I believe in discretion. Privacy. Living with pain rather than laying it on other people. So I will keep it to myself and go forward with the joy of this new moment. I won't look back. The three of us, Bud and Jenny and Lila, heading into the future. A family.

It was risky, but Jenny couldn't stop herself. She ripped out the last page, folded it a thousand times, and stuck it in the key pocket in her bra with the folded up bills. Then, before she had time for second thoughts, she took it out again, tore it into tiny pieces, and flushed it away. She watched the confetti of her birth flow away with a physical pain so intense she had to cover her mouth to keep from crying out.

If Jim Buxton was the good man her mother had believed him to be, why did he try to kill someone he'd once loved? And why was he trying to kill her? Suddenly, she wanted to ask him. Get him on the phone and ask him. She wanted to stop running, get right up in Buxton's face, and ask him why he, or those who worked for him, were trying to kill her mother, and how he could let his goons murder his own daughter.

She closed the diary with a snap and headed downstairs to make that call, but at the top of the stairs she stopped. Araby was on the phone. Jenny held her breath, listening, as Araby said, "Yes, well, this one's pretty far out of touch with reality. She says her name is Jenny Cates. That Senator Buxton, who's running for president, is her real father, and that Buxton and Governor Alfonso killed her uncle, tried to kill her mother, and now they're trying to kill her." A pause, then "Mmm-hmm. It's a story. Rammed on the highway. Sent careening into a fiery car crash, and running all night through forests. Yes, that would be a good idea. I think this is a little beyond my abilities. You can pick her up anytime. She's not going anywhere."

"Like hell she's not." Jenny turned and went upstairs. In the bathroom were clean clothes that Araby had laid out. Everything but shoes. Jenny dressed. As she heard Araby coming upstairs, she pulled the nightgown over them and crawled into bed, pretending to be asleep. Araby came in very quietly, moved the panda, and sat in the chair. Jenny faked being asleep, regulating her breathing to a pace slower than her body liked. *Go away,* she thought. *Leave me in peace. Why are you sitting there?* Araby's eyes, which had seemed warm and mysterious last night, now only seemed untrustworthy.

She sat so long Jenny wondered if the woman had fallen asleep. Finally, apparently satisfied that Jenny was sleeping, she crossed the room and reached for Jenny's purse. The same woman who had said, "I won't touch it. I promise."

Faking restlessness, Jenny suddenly moaned and turned toward Araby. The woman dropped her hand and moved away, waiting to see what would happen next. When Jenny didn't move, she walked swiftly to the door and left.

As soon as the footsteps died away, Jenny threw off the nightgown, shoved the diary into her purse, and hurried down the stairs. She searched everywhere for her shoes, but only found a too large pair of rubber boots. Maybe Araby kept her girls safe from the street by locking up their shoes. She found her jacket on a peg in the laundry room. Still cold and damp, but better than nothing.

Outside the sky was growing light. The world was still a soft gray in the fog, but it was lightening from battleship to dove. Another night with only minimal sleep, but it was time to travel on. As she watched through the window, a dark car pulled around the corner and coasted to a stop at the curb across the street. The door opened and a tall man emerged. A man Jenny had seen before. Awkward in her rubber boots, Jenny went to the back door and slipped out.

"The game is up."
—Shakespeare, "Cymbeline"

CHAPTER NINETEEN

Having traversed the terrain at night in the fog, stumbling along at Fireman Tony's side, she had no idea how far it was back to the river but instinct told her to go that way. Maybe a primitive thing handed down from her ancestors. When you've lost your way, follow the rivers. She felt very lost. The real reason to head for the river? To get rid of the diary.

The ink would dissolve in seconds and her mother's precious words disappear. Her mother's tears had already dissolved some; her tears had muted others. Now, painful as it was, she had to let the water wipe out the written record of that brief, good love. Then all that would be left would be her mother's memories, and Senator Buxton's, if he still gave a damn somewhere in that politicized soul.

Well, the words were in her mind, too. And somewhere there was that vile tape, Uncle Billy's malicious intrusion onto their private joy and Buxton's darkest secrets. If what Billy's girlfriend had said was true, Jenny might know where it was.

She was walking as fast as she could without calling attention to herself, clomping along in the awkward boots. She wanted to kick them off and go free, but freedom in the form of ice-cold, gravelly sidewalks wouldn't be freedom long. As she moved through the drizzly morning, her resolution to find Senator Buxton and confront him hardened into certainty. She couldn't see another way to stop this. She had to go right to the top. The question was how. She'd imagined marching to the phone and calling him. Now that her brain was working, she could see the folly of that. It wasn't sensible to call someone who's trying to kill you and suggest a meeting.

What then? Her mother's voice was back in her head. Don't just impulsively dive into the middle of things, Jenny. Think it through and make a plan. She recalled her mother's eerie stillness, so frightening and unnatural, in the cold light of that hospital room. Her mother hadn't planned. She'd considered the possibility of exposure, but hadn't anticipated danger. Why would she? Having made the supreme sacrifice for Jim Buxton, loving him enough to let him go, how could she contemplate the possibility he might deem her expendable?

Yet she'd given the diaries to Charlie.

The beautiful cadence of the words from Corinthians came to her. 'Love suffereth long, and is kind; love envieth not; love vaunteth not itself, is not puffed up, doth not behave itself unseemly, seeketh not her own, is not easily provoked, thinketh no evil; rejoiceth not in iniquity, but rejoiceth in the truth; beareth all things, believeth all things, hopeth all things, endureth all things.' Her mother had loved much, endured much, forgiven much. Had Buxton, having benefited from that generous love, tried to kill her?

Why did she think it was Buxton? Why not Alfonso? What if it had been Alfonso's people, only intending to find the diaries, or that tape, and the attack on her mother had been a panicked reaction when things went awry? Because of what she'd overheard from Morrissey and Trask? Because though they'd hounded her from pillar to post and made her life a walking agony, she couldn't see them as killers? She knew there were men who were utterly two-faced, who would play whatever role, and do whatever deed was necessary to accomplish their ends, but when she thought of Morrissey in the ambulance, the way, when she broke down, he'd abandoned his questioning to comfort her, she couldn't see him as a killer. He'd been kind and gentle. It was no act. If their goal had been to kill, they never had to bring her out from under that tree. They could have killed her and left her there.

She reached the fire station, looking back as she crossed the street. Their car was speeding toward her. It was no contest. Two men in a car. A tired girl in clumsy boots. But the bridge was just ahead. Hoping she wouldn't fall, she fumbled in her purse, searching for the diary. The car paused at the stop sign, a whisper of a nod toward law obedience, and spurted toward her. She pulled the book out, spilling her possessions onto the street. No time to gather them. As the car pulled up to the curb beside her, and the doors popped open, she kicked off the boots and put on a final, desperate, burst of speed.

The diary was out at the end of her arm, trailing between her fingers. Was she over the water? She glanced down. It rushed below her, roiling from the heavy rain, an ugly final resting place for her mother's passionate words. She turned to face Morrissey.

He rushed at her with impossible speed. An unstoppable juggernaut. Massive. Tough. Official. His face hard and cop-like, his hand automatically going toward his gun as he called, "Stop! Toss that book over here, and put your hands on your head."

Frozen in his path, she felt as a mouse must feel when there is no escape and the cat is pouncing. *Go ahead and shoot me*, she thought. *I haven't come this far, endured this much, to fail my mother now. You don't get this diary.* She felt an electric tingle from the fingers holding it out over the water. She didn't want these words to be destroyed, when there might not be any more. Couldn't open the hand. Clear as bell, she heard her mother's command. "Let go, Jenny. Let go."

Morrissey was almost upon her. "Drop it!" he yelled. "Drop it on the ground and put your hands on your head."

With a pain as sharp as if it had been severed from her fingers by a blade, she let the diary fall. The pain raced up her arm and straight to her heart. Her arm, heavy from the cast, dropped to her side.

"No!" Morrissey's roar filled the morning, rolling over her like thunder, echoing in her ears as though two huge hands had been clapped over them. Dizzy and terrified, still the captive of that singeing pain from letting the diary go, she put her hands on her head and said, "I give up."

Morrissey was already in motion. She watched him launch himself into the air and come at her, his face sweating and furious. The impact carried her helplessly backwards and slammed her hard onto the sidewalk.

Instinctively, she followed her self-defense instructor's instructions. Tuck your head and roll with it. He hadn't anticipated the mass of Morrissey. Her back and then her shoulders slammed into pavement. Her head landed with an ugly crack and bounced like a basketball. The second time, it was her cheekbone that slammed against the pavement. Cheekbone and temple, the delicate bones reverberating, transmitting the blow through her head. Air flew out like a popped balloon and for a time she couldn't even worry about whether her brains were seeping out her ears or whether her face was broken. Her reality was the croaking gasp of her lungs, her consciousness the terrifying sensation of not breathing.

Gradually, she realized she was going to live. Given the savage pain in her head, she wondered why she'd want to. She lay pinned to the ground, awash with strong emotions. High because she'd managed to keep the diaries from his grasp. Desolate because she'd had to destroy them. Terrified because she was back in their hands, and furious at what Morrissey had done. Over it all, she had a passionate desire for oblivion, to enter the darkness swirling through her consciousness that was trying to nullify her senses and take her under.

She looked up at Morrissey, still lying on top of her, looming like an angry lover, pressing her down onto the gravelly sidewalk, and whispered. "Please don't hurt me anymore."

He lifted off her, grunting as he heaved himself onto his knees. The cold wind blew over her. Water trickled down her neck. The new damage from being slammed to the pavement joined all the old aches and pains that had awakened in a chorus of agony. She was ready to let darkness take her.

She looked up at him, searching for some gentleness or compassion. Saw only anger and frustration at losing the diary, at not getting there in time. He stood, staring down at her, huge and silent and grim. Trask handed him his hat and he set it carefully back on his head. Rested his hand on his gun.

Rain splashed into her face as the last of her fight ebbed away. She couldn't run. There wasn't an inch of her that didn't hurt. She pulled her exhausted arms up with painful slowness—they seemed to weigh a ton— and rested them carefully on her aching head. "I give up," she said. "Don't shoot."

GOVERNOR ALFONSO'S HOTEL ROOM

ON THE CAMPAIGN TRAIL

Alfonso was in the shower, soaping his morning erection and thinking about Keris Carlyle's ass, when the phone rang. Reluctantly, he abandoned the pleasures of self-abuse for the duties of the candidate, reached out a soapy hand, and gathered up the phone. "Yes?"

"Van Allen, sir. We've got her. Morrissey and Trask are bringing her in now. They should be at Morrissey's place in about an hour."

"How's our girl, Van?"

"A little the worse for wear, sir. Morrissey says it might be wise to have a doctor check her out."

"What happened?"

"Morrissey had to tackle her, sir""

The Governor pictured the vast bulk of Morrissey landing on anyone, and whistled. "Guess we'd better follow his advice then. This is a VIP guest, after all. I suppose we're lucky she's alive. Not much use to us if Morrissey squashed her flat. Tell him I'll meet them there. Can you arrange for the doc?"

"I'll take care of it."

Years into politics, it still tickled Lou Alfonso to have an upright guy like Van Allen, with his hard cop's face and his cold cop's eyes, calling him "sir." Van Allen knew he hit his wife. Van Allen had driven her to the hospital a couple of times, and still treated him with respect. And gave every sign of believing that whatever Lou Alfonso wanted was what should be done. It was the high that came from having his own way, from people standing up when he walked into a room, hanging on his every word, treating him like what he said was special and important, it was the high that came from all the perks of politics that made him lust for higher office.

After today, things should get surer. After today, when he was going to lay the groundwork to bat poor Jim Buxton out of the ball park. He sure hoped Morrissey hadn't done the girl too much harm. A little sore and shaky was good. It would make her easier to manage. He just didn't want concussions or broken bones, and he needed her face to be all right. No one, looking at a girl with black eyes or a broken nose, was going to see that dazzling blue-eyed resemblance to Senator Buxton.

For now, he'd play it by ear. He hung up the phone and stepped back into the shower, wondering if he should take Keris with him when he visited the girl. Strictly speaking, the girl should have a woman with her, especially if the doctor was going to poke and prod. But he liked the idea of keeping her isolated. Surrounded only by big, mean cops. He'd check out this girl first, then decide what to do.

IN A CAR

SOMEWHERE IN
WESTERN MASSACHUSETTS

Mr. Lopes listened to the last of Van Allen's words and smiled at Mr. Smith. "*Sheeit*, Rocky, wouldn't you think a cop with that much experience on him would know enough to use a land line?"

Mr. Smith touched the ends of his mustache with a fingertip and smiled, just a band of white in the darkness. "Makes our job easier, Bullwinkle, and I never complain when folks make our job easier. Betcha a twenty we follow them right to this guy Morrissey's house and they never notice."

"Bumpkins," Lopes said. "I just hope he doesn't live way out in the country. Country places give me the creeps. Harder to hide and there's always the risk of dogs."

"Think we ought to call Baldy?"

Lopes laughed. "Baldy needs his beauty sleep."

"Baldy pays the bills."

"Can't call Baldy," Lopes said, "unless we use a land line, and how the hell we gonna use a land line when we've gotta follow these guys?"

Smith smiled again. "These guys got a tracking device on the underside of their car."

"Rocky, you are amazing. I ever tell you that?"

"Not since yesterday."

He fired up the battered white van and pulled onto the highway a discrete distance behind the New York state police car carrying Trask, Morrissey and Jenny Cates. On the side, in peeling black letters, it said Houdini Locksmith, and an 800 number. The van had New York plates.

"We'll wait until they get settled. Then call Baldy."

"Otherwise he'll just be wetting his pants."

"His expensive pants."

"And we wouldn't want that, would we?"

"No," Lopes said. "We wouldn't want that." He pulled a gun case from the back and snapped it open. "I think I'm just going to shoot her."

Smith made a sound that might have been a protest.

"Yeah, I know Baldy wants her alive. But Baldy's not being practical, you know. I mean, we've got a good chance of putting a bullet into her through a window and driving away while they're still running around like scared ants. But getting her out alive? I don't know about you, but it's too risky for me. I want to live to see another day. And these New York cops are tough."

Smith gave another snort, this one more like laughter.

"Aw, come on, Rocky. You see what he did to that girl? He ought to get a penalty for piling on like that. Probably broke every bone in her body."

"So? You're going to shoot her."

"At least it's quick and humane. Put her out of her misery. Which I'd bet she's in a lot of right now. I don't like it, you know?"

"Never realized you were such a humanitarian, bro."

Lopes stared ahead at the rhythm of the wipers. "There's a lot about me you don't know." He started fiddling with the gun.

"Stop up the access and passage to remorse,
That no compunctious visitings of nature
Shake my fell purpose…"
—Shakespeare, "Macbeth"

CHAPTER TWENTY

Morrissey at her head and Trask at her feet, they carried her to the car, slung her into the back seat like a bag of laundry, and took off. With her hands cuffed behind her back, Jenny was tossed around the moving car with no more control over her motion than an apple in a pail of water. She could hear them talking occasionally in low voices, and once or twice heard them on the radio, but she couldn't make out anything that they were saying.

It was cold in the car and her sodden clothes sapped her body heat. She shivered uncontrollably, wishing she could return to the deep gray fog that had overtaken her as she lay on the sidewalk. There was no escape from this reality, a reality, to use a word people tossed around carelessly as Kleenex, that sucked. Her head throbbed. Her bruised face was so swollen it hurt to blink or move her mouth. Her back ached. Her shoulders ached. Her cracked ribs ached. The cuffs cut into her arm above the cast on her broken wrist, and that ached. Her torn and bruised feet ached. She was hungry, freezing, and thirsty.

Her heart ached.

There had been times in the last few days when she'd felt powerful or adventurous. She'd enjoyed moments of triumph when she'd once again set herself free, one small woman against a hostile world. Like scoring against a stronger team, she'd relished the feeling of underdog triumphant, even when she was miserable and hurting. Now she felt none of that. Not even a life-time of Lila Friedman's coaching could get her to pull herself together. She didn't feel like a fighter; she felt like a whipped dog, waiting for someone to kick her again, certain another kick was inevitable. Her storehouse of strength and stamina was empty.

She knew despair was her worst enemy. If she let herself wallow in self-pity, she was more at risk of being compliant so they'd be nice to her. But she couldn't help it. How much more down and out could she be?

If only she could sleep. If she got some rest, she might be able to muster some resistance. She closed her eyes and tried counting but each time she'd get herself lulled into a nearly somnolent state, the car would shift lanes or Trask would brake or they'd hit a bump. She'd be tossed around and pain would bring her right back to the surface, gasping, fingers clenched helplessly against her spine.

Besides, she was too cold to sleep. She wanted to ask them for a blanket, a drink, something for the pain, but pride wouldn't let her. Not even when Trask braked so sharply she rolled off onto the floor, her ribs jammed against the hump, her face mashed into the carpet, pain dancing like fire in her swollen cheek. She just lay there, teeth clenched, hurt and hating them, until Morrissey glanced back, saw what had happened, and told Trask to stop.

Morrissey would have just tossed her back on the seat and gone on, she felt it in the hands already digging into her ankles, but Joe Trask stopped him. "Gently, Tom, gently," he urged. The iron hands around her ankles became cushioning hands under her hips, raising her carefully back onto the seat. Trask touched her face, her hands, his own hands so warm she wanted to burrow into them. "She's soaked through," he said. "Freezing. We've got to get these wet things off her."

"It's only another forty, fifty minutes," Morrissey said, the anger still in his voice.

Trask only said, "I'll bring the girl in if that's what Alfonso wants, but I'm not putting her through unnecessary misery because your nose is out of joint." She opened her eyes and looked at him. He looked miserable. "Gotta turn you on your side, Jenny, get those cuffs off so we can get you out of these wet things." He pulled back out of the car and spoke with Morrissey over the roof. "Could you get the blanket?"

She only heard the rumble of Morrissey's reply, and then Trask turned her, undid the handcuffs, and her arms fell free. "Ouch!" she said.

"Sorry," Trask said, and then, "What hurts?"

"What doesn't?"

She must be a mess. He cringed whenever he looked at her. "We'd like to get some of your wet clothes off," he said. "It would be easier if you got out of the car."

"Aren't you afraid I'll run?" she said, and then, "I can't move." Not just talk. Her brain said move and nothing moved. "Don't start being nice to me, okay? It's too late for that. Just get back in the car and drive. Maybe you should put me back on the floor. Like Morrissey said, what's another forty or fifty minutes of jarring to a couple broken bones? The more miserable and beaten-down I am the better, right? It'll make me that much easier to manage. Isn't that what Alfonso wants?"

She was being difficult. She didn't give a damn. She heard the mumble of Morrissey's voice, then Trask stepped aside and Morrissey hauled her out of the car, supporting her with one arm while he pulled off her wet coat and shirt, the way you'd undress a sleepy child. She needed the support. She had the muscle tone of a wet noodle. Then he wrapped both arms around her, pulling her tight against him so she was facing away, and said, "Pants," to Trask in an impatient voice, lifting her off her feet as Trask, having fumbled with the button and zipper, tugged down her jeans and whisked them away.

She was standing beside a highway in her underwear on a rainy day in March, black and blue and shivering, after being publicly undressed by two indifferent policemen. This was part of the manipulation, part of their campaign of depersonalization. She should be in a Russian or Chinese prison, not standing beside an American highway. If anyone ever asked what she did on spring break, she'd certainly have a story for them. Welcome to Gulag Amerika.

"Blanket," Morrissey said, taking it from Trask. He wrapped her as if she were in a papoose, and, scooping her up in his arms, bent and climbed into the back seat, laying her out on the seat with her head and shoulders cradled in his lap. She saw the surprise on Trask's face. "Couldn't stand those bloodhound eyes any longer, Joe," Morrissey said. "You want me to pamper the little princess, that's what I'll do. You wanna pass back her purse and that thermos?"

Both were handed back.

"Now drive. We don't want to keep the Governor waiting. And turn up the heat."

"Little princess?" she said. "Fuck you, Tom Morrissey."

She closed her eyes again, worn out from confrontation, physical manipulation, and humiliation. Too cold to be ashamed, she burrowed into his lap, seeking warmth. He fumbled through her purse, shaking out pills, and unscrewed the top of the thermos. She smelled coffee. "Okay," he said, raising her head a little, "Open your mouth." She felt the chalky sensation of pills on her tongue. Chalky pills and one smooth one she didn't recognize. "Okay. Drink this. Careful. It may be hot. Swallow. Again."

The heat burned her empty stomach. She didn't want to drink it. She wanted to pour it on herself, rub it on her skin, wallow in it. But he took the cup away. "That's good. Now hold on a sec while I put my seatbelt on."

Hold on? As if she could. Her body wobbled like a heavy flower on a fragile stalk. And it hurt. It seemed an eternity before she heard the snap of metal into metal. "Good girl. Now go to sleep." He draped an arm across her and pulled her close. Vaguely, the engine hum and the pills lulled her to sleep, she felt his fingers carefully brushing the hair away from her face, stroking her head like a parent soothing a cranky child.

Slowly, she began to thaw, her body softening like wax as it warmed. His fingers kept up their gentle, steady rhythm. She heard him sigh. Imagined him whispering, "I'm sorry."

She wanted to tell both of them to go to hell. Fly at them in the fierceness of her anger, cry out her outrage at what they were doing. Ask them how they could. Where they got the right. Where her rights had gone. But even as she felt the first faint return of strength, she was drawn down into darkness.

"I pass, like night, from land to land;
I have strange power of speech…"
—Coleridge, "The Rime of the Ancient Mariner"

CHAPTER TWENTY-ONE

The doctor pulled the covers up and turned to the waiting policemen. Jenny, emerging from the throes of a drugged sleep, struggled to listen. Her brain was woozy, perception filtered through cotton. "What did you guys do to her, anyway? Tie her to the back of a car and drag her here?" He sounded young and nervous. His hands on her had felt nervous, too, rough and chilly as he'd poked and prodded, trying not to hurt her and managing to squeeze or jam a finger into every tenderest spot.

Her head hurt. When she tried to open her eyes, the light was too painful, so she closed them again. She didn't think they knew she was conscious. The third pill Morrissey had given her must have been a sleeping pill. She had no memory of being brought here, had woken only to the doctor's insistent prodding. The gray clouds of sleep she had sought now swarmed around her. She had to fight to stay awake.

"What's the bottom line?" Morrissey said, ignoring the question. "The Governor will want to know."

"She's fine. I mean there's no major damage, as far as I can tell, so we don't need to put her in a hospital. Not that I could find broken bones without an X-ray. The bruising is extensive, though. You might try some ice for her face. It doesn't feel like the cheekbone is broken." He trailed off. Jenny wondered whether he thought it was broken and was afraid to say. It sure felt broken. But so did the rest of her.

He cleared his throat. "Mostly she needs rest. Rest and fluids. Lots of fluids. Keep her warm. Pain killers if she wants them. And don't let her move around a lot. If she does get up, watch her carefully for dizziness. That's a big bump on her head. Looks like a minor concussion. You know the drill. Watch for blurred vision. Bleeding. Wake her up periodically. Just, you know, treat her gently… uh… keep her in bed and everything should heal nicely on its own. Those bruises look like a Jackson Pollack. It's too bad about her face…"

He trailed off. Probably Trask and Morrissey intimidated him. "I… uh… need to take some glass out of her foot, and put in a couple of stitches."

"Go ahead," Joe Trask said.

"I… uh… need some things from my car."

"Go ahead."

"Yeah. Sure. I'll be right back." The guy was acting so weird Jenny wondered why they didn't follow him. Maybe they were used to intimidated people behaving oddly.

The door opened and shut. "Weird guy," Trask said.

"Maybe not used to seeing female patients without a nurse in the room," Morrissey said. "And the thought of Alfonso scares him witless. What do you suppose he meant by too bad about her face?"

"Maybe the Governor wanted to take her picture or something."

"Not today he doesn't. Today our pretty little girl doesn't look too pretty."

Jenny resisted the urge to rub her face. She didn't need to know how swollen it was. No. Our pretty little girl wasn't pretty today and she didn't give a damn. Even if she was an unwilling candidate in the Miss Fugitive America contest, today she didn't feel congenial or talented. She'd already amply demonstrated the limits of her ability to run and hide, the skill which had carried her this far in the contest. Which left the swimsuit and evening gown portions. And to hell with those, too.

"Poor kid. Speaking of the Gov, you got an old T-shirt we could put on her or something, Tom?"

"You've got a real thing for this girl, haven't you, Joe?" Morrissey sounded amused.

"You know what a softy I am. He's my boss, Tom, right or wrong, but we both know he's a pig about women."

"So now that we've knocked the crap out of her and dragged her here, you would like her modestly attired for her audience with the Governor?"

"If you want to put it that way."

There was the slide of a drawer opening and shutting, and then Morrissey said, "Here."

"Cops do it standing up?" Trask said.

"My nephew. His idea of a joke, I think."

"You do it," Trask said. "You're pretty good at undressing women. Let's see you dress one."

"Piece of cake," Morrissey said.

She felt the springs wince as he sat on the bed and pulled down the covers. "Hey, Jenny," he said, softly. "Are you with us?"

She opened her eyes. Closed them again. It was still too bright. "My head hurts."

"We're having company soon. We thought you might want to get dressed."

"Can't," she said listlessly. "Can't move. Hurts. Everything."

"No problem," he said. "I'll help." He slipped the shirt over her head, threaded her arms through the sleeves, and lifted her up with one hand while he slid the shirt down with the other. "There you go."

"Maybe I could just die?"

"Not even close."

She felt the shift of his weight as he prepared to leave. "Morrissey. Wait."

"What?"

It was all back in his voice—wariness, distrust, the remnants of his anger. More than she could deal with now. He wasn't about to satisfy her curiosity about Alfonso, or allay her fears. Probably they were justified anyway. Why wouldn't she be afraid of someone who'd go to these lengths to have her kidnapped? "Never mind." There was the infuriating sting of tears against her eyelid. She turned away from him, onto her side, and pressed her face into the pillow. She felt like she'd been zipped in a tight-fitting pain suit. Her own skin. "Never mind," she whispered.

"No," he said impatiently, "what?"

"Alfonso. Is he going to hurt me?"

"Oh, Christ!" The springs groaned again as he got up. "We don't work like that."

She opened her eyes, ready to argue. Saw she didn't have to. Awareness of what he'd just said was all over his face.

"Oh, Christ!" he said again, and stalked out of the room. Over by the door Trask stood, his hands clasped behind his back, staring intently at the floor.

The doctor returned, peeled away the covers, and began to work on her feet. Whatever else he'd fetched from the car, it was clear he'd fetched himself a strong drink. The combination of alcohol and Listerine was overpowering. It seemed to have cheered him up, though. He hummed little off-key bits of tune as he worked, numbing, cleaning, stitching and fishing for bits of glass.

"No dancing tonight, I guess," she said.

He jumped, stabbed her with a needle, apologized, and exhaled loudly. "Am I hurting you?"

"No. No. It's fine," she said, as though he were a normal doctor and she a normal patient.

"How are you feeling?"

"Thirsty. A little bit sick. I hurt all over."

He nodded, poked vigorously at her foot, held up a sharp piece of glass triumphantly. "Got it," he said. "The way you feel. It's perfectly normal, under the circumstances."

"Which are anything but normal, right, doctor?"

"I wouldn't know, would I? We should get you something. Something to drink. Officer." He waved a thin, pale hand at Trask. "Maybe you could?"

"You're aware you don't have my permission to examine me, aren't you, doctor?" Speaking took energy. She swallowed and finished what she wanted to say. "I'm not a minor, nor am I incompetent, and I have been forcibly abducted by these two flunkies working for Governor Alfonso."

"That's enough," Joe Trask said. "No more talking."

She tried to push herself up on the pillow, the better to confront him, but any variation from the horizontal made her sickeningly dizzy. "Joe, you can't—"

He leaned into her face. "I said, 'shut up.' Something about that you don't understand?"

"*Et tu*, Joe?" she whispered. She closed her eyes again. Confrontation took too much out of her. She was a slowly recharging battery. Each time the charge got high enough, she sputtered to life and used up the accumulated energy. She'd never get anywhere doing this. She needed rest.

"How much longer?" Trask asked the doctor.

"Two, three minutes. Another piece of glass and some bandages."

"Well, hurry it up."

The doctor did as instructed. Hurrying, he managed, once again, to poke or squeeze tender, wounded spots, until Jenny, like Trask, was eager to have him leave. Unstoppable tears ran down her face. Finally, he dropped her foot, pulled up the covers, ordered her to open her eyes, and did some things with a flashlight. Then, without comment, he gathered his stuff and left.

In an effort to make peace with Joe, the only person around who'd shown her kindness, she said, "Thanks for the shirt, Joe." He didn't respond. Her tears flowed. *Crying a river*, she thought. It was so quiet in the room she could hear the clock tick. The clock ticking and Trask breathing.

She held out as long as she could, but finally she had to ask. "Joe. I'm sorry. I have to use the bathroom." He came and stood beside the bed, looking down at her helplessly. "Is it far?" she asked. He pointed to a door, looking nervous. "You don't have to carry me," she said. "I just need your arm. I'm so dizzy."

If he didn't move soon, he'd condemn her to the further humiliation of wetting her bed or having to crawl. It was just so damned unfair. She hadn't done anything. Why the hell couldn't he be civilized?

"Look," she said. "I'm not going to jump out the window or fly through the air."

Like a guy whose mother had made him ask an ugly girl to dance, he held out his arm.

Her stomach looped and danced like a bi-plane was practicing in there. Her feet felt like she was walking on hot coals. She thanked him at the door, withdrew her arm from his, and as soon as the door closed, she dropped to all fours and crawled to the toilet. It was pathetic and humiliating. Eventually, business attended to and her stomach wrung out like a wet dishtowel, she crawled to the sink, hauled herself up, and drank from the faucet. The icy water made her stomach writhe. She was too thirsty to care.

The woman in the mirror looked as if she'd been slapped in the face with an oar and had a bad case of one-sided mumps. Or like the before pictures from a plastic surgery ad. In just twenty-four hours, Jenny Cates of Hallowell, Maine will go from looking like an abused chipmunk to looking just like a political candidate.

Of course. If Alfonso couldn't have the diaries, he wanted her face. He wanted to exhibit her like a prize Holstein at the county fair, showing off her astonishing resemblance to her father. He was going to be disappointed when he saw what Morrissey had done. The green skin tone was definitely a plus.

Her legs were shaking and the room was spinning, so she prudently returned to all fours. Too tired to go any further, she stretched out on the floor and pressed her swollen face against the cool porcelain of the tub. Not even the commotion in the other room roused her, where a loud voice demanded, "Where the hell is she?"

Frankly, Scarlet, she didn't give a damn.

The bathroom door banged open and the loud voice exclaimed, "What the fuck! I thought the doc said she was fine? She looks dead to me."

Then, Morrissey was kneeling beside her, gently picking her up and carrying her out. This was becoming a game. Jenny would crawl away and Morrissey would find her and bring her back. A grown-up, high-stakes game of hide and seek. But she was always "IT" yet everyone was always trying to find her.

He put her back in bed, pulled up the blankets, and pressed a towel filled with ice against her cheek.

He wasn't as big as Morrissey, but Alfonso also made the springs groan when he sat down. He smoothed the hair off her face and took her hand in his. "I know you can hear me, Jenny. I'm Lou Alfonso, Governor of this great state, and, I think you know, a candidate for the Presidency. I'm sorry for all that has happened to you. I'm sure you've had a terrible, hellish week, all these bruises, broken bones. I know you've been tired and cold and hungry. And frightened. And all this time, when you may have thought we were chasing you, we've just been trying to save your life, little girl. Just trying to save your life."

He squeezed her hand, shifting on the mattress with an abruptness that sent pain reverberating through her body. "Now I know that when Tom Morrissey landed on you, you didn't see that as a humanitarian gesture, but Tom, here, well, he can be a bit impulsive, and he was afraid you were going to jump right off that bridge, darlin', and that would have been the end of little old you."

One more little girl or darling, one more bullshit bogus word and she'd throw up on him. Not the first time a manipulative adult had tried to tell her that their wrongful acts were "for her own good." A teacher in middle school had accused her of plagiarism and torn up a paper, refusing to give her a grade. Jenny had stood her ground, demanding that the teacher demonstrate a basis for the charge, which the teacher had been unable to do, and then, in a change of tactics, she had told Jenny that her writing was "too mature and sophisticated" and she needed to tone it down "for her own good."

Jenny had gone home and gotten a lawyer. Not hard, since she'd found one in the kitchen. It hadn't been hard to persuade the lawyer to take her case, either, since she'd immediately burst into righteous tears. Right now, she wished most desperately that she could call on that lawyer, or her dad. She wanted to see their faces, to gather them into her arms, to press herself against safe and familiar bodies. She understood the necessity to stand on her own two feet. But her feet were cut and battered, her legs weak and shaky. She was hurt and sick and all worn out, thrown into the ring with nothing to bring to the contest. She was a big girl but she wanted her mother.

"You do understand, don't you, that my competitor, Senator Buxton, thinks it's very important to have you out of the way?" Alfonso continued. "Who do you suppose drove your car off the road?" He bent over her, breathing a hot combination of coffee and breath-mints down into her face. Better than the doctor's alcohol and Listerine, but still a reminder her freedom in the broadest and narrowest senses was being infringed. "Who do you suppose that was? Jennifer, are you listening to me? Are you paying attention to what I'm telling you? Because what I'm saying to you is very important."

She closed her eyes and turned her head away, concentrating on trying not to be sick.

He grabbed her shoulder, the one badly bruised by the seatbelt, and shook her. "Open your eyes and look at me," he commanded, his fingers biting into her skin. Every shake sloshed her brain against her skull. The pain of it brought tears to her eyes. "Jennifer! I said open your eyes and look at me."

She opened them and said, "Stop that!"

"There's my girl," he said. "Now, Jenny, when I'm talking to people, I like them to pay attention. I like eye contact. As I was saying, your father, Senator Jim Buxton, is trying to have you—"

"My father's name is Bud Cates." Asshole. I am not your girl. I am neither simple-minded nor a child, and I am not playing your game. Behind him, she could see several people. A tall, rusty-haired man she didn't know. Behind him, Morrissey and Trask and another state trooper, all watching the interchange with interest. She swallowed. She was so thirsty. So miserable. Trying so hard not to be sick.

Alfonso bounced vigorously, shaking the mattress and sending new tremors through her fragile system, patted her shoulder roughly, and said, "You poor thing. You mean they never told you?"

"Told me what?" She closed her eyes again. She could barely hear Alfonso's voice over the pounding in her head. The way he kept jouncing her around, it was only minutes before she was sick again. "Could I have something to drink, please?" Hating him for making her beg.

"When we're finished," he said. "Open your eyes and look at me."

She tried, thinking maybe, if she cooperated, he'd give her a drink and stop jouncing, but she couldn't do it. "The light hurts."

His rough hand seized her shoulder again, fingers digging in, trying to compel her attention. "This will only take a few minutes, Jennifer, and it's important. I've taken time out of a very busy campaign schedule to come and see you. We've been expending considerable manpower over the past few days, trying to find you. Trying to keep you alive. And it's been no easy task, young lady!"

"No person shall be deprived of life, liberty, or property, without due process of law." A small pulse of rage pushed her words out.

The fingers dug deeper. He hadn't registered her meaning, only her opposition. His voice grew louder. Obviously he believed people understood better if you hollered at them. "And why do we have to work to keep you alive? Because your father wants you dead. Open your eyes and look at this."

She opened them. The light stabbed into her so fiercely it was like daggers in her pupils. He was holding something inches from her face. Too close to focus on, even if she hadn't been crippled by pain. She put up a hand to push it away, but he forced it back to her side. "Look at this," he commanded.

"Move it farther back and I'll try." Hating hearing her voice so shaky and pathetic.

"There! Is that better?" Slowly, cautiously, she tried again. It was a picture of Senator Buxton. A big, glossy color publicity photo. "You know who this is?"

"I'm a registered voter in the State of Maine. Of course I do."

"Now, look at this." He picked up a second picture, so that they were side-by-side in front of her. The second was her own picture. "A picture of you. A picture of your father, Jim Buxton. Your father." He spoke slowly and with great emphasis, as if she were profoundly simple. "Your father who is trying to kill you. Work with us, Jenny. Work with us. We're just trying to keep a man like that out of public office. A man who would murder his own child."

The pain was intensifying, the unholy glow of it filling her head. She felt like it might burst. She turned her head away from the pictures, and closed her eyes. It didn't help. "Sick," she murmured. "Sick, sick, sick."

"It is sick," he agreed. "Senator Buxton is a sick, evil, perverted man. He seduced your mother, sent men to attack her, sending her into an irreversible coma, and now he's trying to kill you. Look at him, Jenny. Look at this man." He shook her again and put her right over the edge.

Morrissey, coming from a lifetime of dealing with people in crisis, understood what was happening. "You'd better move, Governor," he said quickly, "or she's gonna throw up all over you."

Alfonso got out of the way just in time. Off the bed and out of the room, his entourage hurrying behind him. She heard him barking orders. "Get that doctor back here. What the hell's the matter with that man? He said she was fine when what I've got in there is a sick, battered child! How the heck am I going to show that to the press? They aren't going to say, oh, shock, horror, here's Buxton's daughter, they're going to say, looks like Alfonso's beaten up another one. Get that man back and tell him to do whatever is necessary to fix her! And fix her fast."

Jenny, curled in a tight, defensive ball, held her head in her hands and whimpered as the voice went on and on, while Morrissey and Trask silently changed the bed, changed her shirt, and washed her face. "I'm sorry," she murmured. "I tried."

Joe Trask put a cool washcloth on her forehead. "It's okay," he said. "You didn't do anything wrong."

"Joe." She grabbed his hand and hung on. She felt his hesitation, and then a yielding as he let his hand stay. Right now, that warm and human touch was like a lifeline to safety and the normal, even if he was one of "them."

"He scares me, Joe. I'm afraid he's going to hurt me. Hurt me more."
She'd met ruthless people who acted solely in their own self-interest. In
Alfonso she sensed something different. Alfonso didn't just cause harm
and pain incidentally. Alfonso was a sadist. He enjoyed causing pain
and humiliation.

"Don't worry, Jenny. We won't let anyone hurt you."

Dream on, Joe Trask. Dream on.

ON A ROOFTOP

IN THE OUTSKIRTS OF ALBANY, NEW YORK

Greedily, Mr. Lopes pulled the sandwich from the bag, peeled back the wrapper, and bit. Tomatoes, lettuce and onions bounced everywhere as he chewed. "Pretty damned messy," he mumbled, "but good." He peered down at the house across the street. "Awfully quiet over there, Mr. Smith. Anything happen while I was gone?"

Smith shook his head. "Nada. You call Baldy?" Lopes' affirmative was muffled by bread and cold cuts. "What he say?"

"He said he'd really like us to get the girl out of there in one piece. Sounded like he had bad gas or somethin', know what I mean? But Baldy's a tight-ass and a dreamer. No way we get the girl out of there in one piece."

"I'd settle for one clear shot."

"It would help if we knew what room she was in. And there's just the man to tell us."

A pearl-beige Avalon pull up behind the state police car. The doctor retrieved his bag from the back seat and went into the house.

Smith smiled eagerly. "You want this, or can I have him?"

"It's your turn," Lopes said. "Just don't take all night, okay? I do not want to still be sitting on this rooftop, clutching a high-powered rifle, when the sun comes up. Let's just do this girl and get out. I can't believe I'm spending another night on this effing roof, freezing my ass off."

"You barely have an ass," Smith said. "Nothing to freeze off there."

"My nuts, then," Lopes said. "And don't..."

Smith flapped a pale hand daintily. "As if I would." He shouldered a small pack and slipped away through the darkness, moving quietly for such an awkward-looking man.

Lopes watched Smith station himself in the rear seat of the doctor's car. Maybe there'd be a grieving wife and kids at home, but Lopes rather doubted it. The doc had the look of a solitary misfit. It hung on him like the awkward fit of his clothes, the uncontrollable impulse to drink, the defensive way he held his head. No loss, really. Not like the girl. He'd developed a genuine admiration for her. He consoled himself with the thought that one clean, quick shot to the head was probably better than the way she got knocked around by Alfonso and his cops. Either way, he didn't see her walking away from this. You can't beat on a smart kid like that and not have her come back at you.

He ate the rest of his sandwich, drank some coffee, and unwrapped a stick of Black Jack gum. Pretty soon the door opened and the doctor came out, got in his car, paused for a quick nip, and drove away. Never even bothering to look behind the seat.

"My heart aches, and a drowsy numbness pains
My sense, as though of hemlock I had drunk,"
—Keats, "Ode to a Nightingale"

CHAPTER TWENTY-TWO

Time had lost all meaning. Alfonso's nervous doctor had returned, armed with pills and needles. She had been ordered to drink, to swallow, had her arm swabbed with icy alcohol and been stabbed, ineptly, with needles. Almost immediately, she had felt a euphoric wave of pain relief and was plunged into dark sleep.

She was kept prisoner in the realms of sleep, coming to the surface occasionally like a marine mammal coming up for air. Gray and gloomy morning blended into drizzly gray afternoon, afternoon to a gradual lightening and a partly blue sky that faded into dusk, and dusk into a cold, clear night with twinkling stars and a rich, blue-black sky that deepened, finally, to black. In the darkness of the bedroom, she only told one from another when someone raised the shade to look out.

Alfonso came once. Stared, poked and prodded her in ways she was helpless to prevent, and held a muttered conversation with her captors, the only clear word she caught was "clothes." The doctor returned, stabbed her again with drugs, and proclaiming himself satisfied, went away. Alfonso would be pleased. The swelling was already going down. Her color was better. Her chemically-induced sleep was doing her a world of good.

The rest might be healing her physically, but inside her head, prisoner of chemicals she couldn't escape, nightmare followed terrifying nightmare as she tossed, sweating and miserable, in a swaddling tangle of sheets. She was being pursued relentlessly through the caverns of her mind by grunting, blood-drenched, faceless men. She woke, screaming, to find a strange face looming over her. He pinned her to the bed with iron hands and ordered her to calm down. No one was trying to hurt her. *He* was hurting her.

She looked around a strange room. Nothing familiar. She didn't know who he was. Why she was naked in this stranger's bed? She tried to push away the confining hands but they only tightened, pressing her firmly onto the bed. "Calm down," he ordered. "Calm down."

The harsh, shadowy man pinning her to the bed merged with the faceless figures from her nightmare. She struggled to free herself from those confining arms, screaming at him, "Let me go! Let me go!" She flailed at him with her hands, with her fist. He was a stranger, the enemy, and was forcing her down. The need to free herself from this nightmare exploded. She fought with fury and a desperation driven by primitive instinct. Fighting to survive.

"Cut it out. Goddammit!" he yelled into her face, tightening his grip.

She tried to wiggle away. The slippery sheets caught at her legs. Her feet, planted for leverage, stung and burned. She remembered running through fire. Ghostly hands grabbed and clutched. "No!" She screamed into the invisible face. "No!"

With her good hand, she clawed at him, searching for eyes, for something soft and vulnerable, some way to disarm him so she could escape.

The commanding voice of her self-defense teacher reminded her, "You don't have to be polite to someone who has invaded your space, who has grabbed you, who is trying to take you away. Get over your conditioning about not hurting others. He doesn't have it, and if you want to save your own life, you can't either. Look for his vulnerable points. Nose. Throat. Don't bother to go for the groin. Men expect that. But you can take your two fingers and go for the windpipe." The whisper of fingers on Jenny's throat. "Right here, and in a few seconds, bingo!"

Screaming at him to take his hands off her, screaming out the rage built up over days and nights of pursuit and captivity, screaming out her fear of being trapped, pinned down, of being chased, mauled, mangled, murdered, betrayed, awake or asleep. The hands wouldn't let go. He was going to let her go, dammit! No way was he keeping her pinned down on the bed one second longer.

Screaming, roaring, the freeing of her voice giving her a surge of energy powered by a rage so intense it felt like it was breaking right through her skin, Jenny brought her head up and slammed it as hard as she could into his face. He grunted with pain as he released her and brought his hands to his wounded nose. She slammed her fist into his throat. He rolled away from her, choking and gasping, clasping both hands to his face and throat.

The instant his hands were gone, she dashed across the room and locked herself in the bathroom. She crouched on the floor as tremors shook her, the aftershocks of that volcanic explosion. She'd deliberately attacked another person with the intention of doing harm. She'd never known she was capable of such rage, or deliberate violence. They had brought her down to their own level, degraded and terrified her until she had to fight for her life.

She huddled in the corner, her back pressed against the wall, the edge of the tub cold against her skin, arms wrapped tightly around her legs. She stared down at her bandaged feet. They were mottled purple with cold. Goose bumps rose like Braille under her fingers. She closed her eyes and rested her head on her knees. In the aftermath of such extreme anger, she felt fragile and exhausted. If it hadn't been automatic, she would have been too tired to breathe.

She recalled where she was, and who was responsible, but why was she naked? She hadn't been when she fell asleep. And then she knew. Words she'd heard dimly through sleep. She was naked because Alfonso wanted her as vulnerable as possible. Helpless and degraded and unable to run. She probably only had blankets and water because they were necessary to her physical recovery, to help heal her battered face so he could use it. The knowledge reoriented her, setting her right back in the middle of a simmering pool of anger. She would never help him, never cooperate, no matter what it cost her. She couldn't allow him to use her to help him win. She needed food. Clothes. Shoes. A way to escape.

Someone banged on the door. "Jenny? It's Morrissey. Will you let me in or do I have to break down the door?"

She didn't care. It was his door. Besides, to open the door, she'd have to move again. She was too tired to move.

"Jenny? Are you all right?" Another pause. "Please let me in. You know I just painted this door. I'd hate to have to break it but I will if I have to. Sooner or later you have to deal with us. There's no other way out of there."

Morrissey's voice had startled her. She was crying now, involuntary tears, like a fitful pump jolted into action. Big girls don't cry. These tears were anger, not sorrow or fear. Sometimes she thought she was brave. Sometimes she didn't know. She knew only that she wanted to be left alone here unless they were going to treat her decently. She would trade him an unmarked door for the things she needed. And no more drugs. Otherwise, she'd fight them every step of the way.

"Jenny, please. Let me come in and talk to you."

She got up, using the wall for help, and limped as far as the sink, leaning on it heavily. "Make you a deal," she said.

"You're not in a very good position for deals."

"It's your door, Morrissey. Go ahead and break it. What can you do to me that hasn't already been done? Hurt me? Drug me? Humiliate me?"

She undid the lock, then retreated to her corner, arms around her knees, waiting for a repeat of this part of their game, when Morrissey would burst in and carry her off again. Didn't he ever get tired of the same old same old?

The door opened. He stepped in and closed it part way behind him. At least he hadn't brought a battery of staring eyes so that they could all revel in her nakedness. In her abject vulnerability. It was a small room once Morrissey was in it. He crouched down on the floor a few feet away and studied her. "What the hell happened out there?" he asked.

Her mind was a jumble. Perhaps such strong emotions had left a wake of misfiring synapses. She searched for words. "You really want to know what happened out there?"

He nodded.

"Then don't yell at me."

"I didn't think I was yelling."

"I am fragile as tissue paper." She stood, hands at her sides, and looked at him. " "'What happened'? I was so…" Words eluded her. "Scared."

She searched for more words. "I was dreaming. Nightmares. Endless nightmares. All those drugs… I couldn't wake up. Huge, bloody men were chasing me. I ran and ran and I was falling." Tears ran down her face. "Then he grabbed me."

She could see it. She could feel it. But how to convey the frantic terror of it? She was too shaken to go on and hated herself for it, expecting him to yell or seize her and take her back into the bedroom, exposing her to the others, forcing her onto the bed where the needles, the drugs, the nightmares would start again.

He just stayed there, as if he had all the time in the world, as if he sat nightly on cold bathroom floors and listened while terrified women constructed their painful sentences. Perhaps he did.

"He was holding me down," she said. "I thought the people in the nightmare had finally caught me. I was trying... to make him let me go. With all the drugs and everything, I couldn't get out of the dream. I didn't know he was real."

He handed her a wad of toilet paper.

She wiped her eyes and blew her nose.

He took the crumpled paper, threw it away, handed her some more. "Take your time," he said.

"When I realized he was real, I panicked. I thought I was being attacked by a stranger. I didn't know where I was or why I was..." She hesitated. "Naked."

Had hitting her head on the sidewalk damaged her brain? She couldn't find words. "I'm not very experienced. Sexually. I mean, maybe some people, waking up like that... but I've never woken up naked with a strange man."

She didn't mean to tell him this. "All I could think was what was he going to do to me. How could I escape." Her laugh was more like a sob. "I sure got far, didn't I?"

She watched his face. She hadn't said these things for a purpose, but could see she was making a connection.

"You're hell on wheels, Jenny," he said. "There are plenty of big burly men not a quarter as capable as you are. Or as brave."

She pulled in a long, shuddering breath. "Oh, please. Don't."

Being told she was capable and brave wasn't comforting. She was like a rat in a maze. She'd escape and run like crazy, wearing herself out, and then they'd pick her up and stuff her back in a cage. She'd always hated being helpless.

He was crouching. She was standing. She straightened. There was no way to hide it, so just let him how naked she was. How real she was. "Don't say nice things to me. It's not fair. Not with what's going here. I don't know how much..." She finished in a whisper. "How much more I can take."

He stood, like he was going to reach for her, then hesitated. She could feel the heat of his body. She was so cold it hurt. A silent stand-off, facing each other. Jenny made no move to hide her body. It seemed too abject to attempt the meager modesty of an arm across her breasts, a hand across her crotch. It reminded her of Betty, in the kitchen. He'd probably seen it all already. Someone had undressed her.

She put out a hand to steady herself. Took his arm, sensing a shift in the power balance. "I think you're a good man," she said, "and I wonder how you can allow yourself... allow them... to do this to me."

"I'm trying to keep you alive," he said. "There are people out there trying to kill you."

They were only a foot apart now.

"More quickly, you mean. Less painfully. They just want me dead. They aren't planning to exhibit me for public scrutiny first. They want to close my eyes forever; you want to exhibit me to the press like something brought back from the wilds of Africa, so everyone can see how much my blue eyes look like Senator Buxton's. Will you at least let me get dressed first, before you parade me before the press? Or do I appear like this? Mottled and multi-colored?" She twirled slowly, dizzily, and came back to his arm.

"That's not fair, Jenny."

"What's fair got to do with anything that's happening here?"

She took his hand and brought it to her face, to her tender, battered, cheek. "You did this, Morrissey." She moved the fingers to the alarming lump on the back of her head. "And this. And then you threw me in the car and would have left me there in freezing misery, crumpled up like an old suit, because your ego was hurt. Like you might treat a criminal you were mad at. Like a criminal, when my only crime was trying to be free. To be safe.

"You would have left me there, if it hadn't been for Joe. Tender-hearted Joe. I worry about what this is going to do to him. How he'll go on calling himself a good guy?" Jenny swallowed. She wanted to move closer, drawn by his heat. "After what I did to that man, how am I going to call myself a good guy? That's what you've done to me. All of you. Made me more like you. More than this."

Moving his hand with hers, she traced the bruises on her shoulder down across her chest, over her breast, along her ribs and down her stomach. Heard the sharp intake of his breath. He didn't pull his hand away. She stepped closer and slid his hand to her back, tracking his fingers down her spine, every inch of it sore from being slammed onto the pavement. She left his hand just below her waist, in the hollow of her back. Now they were only six inches apart.

"I'm real," she said. "I'm a real flesh and blood person, just like you. I'm not a piece of printed campaign material. I breathe, I eat, I bleed. I suffer. I desire. I dream. Just like you. Can't you feel it?"

She could feel his heat. His trembling. He put his other hand out and pulled her against him. Belt buckle in her chest, shirt button in her ear. She didn't even come up to his shoulder.

His hands cupped her buttocks, ran up her back to her shoulders. Something deep in her belly clenched. A primitive urge to be warm, to be touched, to connect. To blow away all this gritty reality. To make this man want her. Force him to acknowledge her humanity.

Very gently, he pushed her away. "Oh, God, Jenny. You're so real. Don't tempt me." His voice was ragged.

"Tempt you? I didn't chose to be naked, Tom. Someone took my clothes away. Was it you?" She looked down at the floor. "I guess it doesn't matter much. I'm sure you've all seen me." She looked at her bruised body. "Sexy as hell, aren't I?"

She was so cold. He had been so warm. She moved toward him again. Saw him hesitate, then back away. "Please," she said. "I'm just so desperate to be warm. But I won't walk back out there like this. I can't."

She turned away from him. "How can you be so cruel?"

"Jenny, Jesus, I didn't—"

"Did you think it wouldn't matter, because I'm not someone you know? Because you were just following orders?"

She needed to lie down. Her legs felt like spaghetti.

"You never let a guy get a word in, do you?"

Like they were just two people talking. Well screw him. All her life she'd been letting the guys get in most of the words. "You're not just a guy, Morrissey. You're a kidnapper. You're a guy so twisted he'll knock a poor beaten down girl to the pavement and half-kill her. When you found me after the car crash, I thought you were a nice guy. I thought that you were kind. Hard to say which of us is the bigger dope. Me, for thinking that you're one of the good guys, or you, for believing it."

She wrapped her arms around herself, shivering. "Why don't you just go away?"

"I can't leave you like this."

"Oh, please, Morrissey. Why the hell not?"

He touched her shoulder lightly with a warm hand. "You're freezing in here. Come back to bed."

"And then it starts all over again?"

"At least you'd be warm."

"I'm afraid of the dreams."

"You can't stay here."

She knew it was true. Sooner or later, he'd run out of patience and do whatever he wanted anyway. "I'll make you a deal."

"What?"

"Send them out of the room. Anyone who's waiting out there. Then I'll come out."

"Sure."

"You haven't heard the rest. I want a cup of cocoa. Lovely, warm cocoa. And I want you to be the one to stay with me. So if the dreams come back, at least the face I see will be familiar."

He fingered his nose cautiously. "I've always rather liked it the way it is."

"I can't make any promises. And I want some clothes."

Morrissey was silent for a while. "Oh, hell, yes!" he exploded. "I'll send Joe for cocoa. I'll tell the other guys to wait outside. Will that do?"

"You make it sound like I drive a hard bargain."

"I'll be right back," he said. "And don't lock the damned door again."

He was gone a while. Jenny didn't think. Didn't plan. She huddled in her corner and waited. She was getting out of here somehow. And Morrissey would be the key.

Eventually he came back, carrying a blanket, and held out a hand to pull her up. He wrapped the blanket around her and she limped back to the bed. On a chair across the room was a small pile of clothes. He pointed to it. Then he went to his drawer and got a T-shirt, tossed it to her, and sat down in a chair, watching her like he was afraid to get too close.

Joe Trask knocked on the door and came in with a mug of cocoa. She had to hold it in two hands to keep it from spilling. "Thanks, Joe."

He gave her a cautious smile. "No problem."

Cocoa flowed into her like a voluptuous chocolate river, tasting better than she ever remembered anything tasting. She struggled into the

T-shirt, feeling almost normal, and wiggled down into the pillow. Sleep was tugging at her again. "Is it day or night?" she asked.

Morrissey raised the shade a little so she could see. "Night," he said.

She closed her eyes and slept. It wasn't long before the nightmares returned. When she woke, whimpering, Morrissey was lying beside her, stroking her like he'd done in the car. She reached over and pulled his head to hers, seeking the warmth of his lips. Knowing what she needed and knowing that never in life could logic explain it. In a world of dislocation, connection mattered. "I am human," she'd said.

He didn't argue. He didn't mention temptation, hers or his. He just said, "Jenny, are you sure?"

Her mumbled affirmative must have constituted informed consent. He switched off the light. Seemed to be able to find her just fine in the dark. Before she'd slept with Drew, Jenny had imagined a lover a lot like Morrissey. Gentle, tender, careful. Maybe he'd had to learn to be, because of his size. She heard the sound of tearing foil, and the latex snick of a condom. He said, "Jenny, I promise I won't hurt you," and slid slowly in. Just as he reached the first shuddering gasp of his climax, the headboard above them exploded in a shower of splinters.

Grabbing her, he rolled them both sideways off the bed. They landed on the floor with a jarring crash, Morrissey on top. At first, Jenny thought that his sudden somnolence was simply post-orgasmic bliss, until she felt his blood dripping onto her face. She struggled to get up, but she was trapped beneath him. Still intimately connected when she didn't know whether he was alive or dead.

She began to scream.

"Only the deep sense of some deathless shame…"
—John Webster, "The White Devil"

CHAPTER TWENTY-THREE

The door burst open and the room erupted with activity. Lights going on, men and noise, a commotion of shocked faces, unintelligible voices, staring eyes. She was as dumbly helpless as a punch-drunk boxer. When they hauled him off her, she curled up on her side and threw an arm over her blood-drenched face, lying there until Trask hauled her to her feet, draped a blanket over her shoulders, and led her away.

"Are you hurt?" he demanded. He had the sick, worried look her father had worn in the hospital, the face you wear when someone you care about is struck down.

She touched her cheek with a hand that didn't seem to belong to her, stared at her bloody fingers, and shook her head. Wounded in spirit, perhaps beyond repair, but not any more physically hurt than before. Before what? She couldn't make sense of things. What she'd done. What he'd done. How they'd come to it. How everything led to betrayal and violence.

Trask dragged her into the kitchen and opened a door. She expected another place to lock her up until they decided what to do. They were bound to be angry about what had happened to Morrissey. And besides, she was their kept woman. Transported across state lines for immoral purposes.

The door opened into a tiny half-bath. Flowered wallpaper, warm yellow tiles. He shoved her inside. "Wash that blood off. Hurry."

She had to use the mirror to clean off Morrissey's blood but couldn't meet her own eyes. Some people went through life being as willful as they wanted, and nothing ever happened to them, while when she tried to exert her will, things got worse. Now look what she'd done. By wanting something in this unending morass of pain and fear that felt powerful and rejuvenating and good, she'd probably killed him. No wonder Joe Trask was mad at her.

He banged on the door. "Hurry up in there."

Hastily, she wiped her face and stepped out. He wasn't nearly as big as Morrissey, but he towered over her, stern-faced, square-shouldered, and fierce. Head bowed, she stood there, waiting for her next imprisonment, the next indignity, the next infliction of pain. On the floor beside him lay a large duffel bag. Beside it, several lethal-looking guns. He pointed to it. "Get in." His face was so twisted with anger she just dropped the blanket and crawled into the bag, afraid to argue. He dumped the blanket on top of her, and started putting in the guns.

She heard footsteps and a stranger's voice. "That's a lot of firepower, Trask."

"And I've got to get it out of here before the press starts snooping around and someone wonders why a state cop has stuff like this in his kitchen."

He dropped another gun on top of her and zipped up the bag. Another prison. If she wasn't claustrophobic coming into this, she sure was now. If she ever came out. She was sure the bullet that had hit Morrissey had been meant for her. He'd said, "I'm just trying to save your life." What incredibly ironic meaning this last hour gave to the words, "serve and protect."

She tilted wildly as he lifted the bag. "I'm putting you in my trunk," he said. "Don't move. Don't yell. Don't say a word. Do nothing until I come get you. Understand?" His words flew at her with brisk precision.

She didn't understand anything. How do you go from drug-induced nightmares to passionate love-making to being pinned to the floor by a dying man and make sense of the experience? She'd fought her way back from that awful drugged haze to this?

A door opened and closed. Through the canvas, she felt the cold. A rough jolt as he set her on the ground. Keys jingled. She was lifted again, set down on a hard surface, the heavy guns pressing down on her. The blanket slipped. She felt cold metal on her naked back. In minutes, she'd run the gamut of intimate contacts from warm flesh to cold steel.

The trunk lid slammed and she was sealed in icy darkness. A miserable sheaf of time passed. Folded embryonically in her canvas womb, she lived and relieved the last days, the last hours, all the awful, dislocating events, beginning with Drew in the kitchen. Her never-still mother deathly still in a pool of blood. The adrenaline spike of fear when that car smashed into her. The scream of tortured metal and crashing glass. Crawling away through the darkness. Being chased through the woods at night. Standing by the roadside, staring up at the massive truck behind those piercing lights, hoping it would stop. The stranger bending over her, forcing her down onto the bed. How many times had fear stopped her heart and stolen her breath?

No wonder she'd had nightmares. She'd lived a nightmare. It was icy cold here, taking her back to that night on the streets, wandering into the Dunkin' Donuts, taken up by a friendly fireman and led to another safe house that turned out not to be. Would she ever trust anything again?

She'd felt pain in its many guises, sharp, intense, global, diffuse. Pain that woke her. Pain that movement woke. The pain of dislocation, of betrayal, of an information void, of not knowing what to do, whom to trust, where to turn. She thought when she was done with this, if she survived, academics would have to wait. First, she'd sleep for a year. Sleep for a year, get some therapy, and never, ever, have sex again.

She saw herself huddling in the bathroom. The cold sensation of the tiles against her skin. Trying to communicate with Morrissey and not being able to find words. The strange impulse that had made her take his hand. The inexplicable mixture of anger and attraction she'd felt. A mind and body engorged with feeling, wanting to counter her fear with the heated release of intimacy. And her awareness that at that moment she'd had power—the power of his attraction to her. His own need. He would've helped her, she thought, when it was over. But not when it ended this way.

Suddenly, the car lurched into motion and shot down the street, Jenny a helpless piece of baggage, rolling around the trunk like unsecured groceries. This time she was beyond anger, lacking the capacity for any more passion, any more feeling. Pressed into the apathy of despair by the sensation of Tom Morrissey's lifeless body on her own, by the weight of the cold steel that pressed down on her now. She'd given up.

It had been hard to let herself go with Drew. It had taken a lot of pressure from him, and several glasses of wine, to finally get them together. With Tom Morrissey, the will to do it had been so much stronger it had felt almost external. Then, just before they came together, she'd been scared. Only her second man, second lover, barely known, the circumstances so strange. He had known it at once. He had stopped his soft kisses, stopped touching her, and asked, "What's wrong?"

She'd told him she was scared. Didn't know what she was doing. Afraid she wouldn't be good at it. Feeling small and stupid for saying it. He'd told her they could stop anytime she wanted, neither of them had anything to prove, and she was doing fine. Then he'd kissed her gently and gone back to making love to her, and everything had been so nice. She'd been swept away and then it had all ended in a pool of blood, a roomful of staring strangers, and total humiliation.

She'd never have sex again. There were other things in the world. Books. Sports. Work. She tried to chase away the image of Morrissey being lifted off her, of the fish-belly white condom dropping to the floor between her legs, of the remark she'd caught as Joe Trask led her out of the room. Something about it looking like she had "fucked his brains out."

The car swerved, flinging her hard against the car wall, bringing tears to her eyes. Maybe it wasn't time for a new plan yet. Maybe she needed a more R&R. But probably mean, pig-faced Alfonso would be waiting at this new destination, ready to stare at her body, treat her like a simple fool, and bring back the doctor to drug her again. The car braked abruptly to a stop, there was the electric hum of a garage door opener. Then the car lurched forward, stopped, and the hum brought the door down again.

She was being carried again. Up some stairs, through a door, and plop, onto another hard floor. She wished their positions were reversed. She'd kick him all around the room. There was the whir of the zipper, the clatter of guns, and he reached in and hauled her out. They were in another kitchen. Just like a pizza delivery. Kitchen to kitchen. Fresh, cold, naked girls. Or, in this case, slightly used.

She couldn't look at him. Too aware of how he'd seen her, lying on the floor after they'd lifted Morrissey off, before all those staring eyes. "Is he dead, Joe?" she asked. "Is he going to die?" And then before he could answer, "Where's Alfonso? In the next room? Waiting for me?"

She grabbed his arm. "Please, Joe, please. Give me something to wear. One of your shirts. Anything. I can't..." Her hands fluttered up and down. "Can't be like this anymore. I've been humiliated enough."

He picked up the blanket and draped it over her shoulders. "This way," he said gruffly. He led her down a short hall and into a bedroom. Another man's bedroom. Neat. Utilitarian. Double bed with no headboard. A desk. A bookshelf with a bubbling fish tank. The only decoration was hats. Rows and rows of them on nails around the top of the walls. He put his hands on her shoulders and steered her to the foot of the bed. "Sit."

She sat. He went out and returned with a large paper grocery bag. "Clothes," he said, his manner stiff and awkward. He was as ill-at-ease dealing with her as she was with him. He jerked opened a door. "Bathroom. I thought maybe you'd like a bath?"

Her throat tightened with the threat of tears. "Don't be nice to me. Not if you're about to turn me over to Alfonso. I've had enough of tricks and fake." Tears warred with her anger. "Just keep treating me badly."

"I've been treating you badly, Jenny? I don't think so."

"Come on, Joe. You drag me out of the room. Shove me into a bathroom and order me to wash. Stick me in a bag, naked and cold. Dump guns on top of me and throw me in your trunk. Bring me here without a word of explanation."

"I had to get you out of there."

"Get me out of there?"

"Make it look like you'd run away again in all the confusion. Tom was going to let you go as soon as you could manage on your own, see. I don't know what you said. How you did it. Somehow you got to him. Tom's a straight-arrow, a hundred percent for Alfonso, a hundred percent for doing his duty. It blew me away when he said what we were doing was wrong. But then—"

Too much for her to follow. She made a time-out sign. There was something she needed to know right now. "I'm sorry about Tom," she said. "You probably don't believe me but I didn't mean for anything to happen to him. Is he? Will he..." She swallowed and pushed the word out. "Die?"

Trask's shoulders slumped beneath his crisp uniform. He sat down beside her and took her hand. "Poor little Jenny. You have no idea what's going on, do you?"

"Don't call me that," she said, pulling her hand away. "It makes me sound so trivial." She swept a hand to take in her battered body. "Why would you bother with all this if I'm so trivial? And why would you want to be nice to me, after what happened to Morrissey?"

"The bullet didn't penetrate his brain," Trask said. "He's okay. There may be some concussion and he'll need stitches." He stopped. "Look, let's start you a bath. While you're in the tub, I'll fix us some food, then maybe I can explain."

He checked the clock on the wall. "I'm supposed to be stowing these guns and then going to the hospital, so we haven't got a lot of time."

She didn't trust him. Whatever this new game was, she wasn't playing. "Forget about the bath. I don't want it. I don't want you being nice to me when you're just cleaning me up to hand me back to him. When kindness makes me more vulnerable. If you've got a decent bone in your body, just tell me straight, then hand me over."

He seemed genuinely surprised. "I'm not handing you over to anyone."

She really wanted to believe him, but too many people had told too many lies. "God, and you look so sincere, too. So goddamned believable with your boyish face and sweet brown eyes."

She shook her head. "It's just another game, right? Lull me into a false sense of security and it begins all over again. Get me at rock bottom, then be nice to me and whoopee, little Jenny becomes cooperative. A stand-up girl for Lou Alfonso, ready to tell all to stop the evil father who seduced her mother and deserted her. Loaded for bear against the Buxton campaign. That's what this is about. Sorry, you're too late. Governor Alfonso is scum. I wouldn't help him if he were the last man on earth."

She stood up. "Let's just get it over with. Where is he? In one of those rooms down the hall?"

She headed for the door, trying for tough. Every step agony. Her legs rubbery, she walked unsteadily as far as the door. She stopped, leaning heavily against the door frame. It wasn't courage that failed. Her body simply gave way. She melted, a strange boneless descent, spilling her onto the floor like a dancer's final curtsy. She stared at him bleakly. "I'm too tired for any more bullshit. Go ahead. Do what you want." She pulled her legs in, laid her head on her knees, and closed her eyes.

He went into the bathroom and a moment later she heard the roar of water. When he came out, he sat down beside her and drew in his legs in imitation of her. "Look, I'm doing this all wrong. I'm not much of a talker," he said.

She waited, past the point of polite responses.

"But I've got to explain."

He seemed to be hoping for words of encouragement, but she was out of words. Just being took all her effort. Being upright, staying alert, waiting for the next injury, insult, humiliation. The next moment when someone would try to exploit her. Or kill her.

"I know you're embarrassed about what happened with Tom."

She lifted her head, couldn't think of what to say, so she put it back down. What would she do, ask him not to talk about it? Tell him mentioning it was like pouring salt in a wound? The blanket was rough against her skin, a chafing bit of reality. Otherwise, she felt only lethargy and the enormous weight of her shame.

"You won't believe this," he said, "but we, people who care about Tom, are grateful to you."

She didn't even raise her head. "Bullshit," she murmured. "Nobody wants a man like that to get shot. It would be different if he was hateful. But anyone could see he was special."

"No," he agreed. "No one wanted Tom to get shot."

His long, empty silence seemed tangible in the room. Outside, the dark sky grew gray. Cars began to pass. Another long night's journey into day. He went and shut the water off. "Tub's ready," he said.

"I'm fine right here." Now that she knew what FINE really meant.

He reached toward her. "You'll feel better if—"

She flinched. "Don't touch me," she said. "I've been hauled around so much I feel like a piece of luggage." She saw herself standing in the dim bathroom, inches from Morrissey.

"I just thought you'd feel better," he said.

"As if you cared."

"But I do," he said, sounding hurt. "And like I said, I'm grateful to you."

"If I believe that, you've got a bridge to sell me, right?"

"I'm serious."

"About what? My needing a bath?" She probably did. It had been days, hadn't it? She'd lost count.

"That, too," he agreed. "Why don't you get in the tub, then I'll explain the other thing. About Tom."

"Why do I have to get in the tub first?"

"Because my mother, the very wise Mrs. Trask, says nothing restores the spirits like a nice bath. And yours could use some restoration."

"It's too far to walk."

"And I can't touch you. Per your orders."

"All right. You can help," she said, but as he reached for her, she said, "Wait."

His extended hand stopped. "This is not a trick," he said. "The Governor doesn't know you're here."

"Everybody lies to me," she said. "Why should I believe you?"

The stricken look on his face told her she'd scored a direct hit.

He lowered his eyes, unable to meet her gaze. "Tom Morrissey is a good guy," he said. "A straight arrow, by-the-book cop who believes in duty and loyalty and a bunch of other old-fashioned virtues most people have forgotten. If Morrissey believes it's his duty to follow the Governor's orders, that's what he does. Alfonso is his boss, right or wrong. So if Morrissey decides he's going to disobey the Governor's orders, that's a big deal for him. A real big deal. And that's what Morrissey decided."

He dropped the outstretched arm. "I don't know if you can imagine what it's like for a man like Morrissey to decide to disobey orders. To risk his whole career for you."

"Spare me the melodrama," she said. "He was ready enough to slam me to the pavement and let me freeze and suffer."

He didn't like that. "Tom was just doing what he was ordered to do."

"It must be awful, having a hard job like yours, while I get to be a carefree college student on her spring break. I feel so sorry for you both."

"Look," he said, "We do lots of things that would seem cruel to outsiders. But this time, in Tom's mind, we were asked to go too far."

What about in your mind? She said, "Everyone I've dealt with lately has been looking for a chance to sell me down the river. Kill me or use me. Including you and Morrissey."

"We changed our minds," he said finally.

"Both of you, or did Morrissey change his and you just followed along?"

He gave her a "that's not fair" look. She thought it was entirely fair. "When did this change of heart occur?"

"When you were sleeping, he was out in the hallway, pacing back and forth. Trying to decide what to do. Whatever you said to him in the bathroom really got to him. He was ashamed. Uncertain. Not like himself. Tom's a guy who knows the answers. Persuading you to cooperate was something he could go along with. Why shouldn't you, if your own father is trying to kill you? We want Alfonso to be elected.

We believed in the necessity to protect you from the other side. But when Alfonso was bullying you, Tom didn't like it. And drugging you, taking your clothes, the whole campaign to make you helpless and vulnerable? Tom refused, so Cardullo had to do it. That was before you broke Cardullo's nose."

"I didn't mean to," she said, taking some comfort in knowing she'd broken the right nose. "You thought you were protecting me? Really? This is how you protect?"

"We aren't proud of ourselves," he said.

"Before we both grow old and die, tell me. What is it I did that you are all so grateful for? It can't be getting him to put his career at on the line."

His face got red. "Having…" He took a breath, a tough cop reduced to monosyllables. "Having sex."

She couldn't have heard him right. "You're grateful because I had sex with Tom Morrissey?" Now her face was red, remembering what all those grateful cops had seen. "It was so humiliating."

"I can't imagine."

"You don't want to. Look, I can't talk about it," she said.

If her life hadn't become completely unbelievable, she wouldn't have believed this either—she was sitting on the floor, naked except for a blanket, talking with a strange man, about her life's most embarrassing moment. At least in the kitchen, it had been Drew and Betty who were naked. Oh. Jesus. She did not want to think about this, talk about this, to have lived this. She wanted to type "THE END," rip these memories from her life's typewriter and burn them.

But Trask wasn't letting it go. He was going to explain, whether she liked it or not. By now she should be used to people running rough shod over her wishes, shouldn't she?

"No," he said, "I suppose you can't. Why we're grateful? It's almost a cliché, I guess. Tom had a wife, Peggy. High school sweetheart. She looked a lot like you, actually. Small and delicate, with long dark hair and blue eyes. He adored her. They never had any kids, so maybe that made them closer. I don't know. I never saw a man who looked at his wife the way Tom looked at her. Like he was always seeing her for the first time and falling in love again. I thought it was nice."

He ducked his head, the tough cop going all blushes and embarrassment. "Oh, hell, Jenny, I guess I'm a closet romantic. Two and half years ago

Peggy was driving home from work. She was a nurse, worked 3-11. A drunk driver ran a stop sign and killed her."

The phone rang but he made no move to answer it. "Two and a half years and he hasn't even looked at another woman. He goes through life like a dead man. Alive only at work. You think you've killed him, but maybe you've saved his life. So when you're sitting there thinking you've just had the most humiliating experience a woman has ever had, think about what you've done for Tom. Maybe it will help."

His face was as red as hers. He swallowed. "Now, how about that bath?"

With his help, she navigated the distance from the doorway to the tub, dropped her blanket, and cautiously lowered herself, bandaged feet and all, down into the suds, wondering about a single guy who had bubble bath. Well, Trask was attractive. He probably had lots of women stay over. She closed her eyes and lowered herself deeper. The heat stung her feet but soothed the rest of her. She stopped thinking about what lay ahead and concentrated on restoring herself. She couldn't run. She couldn't hide. She didn't have shoes. Until her brain was rested and her body fed, she couldn't plan.

Relaxing at last, after the nightmare days, brought her mother back into her head. Maybe you never know how much someone is with you until you face the threat of losing them. This had taught her so much about being Lila Friedman's daughter, and a lot about Lila Friedman.

Lila fired off a quick question. Did Jenny believe that male bullshit about Tom Morrissey being redeemed by sex? Jenny wasn't sure.

A compelling need for sleep stole over her. Time to leave the warmth of the tub for the warmth of a bed. She lifted her head and met his watchful eyes. "Got a towel?" she asked.

"Come Sleep! O Sleep, the certain knot of peace,
The baiting-place of wit, the balm of woe,
The poor man's wealth, the prisoner's release…"
—Philip Sidney, "Come Sleep, O Sleep"

CHAPTER TWENTY-FOUR

She was awakened by a streak of late afternoon sun slanting through the shades and stealing across her pillow. She moved out of its reach and opened her eyes. She was in Joe Trask's bed, still dressed in what she'd put on after the bath, and entirely alone. No one was watching. No one hovered to stick her with needles or force pills down her throat. No one waited to ask her probing questions.

In a glass by the bed was a single red rose and she remembered Trask had said he was romantic. Probably a ploy. Nothing these people said or did could be trusted. Cautiously, she sat up. The past week had taught her to treat her body gently. A small chorus of pains began singing out their woes, but the world wasn't filled with the cacophony of her pain.

She limped to the bathroom, her bandages still damp from the night before. On the sink was a vial of pills and a new toothbrush. No fool, she took a pill, brushed her teeth, and attended to the necessities with only the quickest of glimpses in the mirror. The woman she saw was pale and sickly, with grayish skin and deep circles under her eyes. A spidery line of stitches at the hairline. Wild, uncombed hair. A bruised and slightly swollen cheek. She looked an unhealthy, dissolute thirty. He'd left out antiseptic cream and a roll of gauze, but that was more than she was up for. She drank water and limped back to bed, ready for more sleep.

She'd just settled herself and pulled up the covers when the door opened and a man came in with a tray. He looked like Joe Trask—same eyes, same square jaw, and same slightly worried look, but this guy was taller, broader, and younger, with masses of curly hair, an earring, and attitude. "I don't know if you'd call this breakfast, lunch or dinner," he said, "but I've brought food."

She realized she was clutching the covers to her chest like a timid virgin. "Who are you?"

"I'm Terry, Joe's baby brother, assigned to baby-sit you. Joe's at the hospital with Morrissey." He slid the tray onto the bedside table beside the rose. "You hungry? Joe said keep it simple and light, so you've got scrambled eggs and toast. No butter. And cereal. Not exactly the breakfast of champions, but hey... who really cares that much about being a champion? If you lean forward a sec, I can stick this other pillow behind you. That'll make it easier to eat."

Overcome by the barrage of words, she did as she was told, and found herself sitting up with the tray on her lap, staring at the food. Eating seemed like too much trouble.

"You okay?" he asked. "Joe didn't tell me much, except I wasn't to let anyone near you. I mean, can you feed yourself or do you, like, need some help? 'Cuz I'd be more than glad to help, if that's what you need. You look pretty beat up." He watched her fumble with the fork, then sat heavily on the edge of the bed, took the fork and speared a clump of egg. "Open wide," he said, and dumped it in her mouth. "Good job." He speared another clump and did the same thing. "I see you're hungry."

She couldn't talk around the egg, and she was hungry, so instead of answering, she went on eating. It was amusing, in a bizarre way, being hand-fed by a stranger. Especially a sweet-natured one. Sort of Joe Trask Lite.

"Orange juice?" He lifted the glass. "With the added convenience of a straw?"

"You've thought of everything."

"Big brother Joe thinks of everything," he corrected. "He's a paragon of virtues."

She refrained from comment, settling back against the pillow and closing her eyes. Thinking about her next move. "Can I get you anything else?" he asked. "More toast? Coffee? Water?"

"You sound like a waiter."

"Bingo!" he said. "That's me. Terry Trask. Waiter extraordinaire and occasional musician. So." He bounced to his feet and picked up the tray in an exhausting display of energy. "You all set?"

She sighed. "Yes. Thank you." When she was alone, she'd work on her plan. Instead, she fell asleep. She woke because someone was shaking her. "Go away," she muttered, burrowing into the pillow.

"Rise and shine, sleepy head," Joe Trask said. He held out a paper bag. "Got some clothes for you."

"Go away." She burrowed deeper.

"Come on, Jenny. Wake up. Got to get out of here before the bad guys come."

Instantly she went from deep sleep to wide-awake panic. "What? Jesus, Joe. Tell me what's happening."

"That's pretty good, the way you go from totally asleep to totally awake," he said. "You ever consider becoming a cop?"

"Haven't had good role models," she said. "What's going on?"

"Nothing yet. But sooner or later, someone will wonder about that bag of guns I put in my trunk. Why it took so long to get to the hospital even if I did have a flat tire. And start asking questions. And there are the bad guys who were trying to shoot you. You should go, before they pop up again."

"You all do that. Besides, if they keep finding me no matter where I go, what difference does it make where I am?"

"Maybe none." he said, "It still helps to stay ahead of them." He shrugged. "And I'd sort of like to keep my job, hard to do if the Governor's looking all over hell and gone for you, and you turn up in my bed."

She could imagine Alfonso's dirty little snicker. First Morrissey, then Trask. The girl's hopping beds like a lusty cricket. What's the girl got that's so special? Who'd wanna screw a gal who looked like she'd run full tilt into a door?

"So what do I do? Walk out the door and hitch a ride to somewhere? I don't even know where I am."

She dumped the bag of clothes. A sweatshirt. Some jeans. A pair of socks. Underwear. All she had in the world. None of it really hers. At least the underwear was new. "I don't even have shoes."

He turned away. "You think I'd just put you out on the doorstep?"

"My perceptions of what people will and won't do have been significantly altered in the last week. You seem nice. But this could be another trick. Don't ask me why or for what. But you have to understand. No matter where I go or what I do, I keep getting caught."

"And you keep getting away."

"I keep getting caught," she repeated, "and I keep getting hurt. So if this is just 'let Jenny go, see where she runs, and pick her up again,' I'd rather skip the 'see where she runs' part. I feel awful. Everything hurts. I've had enough, Joe. I just want this over."

"Buxton's people want you and your mother dead."

"And my Uncle Billy. And they want the video tape. Alfonso wants the tape, too. And me." She considered her utility to Alfonso. "Does he really need me?"

Trask shrugged. "He might use the story anyway." Responding to her puzzled look, he added, "Blood tests? Pictures? People you confided in."

"There are no such people."

"Jenny. Jenny. This is politics."

"If he never needed me, why do this?"

"He wanted the diaries. If he couldn't have them, he wanted you. He wanted your sweet face with Buxton's blue eyes." Trask hesitated. "He wanted your blood."

She looked at the purple bruises on her arms. "It's ghoulish, you know. Sick. But if Alfonso can use the story without me, then Buxton no longer has any reason to kill me."

Talking to herself. To her hopes of this being over. Of going home and returning to a normal life. Hope flared up and died as quickly. It wouldn't end things. Breaking the story would only put her mother and herself in greater jeopardy. The story wouldn't be much without people to confirm or deny it. Someone for the press to sling their microphones at. It's hard to make a scandal about something that took place twenty years ago with a woman who's dead, or to raise a ruckus around a daughter who can't be found.

There was still the tape. By killing Billy, they probably thought they'd put it beyond reach. But Alfonso's people, or Buxton's, could find Jasmine Smith and get Billy's reassuring message. A few bucks, some booze and cigarettes, Jasmine would tell them she'd delivered Billy's message to Jenny and they'd be back on her tail again. Alfonso knew about the tape. He just didn't know what was on it. Probably expected a lurid sex tape.

She was jerked to the present by Trask pulling the tape off her feet. "Ouch!" She glared at him.

"Gotta get you taped up for the race," he said.

"Race?"

"Gallows humor," he said. "Race for your life."

"Sick," she agreed. "Are they bad?"

"No prettier than the rest of you, but you'll manage. You'll need a couple pair of socks to wear Caitlin's shoes, anyway. You've got awfully small feet. Caitlin's our sister."

"Older or younger? OUCH!"

"I'm the oldest. Mom and dad wanted a baseball team. They got a basketball team and quit. You have brothers or sisters?"

A painful question, given the recent revelations about her parenthood. Somewhere out there, she had three half-sisters. She'd stick to simple. "I'm an only."

He smeared the sole with cream and wrapped her foot until she looked like a mummy, then did the other. He looked like he knew what he was doing. "Good. Now get dressed."

She swung her feet over the side of the bed, seized the jeans, and began carefully threading her feet into the leg, feeling graceful as a baboon putting on pantyhose. "You okay with that?" he asked. "I could help."

"I've had enough strangers' hands on my body this week." She stood, gingerly testing her mummified feet while she pulled up the jeans. These hung on her hips, showing a good four inches of purple, yellow and green bruises, and piled up around her feet. "28 x 28," she said ruefully. "What are you, a race of giants?"

"Guess I blew it, huh?"

"Not if you've got scissors and a belt. But Caitlin's going to have to kiss 'em good-bye." She pulled the sweatshirt over her head. It came almost to her knees.

"I'll look again." After some digging he held up a navy and white hockey shirt. The size was right, but when he turned it over they both said "No." Across the back it said TRASK. In the end a baby blue hooded sweatshirt emerged. She pulled it on. A few minutes with the scissors, he punched a new hole in the belt, she was done.

She bent to put on her socks. Nope. "You do the socks."

He bent to the task and she had a flash of a solemn-eyed young Joe putting socks on wiggling little brothers and sisters. He went out and returned with a pair of Dr. Martens. The world's most ungraceful shoes. He carefully slipped them on her feet and tied the laces. "Now for the test. Can you walk?"

She crossed the room, trying not to wince. "They're fine. You wouldn't have an elastic and a spare baseball cap? One that doesn't say Police Academy?"

"You bet." He got them both and followed her into the bathroom, watching as she clipped some bangs to cover the stitches, gathered the rest into a ponytail, and put on the baseball cap. "Cute," he said. "You look like everybody's kid sister."

She studied herself in the mirror. Pulled some pieces of hair loose so she didn't look so neat, and turned to him. "Jacket?"

"Terry's bringing something."

"Terry?"

"You met him. My brother. He's going to Boston with you."

"I'm going to Boston?"

"Actually, I think you're going to Maine. But Terry's going as far as Boston. On the bus."

"I'm going to Boston on the bus with Terry. I get no choice?"

He shook his head. "No choice. In Boston, you'll meet a driver from Mason Brothers Trucking. He'll take you home."

She turned away from the mirror, not wanting to watch the poor girl cry. It was the word "home" that did it. "I can't go home. It's not safe."

Joe Trask shrugged. "Someone as resourceful as you, you'll have something figured out by the time you get there. You've got hours on the road to think. And this guy. The trucker. He sounded pretty sure he could get you back safely. I figured they'd be less likely to be watching buses, or be looking for two people traveling together."

The door opened and Terry came in, a very different Terry from the one she'd seen earlier. His hair was washed and moussed, framing his handsome face in a halo of curls. He wore a black leather jacket and black leather pants. Under the jacket was something skintight and black, and some chains. Black boots added a couple inches to his height. He was simply gorgeous. He carried a leather backpack and a guitar case. He grinned and stuck out a hand. "Terry Trask," he said. "Musician."

"Hot damn!" She shook her head, and sat down on the bed. She looked too frumpy. The contrast was too great. People would notice.

He studied her critically. "Nice try, bro," he told Joe, "but she needs a tune-up." He set the pack on the bed and started pulling things out. A tie-dyed long-sleeved shirt. A long brown crocheted vest. He handed them

over and called, "Shireen." A lanky girl with the trademark Trask eyes
stalked in, leaned against the wall, and folded her arms. Posing. Her hair
was very long, very straight, very black. She was wearing double-breasted
brown leather jacket, like one Jenny's mother had worn twenty-five years
ago, and a brown velvet hat with a tattered pink rose.

Terry grinned wickedly at his sister. "Voila, everything the fashionable
musician's dolly needs, yes?" The girl didn't moved. "Shireen, the jacket,
please. And the hat." She sighed, removed the jacket off with an irritated
wriggle, and handed it over.

Jenny scooped up the clothes and took them into the bathroom. She
shook her head at the confused face in the mirror. This seemed unreal and
untrustworthy. For now, she'd play along. The shirt smelled of cigarettes
and sweat. The vest of mothballs. She tucked the shirt in, put on the vest
and jacket, and last of all, the hat. Shadowed by the brim, her face didn't
seem bruised. The look cried out for make-up. She didn't have any.

She picked up the pills and the toothbrush, went back in the bedroom,
and handed them to Terry. "For the pack," she said. "I hope this works. If
not, I hope your family's willing to die to protect your job."

"Goes without saying. Trasks stick together."

Terry look at his watch. "If team Trask doesn't get rolling, we'll miss
that bus."

"Bye, Joe. Tell Morrissey bye, too." Morrissey, about whom she had
such conflicting feelings. Unlikely she'd ever see him again. She slipped
her arm through Terry's, her leather creaking pleasantly against his, and
they went out into the night.

THE BUXTON CAMPAIGN

ON THE ROAD

Frank Follett was busy as a one-armed juggler. He had so much on his mind he wished he had two heads, or at least two mouths so he could talk on two phones at once. Sleep had become something other people did. He'd drunk enough coffee in the past twenty-four hours to sink the Titanic. His shirt was wrinkled and sour. The latest poll showed Alfonso creeping up and Maggie Buxton blamed him. The Senator seemed distracted, and Frank couldn't get his attention. He'd been closeted with his hick buddies, Bean and Bass, for the past hour.

When the phone rang for the thousandth time, he grabbed it and growled a curt hello, hoping whoever it was would just go away.

"Bit of a dust-up, I'm afraid." Lopes' unwelcome voice, snide as always. "Thought we had a good chance to take her out tonight, Boss, when we caught her boffing a state trooper."

Frank wished he had time for the details. But it sounded like Lopes hadn't been successful, and he was pressed. "And?"

"Just as I'm ready to plaster her cranium all over the headboard, they changed position and... I shot the trooper. Needless to say, Mr. Smith and I are no longer in the area."

"Shit! You left without finishing the job?" Frank said.

"We'd just shot a cop. You wanted us to stay on that rooftop and wait for the sun to come up? You didn't hire us because we're stupid." Lopes paused. Frank knew there was more coming. The pause was to make him sweat. "Messer and Trudeau are on the case. In the confusion, it looks like the girl got away. We think she's had enough. She'll head for home."

"Based on?"

Lopes laughed. "Killer's intuition. You want us to see what she does or you want her terminated?"

"You know where she is?"

Lopes made an affirmative sound.

Frank ignored his other phone, thinking about the intel from his source in the Alfonso campaign. There was still that video tape and Alfonso's people believed the girl knew where it was. It did no good to kill the girl and her mother until they had the tape, if there was any chance she knew where it was, or that Alfonso might find it. So Lopes' missed shot wasn't such a bad thing.

"She's a smart cookie. Bound to go for the tape. It's her insurance policy at this point. Too bad she has to be eliminated. I'd hire a kid like that in a minute. Stay on her, Lopes. All of you. Wait until she has the tape, then you know what to do."

Lopes' laugh was harsh. "You bet we do, Frank. You want we should send you her hands or something, as proof we did the job?"

"Just send me the tape. That will be fine." He disconnected and went to wash his hands. Talking with Lopes always did that.

Lopes called Messer and Trudeau, gave them instructions, backed out of the phone booth and came back to the car. A different car. Their former ride was now sitting in the bottom of a quarry with a dead cop in the trunk. Mr. Smith was dozing against the window. Lopes nudged him awake. "Fearless leader says follow, don't shoot. I think he's pleased I missed."

Smith yawned. "The fates look after you, Lopes. You live a charmed life."

"And you're a trigger-happy asshole. You oughta see someone, you know. You've got a bad problem with impulse control." He fired up the engine and rolled back onto the highway.

"Beware the Jabberwock, my son!
The jaws that bite, the claws that catch!"
—Lewis Carroll, "Jabberwocky"

CHAPTER TWENTY-FIVE

Their trip to the bus station had been unreal, a cold ride in a jolting old car with a stiff, unsmiling Caitlin at the wheel. When they got out, she'd hesitated barely long enough for them to grab the pack and guitar before taking off with a squeal of tires. Terry had stared after her, grinning. "She's at a charming age."

They'd timed it so closely they walked right into the line waiting to board the bus, the night air bitter cold and biting. There was snow on the ground and flurries in the air. The bundled, shuffling passengers around them looked like refugees. Terry handed over their tickets and then they were down the aisle and into their seats, Jenny by the window, Terry on the aisle.

In her absurd costume and the absurdly handsome Terry beside her, she felt like she'd simply traded one unreality for another: the unreality of flight and the grim unreality of capture for the unreality of play-acting and dress-up. She didn't believe she was going home, nor that she'd been rescued. It felt more like Halloween, dressing up in funny outfits and running around in the night. A silly interlude between dark adventures. In her current state, the prospect of a mindless interlude was appealing, but a wary part of her mind warned her not to trust this.

She hoped he wouldn't expect her to talk. She wasn't comfortable with strangers, especially handsome strangers everyone stared at. She meant to use the long journey to make a plan. Instead, they'd barely gotten underway before her head dropped against his shoulder and, soothed by the muted roar of the engine, she fell asleep.

When she woke, dry-mouthed and disoriented, the bus was stopped and Terry wasn't there. For a moment she panicked, looking frantically around until the woman across the aisle leaned toward her. "He said if you woke up to tell you he went to get something to eat."

It seemed like a good idea to stretch her legs and see if she could shake off this haze. "I was asleep when they announced the stop," she said. "Do I have time to get off the bus for a few minutes?"

The woman checked her watch. "Go ahead, honey. You've got another ten minutes."

She was stiff and sore. When they got to Boston, she wanted to move swiftly, so she decided to get her pain pills from Terry's pack. The pills weren't on top, so she dug down. What she found, beneath the top layer of clothing, was a gun. She found the pills and stuffed them in her pocket, feeling like her head was wrapped in cotton. A fierce wind snatched at her hat and carried snow under her short coat, piercing the thin shirt and crocheted vest.

The rest stop had the cold, uninviting blue-white light that makes night seem bleaker and makes you feel lonely and sad. She passed Burger King and wondered if she should eat something—those eggs seemed long ago—but the smell of food turned her stomach. Besides, she didn't have any money.

Terry was on the phone with his back to her. As she passed, he said, "Evans is on the bus keeping an eye on her but she won't wake up. Those pills worked like a charm. She was out like a light before we'd left Albany."

She didn't wait to hear more. She hurried into the bathroom and locked the stall door with trembling hands, recoiling with shock. The Trask brothers made all the other bastards she'd met recently seem like Boy Scouts. And she was the fool who'd been conned into another game of "See Jenny Run."

She struggled to get herself under control, her mind taunting her with pictures. She saw herself sitting on the floor beside Trask. Him helping her out of the bath, wrapping her in a towel. Bandaging her feet. Tenderly tying her shoes. Remembered the cheerful way he'd composed her costume, conspiring with his brother and sister to help her escape. Letting her go so they could follow her home to get the tape.

Revulsion shook her. She bent over the toilet, the muddy water from many feet pooling around her feet, being sick. When she was finally wrung dry, she rose and went to the sink. Awful as she'd looked before, it was nothing compared to this. The stricken eyes of a terrified creature stared back from a dead white face. Everything about her screamed desperation. With shaking hands, she cupped some water and rinsed her mouth.

She couldn't get back on that bus and sit beside the perfidious Terry for hours, but panic had frozen her brain. She clutched her poor fuzzy head between her hands. Oh, brain. Please, please work. She had no ID. No money. Nothing of her own. Not even the clothes she wore were hers. They had stripped her of everything. Family, friends, identity, pride, privacy, bodily integrity. She laughed bitterly. Liberty and the pursuit of happiness. And aiming at life as well. It was time to get mad. Come alive. Rescue herself.

An older woman at the next sink said, "Excuse me, but are you all right, dear?"

"Oh. Thanks for asking. Someone on the bus stole my purse. You know what a shock that is. I can't get back on the bus. Not after that. So I have to call my mom to pick me up, and I don't have a quarter for the phone."

"That's dreadful," the woman said, rummaging through her purse. She handed Jenny several quarters, and then added a ten dollar bill as well. "Just to be safe, you know."

It was almost time for the bus to leave. If she didn't appear, Terry would look for her. Or the person he'd referred to as Evans. She had to find somewhere to hide. Fast.

Four laughing girls burst through the door. Two headed for the stalls and two came up to the mirror. They were wearing matching athletic sweats from some high school team. Maroon and black and white. They looked healthy and happy and so carefree it hurt. An idea forming in her head, she waited until the girls weren't watching, then snatched a jacket lying on top of a duffel bag, balled it up under her arm, and went into a stall. She shucked the leather jacket, crocheted vest, and hat, put her hair in a ponytail, and stepped out of the stall again, the stolen jacket tucked under her arm.

She left the bathroom, heading toward the rear, where another door led into the parking lot used by trucks, slipping on the jacket as she stepped into the cold. A cluster of men stood just outside the door, smoking. She scanned the group, looking for someone she might approach. Farthest away, to her right, was a man bigger than the rest of them. A man who looked familiar. She stepped up to him and said, "Got time for another rescue, Jerry?"

His face split in a grin. "Dunno," he said. "Are you a hooker?"

Jenny matched his grin. "Whatever it takes to hitch a ride home," she said. "It's been a bad bunch of days since we last met."

"Cops catch you?" he said.

Jenny realized the other men were staring. "I've been caught and gotten away so many times I feel like a prize trout in a catch and release pond," she said.

"I was just heading out," he said, dropping the cigarette. "You can come along, if you're going my way."

"Boston? Maine?" she asked, wishing she'd stolen a warmer coat.

"Boston. Then Maine. Let's go." He started off across the lot so fast Jenny had to trot to keep up. She was going around to her side of the truck when she heard a metallic pin and then felt something sting her shoulder. In the distance, she heard a gunshot. She scrambled up the side and into the truck, slamming the door as Jerry started moving.

Someone shooting at her was very bad news. It wouldn't be Trask, he wanted her alive. Buxton's people must have found her.

Jerry was on his radio, talking to other truckers, giving a description of the car the shots had come from. Jenny was pretty sure he was getting assurances that the car's progress would be slowed by other trucks on the road and fellow truckers would notify the police about the gunshots.

"If I call it in," he told her, "I'll be stuck for hours. We both will."

"Thanks," she said. "Now I need another favor."

"Why am I not surprised," he said.

"I need to get in touch with the Masons, and I think their phones are tapped. I'm supposed to meet Hugh in Boston, but it's a trap."

"They gonna arrest you?"

"Follow me back to Maine. There's a tape they want. I think I know where it is. They plan to follow me there and grab it."

"All sounds like something from TV to me," he said.

"I wish it were just on TV. Someone shooting at me feels way too real," she said.

"I shoulda asked," he said, cursing a driver who drifted into his lane and shifting to another. "You okay?"

She wasn't okay. Whoever shot at her hadn't missed. But it only felt like a bee sting, and after what she'd been though, a bee sting was nothing. Besides, Jerry didn't like trouble and he'd already gone through enough for her. She just hoped she wasn't getting blood on his seat. She didn't have anything to mop it up with. "I'm okay."

"I can call Hugh on the radio, let him know that I've picked up the package he was supposed to get, and I'll be delivering it."

"Thank you, Jerry."

"You don't sound so good," he said. "You aren't over there bleedin' on my truck, are ya?" He reached behind him, grabbed a blanket, and shoved it at her.

"I didn't mean to."

His laugh was huge. "You sound like my little granddaughter."

It hurt to laugh, but she couldn't help it. "Sorry, Grandpa." Then she said, "Can I use your phone?"

"Now you sound like my other granddaughter. She's ten." He gave Jenny his phone. She did a search, and made a phone call.

When she was done, Jerry said, "You've been through a lot. I shoulda taken you with me back when I first picked you up. But I never thought—"

"Me neither, Jerry. I had no idea people could be so ruthless and anyway, I couldn't go home. But people are also kind. Like you. And now I kind of have a plan." She gave the phone back. Her "thank you" as she wrapped herself in the blanket was barely audible, and it wasn't long before the thrum of the engine put her to sleep.

GOVERNOR ALFONSO

ON THE CAMPAIGN TRAIL

After he left Alfonso's office, Joe Trask sat in his car and stared at the dashboard. During his eight years as a cop, he'd done things thing he wasn't proud of, they all did, but this was the worst. Always before he could see the end justified the means because the end was justice. Justice as he defined it, which meant stopping crime and putting bad people where they belonged. He liked making the world a better place. Occasionally someone who wasn't particularly bad got swept along when it was necessary to get the real bad guys. Besides, Joe believed you lie down with dogs, you get up with fleas. Those not so bad people were where they were for a reason: to buy the dope, make the deal, get the fake ID, find the hooker, get the money.

He'd also done things because he'd been ordered to, some of those less savory. But in every case, he'd had the justification he was following orders and following orders, like promoting justice, was a vital part of the job. If you couldn't follow orders, you couldn't be an effective part of the team. The best cops were the ones who had the instinct, an innate understanding of criminals and a special sense of what was going on. But even those guys couldn't make it if they weren't team players, because no one could watch his own back. And everyone was out to trip them up. It was a big cat and mouse game. Stick with the pack or maybe you get eaten. So cops looked out for each other, cops did what they were told.

Joe had done what he was told to do. Used his big brown eyes and his boyish charm to get Jenny Cates to trust him. It ought to have been simple. The Governor needed Jenny Cates to help him get elected. Joe worked for the Governor. So Joe had done what he could. Now he felt like a skunk. They'd been supposed to treat the girl like a pawn. A piece on the chess board of Alfonso's election strategy. But from the moment he'd parted those branches and seen her curled up there, from her trembling request to see some identification, she'd been more than a pawn.

It wasn't a sex thing. Joe had seen plenty of naked women. Naked hookers. Naked spouses tossed out of their homes by abusive husbands. Partying teenagers, high as kites. None of that aroused him. And women who'd gotten naked voluntarily—girlfriends, would-be girlfriends, cop junkies—they aroused him just fine. Jenny's nakedness had been different. First, when they have brought her in, battered and freezing, it had been a terrible vulnerability, that delicate, finely-made body so disfigured by bruises. He'd felt an almost paternal need to cover and protect her. He'd shared Morrissey's anger at the Governor's decision to expose her and keep her vulnerable. Known, with his cop's instinct, that humiliation and intimidation wouldn't work.

At his apartment, it had been something else. There he'd seen a surprising maturity, a wisdom in the way she wore her nakedness with dignity. Instead of being bowed by it, she had made it something proud and her own instead of something thrust upon her to undermine her courage. She'd worn her nakedness the way someone comfortable with herself might have worn jeans and a T-shirt, saying "This is who I am. It needs no amplification." A lovely woman with quiet inner strength and integrity, just beginning to feel the force of who she was.

And she had managed to make a connection to Morrissey. In a world nearly devoid of heroes, Morrissey was his. Jenny pooh poohed the notion of redemption through sex. But Joe believed. And he believed that despite the blood bath in which things had ended, Jenny had made a difference. For that alone, he wanted this ordeal ended for her. Yet he'd delivered her up, once again, at the Governor's request.

His reverie of self-flagellation was interrupted by his phone.

"Joe? Terry. Can you fuckin' believe this? We've lost her." Terry, who'd set off on this mission so cocksure, didn't sound so cheerful now.

"Jesus, Terry, I told you not to make assumptions based on how she looked. How in the hell could you lose her?" He listened again. "This is a bad career move, Ter. How long ago? Any idea where she went? How she got away?" He listened and nodded as Terry described the truckers and how she might have gone with one of them. "Okay. You and Evans follow that up. And keep us posted. I've got to tell Van Allen. Call me in an hour.

He pounded once on the steering wheel in frustration. Then, smiling at Jenny's resourcefulness, he called Van Allen.

THE BUXTON CAMPAIGN

ON THE ROAD

When Ken Bass's phone rang at ten p.m., he had a premonition big trouble was on the other end. Trouble in the form of a voice so small and soft he could barely hear it. "Speak up," he barked.

She spoke up. "Is this the Ken Bass who works for Senator James Buxton?"

"Yes."

Faintly down the line he heard a sigh. "This is Jenny Cates." When he didn't say anything, she continued. "Twenty-two years ago, you were Jim Buxton's driver when he was attorney general. Twenty-two years ago, you let Jim Buxton and Lila Friedman use your trailer to have sex, Mr. Bass, didn't you?"

"I don't know what you're talking about."

"Bullshit, Mr. Bass, you know exactly what I'm talking about. My mother told me all about it. I think you know who I am, but in case your memory fails you here as well, I am Lila Friedman's daughter. And Jim Buxton's daughter. Do you remember the time she spilled coffee on herself and you had to drive her home to change? My mother used to think a lot of you, Mr. Bass."

Ken Bass was wide awake and sweating. "Hold on a minute," he said. He pulled out his cell phone and punched in Linwood Bean's number. "These are pretty wild things you're saying."

"I'm not calling to get an earful of crap and denials, Mr. Bass. I'm calling because I want my life back. Twice now the Buxton campaign has sent someone to try and kill me. I'm bleeding right now from one of those attempts. I want you to give my father a message."

"Ms. Cates, you can't just call up a political candidate, claiming to be his illegitimate daughter and making wild claims like this."

Woody answered on the other phone. "Hold on a minute," he said. "I'm setting the phone down. I've got to turn on a light."

Into the other phone he said, "Woody, I've got Jennifer Cates on the line, get down here now."

He darted across the room and opened the door, then picked up the phone up again. "Listen, Ms. Cates..." as he watched Linwood Bean coming down the hall. Bean slipped past him and picked up the extension.

"No, you listen. I'm no one's illegitimate anything. You tell the Senator I'm not waiting for third time lucky. I called you because my mother thought you could be trusted. She considered you a friend. But you're no friend of mine. After my car was forced off the road and I nearly died in the crash. After a bullet came through the window and smashed into the headboard of the bed I was in, after the week I've just gone through, I'm not sure who my friends are. But I know who my enemies are. I know who has the greatest interest in exposing what happened between my mother and the Senator, and I know who has the greatest interest in keeping it quiet."

She was silent for a minute. Ken Bass thought about the girl who was speaking. How small and young she was. He heard the strain in her voice and the fear. He heard something else, too: strength and anger. And across the years, he heard Lila Friedman. He wanted to say, yes. I know. I'm sorry. He wanted to tell her that she was wrong about the Buxton campaign's involvement. But he didn't know that she was.

"Look," he said, "this is a total bolt from the blue. We need to talk about this. We need to sit down and talk. You, me, the Senator, all of us."

"Neat idea," she said. "We set up a meeting. I show up. Your guys shoot me. Problem solved. A week ago, I might have been naive enough to agree, but it's been a bad week, Mr. Bass. And if this is a bolt from the blue, you guys are too dumb to run a political campaign."

"What do you want?" he asked.

"I want to be left alone," she said. "I want my life back. What I don't know is how to get it. There is a tape of my mother and Senator Buxton in... uh... a compromising situation. I know my mother doesn't want that video seen. I also know that from Senator Buxton's point of view, that tape represents an insurance policy for me. For her. For us. We could all agree that, so long as everyone leaves us alone, the tape stays hidden. But if anything happens to my family, it is given to the media along with affidavits about my paternity."

He tried to interrupt. She cut him off. "The trouble is Governor Alfonso is also very keen to get his hands on that tape. And the Governor is at least as ruthless as my biological father about what he'll do to succeed. So that, while as long as I have the tape, I'm safe from you…"

Her voice faltered, then continued, "As long as I have the tape, I'm not safe from him."

"We could protect you," he began.

"Don't make me laugh," she said. "Alfonso has had me kidnapped. Taken across state lines. Imprisoned. Drugged. He has forcibly taken samples of my blood, so if he can get his hands on Senator Buxton's, he can establish paternity."

"Jesus!" Bass said. "What do you want us to do?"

"You've got the resources of the federal government at your disposal, maybe you can figure it out. I called to say one thing: Call off your killers."

"But we don't have…"

"Mr. Bass." Her voice embodied weariness, cynicism and pain. "Buxton's people and Alfonso's people, in the name of political ambition, have taken one small citizen and stripped her of everything. I've lost my books, my clothes, my money, my identity, my freedom, my peace of mind, my trust in other people. I may have lost my mother. I've lost my Uncle Billy. I've lost my innocent faith that a wonderful man named Bud Cates is my father. I've nearly lost my life. I'm hurt and I'm tired and I'm scared. I have stitches in my head and my bones are broken. I want you to stop. That's all. I want you to leave me alone."

"Ms. Cates," he said, "you've got it all wrong. Senator Buxton is not your father, and the Buxton campaign has never…"

"Tell that to the judge," she said. "No. To the press," and disconnected.

GOVERNOR ALFONSO'S OFFICE

ALBANY, NEW YORK

Alfonso's thick, hairy hands pumped against the desk like starfish doing push-ups. O'Malley watched them with a grim fascination as he waited for the Governor to speak. He'd told the Governor they were spending too much time on Jennifer Cates and needed to concentrate on other things, but Alfonso took things personally. Alfonso was such an ingrained chauvinist he couldn't accept defeat at the hands of a mere girl. O'Malley could relate. He needed to beat Frank Follet just because Frank was Frank.

They were waiting for Van Allen. Keris Carlyle had slight parentheses around her mouth showing strain and disapproval. She wanted to talk about his wife, Angie and his daughter, Gina. Her ideas for bringing Gina on board, but Alfonso wouldn't listen. O'Malley was surprised she was still speaking to the Governor, after all his nasty cracks, but what made Keris effective was her driving ambition. She did her job and didn't let Alfonso knock her off her feet. Yeah, she hissed when the guy was pig, but she'd hitched her wagon to his star, and was along for the ride.

At last, Van Allen arrived, his cheeks and nose red from the cold. He set down his coat and rubbed his hands together. "I don't think spring is coming this year."

"Send the Trask brothers to Siberia," Alfonso said. Van Allen's look was sour but he only nodded. "And what's the story on Morrissey? He fit to travel? I want that tape and I want the girl. He's the one to do it. If she'll sleep with him, she'll trust him."

It was too much for Keris. "You've got to stop underestimating her, Lou," she said.

"What the fuck's that mean?"

She shrugged. "It never occurred to you that maybe she was using him?"

Alfonso's look was uncomprehending. "You're kidding, right?"

She shook her head. "And that this could all blow up in our faces? Smart as she is, she's bound to figure out that the media would love her story… the story of what two political candidates have done to her. How they've used and abused her in their quest for victory."

"You forget something," he said. "Two things. Her mother's still at risk. And the girl will want to protect her mother's reputation. Keep her mother's story hidden. Why else destroy the diaries? This kid idolizes her mother."

Keris nodded thoughtfully. "The second one maybe I give you, but why would talking to the press put her mother at risk? The way she'll figure it, it would remove risk. Once the story is out, there's no reason for anyone to bother either of them."

O'Malley stuck his own oar in. "She's a smart girl. If going to the press and telling the story would have settled this in the beginning, she would have done that." He shook his head. "No. Her mother sat on this story for twenty-two years for a reason. Because she wanted to protect Senator Buxton. And her daughter wants to do the same. Protect her mother. Protect Buxton."

"Exactly. So we still have to convince her that Buxton is her enemy."

"Oh, please," Keris said. "After what we've done to her?"

Alfonso's eyes glittered. The starfish jumped. "Which is why we want the tape. Once we've got the tape, we don't have to give a damn about the girl or the mother. Oh, yeah, sure, I'd love to see her on the evening news, wearing Buxton's eyes in that sweet little face, telling how her father tried to bump her off so she wouldn't embarrass him. But I'll settle for a nice grainy video of Buxton and the lovely Lila Friedman doing the beast with two backs."

"You think she knows where it is?" Van Allen asked.

O'Malley's smile transformed his plain face. His wife once told him that even when she positively hated him for something he'd done, the smile so disarmed her she'd forget why she was mad. She blamed their third child on the smile. "She told Buxton she does."

The starfish collapsed onto the desktop. "Do tell."

"The buzz in the Buxton camp is Jennifer Cates called him up and said if he didn't give her her life back she would use the tape."

"Could be a bluff," Keris said, but on her face was admiration for how he'd infiltrated the Buxton camp. He was pretty pleased with himself.

"Could be the truth."

"But she doesn't have the tape," Van Allen said.

"That's where she's heading," O'Malley said. "Why we let her go, remember?"

Alfonso clapped his hands. "So are we on top of this?"

Van Allen nodded. "Someone is watching and listening to anyone we think she might contact. What do you want Morrissey to do?"

"Once we pick her up again, we send him in. To get the tape. To get the girl, if possible."

Van Allen nodded. "Right." He rose from his chair and left the room.

"...If you prick us, do we not bleed?
If you tickle us, do we not laugh?
If you poison us,do we not die?
And if you wrong us, shall we not revenge?"
—Shakespeare, "The Merchant of Venice"

CHAPTER TWENTY-SIX

After she'd told Jerry her story, he'd sighed and told her to get into the bunk. From time to time, she heard him on the radio, but it was only a blur of sound. She slept through all the merges and exits, through the toll booths. She woke briefly in Boston, where Jerry gave her a bottle of water and asked if she needed a bathroom. She thanked him and said no, and slept again, even though she knew she should ask about a plan for when they got to Maine. If he took her to Mason Brothers trucking, she was sure there would be people watching and it would start all over again.

She only woke when she heard a familiar voice calling, "Hey, Spit," and felt a warm hand on her cheek.

Without fully opening her eyes, she wiggled out of the truck and right into Andy Mason's arms. She snuggled her head into his neck as his arms tightened around her. "My hero," she whispered sleepily. "All my life. My hero."

He set her on her feet. Still emerging from the throes of sleep, she leaned against him for support, secured by the strength of his arm. He represented home and all that meant. "Welcome back," he said.

"You'll make me cry."

"You, Spit? My little tough as nails?"

"Oh, Dandy. You don't know how good this feels. It's been so awful." She wrapped her arms around his waist and hugged him, wanting to stay right there forever. She felt his hesitation before he hugged her back. "What do we do now?"

"*We* don't do anything. We say thank you to Jerry, and then Sonny's going to take you—"

"Sonny? Not you?" she interrupted. "Who is Sonny, anyway?" She couldn't keep the disappointment from her voice. Of course, he would be watched. Probably his phone was tapped. But seeing him opened a lake of yearning. For her father. For Rose and Charlie. For people she could trust. For home, though she knew home wasn't safe.

She looked around. They were in standing in front of a house she didn't recognize. A neat split-level with blue shutters. Jerry's, she supposed. She didn't see Andy's truck anywhere, though an unfamiliar pickup idled out in the street. "I know you can't, but won't they be watching Sonny, too?"

She felt Lilliputian, standing beside Jerry's huge rig. In the distance, something clanged metallically into something else and she jumped. A tiny thing but it was all she needed to remind her of the situation. Back in Maine or not, all that had changed was her location. She was still in danger.

"Maybe, if they were able to follow Jerry's truck or the twisting and turning way I got here. Good thing you're small." He looked away as he said it and her heart sank. It would be the disappearing Jenny act again. What would it be this time? Oil drum? Cooler? Another duffel bag? Maybe the toolbox built into Sonny's pickup. Why not? Hadn't she spent the last week being treated like a tool? For Alfonso, a lever to lift his campaign; for Buxton, a drill to sink his ship.

"We've tried to make it comfortable."

The look on her face stopped him and when he spoke again, something in his voice almost broke her heart. It was low as a whisper but thick with anger and frustration. "You think I want to do this? That I don't know what you've been through and it doesn't make me angry. Hell, Spit, angry isn't a big enough word."

"Mad as wet hen?" she suggested, using one of his mother's favorite expressions.

But he wouldn't be humored. "I want to take you home to your father, tuck you into your own bed, and sit there with my gun, ready to shoot anyone who comes near. You know I'd move heaven and earth for you, Spit. We all would."

It was very early in the morning, just at that time when the birds start up. Even in the poor light, she could see how awful Dandy looked. Unshaven and unrested.

While she'd been racing desperately from place to place, they'd had their own kind of desperation here. The desperation of the helpless. Needing to know and having no information. Longing to help both Jenny and her mother, and in each case, unable to. They also serve who only stand and wait.

She touched his face with gentle fingers. "Poor Dandy. It's been bad for all of us," she said. "But it's almost over." She slipped her hand behind his neck and pulled his head down to hers. He stiffened. Resisted. "It helped to know that you were here."

"Jenny, don't! You don't know how…" He expelled a breath with something like a groan and never finished the sentence. She felt his rough whiskers brush her face, his warm, chapped lips on hers. In the passion of his kiss, she felt all the fear and worry, all the love of a lifetime of friendship, all the care he wanted to surround her with. It surprised and moved her. An unexpected moment when, like the peace in the eye of a hurricane, everything temporarily felt right. Safe and good and whole. When the people in the world could be relied on and trusted again.

This was not Trask and Morrissey's redemption through sex, either. This wasn't even about sex. This connection was a feeling flowing back and forth along a web of love and attachment that had been spinning between them all their lives. Ever since she'd toddled over to him and demanded that he pick her up. She was still toddling over; he was still picking her up.

As suddenly as he'd kissed her, he pulled away, red-faced and flustered. "Sorry, Jen," he said, his voice rough with feeling. "I never meant to do that."

"Don't apologize, Dandy. Sometimes, especially when things have been as bad as they are here, it's important to know there's still love and goodness in the world."

He wouldn't look at her. Poor Dandy. Big brothers aren't supposed to do what he'd just done. "Anyway," he said. "Sonny's going to take you in his truck up to Liberty."

"What's in Liberty?"

"Dizzy's snowmobile. Dizzy will take care of you until… until we've figured out what to do."

"I know what to do. I just need wheels. A gun. And some clothes. Please tell me you've got clothes. My clothes. My shoes." A catch she shouldn't keep from her voice. She'd worn stranger's clothes long enough.

He shook his head and held up a brown grocery bag. "Got a few clothes from your dad. We figured you'd probably lost what you had." He chuckled. "Stuff went back and forth between our houses in a pie basket. Adele thinks you can never say enough good things about a pie basket."

"I don't suppose there's a toothbrush in here?"

"Oh, ye of little faith."

She hugged him again. "Me and my little coated teeth are grateful," she said.

He made no move to go. "Dizzy's kind of a funny guy. Scary, maybe. Don't be put off by his looks, okay? He's a straight arrow. Got no patience with politicians. And he's a big fan of your mom."

"Like half the state,' she said, trying not to let Dandy's description alarm her. "Speaking of mom's fans, Dandy, do we know any big fan of my mom who's a TV reporter?"

He shrugged.

"Ask my dad, will you?" Suddenly she had a million questions. "How do we stay in touch? How do I get around? I've got things to do, people to see. Am I staying with this Dizzy guy?"

He made a time out sign. "Slow down, Spit. Your mouth works faster than my brain, okay? We stay in touch by me using a pay phone to call Dizzy at his shop. But listen, Spit, you're all beat up, even in bad light without my glasses I can see that. You ought to take a couple days and rest up."

"Haven't got a couple days."

He gave her his 'don't be a brat' look, but shrugged. "Yeah, you're staying with Dizzy. Can't be worse than what you're used to. You need to go somewhere, Dizzy's nephew, Gus, will take you."

Jenny thought about cold streets, bathroom floors, gunshots in the dark. Whatever awaited her couldn't be worse. "Bet your ass," she said.

Dandy winced, big brother enough to object to her language. "We figured that you could lie on the floor behind the seat. There's lots of room. He's got those two little seats back there. And we've put in lots of padding."

She flashed to other back seats. To the bizarre combination of agony and elation when she'd escaped from the hospital on Britt's car floor. The even more bizarre and agonizing ride with Trask and Morrissey, tossed in like a piece of luggage, utterly helpless. And Trask's trunk. She'd be a long time getting her head back to some healthy place, and that was if this ended happily.

"No problem," she said. "Are we keeping him waiting?" Then, "Hold on. I need a gun. A shotgun. Too out of practice for a rifle."

"Already in Sonny's truck," he said. "One you've used before, and don't wreck it, okay. It's got sentimental value."

"Word of honor," she said, examining the shells and finding #4 buck. "I'll be careful."

"Just don't shoot your foot off."

"Never have yet," she said.

"There's a first time for everything."

"My hero," she said. She'd been defenseless long enough. "Tell my dad to find me that reporter, okay. Someone honest, reliable, ambitious and on our side." She started toward Sonny's truck and turned back. "Tell Daddy I love him, please? And hug Adele?"

He put his arms around her, nuzzling the top of her head with his chin. "When this is over—"

"We're going to share the biggest hot fudge sundae in Augusta. I get all the cherries."

He released her, shaking his head. "Some people never change." He walked her to Sonny. "Okay, pal," he said. "She's all yours."

Jenny climbed into the truck, slow and awkward as she lowered herself onto the floor. When she was in, they slid her gun in beside her, dropped blankets over her, and piled some light junk on top. She heard the murmur of their voices. Then the truck started with a roar and the metallic clang of something rattling underneath and she was on the road again.

GOVERNOR ALFONSO'S OFFICE

ALBANY, NEW YORK

Alfonso never got over being surprised at how big Morrissey was. Right now, as Morrissey sat pale and silent in front of his desk, his head still swathed in bandages, Alfonso was trying to picture how all that bulk had managed to connect with Jenny Cates' small frame. A small man himself, he'd always wondered if there was a connection between body size and penis size. God, Morrissey looked like hell. He leaned forward solicitously. "Tom, can we get you anything? Coffee? Tea? A soft drink?"

"No."

Morrissey never embellished. A real 'just the facts, ma'am' guy. Firm jaw. Firm principles. It amused him to have a guy like Morrissey do his bidding, though some vestigial scruple kept him from using Morrissey to assist with his liaisons.

"You know that the idiotic Trask brothers lost the girl?"

"Terry Trask lost the girl. Terry Trask and Jill Evans."

Protecting his partner, Alfonso thought. Good old fashioned cop loyalty. He liked it. Maybe, when they had the girl again, he'd relent and bring Trask back. "She's going back to Maine. Going after that tape. We want you to go after her. She trusts you."

Morrissey looked down at his hands. "Not a good idea, sir," he said. "The doctors don't think I'm ready to travel."

"Since when did you start playing prima donna?" Alfonso said. He liked his cops macho tough. Adventure novel, Jason Bourne, bash the bad guys with their casts or crutches types. "Come on, Tom. Superman's doctors don't try to keep him in bed when there's a job to be done."

"She'd be a fool to trust me, after all we've done to her. And she's no fool."

That was the truth. Better appeal to Morrissey's protective side. Alfonso leaned across the desk, putting on his most serious face. "You're right. She is smart. But she's very young. She's hurting and scared, by now she's got to be exhausted by all this, and Buxton's people are still trying to kill her. She's out there on her own, Tom. She needs someone on her side. Someone who's got a shot at keeping her safe. You won't be alone. I've sent other people. But she knows you. Knows you're a good guy. A good cop. In a pinch, she'll look to you."

Morrissey shook his head and a look of pain not just from the motion crossed his face. "She's got no reason to trust me. Especially me."

"Bullshit!" Alfonso said. "She slept with you. A young girl like that under those circumstances? Hell, Tom, it means something. It means you've made a connection."

"I disagree," Morrissey said.

He didn't explain. Alfonso wouldn't understand about humiliation. About trust and personhood and how Jenny Cates felt. She probably hated him now more than ever. But he could talk forever and Alfonso wouldn't listen. When he wanted something, that was that. "If it's what you want, I'll go. Can't guarantee I'll be much use. I've still got a headache so bad I can't think straight, never mind drive or shoot straight."

"All we'll need is for you to talk straight," Alfonso said, "and you seem to be able to do that. Get whatever prescriptions you need from your doctor and get ready to leave. Someone can drive you."

Morrissey closed his eyes. It took most of his will power to stay upright when his head hurt this much, the rest not to leap across the desk, seize Alfonso by his thick neck, and pound his head against the wall. "I want Trask to drive me," he said.

"Trask's in Siberia."

"I want him." Let Alfonso think it was because he was loyal. Alfonso loved loyalty. The Governor's irritation was replaced by an amiable smile. As long as he was getting his way, Alfonso could be generous.

"Sure," he said. "Sure. Whatever you need, Tom. Just remember. Bring me the tape or bring me the girl. Okay?"

Morrissey knew what Alfonso wanted to say: that maybe, if Morrissey got lucky, he'd get to screw the girl again. But Alfonso was wrong. If Morrissey got lucky, Jenny Cates would get to screw Alfonso. Big time. And she wouldn't even have to take off her clothes.

THE BUXTON CAMPAIGN

ON THE ROAD

Entertaining Maggie Buxton in his hotel room was not Frank Follet's idea of a good time. Frank liked the women in his hotel rooms to be barely clad, nubile and talking dirty. Maggie was wearing a thick velour robe over a flannel nightgown and fuzzy pink slippers. She had never been nubile. She was talking dirty, but not in a way that aroused anything but his temper.

"Jesus H. Christ, Frank! Are you a fucking incompetent moron? I thought these people you'd hired were supposed to be the best, and here we've got this inexperienced little college girl flitting away from them like Tinker Bell, while they're busy shooting New York state cops."

"Maggie. Maggie," he said, trying to calm her. "Contrary to what you see on television, killing people isn't always simple."

She wasn't paying attention. As she paced the room, she'd passed his desk, where he'd stupidly left out the pictures of Jim Buxton and Jennifer Cates. She snatched them up and snapped on a light. She immediately saw what the pictures were meant to convey. She dropped them on the desk as if they were hot and whirled around. "You weren't planning to tell me this, Frank?"

He hated the way she made him feel like an idiot. This whole thing was getting out of hand. What had looked like the efficient elimination of a minor political problem had turned into a three-ring circus.

"What difference does it make" he said.

"Except she had the diaries, which our intelligence…" She paused on the word 'intelligence,' to highlight her doubt about its applicability, "…tells us the girl has destroyed; eliminating her was just a belt and suspenders thing, Frank. Let her lead us to the video tape if she could, but eliminate her if it became necessary. But now, Frank. NOW!" Her rage boiled through. "It was one thing. One thing that Jim was infatuated with Lila Friedman and slept with her a few times. But that she had his baby! Jim had a child by another woman and never told me? Frank, I'd kill her myself!"

"Quiet down!" he ordered. "You want everyone in the hotel to hear this, Mags?"

Even in a blinding rage, she was a politician. "Do you know where the girl is?" she asked.

"We did. She disappeared at a rest stop on the Massachusetts Turnpike. But we think we know where she's gone."

"Find her, Frank. Find her and kill her before that despicable Lou Alfonso hauls her face up before every TV camera in the nation. No more mistakes. You hear."

He sketched a bow. "To hear is to obey. You want her head?"

"On a silver platter," she said, snatching the pictures off the desk. "I'm going to see Jim." Clutching the pink robe tightly at the neck, she went out.

Frank picked up the phone.

"...you stand like greyhounds in the slips,
Straining upon the start. The game's afoot..."
—Shakespeare, "Henry V"

CHAPTER TWENTY-SEVEN

She wondered how he was going to unload her once they got to Dizzy's without her being seen, in case they were being followed, but long before they got there, she'd been lulled by engine sounds back into a deep sleep. She never heard them arrive; never felt herself being moved. The drugs Trask had given her must have been very powerful. She was temporarily narcoleptic. After days of being jarred awake at the slightest sound or movement, fleeing only minutes away from capture, suddenly she couldn't stay awake.

When she did wake, it was to her own screams. She burst, sweating and terrified, from a nightmare in which she had to choose between being crushed by an oncoming truck or jumping into an icy river. A door burst open and a man came toward her. When he bent over her, she almost screamed again. The man had a long skull, skeletally thin and shaved. Thick graying black eyebrows that rose in arches over eyes that gleamed darkly from deep sockets. A long and pointed nose; a mustache silky black and straight, dripping below the sides of his face like Fu Manchu. One ear was missing and that side of his face was contorted by a thick, purplish-white scar.

He put an icy hand over her mouth. "Silence!" he commanded.

"Dizzy?" she whispered.

He inclined his head slightly.

"Sorry. It was a nightmare."

Another inclination of his head. "Do you need something?" he asked. "Food? Water?" He had a faint accent.

"Bathroom?" She tried to keep her voice steady. Though, after his offers of food and drink he seemed marginally less fearsome, her heart was still pounding.

He peered into her face and she tried not to flinch. "You look like your mother." He turned toward the door. "Come," he said.

Cautiously, she peeled back the covers to follow, not sure what state she'd find herself in, grateful to discover this odd man hadn't joined the ranks of those who'd undressed her. Except for shoes, she was dressed exactly as she'd been when she crawled into Sonny's truck. She followed him, stumbling slightly from the remnants of sleep, her torn feet tender, still jazzed from the adrenaline rush of fear.

He led her to a tiny, pine-paneled room. "Wait," he said, lowering a shade and closing the curtains. He bent and lit a candle sitting on the toilet tank, his face, in the flickering light, all spooky planes and shadows. "The power. Sometimes it works, sometimes not." He stepped past her, pausing in the doorway where he knelt to pick up something outside the door. He thrust her paper sack at her. "Here. Your things. Maybe there is some hot water. I cannot guarantee."

"I'll be fine. Thanks," she said, wishing her voice didn't sound so small and scared. She attended to business, brushed her teeth and her hair—her first hairbrush in days—and dug in the paper sack for clean clothes. It felt miraculous to dress in clothes that fit.

He was waiting outside the door. Silently, he escorted her to the kitchen. It was daytime now. Her brain, goosed by that adrenaline jolt, was racing, trying to plan what to do next. Finding the tape was important; equally important was finding a way to tell her story. Once the truth was out, Buxton lost his incentive to destroy her. She'd developed an affection for him while reading her mother's words, so it would hurt to tell a truth that could destroy him, but Buxton hadn't thought twice about hurting her, or that bee sting on her shoulder wouldn't be throbbing. She'd asked them to give her her life back and they'd denied knowing anything about her or any attempts on her life. She wasn't waiting around to see if they changed their minds.

She didn't even consider trying to get Alfonso to back off. The idea of taking the wind out of Alfonso's sails pleased her. Her only regret was Tom Morrissey. About revealing his role in things. She didn't understand her hesitation about that. Morrissey, as much as any of them, had used her. Hurt her. Ridden rough-shod over her rights. He'd slammed her to the pavement and slung her into the car like a sack of wet laundry. Yet something had happened. She'd used him, too, and created a connection. Knowing Trask was a traitor hadn't made her certain Morrissey was one, too.

Only the second man she'd ever slept with. They always talk about memorable first times. Jenny's best memories would always be held by her second. She felt a blush steal up her face as she thought about them together in the icy bathroom. Picking up his hand and guiding it along her body as she detailed the damage. She might be scornful of the redemptive power of sex, the idiotic idea that a brief physical connection could change Morrissey's life. But how different had it been for her? Hadn't she wanted to make a connection? Hadn't she been trying, in wanting to have sex with Morrissey, to save something about herself? Give herself some power?

That was the good part, before bullets shattered the headboard and nearly shattered Morrissey's brain. No way to romanticize that. She could see his stricken, gory face lolling beside her, blood pooling on the floor. It was a pictorial memory. Sensory. She couldn't be sure that she'd spoken to him as she reached out to touch that wounded head. But she could remember the wet plop of the condom falling, just as she remembered the distinct latex snick as he'd rolled it on. The ecstasy and the agony, between a snick and a plop. Her father always said you had to have a sense of humor to survive this life.

How would she concentrate on papers and lectures, return to a mundane life after this? How could she plan for her future with her head so full of these images? Drew and Betty in the kitchen. Her mother lying still and white in her own blood. The smell of crushed flowers. Swirling snow mixed with swirling blue and red lights. Rose's flowing tears and Charlie's stoic calm. Her father's pained confession a stab to her heart. So many pieces of her life that would never be the same.

The kitchen was a dark, pine-paneled room. A summer camp that was barely winterized. Her shotgun was propped against the wall beside the door. On the wooden crate that served as a side table sat the box of shells. Dizzy motioned her into a chair and poured her coffee from a big graniteware pot on a woodstove.

"Milk or sugar?" he asked.

"Both. Please."

He fixed it and handed her the mug.

She felt like she was getting the flu, along with the stiffness and soreness she was becoming accustomed to. She hoped he'd have aspirin.

The place was small. Only a living room, small kitchen and a second bedroom. And empty. The living room door opened to a small porch with steps leading down to a path and beyond it, a wide, frozen lake. The lake, even this late in the season, was dotted with ice fishermen's shacks.

She pulled her chair closer to the stove for warmth and wrapped her hands around the cup. There was no clock, radio or TV, and she had no watch. She thought she should eat something but wasn't hungry. This isolation spooked her.

Dizzy was out on the porch, staring toward the lake. She poured herself a second cup of coffee and joined him. Except for the occasional rustle of leftover leaves and the busy noises of birds, the world was quiet. She should enjoy the tranquility. How often had she longed to be someplace like this, deserted and untouched? But right now she needed to be out in the world. And anyway, she'd gotten so conditioned to having all hell break loose she didn't trust this quiet.

A distant whining noise, like a chainsaw across the lake, gradually got louder, and a small black dot on the lake became a moving object, heading toward her. No sense in taking chances. She turned to get the gun, but Dizzy shook his head. "It's only Gus," he said. "Coming to help us."

Obediently, she put stayed put, but visualized hauling it up, settling it against her shoulder, and siting down the barrel. Thanking her few remaining lucky stars she hadn't been shot in the right shoulder.

A chunky man in a puffy white snowmobile suit, decorated with chevrons and gaudy stripes, climbed awkwardly off the machine and headed toward the cottage. Dizzy said. "Come inside," without even looking at her. Ever the polite guest, she did as she was told.

"You slept well?" he asked.

"No."

He pointed to the man who'd just arrived. A heavy-set youth around her own age. "This is Augustine. My nephew. He will drive you."

She held out her hand. "I'm Jenny."

The boy's hand was hot and damp. "Gus," he said.

In full daylight, and with her eyes open, Dizzy looked much worse. No wonder Andy had worried. People joked sometimes about appearances being bad enough to scare babies and small children. Here it was true.

He picked up the pot and held it over her cup. "More coffee?"

She shook her head. "No. Thanks. Do you have any aspirin?"

Abruptly, as if someone had told him to care for her and he'd forgotten, he was attentive. He examined her closely. "What hurts?"

"My shoulder, where I was shot."

"Shot?"

She nodded.

"Left? Right?" Without waiting, he said, "Take off your shirt and let me see. Augustine. Into the living room, please."

As Gus went reluctantly out, he said, "Your modesty. He is just a boy. There is no need." He pulled off her sweatshirt, unbuttoned her shirt, and stared intently at her shoulder. This must be what it was like to have a chronic illness. New strangers always wanting your clothes off to examine you. She closed her eyes, trying not to look at his ravaged cheek, the shredded stub of ear, trying not to feel naked. Trying not to shiver as her skin puckered up in a million goose bumps.

He grunted and straightened up. "You need a doctor."

"I can't," she said. "Doctors have to report gunshot wounds. There would be cops and questions and I have things to do."

He shrugged. "I'll do what I can, but this is stupid. Your mother wouldn't want this. It is enough for your family to have one person stricken."

He left the room. She didn't know whether he was leaving to get some medical supplies or walking away because he was upset. She cast a wary glance at her shoulder. It was ugly. Red, raw, and oozing. Sickening in a way the bruises hadn't been.

He came back with gauze and tape and a big brown bottle of Peroxide. He showed it to her, as if to punish her for her willfulness in refusing a doctor, and said, "I'm going to use this. I have no choice."

"Go ahead."

Pure bravado. She took a deep breath and braced herself. He didn't mess around with wads of cotton and dainty dabbing; he just poured a slug into the wound. She tried not to scream but she couldn't help it. She groaned and gasped and found that she was gripping his hand tightly as she waited for it to be over. As he went to work, bandaging her shoulder, she blinked away her tears and felt her resolve harden. Any last qualms she might have had about striking back at Alfonso and Buxton had boiled away in the sizzling peroxide foam. She gazed at the shotgun and flexed her trigger finger. Most of the girls she knew at school didn't have trigger fingers. Maybe Betty should watch out.

"There. It's done," he declared, helping her carefully back into her shirt and turning away.

"Gus will take me wherever I want to go?" she asked.

"Yes."

"Does he know what's going on?"

"He only knows you've had some trouble. Some men are threatening you and so you are staying with me for a while. That's all he needs to know. But don't underestimate my nephew. He may look soft but he isn't soft. He can take care of himself, and you, if necessary. I ask only that you don't get him killed. My sister would not find that amusing. She is like you. Small but rather fierce."

An odd compliment that pleased her. She smiled. "I'll do my best not to get either of us hurt, Mr. Pelletier."

"Dizzy," he corrected.

She stood up. "Then I guess I should be going. What time is it, anyway?"

He pushed up the thick padded sleeve of his suit and consulted his watch. "Eight-thirty. Andy calls me at the shop at nine. You should eat some breakfast."

"I'm not hungry. I could use some aspirin, though."

"Of course. You asked and I forgot."

He went to a cupboard, rummaged a bit, and came back with a bottle. He handed it to her, ran a glass of water, and set that beside her. "Augustine?" he called. He followed it with some instructions in rapid French, too hard for her high school French to follow, and Augustine came back into the room. He looked at her curiously but said nothing, only pulled out a chair and sat down at the table. "I'll fix Augustine some breakfast and you can be on your way. Sure you won't eat some toast and eggs?"

She shook her head and swallowed the aspirin. She felt too sick to eat, and extremely tired, though not at all sleepy. There was only one thing that would make her feel better. For all this to be over.

She couldn't stand the smell of breakfast, so she went into the other room to wait. Standing there, staring out at the lake, she was suddenly seized by a terrible trembling, by fear of the danger she was in. When she was running, she'd had no time to reflect, simply reacted. Now there was a different pressure. She had to become confrontational. She had to make the moves to end this, or go back on the run again.

It was all very well to talk of seizing the bull by the horns. Most people who used the expression had never been close to a real bull, but Jenny knew how frightening it was to get close to something powerful, something ruthless and instinctive that could destroy her. Yet she didn't see any choice. She couldn't run forever. Couldn't keep taking this level of abuse. She had to be the one on the offensive. She had to find a friendly TV reporter who would put her story on the air. She had to be willing to take the risk of destroying their reputations and their campaigns, without second thoughts, without nice girl waffling, without regrets or remorse, as they'd had none for her.

She'd followed Lila Friedman's advice. She'd made a plan and she was on the verge of carrying it out. But now her courage was failing. She was scared. She wanted to stay in this chilly cabin. Crawl into bed and pull the covers over her head. She didn't want to go back out there where people were waiting to hurt her. Where her vulnerability made the skin on her back shrink with anticipation of what might happen. Contemplating the next shot, blow, or capture, made her feel weak and sick and desperately low on courage. If only she could write it all down and give it to someone to read. But the impact came from the personal drama. The only way this would work was with her face, with the very display of Buxton's eyes that Alfonso had wanted to make, the cast on her wrist, as well as her cuts and bruises, and the ugly wound on her shoulder.

One more humiliating striptease before cameras and reporters. One last graphic shot of their cruelty. And she had to do it before she healed. It was maddening to have to violate her privacy to save her life. Her life and her mother's. Slowly, as it had in Trask's apartment, her body folded until she was kneeling on the floor. She wrapped her arms around her knees, tears she couldn't stop dripping onto the legs of her faded jeans. She wasn't well. She needed rest. She shouldn't have to do this now.

Crying hurt. The spasms taunted every ache and bruise and that made her cry harder. Fighting the tears, fighting to get her control back, did no good. It was like trying to fight some huge amorphous creature that kept changing its shape. In the end, she gave up and let it all pour out.

That was how Dizzy found her. Curled up on the floor, leaning against the wall, sobbing like a broken-hearted child. "It's time to go. We must get to the shop. Andy will be calling."

"I can't," was all she managed to say.

"You are Lila Friedman's daughter," he said. "You will do what must be done." He pushed a clean, faded bandana handkerchief into her hand.

She pressed it hard against her eyes and breathed deeply, striving to control the sobs. "That could be my motto," she said between spasms. "I am Lila Friedman's daughter. I will do what must be done."

"You want to quit," he said, squatting down until his head was level with hers. "I know. I'm sorry. No one would like better than I to tell you to forget all this. You are so young for such trouble. But you cannot until you've stopped the ones who hurt your mother, who are trying to kill you. Your mother deserves no less. You cannot let her suffering go unavenged. So much suffering. Your mother's. Your Uncle Billy's. Your father's. Your own. These people will destroy your life unless you stop them."

"But I can't!" she wailed. "There's just me against all of them. And I'm so tired."

He put his hands under her elbows and stood, raising her with him. "When this is over, you can rest," he said. "Come along. Gus is waiting and Andy will be calling. We must not be late."

"I can't."

"Of course you can," he said firmly. "Would your mother be cowering in a corner if what happened to you had happened to her?" His eyes were fierce. "Of course not. So you will do it. You can do no less for her than she would do for you. You are not a child anymore."

He hesitated, searching for the right words. "No one, setting out to make things right when the situation is dangerous, is without fear. If there were no fear, no risk, you wouldn't need courage. But I see your courage. It is what sets you apart, you and your mother."

He made a gesture with his hands that meant "this is bigger than I can express" and said, "Your mother. She is, to so many people, someone very special."

He lowered his eyes, as though considering whether he would continue. "I have not known you long, and all this is personal so please forgive me, but I see so much of your mother in you. Small women with big courage. And I think, like her, you are a righter of wrongs. And a very big wrong has been done to you and your mother."

She felt too young and inept to match such big expectations.

"So, we go? Are you bringing the gun?"

She nodded absently, not thinking about the gun. She was thinking about what he'd said. She'd always thought about what her mother would want *her* to do, but never about what her mother would do. She'd thought of herself as her mother's child and never as an adult with her own responsibilities to protect the people she loved. Now she took a deep breath and tried it on, the idea of doing what she had to do to protect, and avenge, her mother. Trying on the notion of doing for her mother what her mother had always done for her.

Slowly she let the breath out, feeling the sobs subside. It wasn't a dramatic transformation. More like a changing of the tides. Before her courage had been on the ebb, her strength and determination draining away. Now she felt them flowing back.

She shoved the box of shells into her pocket, and picked up the shotgun. She'd already put the money she'd found in the sack into her pocket. She tossed her hair back and met Dizzy's eyes. "I'm ready," she said.

THE BUXTON CAMPAIGN

SOMEWHERE ON THE ROAD

Andy Mason, having made his nine a.m. call and delivered the information Jenny had requested, backed out of the phone booth and headed for his truck. It was a beautiful day, finally, after months of crappy weather, and he couldn't be completely depressed, even by Dizzy's report that Jenny's wound was infected and she refused to see a doctor. He stopped beside the truck to light a cigarette. As he shoved the lighter back in his pocket, he felt something cold and hard press against the side of his neck.

"Get in the truck, and no funny business."

He tried to turn his head to look at the speaker but the gun pressed more insistently. "Don't look around. Just get in the goddamned truck."

He weighed his escape options as he opened the door. They didn't look good. He'd picked this phone booth because it was deserted. Only one road. Not a lot of traffic. And there were two of them. The second man was already sitting in the truck. That's what he got for leaving the thing unlocked. He opened the door and climbed into the driver's seat.

"Shove over. I'll drive," the man said, and put his gun in his pocket. Andy didn't get a chance to relax. As he slid along the seat, another gun nestled into the other side of his neck. The first man slammed the door and held out his hand. "The key, asshole."

Struggling not to lose his temper, Andy gave it to him.

The truck rumbled over the rough parking lot and onto the road, heading north as though the driver knew where he was going. He was middle-sized, with ordinary features, ordinary hair and ordinary clothes. Deliberately nondescript. Even the mustache was plain. The gun in his neck kept him from turning to get a good look at the other man.

"Where are we going?" he asked.

"You'll see when we get there."

The second man was a mouth breather. Bigger, beefier, darker, with a noticeable inability to sit still. Andy wondered how the first man stood it. But he knew why they were here and what they wanted. He hoped he'd be brave enough not to give it to them, and whether he could possibly be lucky enough to come out of this alive. It no longer seemed like a nice day. It was too hot for comfort. His skin, beneath his clothes, was growing slick with sweat.

Andy kept hoping they'd pass someone he knew, someone who might notice two strange men in his truck, but they only passed two vehicles, a florist's van and a little old lady in a Chevette, before the driver snapped on his signal and turned down a rutted dirt road.

Andy's heart sank. These guys were good. They couldn't have been in town for long, and they'd managed to find the perfect spot—the decrepit remains of a junkyard, long out of business, a spot so ugly and devoid of interest not even teenagers bothered with it. And no one came here at nine in the morning.

The truck stopped in front of what had once been the shop. The driver shut off the engine. "I'm going to assume you're not a stupid man," he said, "since you're friends with Jenny Cates, and she's not a stupid girl. We want to know where to find her. We know you have that information. We can do this the easy way—you tell us and you don't get hurt—or we can do this the hard way. Rest assured that my associate, Mr. Smith, is an accomplished persuader. He will make the hard way as hard as he needs to."

The gun in his neck dropped as Mr. Smith made an elaborate show of pulling on a pair of gloves. He hadn't spoken, but now he made a low sound in his throat, like the growl of a menacing dog.

None of it—the attack on Lila Friedman or Jenny's ordeal—seemed as real as this. He understood that they couldn't afford to let him live. He didn't have any real choices other than not tell them where to find her, and die, or tell them and die. No superheroes would appear at the last minute and save him. No one knew he was here except his mother, and she'd expect him to go on to work.

He loved Jenny Cates but he wasn't sure there was anyone in the world he was willing to die for, except his daughter Diana. He wasn't ready to die. Crappy as his life had been lately, he'd rather have a crappy life, hoping things would get better, than no life at all. Not being given a choice in the matter made him mad.

"What'll it be?" the driver asked, as if Andy might have been seriously considering his offer.

"Give me liberty or give me death?" he said.

"How about, I'll give you misery and then I'll give you death, unless you give me the girl."

The driver had his gun back out now, using it to motion Andy out of the truck. The other man had already gotten out and was heading for the building, walking with the simian lope of the muscle-bound, rounded shoulders thrust forward, working one gloved hand into the palm of the other.

The driver prodded him through the door into the wrecked shop, straight into a fist that smashed his stomach into his backbone, a second that smashed his head into the wall, followed by kicks to his groin and kidneys that made him see stars and left him quivering on the floor like a jellyfish. As he lay retching on the filthy linoleum, the driver bent over him. "That was just the appetizer, Mr. Mason. Care to tell us what we want to know, or shall we move on to the salad course?"

He didn't have the breath to reply, which they must have taken for refusal, because he quickly found that the salad they had in mind was tossed, and he was the main ingredient. The mouth-breathing animal, Mr. Smith, was like a caged beast let out an hour a day for exercise. Another swift series of kicks and blows smashed his nose and probably several of his ribs, left his lips crushed and bleeding. One shoulder felt dislocated. By the time they'd paused for another Q&A, his senses were so dim he had to strain to hear what they were saying

"Mr. Smith," the driver was saying, "Mr. Mason doesn't seem to be responding. Perhaps we'd better take a different tack."

"Gimme a break, Lopes. I've almost got him. A little bit more and he'll sing like a bird." By way of illustration, he slammed his monumental fist into Andy's jaw.

"Smith. Smith," Lopes chided. "How is the man to tell us what we want to know if you break his jaw so he can't talk?"

"Now then, Mr. Mason," the man called Lopes went on in his calm voice, "this doesn't seem to be working, does it? Perhaps we can find a way to circumvent these unnecessary heroics. None of us, except Mr. Smith, enjoys unnecessary pain."

The cheerfully ironic tone was more terrible than Smith's violence. An animal Andy could understand. Lopes was harder. People who thrived on causing pain were sick but people who watched it with amused detachment were scarier.

Lopes squatted down so that his face was near Andy's ear. "You like little Jenny, don't you? She's a lovely girl. Very smart. Very brave. Alas, we're going to find her, and we're going to kill her. That's our job. Still, while the result is inevitable, you have some choice about how it is achieved. You tell us how to find her, and we promise that her end will be as swift and painless as possible. Make us find her ourselves, and I will let Mr. Smith do it his way."

Deep inside his cocoon of pain, Andy Mason felt a deeper chill.

"Shall I tell you how Mr. Smith will proceed?"

THE ALFONSO CAMPAIGN

ON THE CAMPAIGN TRAIL

Morrissey and Trask had done most of the drive in silence, Trask driving and Morrissey trying to ignore the pounding in his head. Other than thanking Morrissey for getting him back from the boonies, Trask had kept his mouth shut. It was a hard silence. Morrissey could see that Trask was brimming with apologies, explanations, and excuses. He didn't want to hear them.

The black florist van borrowed from the detectives' division was great cover but a miserable ride, drafty and badly sprung, with stiff vinyl seats that didn't adjust and no leg room. By the time they got to Maine, Morrissey felt like he'd just done a coast-to-coast red eye in coach and was in a piss-poor mood.

He was too old for this. The days when the excitement of the chase outweighed the misery of hours with his knees in his ears were gone. He felt a depressing certainty things wouldn't end well. In the battle of young Jenny Cates against the world, despite her successes to date, the bad guys had the edge. Ravaged by an aching head and a bleary brain, he felt old, jaded, angry. Still touched by a lingering shame at allowing himself to sleep with a woman so young and vulnerable. It was no state for a cop to be in when he needed to be on top of things.

More than anything, he would have liked a huge breakfast and a soft motel bed, but his cop's intuition told him the situation required immediate attention. They gulped an indigestion-inducing McD's breakfast heavy with grease, butter and cholesterol and joined the team watching the Mason and Cates houses. When Andy Mason came striding out and jumped in the red truck, he had signaled that they'd follow.

The place Mason had chosen to stop, a stark phone booth at a closed roadside restaurant, gave them nowhere to hide. They'd had to settle for driving down the road and doubling slowly back in time to see the truck, now with three passengers instead of one, heading in the opposite direction. They'd done their own about-face and followed the truck down the dirt road, stopping out of sight and going forward on foot. They had seen Mason taken at gun point into the derelict building by two men, a smaller one who appeared to be the leader, and a larger, a slope-shouldered Neanderthal.

Now, crouched behind the stripped carcass of a panel truck, they were discussing what to do. "Dollars to doughnuts those are the guys who shot you," Trask said.

"Not a betting man," Morrissey grunted, though he agreed.

He was more concerned with how they'd get inside and grab the guys before they wasted Mason. Even at a distance, he heard the sounds of violence. He knew from experience the kind of damage that slope-shouldered sadist could inflict and how little time it took. He gestured toward the building. "They're gonna kill him. We've got to go in," he said. "You take the back."

"Let me take the front," Trask protested. "You're in no shape…"

"The back," he said. "Go."

Trask went.

Outside the door, he listened to the voices. First the one finishing an ugly and graphic description of what they would do to Jenny Cates if Andy Mason didn't cooperate and they had to find her on their own. The voice so light and cheerful, the threat stomach-turning and utterly believable. Morrissey had seen plenty of things in his life most people couldn't conceive of one human being doing to another. People so badly cut they looked like hash. A baby that had been boiled. An eighty-year old woman raped with a broom handle. And they'd been people he didn't know. Jenny Cates he knew too well. There was a silence, the sound of a blow, and a thick, stumbling voice he assumed was Mason's, strained with pain and tinged with helpless rage, telling them what they wanted to know.

Acting on the information overheard, he could have slipped away to find Jenny Cates, leaving Mason to his fate. But Morrissey'd been a cop twenty-five years. Leaving a civilian, particularly one whose only offense had been to try and protect someone, to a brutal death at the hands of two thugs wasn't in his personal code.

He drew his gun, raised his foot, and kicked in the door.

SENATOR BUXTON'S HOTEL ROOM

ON THE CAMPAIGN TRAIL

Buxton opened his door to Ken Bass and Linwood Bean at their first knock. He had the politician's knack of being "on" at a second's notice. He took in their anxious faces and waved them into chairs, automatically going to the coffee machine and setting about making the first pot of the day. "I just had a phone call from Jennifer Cates, Jim," Ken Bass said. "She says she wants us to stop trying to kill her. She says she wants her life back."

Only the whiteness of his knuckles gave away Buxton's anxiety. "Are we trying to kill her, Ken?"

"Someone is."

"That isn't much of an answer."

Linwood Bean sighed, glanced at Bass, and took over. "Our information is that there have been a couple of further attempts on Lila Friedman, so an officer is now posted there 24/7. And someone forced your daughter's... Jennifer Cates'... car off the road. She suffered minor injuries in the accident and then disappeared from the hospital the next day."

He already knew about the accident. "How minor?" he interrupted.

"Concussion. Broken wrist. Scalp laceration. Severe contusions."

Buxton nodded. "Go on."

"She next surfaced in a camp outside of Elmira. The camp was surrounded by New York state cops, but she got away. Excuse me, Jim, you want the whole chronology or just the bottom line?"

"Bottom line," Buxton said. He was thinking about the girl in the video. The proud Valedictorian. Delicate and fine boned. He was thinking of Lila Friedman's body. He was thinking about how contact with him was bringing heavy damage to these two women. Of how they possessed the ability to do heavy damage to him. Was it possible his campaign manager had decided to eliminate them? And what the hell was he supposed to do now?

"Okay. Well, I'll back up just a little. We have reason to believe that Alfonso's people had her stashed in a house belonging to one of Alfonso's pet troopers, waiting for some damage to her face, sustained when she resisted the troopers, to heal. The trooper was shot inside the house. We believe the shot was intended for Jennifer Cates. She was then removed from the premises in the trunk of a car, in order to..."

Buxton dropped his head into his hands. "That girl. My daughter..." he began. The words were awkward. "My daughter is being stalked like an animal. Do you think we have something to do with this?"

"Let me finish," Bass said. "She was last seen getting on a bus in Albany, headed for Boston, with a young man carrying a guitar case. The young man is believed to be an undercover cop named Terrence Trask."

"So she's on her way to Boston with a cop? Why? Why would Alfonso let her go? And why on a bus? Why not just drive her home?"

"If she's going for the tape," Ken Bass said, "she'll only do that if she thinks she's getting away." He looked at Buxton. "That goddamned tape again."

"We assume she didn't know the guy was a cop" Woody said. He set a small tape recorder on the table. "But somehow she figured it out. They recorded this conversation a while ago." He played Jenny's conversation with Andy Mason.

Buxton listened eagerly. Her first words. His daughter was twenty-one and he was hearing her words for the first time. She sounded exhausted, beaten down, at the end of her tether. She sounded like Lila Friedman. "You think Frank is involved in this?"

They nodded.

"Which means I'm involved."

Ken Bass looked abashed. "We weren't sure. Well, we still aren't sure, but tonight, after her call, we... Our FBI sources have linked calls on Frank's cellular phone to a Dino Stormont. Mr. Stormont is believed to be in the... uh... elimination business."

Buxton saw the ashes of his bright hopes piling up around him. "Ken? Woody? What the hell do we do? Can we contain this?"

He paused, considering how cold that sounded. Containment was necessary, though. He hadn't come this far to fold his tent now, leaving the field to Alfonso. Alfonso was a selfish, ignorant scum-bag. Possessed of the necessary ambition and a vast well of artificial charm and charisma. And well advised. But he would be a bad leader. Bad for the people. Bad for the country. And he was willing to stalk and imprison this young woman to use her for his own purposes. But was it any worse than what he, or his campaign was doing? Of course not. Alfonso wanted to use her; Buxton's people—his people—wanted to kill her.

He struggled to quell a rising panic. In his entire career, he'd never panicked. This was not the moment. He didn't want to quit. He promised himself if he went down, Alfonso was going, too.

"She says if we don't leave her alone, she'll use the tape," Ken Bass said. "I think she's going home to get it."

"Jesus!"

"I don't think she wants to use it. Because of her mother. But she doesn't see she has a lot of options. She's got her back to the wall."

"Can we contain it"" he repeated.

If she got the tape, Alfonso might get it from her. Damn! He'd never imagined it might come to this. That tape was supposed to have been destroyed. "For God's sake, call Frank off before—" He hesitated. 'What the hell do we do now? You'd better get Frank in here. We need to talk."

The door burst open. Maggie Buxton, her face as pink as her robe, stormed in, Frank Follet right behind her. She pointed a finger at her husband, so angry she could hardly speak. "You! You lying, cheating bastard! How could you do this to me! How could you have a child with another woman and never tell me? How could you!"

She slammed the pictures down in front of him. "And try as I may, the goddamned girl won't die!"

"For Christ's sake, Jim. She didn't mean it literally. You can't seriously think we're out there gunning for the girl."

Buxton looked up from his contemplation of the carpet. He swallowed, perhaps for the first time in his political career at a loss for words. He took a deep breath, opened his mouth, then, without speaking, resumed his study of the carpet.

"Jeez, Jim," Frank continued. "You can't imagine I'd take a chance like that with your campaign. Sure, I've been accused of being willing to do whatever it takes, but there's ruthlessness and there's insanity, which is what you seem to be accusing me of." He carefully adjusted his suspenders.

"I've never been accused of insanity. Why, if I didn't recognize the stress we're all under, I'd be deeply offended at your lack of faith."

"Save it, Frank."

They say when you're drowning, your whole life rushes before your eyes. Buxton felt like he was drowning now, drowning in a filthy pool of political duplicity, ambition and corruption, in the meltwater of his own high hopes and personal failures. Drowning because he'd neglected to check the equipment himself and now he was stuck in a leaking lifeboat with no life jacket. He was drowning in the conflicting currents of his own emotions, with a lifetime in politics floating through his mind like old news clips. Highlights of a career he wasn't ready to see end.

Incredible as it seemed, even though he was running for the Presidency, a race that represented the consummate exercise of political ambition, he hadn't understood until now how ambitious he was. Ambitious enough to want to believe Frank Follet, believe Maggie hadn't meant what she said. He wanted to believe the woman he'd shared thirty-five years of his life with couldn't cold-bloodedly contemplate the murder of two innocent people, one of them his own child. Wanted to believe, but didn't.

They were all waiting for him. He could feel their eyes on him. He wanted the presidency, a job that called for a decisive nature, for a ruthless—Frank's good word—ability to make decisions. Courage under pressure. He didn't feel presidential. He felt like throwing up. In this room with his wife, his two closest friends, and the campaign manager he despised, he didn't see any of them.

He saw Lila Friedman's face in the doorway of his office, her shining eyes slightly slick with tears, her brilliant smile a little shaky. Saying, in her husky voice, "You give 'em hell in Washington, Jim. The only way I can bear having my heart broken, the only way I can bear losing you, is knowing that every one of us who cares about Maine, about honesty in politics, and about vulnerable people, gains by having you looking out for our interests in Washington." One tear running in a shining river down her cheek.

"I'm not coming to the party," she'd said. "I'd cry and make a fool of myself. I don't like making a fool of myself and I don't like people knowing my business. I haven't got a politician's face. I'd look at you and everyone would know this silly baby lawyer has fallen in love with her boss."

He'd wanted to brush away the tear, take her in his arms, and swear he'd never leave her.

But Lila had been good at reading his mind. "Don't even think it, Jim. You can't turn back now. So few decent people get a chance at a higher calling like this. You've been honored with a very special opportunity. Take it and don't look back. And don't worry about me." She'd touched one small fist to the breast of her jacket. "You will always be in my heart. My own private hero. I'll be fine. I'm getting to do what I love."

She'd shut the door and kissed him one more time, leaving the wetness of tears on his face. "Go out in the big bad world and do good, Jim. And don't lose your soul."

He'd never seen her again.

Don't lose your soul. Buxton looked into the well of emptiness inside him and wondered if he had. He raised his eyes from the carpet. "Let's assume you are more ruthless on my behalf than I am for myself, Frank. And have taken certain steps to prevent embarrassment?"

Frank Follet managed a sickly smile but said nothing.

"Call off your jackals, Frank. Leave Lila Friedman and my daughter alone." The only response was a low growl from Maggie when he said "daughter." She bared her teeth and he fought the urge to shield his throat.

When none of them moved, he shifted to the issue that consumed them all, and snapped out his questions. The beginning of damage control. "Do we have complete deniability on this? Can anything be traced back to us? What else do we need to do?"

Frank had located his voice. "Find the girl. Find the tape. And find a way to keep her from talking."

Jesus, Buxton thought, he hasn't heard a word I've said. Nor did he miss the look that passed between Frank and Maggie. So it was true. He should fire Frank right now and file for divorce.

"Call off your jackals," he repeated.

"Here must all distrust be left behind;
all cowardice must be ended."
—Dante Alighieri, *The Divine Comedy*, "Inferno"

CHAPTER TWENTY-EIGHT

Jenny waited in an impatient silence while Dizzy opened the shop, stoked the Russian fireplace that provided heat, and went to work on a snowmobile sitting with its guts exposed in the center of the room. Gus went to work restocking shelves, loading the soda machine and sweeping the floor. She wished he'd given her a chore, something, anything to distract her from nervously watching of the phone.

Part of her wanted to collapse in a giggling heap at the image of herself as an avenging angel. If he hadn't been so fierce and formidable, she would've poked Dizzy in the ribs and asked how he could seriously believe she had the ability to avenge her mother? Yet there was something inspiring in the idea that this taciturn man who had such a worshipful vision of her mother imagined she possessed similar abilities.

She was deep into imagining herself an avenging angel when the phone rang. Dizzy dropped his wrench, wiped his hands on a greasy rag, and answered. She froze, suspended, her head cocked toward him even though she couldn't hear a thing, as he listened, scribbled something, and asked a few questions. Then he hung up the phone.

"Your reporter," he said. "Andy says you're to meet someone named Marcia Shelton at eleven-thirty at The Brewery in Augusta. You know where that is?"

She nodded. "Anything else?"

The unscarred half of his face lifted in what she took for a smile. "Your mother opened her eyes."

An electric tingle rushed through her, bringing tears to her eyes. Dizzy hugged her carefully. "This is very good news," he whispered. "But she is not safe until—"

"I take care of business," she finished.

"Where do you go, then?" he asked.

"Waldoboro, then Augusta."

"Okay, then Gus knows where to take you. Gus!"

His nephew set down his wrench and wiped his hands. Once again, Dizzy gave a series of instructions in French. This time she followed enough to recognize that Dizzy was not just giving instructions about where they were to go, but also reminding Gus to take care of himself and of her, so as not to get Dizzy in trouble with Gus's mother, or Jenny in trouble with her mother. Under the circumstances, a hard set of instructions to follow. When he was done, Dizzy turned back to her. "You will both be very careful, yes?"

She nodded.

"Watch out for each other? And don't be foolishly heroic?"

"I thought that's what you wanted?"

"Heroic, yes. Foolish, no." He set a gentle hand on her shoulder. "May goodness watch over you, Jennifer Cates." He picked up his wrench and returned to work.

She climbed into the VW beside Gus feeling like she'd been given a blessing. She'd need all the watching over she could get. She fastened her seatbelt and they set off, the ancient bus surprisingly smooth on the frost-heaved roads. The heater didn't seem to work, so she shoved her hands into her pockets. They rode in silence, Jenny occasionally glancing at the road behind them, looking for someone who was following. As far as she could see, the road was empty.

"You think someone will be following?" Gus asked.

"How would anyone know where we're going? The only person who knows is your Uncle, and he would never tell. Yet everywhere I've gone, someone has been there. Either they're waiting there, or following."

"But you keep looking. And what do you see?"

"Nothing."

"I, also, see nothing. But just to be safe, we will be changing cars soon."

"Your uncle didn't say anything about changing cars."

"It is never wise for one person to know the whole plan, yes?"

Brighter than he appeared, as Dizzy had said. "Yes."

They stopped at a garage in Union and Gus went inside. A minute later, the door opened, he drove inside, and the door closed. "Come on," he said. Jenny got out and followed him through the back door, where they both got into the capped back of a rusty old pickup. It roared to life and went rocking off down the road. A few bumpy miles later, they emerged in a farmyard. Gus thanked the driver, then the two of them, Gus's rifle, and Jenny's shotgun, got into a dark Subaru and drove away.

She didn't ask about his rifle. "I feel like someone from a spy novel," she said. She didn't add that it was a bad spy novel with a frighteningly young and inept heroine. Nor did she use the time to rehearse what she would say when she finally met with the reporter. When she got there, whatever came out was what she'd say.

"Me, too."

Jenny was troubled about dragging him along. Even though he'd given some thought of his own to planning, she wondered if he had any idea what she might be getting him into. But she had no space for guilt today. She reached down and ran a hand along the stock of the shotgun. She'd use it in a breath if she had to.

She settled into impatient waiting until Gus stopped beside the cinder-block building housing the butcher and storage facility where her grandfather and uncles had brought sheep, steers, and the deer they shot to be butchered, wrapped, and stored. "Wait out here, please," she said. "And keep an eye on things."

Gus nodded. She got out of the car, fear lying in her stomach like a big lead weight, and went inside. This was too important. If she didn't find the tape here, she had no plan B. The walk from car to the door seemed endless. Any second, she expected something to strike her between the shoulder blades. A voice in her head cried, "don't make me do this."

By the time she reached the door, she felt like she'd done a marathon. She turned the knob and entered, the door closing behind her with a *whomp*. As she looked around for someone to direct her, she let her breath slowly out, hoping this was what Uncle Billy meant when he said he'd "iced" the tape.

When she came out, the wrapped, frost-rimed video tape in her pocket cold against her side, a police car was parked beside the Saab. A man in uniform leaned in the window, talking to Gus. She would have retreated back inside, but the man straightened and looked right at her, one hand on his gun, the other giving what looked like a friendly wave.

She'd had too much experience with the friendliness of the police. She struggled to quell rising panic as she considered her options. There might be a back door, another way out, a chance to run. There also might be another police car on the other side of the building. She was in Buxton's territory now, just as she'd been in Alfonso's before. No way of knowing how much these people stuck together.

She hadn't come this far to quit without a fight.

She took another step backward, fumbling for the doorknob as the officer took a few steps toward her. She found the knob and stepped backward. In an instant, she'd slipped through. The man behind the counter who'd led her to Billy's locker was staring curiously.

"Forgot something," she said. "If I could just have the key again."

Impatiently, she held out her hand, feeling the weight of the seconds as he fumbled for the key. As he slipped it off the hook, she heard the crunch of feet on the steps. "Here you go, honey. You know where—"

She snatched it from his hand and dashed through the door, but it was too late. No sooner had the door closed behind her than it opened again, and Gus and the officer were there, looking for her through the frosty haze. There was no other way out. She looked around for something to use as a weapon. In one corner, a man was stacking wrapped packages into a freezer. A slab of frozen meat would be good, but this meat wasn't frozen. Slowly she backed away from them, deeper into the haze. Step by step they kept advancing.

Something clanged by her feet. She bent down and picked up a rusted crowbar. Not much against a gun, but it was something. "Don't come any closer," she called.

"Jennifer." It was Gus's voice. "I didn't mean to frighten you. I only wanted you to meet my Uncle Stephen. He is loaning us some bulletproof vests."

"How do I know I can trust him?" she asked.

"Please, Miss Cates," the second voice said. "I didn't mean to frighten you. I'm just helping Gus out."

They sounded so innocent, so sincere. But she'd trusted people before and it had gotten her beaten and battered. Now she was standing in the haze of a gigantic freezer wielding a crowbar she could barely lift against two big men, one with a gun. Her own gun outside in the car.

Their feet crunched slowly toward her.

"Look, Jenny," Gus said. "Honestly, no one's trying to hurt you. Anything happens to you and Uncle Dizzy'll kill me, you know that. Why would I go to so much trouble, switching the cars, the whole thing, just to hand you over to the cops?"

The answer involved handsome cops and their even handsomer brothers. It involved generous women who took in strays and sold them out. It involved chatty artisans who lied. It was written in their Braille on her body and singed by pain and fear into her mind.

They were off to her left now, moving not separately to trap her but together. Not smart, unless they were telling the truth. She wasn't sure she even knew what truth was any more. She threw the crowbar behind them, knowing they'd turn to follow the clang, and when they did, she rushed for the door and let herself out, throwing the key at the astonished man behind the desk as she raced for the car. She wrenched the door open, staring in disappointment at the empty ignition.

She grabbed the shotgun, quickly jacking two shells in. She raised the gun to her shoulder and trained it on the steps, watching as Gus and the man he claimed was his uncle came to an astonished halt.

"Young lady," the officer called. "So far, there isn't any trouble between us. So far, it's fine with me if you and Augustine just get back in that car and go on your merry way. But pointing a loaded gun at a police officer can get you into serious trouble."

He waited to let her process, though to Jenny's mind, her trouble was no more serious than it had been before he made the speech.

He was a short, round man with thick, dark eyebrows and a small, dapper mustache, except for the mustache the physical opposite of Dizzy. She was shaking from nervousness and being in the freezer, but he seemed perfectly calm. "Here's what we'll do," he said, "so you'll know you can trust me. I'll put down my gun. Then you put down your gun. How's that?"

He didn't wait for her to answer. Before she could react, he flipped his gun out of the holster, laid it on the ground, and stepped away. If she'd truly been as crazy and trigger happy as she wanted him to believe, she would have shot him the instant he went for his gun. He had taken that risk. With shaking hands, she set her own gun on the ground at her feet and turned away, sick to her soul at how close she'd come to violence.

She sensed rather than saw Gus come and pick up the gun, eject the shells, and put them in his pocket. "My uncle, Stephen Pelletier. Jennifer Cates." Introducing them as though nothing had taken place.

Jenny, still caught up in the enormity of what had just happened, couldn't meet the officer's eyes. She rested her head on her arms. "I'm sorry. I'm so, so sorry."

He lowered the outstretched hand but didn't back away. "How I know you're what Augustine says, and not some gun-crazed nut, is that you're feeling bad about what you did, aren't you?"

She nodded, still not meeting his eyes. Some tough cookie she was, marching boldly forth with a shotgun and then afraid to use it. No. That wasn't true. She'd used her judgment, like people are supposed to. She hadn't shot an innocent man just because she was scared and had a gun in her hands. They hadn't entirely succeeded in turning her into a monster.

She pushed herself away from the car and turned. "Yes, Mr. Pelletier. Officer. You're right. I'm feeling terrible. If I were to explain. If I had the time and you believed the crazy story I have to tell, you'd understand."

He patted her shoulder in a fatherly way. "You two better get going, if you're going to be in Augusta by eleven-thirty. Threatening a peace officer with a loaded gun is bad enough. I wouldn't want you speeding, too."

He was letting them go? She couldn't believe it. Gus opened the door, put the gun in the car, and waited for her to get in. He pointed to the back seat. "Bulletproof vests. Uncle Stephen loaned them to us."

"And don't make me be having second thoughts about it, either," the officer said. "I want 'em back unharmed and I don't want to be reading in the papers about some gun-happy college girl home on spring break going around shooting any cops, either, you hear?"

She swallowed. "I'll do my best, sir." She shook his hand and climbed into the car. Gus waved good-bye to his uncle and they rolled out onto the highway.

"Through sense and nonsense, never out nor in.
Free from all meaning, whether good or bad,
And in one word, heroically mad."
—Dryden, "Absalom and Achitophel"

CHAPTER TWENTY-NINE

"Find what you were looking for?" Gus asked, as though nothing had just taken place.

"I think so." She leaned back against the seat. Closed her eyes. It could be weeks before she stopped shaking and her mind cleared, and in a little over half an hour she was meeting a reporter who'd expect her to be coherent. "I can't believe I did that. I could have shot him."

"You wouldn't have." Gus shrugged. "Uncle Stephen's cool, isn't he?"

"Yes. This restaurant. The Brewery. Do you know it?" she asked.

"Been there," he said.

"What's the set-up?"

He frowned, then said, "Oh, right," and considered. "It's in kind of like a strip mall. Just a couple stores. There's this semi-circular drive that comes in, with parking around the sides and a little patch of green lawn, well, green in the summer, between the drive and the street."

"No parking or entrance in the rear?"

He shook his head. "I've never actually looked, but I don't think so. Don't see how there could be. There's buildings off another street right behind."

"So if we drive right up to the door and you let me out, there could already be other people there in the parking lot, waiting for us, knowing it's the only way in?"

He shrugged. "I guess so."

"I don't like it," she said. "It doesn't sound safe. You didn't happen to bring binoculars, did you?"

"No. Sorry."

"Cell phone?"

"Sure."

"It's just I have this feeling that unless I change the course of events, this is going to be a very bad day. That it's already a very bad day."

"Premonition?" he asked.

"Educated guess based on past experience."

"So what do you want to do?" he asked, holding out his phone.

"Call the restaurant, find this woman I'm supposed to meet, and arrange to meet somewhere else."

"Like where?"

"Someplace public where there will be people around, where there's more than one way in. The TV station or the State House or the State Library. I'd like to lower my chances of getting shot."

"Sounds like a plan." He checked his watch. "So when do you want to do this? You're supposed to meet her in what? Ten minutes? And we're about five minutes away. You want me to pull over?"

"Guess you'd better."

She tried not to let on how tension was winding her up. She felt like the cowboy in an old western beginning that long, lonely walk down Main Street, hand hanging by the holster on her hip, heading for a showdown. The daylight, things they passed, impressions, sensations, had all taken on a strobe-light quality, coming to her in bits and pieces, intense flashes that briefly penetrated the density of her fear.

He pulled off at a Dunkin' Donuts—there was no way he could know how that spooked her—and she made the call. Her movements also had a strobe quality. Tense and jerky. She had to think about how to use the phone. The fingers punching in the number seeming not to belong to her. The world felt distant and black and white; the air had an electric charge. People in cars passed, going about their normal lives.

The girl who answered at The Brewery seemed to consider it a huge imposition to find a patron who was waiting for someone. "Look," Jenny said harshly. "I wouldn't bother you if it wasn't important. Tell her it's a matter of life and death." She thought if someone called, sounding upset and said something was a matter of life and death, she'd hop to it, but the girl's bored response was she'd go see.

Good thing Jenny, a madwoman on spring break with a shotgun, wasn't actually at the restaurant. Morality or no morality, she was no longer responsible for her actions. This whole thing had been set in motion by others, but she had a major role to play and soon it would be her turn to go on stage.

She sat in the borrowed car in the middle of her disjointed reality, listing to distant voices and clattering bar sounds, fear roiling inside her, until finally a voice on the other end said, brisk and businesslike, "Marcia Shelton."

"Ms. Shelton, it's Jennifer Cates."

"Yes?" Cautious. Reserved.

"I'm sorry about this but we need to meet somewhere else."

"I've already rearranged my day so that I could meet you here. I wouldn't have bothered except I was asked as a favor to your mother. What's the problem?"

"The problem is that there is a man, maybe more than one, outside the restaurant waiting to kill me, Ms. Shelton."

"That's a bit dramatic isn't it, Ms. Cates?"

"Does that mean you don't believe me?"

"I only said—"

"Someone attacked my mother and tried to kill her, didn't they?" Jenny interrupted.

"Well, yes, but—"

"That was dramatic, but it was real, wasn't it?"

"Uh. Yes." Hesitant, as if Ms. Shelton didn't get it and didn't want to.

"But if I say the same people are trying to kill me, that's too dramatic?"

"I only meant that it seems highly unlikely that someone would attempt to attack you right here, in broad daylight, in front of many witnesses. What's this all about, anyway?"

"I'll explain all that when we meet. I'm just saying we need to meet somewhere else, Ms. Shelton."

The reporter wouldn't budge. "I'll wait fifteen minutes. You can meet me here or not. I don't have time to meet you someplace else." All snooty and dismissive. This woman was no friend of Lila Friedman. Lila Friedman's friends cared.

"Do you have a camera person with you?" Jenny asked.

"No. Why?"

"Because I'd hate to get shot down in the street without someone there to record it. How long will it take you to get one?"

"Is this some kind of a joke?"

"Depends on your sense of humor. I haven't found very much funny lately. I doubt if I'll find this amusing either. But if I were you, I'd call a camera crew. It isn't every day that you get a political assassination on the streets of Augusta. It might make your career."

"I'm sorry but I don't understand," the reporter said. "Explain what the hell's going on or I'm leaving."

"I'm only doing it once. Face to face," Jenny said. She hung up before she lost it completely. She was patient, but there was a time and place for everything. She'd had such high hopes that this woman would put her on the air and give her a chance to make everything right. She's ready to deliver her soul and she's delivering it to a clueless idiot? This was complicated enough to explain to someone with a brain. She flashed back to trying to explain things to Araby. Jenny had sounded totally demented. Today, though, she had no choice. She'd have to try. If she made it that far.

She disconnected and looked around. The world hadn't righted itself. It was black and white with splotches of color, like an old hand-tinted photograph. The passing traffic seemed part of a different reality, moving in a different plane and at a different speed. She couldn't lose it now. She scrambled to pull herself together.

She was Lila Friedman's daughter, the maker of plans. But how can you plan for death and disaster? How can you organize the way you walk into a blood bath? How can anyone, even your mother, expect you to be coherent when dealing with a completely incoherent experience?

She would be late, but there was something she had to do. She called all the newspapers she could find, as well as Shelton's TV station and the local cable station, telling them there had been a shooting in The Brewery parking lot, hanging up when they asked for details. If something happened, she hoped to have an audience.

Gus turned on the engine. "All set?"

"She won't change her plans."

"So don't meet her."

In her mind's eye, the cowboy hero—always cowboy, never cowgirl—striding slowly and deliberately down Main Street, hand poised above the butt of his gun, suddenly turned to the on-lookers and said, "I've changed my mind." It wouldn't go down that way. The other guy would shoot him out of sheer frustration.

"No," she said. "It's now or never."

"You're crazy," he said.

"I think you're right."

"Better put on your vest, then. And load up the old blunderbuss."

They helped each other into the uncomfortable garments. Even over her clothes, Jenny was so small she couldn't pull the vest tight. It curved far out over her breasts, leaving several inches on either side exposed. Still better than nothing. She hoped policewomen got their vests custom-made.

"Aren't you scared?" she asked as she pulled her coat back on.

"Shitless," he said. "Doesn't it show? You?"

"Likewise."

"And I'm turning you loose with a shotgun?"

"Think of it…" Her throat was closing. "…as an adventure."

"Here, let me do that." He took the gun from her fumbling hands and loaded it. Good old Remington semi-automatic 12-gauge. Noisy as hell. She watched him load five rounds of #4 buck. Twenty-seven pellets of venom in each round. "Just don't shoot yourself in the foot," he said, handing it back.

Not the first person to tell her that. "I'll do my best."

Right now, she couldn't marshal enough coherent thought to tell someone her name, much less explain her complicated story to a hostile TV reporter. Maybe she should put this off another day. Stride back down Main Street, unload the gun, crawl under Dizzy's bed, and try again tomorrow.

She checked her pockets. Video tape. Butane stove lighter. Shotgun shells. She patted the gun. "Attack when ready, Commander."

THE ALFONSO CAMPAIGN

ON THE CAMPAIGN TRAIL

Morrissey wasn't easily shaken, and he wasn't shaken now, as he looked from Joe Trask, lying on the floor bleeding, to Andy Mason, curled up in a quivering ball. He stared for a moment at the retreating truck, eager to give chase, but his job was here, taking care of his partner and Jenny Cates' battered champion. With a sigh, he holstered his gun and bent to inspect the damage.

Trask had an ugly shoulder wound and he was sorry. Just because you were pissed off at someone didn't mean you wanted them shot. Mason was pretty badly beaten but barring severe internal injuries, would survive. He only wished he weren't hundreds of yards from the car, so he couldn't call in the rest of the surveillance team and leave this situation in their hands while he went after the bad guys.

It wasn't the first time he'd been up against pros. Probably wouldn't be the last. But he felt stupid for not having managed things better. He'd given Trask the back door because he thought it would be safer. No one could have predicted a shooter like the Neanderthal. A wind-up killing machine who didn't stop even when he'd taken several bullets. He'd gotten away but Morrissey didn't think much of his chances.

Morrissey had come here to find Jenny Cates. Now he was stuck working clean-up, with the hours of explaining surely involved, while a cold-hearted killer had gotten away and Jenny's life was still at risk.

He murmured some comforting words to Mason and loped back to the van, hoping in their rushed departure Buxton's men hadn't disabled his communications equipment. They hadn't. He got on the radio, and gave the others the information he'd overheard Andy Mason give Alfonso's thugs: the place and time of Jenny Cates' rendezvous. Then he called the local police and requested cops and an ambulance. He did what he could to make them comfortable, told Trask and Mason help was on the way, and left them in the dingy office, bloody and hurting.

As he rumbled off down the road, his head pounding, he regretted that he hadn't sent Buxton's killers to hell. He believed in hell. Not sure about heaven but he was sure of hell. If there was anything in the world like justice there had to be a place for scumbags who got off too easily up here. One of them, the Neanderthal, was on his way. By now, his partner would have put him out of his misery. Purely a business matter. With a job still to do, he couldn't afford to have the other vulnerable. Watching blood gush from the man's chest, he'd never been more glad he'd taken the time to put on his vest.

He passed a police car, an emergency response team and an ambulance heading the other way. He checked his watch. Ten forty-five. Plenty of time to get into place and wait for Jenny Cates. His eyes slid down to his hands, gripping the steering wheel, the creases limned with blood. He'd have to stop somewhere and wash.

THE BUXTON CAMPAIGN

ON THE ROAD

Mr. Lopes looked across at Mr. Smith, who sat gray-faced and vacant, mouth breathing more pronounced as blood flowed past the compress Smith held weakly against his chest. Lopes pulled out his phone and dialed. "Messer? Lopes. Yeah. Bit of a dust-up, I'm afraid. Nothing to worry about, but you need to take over for a bit. Yeah. Girl's heading for a meeting with a TV reporter at The Brewery. A restaurant in Augusta. Eleven forty-five. She is not to keep that appointment. Do whatever is necessary."

He listened for a moment. "I know what Baldy wants, but there's no way we're going to try to obtain a tape or documents. If you get a chance, of course you'll search the body for the tape or whatever, but likely there will be too many people around. Shoot to kill and get the hell out."

He pressed "end," shaking his head. He couldn't remember a more botched job. He turned to his companion. Smith looked awful. "Jesus, Smith," he said. "How could you?"

Smith's rictus didn't much resemble the smile he'd intended. "Rotten luck," he breathed. "Fuckin' cops. Get me… hospital, Lopes. 'kay?"

Lopes pointed the gun he'd been holding under his coat at Smith. "Sorry, old buddy. Survival of the fittest and all that, eh?"

Smith slumped against the door and was still.

God! Another few hours listening to that breathing and he would have done this even if Smith hadn't needed to be eliminated. The man was an animal. He was going to have to speak to Dino. Smith hadn't been a bad guy to have watching his back, and he hadn't flinched at the dirty work, but the man took too many chances. That last cop, for example. Smith hadn't needed to kill him, and he'd cost them both time and a car. Every time you killed someone, every time you had to change cars, it created risks. And risks were what got you caught.

"Sorry, buddy," he told the corpse beside him. "Hope you carried lots of life insurance."

An hour later, Smith and the hick's pickup had gone for a swim and he was ready to join Messer and Trudeau and end this thing. It had gone on long enough.

"...from all the deceits of the world, the flesh, and the devil,
good Lord, deliver us...
from battle and murder, and from sudden death,
good Lord, deliver us."
—"The Litany," from *The Book of Common Prayer*

CHAPTER THIRTY

Gus started the van, but before they moved, Jenny put a hand on his arm. "Wait."

He gave her a curious look. "Thought you were on a deadline?"

"First things first," she said. "This whatever it is we're... I'm about to do, Gus? My intuition tells me it's going to be very dangerous. But it's..." She fumbled for how to say this without offending him. "This is my problem, Gus. Something I have to settle before I can get on with my life. Grateful as I am for your help, I don't want to drag you into something that could get you hurt or even killed. Your uncle made me swear I wouldn't. He said your mother would kill him if anything happened to you."

Gus still looked puzzled, on the verge of insisting that he had to follow her because his Uncle Dizzy had told him to.

"Look, probably I'm doing this all wrong," Jenny said. "I'm just trying to say you don't have to come with me. I don't want you to come with me. Just drop me at the door and drive away. I've seen too many bad things happen in the last week. I can't be responsible for something bad happening to you."

His face, the frowning brow and stubborn chin, the eyes that wouldn't look at her, said it wasn't working. She gripped his arm tightly. "Gus, please understand. This isn't about whether you're brave enough or tough enough. That's not why I'm asking you to stay out of this. It's not even because your mother and my mother would be mad. It's because I've got too much on my mind already. There's too much hanging on this without the distraction of you getting hurt."

She waved her hands helplessly. "Put yourself in my place. I need my mind clear for what I've got to do. If you're there to back me up, I'll be thinking about you, watching for you, wondering if you're okay. I can't do what I have to do if I'm worried about you."

"Yes, but—"

"That's just it, Gus. I can't have any 'yes, but.' I need a clear yes. That's all. I need you to drop me at the door and drive away so I'm not distracted by worrying about you. Okay?"

Sullenly he said, "Okay."

"Good. Thank you. I guess we'd better get going."

"Whatever you say."

What did she expect? She'd asked him to stay out of the biggest adventure of his life. He wasn't going to thank her.

The car began to move slowly down the street and it was back in her head again, the stately walk down Main Street toward the showdown. Lunatic delusions of grandeur. It was probably a stately walk into a bad restaurant to talk to a hostile reporter and she'd wasted a couple minutes. But she had to trust her intuition. At worst, Buxton's team would win and she was enjoying her last minutes on this planet. At second worst, she'd get out of the car and there would be Morrissey and Trask waiting to drag her away and lock her up again.

She felt like throwing up.

She reminded herself of what Dizzy had said when she wanted to run away from this. Her mother would never let her be hurt and walk away; now she was the one who couldn't walk away. Was this what people had in their heads when they walked into perilous situations? Did they go in conscious of their missions or with nothing in their minds except the pounding of their hearts and an overarching sense of unreality? Did they recite mantras to themselves to keep them brave? Did their own personal war songs run through their heads?

Soon she'd know.

She flexed her hands as she mentally reviewed how to fire the gun. When she got there, things would happen fast. She'd have no time to think. It was a heavy thing, about eight pounds, but it didn't have the kick some guns had. Dandy had chosen carefully, knowing she was black and blue enough already. He'd had the gun there waiting for her. Dandy. Other than her parents, her first and always hero.

She closed her eyes and imagined swinging the gun smoothly to her shoulder, aiming and firing. What was it called? Visualizing. She visualized shooting another human being. Ran through it again. Teeth clenched, she shot Governor Lucius Alfonso. Shot James Buxton, the father who had abandoned them, setting all this in motion. Felt the anger start, the adrenaline beginning to flow. Felt the stiffness leaving her fingers as the deadly sarcophagus of fear shattered and fell away, freeing her for action.

"Here we are," Gus said. "Are you sure you want to do this?"

Her "yes" was more growl than affirmation. She wriggled down until she was out of sight. "Drive through once and tell me what you see."

He flipped on his turn signal and cruised with agonizing slowness through the parking lot. "We come in from the right as you're facing the door. A couple cars away, there's a big guy sitting in a black van. About six cars down, on the left hand side of the door, there are two men sitting in a silver Taurus. Down toward the far end, another guy, sitting by himself. That's all I saw." He hesitated. "Jenny, that's too many people."

"I'm just running up the steps and in the door, Gus."

"If you make it that far. I have to—"

"No, Gus. What you have to do is let me off and drive away."

Silent and with jaw set, he circled the block, turned on his blinker, and drove slowly back into the parking lot. She picked up the shotgun and stuck it under her coat, one hand on the gun, the other on the door handle. She didn't think she was breathing as she scanned the cars, looking for the men Gus had spotted. Then they were at the steps. The van stopped and she opened the door. Stepped out awkwardly, trying not to trip over the gun. Too bad they didn't make them in petites. The Barbie pink 12-gauge blaster.

She started up the steps, eyes darting in both directions. Someone on her left moved, then someone on her right. A voice yelled, "Jenny, watch out!"

Morrissey. Why was she not surprised? She turned in that direction as she reached the top step, just as something slammed into her back with such force it plastered her against the door, taking her breath away. She bounced off and was falling, terrible pain in her back. She'd been hit by a battering ram. Gasping, mad as hell, furious adrenaline pumping, she forced herself back up, raised the gun, turning to her left, hand already on the trigger. A man was running toward her with a gun in his hand. Head, body, legs, she thought, squeezing the trigger. One. Two. Three. He looked so surprised as he fell, blood blooming, the gun dropping from his hand.

Deafened by the gun's blasts, she couldn't hear anything except echoes of the roaring that seemed to go one and on. But he wasn't alone. Another man was getting out of the car. How many shots left? One? Two? Had she loaded five? She didn't have time to reload. Vaguely, then, she heard voices shouting, people screaming. A woman standing in the doorway, staring at her, who had to be Marcia Shelton, her mouth moving. A TV talking head with the sound turned off.

Her back felt like someone had fired a cannon right through her. Vest or no vest, she was sure she'd been blown up. She could feel the tear in her skin, the burning agony of it, sure these were her last minutes and she had to make the best of them. The second man, like the first, was running at her with his gun out. Jenny "John Wayne" Cates lifted the heavy gun again. Playing through the pain. Fuck 'em. She might be dying but she wasn't going down alone. She shot again. He zigzagged. She followed, tracking him like a can through the air, aimed where he was going to be, and squeezed. Watched the gun fly out of his hand in an explosion of blood. If the TV cameras hadn't gotten here, too bad for them.

"Jesus, Jenny, get down!" Morrissey came flying at her, snaked an arm around her waist, pulling her down onto the cement, back behind one of the thick pillars that supported the roof over the entrance. Bullets slammed into the bricks where her head had been, bits of brick and dust flying. The woman in the doorway was still staring.

"Get back inside," he barked, loud enough so even Jenny, in her deafened state, could hear.

Still the woman stared.

"You wanna get your fuckin' head blown off?"

She retreated.

"Third guy's got a rifle," he said. He was panting, breathless. "You got hit. I saw it. How on earth did you?"

His hands went under the coat, feeling for the wound, finding the vest. He smiled, proud as a dad at his kid's first steps. "Wearing a vest."

"They made me. My friends." It hurt to talk. Hurt to breathe. She'd come here to talk so she could keep on breathing. So her mother could keep on breathing. So they could stay alive. And now she couldn't talk. "Hurts," she said.

"You bet it hurts," he agreed, "but it's a hell of a lot better than being dead. Which you otherwise would be."

"I'm not dead?"

"No, Jenny. Far from it." He was speaking very loudly, and close to her ear, so she could hear. "Stay here. I'm going after him."

"Morrissey, why?"

His eyes were scanning the parking lot. "Later," he said, then added, "Serve and protect. Protect you. Living, breathing human being, remember?" He squeezed her hand. "First hero I've had in years. I had no choice."

He began edging away.

"Morrissey. Tom. Don't go."

But he was moving away from her.

She tried to put her urgency into her voice. "Wait…"

He hesitated, turned toward her. She reached up, trying to grab his sleeve. "You'll get shot."

Her voice was too soft. Not enough to stop anyone. The cement beneath her was cold and gritty. She'd been here before. Lying on the cold, cold ground, wrapped in pain. She turned her head sideways, watching as he crept away. The gunman she could see, that he couldn't, raising that lethal rifle again, pointing it, aiming it.

She reached in her pocket for shells, fumbled for her gun. She'd never make it in time. Couldn't force herself up again. She was right here and yet it seemed unreal, unfolding before her disbelieving eyes like a TV drama. Watching Tom Morrissey heading toward death, watching death get ready. Suddenly, the gunman's body jerked, the rifle flying up, the shot that was to have ended Morrissey's life sailing wildly away into the air. The gunman seemed to hang there, clutching the rifle, as if suspended in the air, before finally falling to the ground and staying there in a boneless stillness that could only be death. At the far end of the lot, she saw Gus emerge from between two cars, his rifle still pointed at the sprawled figure.

She exhaled and closed her eyes. So much for not getting involved. Gus had gotten his adventure after all.

A woman in an apricot blazer was kneeling beside her. "Jennifer Cates? Marcia Shelton."

"You'll have to speak up."

"Marcia Shelton."

"Now do you believe me?"

"Yes. Yes, of course. Look, I see my camera crew over there. Let me get them and then we can do that interview."

This is what she'd come here for but she wasn't Superwoman. She wasn't even Jane Wayne. She would have loved to get up. To speak eloquently for Shelton's cameras. She couldn't move. Not when all the bones in her back were broken.

Shelton was starting to fuss. "Why are you lying here? Are you injured? Why don't you get up? Come inside? I could help you."

The reporter's busy hands pawed at her. "What's this? You're wearing a bullet-proof vest? That's what this is, isn't it? You really were expecting something like this to happen. Where are you hurt?"

Stupid bitch, Jenny thought. *I told you, didn't I?* "Shot in the back."

Shelton was trying to turn her over, and Jenny was trying to fight her off, when Morrissey returned. "Excuse me, ma'am," he said, "but you shouldn't be doing that, you know."

Shelton's eyes narrowed as she looked around for the microphone she hadn't brought. "Who are you?"

"Lieutenant Tom Morrissey, New York State Police, retired," he said.

Jenny stared. "Retired?"

Shelton beckoned wildly to her camera crew. "All right," she said. "I'm confused. What's the story? What's going on here?"

"I'm afraid, ma'am, that it's Miss Cates' story, but at the moment, she's in no shape to tell it. Right, Jen?" He reached down and took her hand. "Medcu's on their way. Don't talk. Take it easy."

She hadn't come so far to quit now. "But I came here to talk."

It wasn't going to happen.

"You can talk later," he said. He looked like hell. Dull skin and bandaged head. He needed a shave. But his eyes were smiling. Proud. "You wore a vest. You are just so damned smart, Jennifer Cates."

Don't sidetrack me, she thought. *I'm on a mission here.* "Story," she said. "You tell it."

"Me?" he said. "But I'm the bad guy."

Marcia Shelton was so eager she was practically drooling. "The bad guy?"

"One of the bad guys," Jenny said.

"Well, ma'am," he said, and if Jenny hadn't felt like she'd just been kicked by a horse, she would have smiled at his deferential, shy-guy trooper act, "It all began about twenty-two years ago."

THE ALFONSO CAMPAIGN

ON THE ROAD

Keris and O'Malley watched Alfonso pace the room like a hyperkinetic Energizer Bunny, storming from wall to wall, pausing occasionally only to whirl and yell at one of them. Both of them, running on too much abuse and too little sleep, were close to quitting. The more he paced and the more he yelled, the more his language deteriorated until he sounded like a thirteen-year-old trying it out because swearing was a newly acquired skill. In a young boy, it had a bit of innocent charm, in Alfonso it was just ugly.

Finally, O'Malley had had enough. The next time Alfonso turned on him, he held up a hand. "Shut up, Lou," he barked. "Shut and listen."

Alfonso did stop, astonishment all over his face. Then he took a few paces, muttered, "What the fuck? Who works for whom around here, O'Malley?"

O'Malley said, "Shut up, Lou," again.

Keris watched, fascinated, rooting for O'Malley, hoping he'd get a chance to have his say before Alfonso sent them both packing, because she was here to work with O'Malley. She couldn't stomach Alfonso on her own. Half the time, he wouldn't listen no matter how good her advice was. She'd busted her ass trying to broker a potential truce between Alfonso and his daughter, and he wouldn't give her five calm minutes to hear the details. If he didn't listen soon, she'd lose Gina again. She'd had enough of loony abused wives and bitter, manipulative daughters.

"This whole business with Senator Buxton's daughter has gone too far, Lou," O'Malley said. "It's gonna come around and bite us on the ass. It's time to concentrate on your campaign. Focus on who you are and what you're going to do for this country, instead of trying to find an underhanded way to destroy your opponent."

"Don't lecture me, shithead," the Governor said. "I want that girl!"

O'Malley's pale face flushed red. "I've cut you all the slack I'm going to, Lou. I'm not your office boy. I'm your campaign manager. If you won't listen, maybe it's time…"

The phone rang. "Betcha they've got her," Alfonso grinned. A minute later, his countenance considerably grimmer, he set it down, shaking his head. "Trask's been shot."

"Call it off, Lou," O'Malley said. "This is not worth wasting more good men over."

Alfonso shrugged. "Don't know how I can. Morrissey's disappeared. Gone after the girl, I'll bet. Besides, I don't want to call it off."

"Morrissey wouldn't…"

Keris Carlyle cleared her throat. Maybe it was time for a distraction. "Lou," she began, "if I could have a few minutes of your time."

Both men turned and glared at her. "Not now, Keris," O'Malley said.

"Not now, Keris," Alfonso mimicked.

She straightened her shoulders and looked down at the loathsome man. "Jennifer Cates will be the least of your problems if you don't listen to me."

As if sparked by an erratic plug, Alfonso suddenly resumed his pacing. "Don't you two get it? I knock Buxton out of this race, I'll hardly have to think about issues."

In spite of her resolve, Keris heard herself saying, "Oh, come on, Lou. Not even you are that stupid."

The Governor pointed a thick, hairy finger at her chest, marching up to her until it was touching. "You've gone too far this time, you stupid cow. You are fired," he said.

"Go ahead. Fire me, you ugly little pig," she said. "And when your wife and your daughter nail your balls to the wall, don't ask me to sew them back on. I won't. And Mikey won't."

She backed away from the finger, trying not to look to see if he'd left a spot on her jacket. Backed right to the door, not out of deference, but of a desire not to expose her back to the man, and walked out.

Mike O'Malley stared down at his boss. "You listen to me, Lou, or I swear, I'm next. Call this thing off."

"I can't," Alfonso smirked. "Can't reach anyone. Don't know where anyone has gone."

"Who was that on the phone?"

"Van Allen, relaying word from the hospital."

O'Malley, envisioning a disaster worse than the disasters he imagined every day, squeezed his head between his hands and glared at the Governor. "What does it take to get you to see the light? We've got two troopers wounded and one dead, all tied up in this Jennifer Cates thing. If the press gets wind of it, how do we explain New York state troopers getting shot up in Maine, when the Maine cops don't even know about it. You're a governor, you know how this works. We don't go pissing in someone else's back yard. Call Van Allen and tell him to call it off before it's too late."

Alfonso stuck his hands in his pockets, like a kid playing innocent, and tried for an engaging grin. "Nope," he said. "No, Mikey, I won't."

The phone rang again. Alfonso answered. Too frustrated with his boss to care what the man thought, O'Malley picked up the extension as Van Allen said, "Governor, I just found Morrissey's retirement papers on my desk. You know about this?"

"Heck no. I don't care when he retires, once he brings me back the girl."

Van Allen said, "He's not on the job, sir, he's on vacation."

"What the fuck's that mean?" Alfonso growled.

O'Malley replaced the receiver. He knew exactly what it meant. It meant they were about to get bitten on their collective asses. He wished he'd quit, like Keris. But there was a part of O'Malley that wouldn't let him. He was tired, and his head hurt, but he was already searching for a way to put a good spin on this.

THE BUXTON CAMPAIGN

ON THE CAMPAIGN TRAIL

Buxton sat by himself in his room, chin on his fists, and stared at the nondescript carpet without seeing it. All he saw were Lila Friedman's face, that last day when she'd kissed him and walked out of his life, and her daughter's eyes. His daughter's eyes, staring up from the stiff studio photo. Sometimes, when he closed his eyes, he saw their heads exploding. Saw bursts of blood, cascades of blood, ribbons of blood. Blood so vivid he half-expected to see it running between his fingers.

Someone knocked on the door, tentatively at first and then more loudly. "Come in," he called, glad to be interrupted.

Woody opened the door and took a step into the room. It was dim enough so Buxton couldn't see his face but he'd known Woody so long he could almost predict the words before they were spoken. "You have to fire Frank," Woody said. "This whole thing is going to break wide open and he's going to be at the center of it. He's going down, and you're going down, too, if you don't act now."

"Fire Frank because of what I suspect?"

"Fire Frank because of what you know."

"What do I know, Woody?"

"That he tried to kill at least two people, maybe three."

"On my behalf."

"You didn't ask him to."

"No. I didn't ask. But is that my virtue, Woody, or my vice, that I didn't ask soon enough?"

Woody dropped his lean frame into the chair. "I don't know if we can save your candidacy, Jim. I just don't know. But in the long run, it will certainly look better for you if you act before you're forced to."

"You think I'm going down too, don't you?"

Woody nodded sadly.

"But I never knew."

"It isn't always true that what you don't know can't hurt you, Jim. And your wife knew."

"She never told me," Buxton said querulously. He couldn't help it. He'd spent his whole life climbing this mountain and suddenly, just a few hundred yards from the summit, they were telling him they were sorry but he had to go back down. Maybe he could start over and climb again, maybe he'd just have to stay down there. It wasn't fair. He'd given his whole goddamned life for the state of Maine, for the people of Maine, and now they were going to yank the rug out from underneath him for something he hadn't known about. For something he hadn't done.

As if he'd said it aloud, Woody said, "Yes, Jim, but you set the whole thing in motion."

"Jesus Christ, Woody, it was twenty-two years ago! And I loved her."

"You were a married man. You had sex with an employee, a woman who wasn't your wife."

He heard Kenny Bass, reporting on Jenny Cates' phone call in his calm voice. "She says she just wants her life back." Saw his wife storming through the door saying furiously, "...and I keep trying to kill her and she just won't die." And what had he done? Had he tried to save her? No. He'd gathered his advisors and asked how to contain things, leaving her at risk. At risk from his campaign manager. At risk from his wife. At risk, because he'd refused to act, from himself.

As if it were yesterday, he heard Lila's voice. "You give 'em hell in Washington, Jim." Saw her eyes rise and fall, and felt, across the years, the rush he got when their glow fell on him. Those eyes with total faith in him. Love and admiration and an absolute certainty that he was something special.

He looked down at his aging hands and saw her blood on them. He took a deep breath and let it slowly out. He wanted the presidency so badly he'd let it corrupt him entirely, and now he felt that corruption in his mind, in his soul, and he wanted it gone. Maybe he'd waited too long. Maybe the devil had already signed and filed the papers, but maybe it wasn't too late to do the right thing.

He shook his head. The inside felt dusty and he thought it was his expectations and hopes, crumbling. "Call Frank," he said, "and tell him he's fired. Then call my lawyer. Tell him I want a divorce."

"Let the great world spin for ever down
the ringing grooves of change."
—Tennyson, "Locklsey Hall"

CHAPTER THIRTY-ONE

They insisted on putting her in the hospital overnight. "For observation," they said. Jenny thought she'd had enough of being observed, but she was happy to accept the antibiotics for her shoulder and the painkillers for her ruined back. She was even glad to get a new cast for her wrist, having pretty much destroyed the first one. All the rest was old news.

She ought to have been more grateful. The medicine did make her feel better and enabled her to finally have a conversation with Marcia Shelton, on camera, now that the ringing in her ears had faded to a dull hum and she could hear well enough to converse. A complete dog and pony show, with close-ups of wounds and bruises, and a frank, unembellished narrative of what she'd been through in the past week.

It was disagreeable in the telling, not therapeutic, as she'd hoped. For the modest person, there's no satisfaction in publicly baring the soul. It's just another painful exposure, like cold air on a sensitive tooth. Jenny did it because she had to finish the job, and endured the ache in her soul that came from violating her own privacy, and worse, from violating her mother's. And her father's. Her real father, Bud Cates, the man who'd been there for her her whole life.

What it meant to Alfonso and Buxton she no longer cared. She could only hope, the tale being told, that neither side any longer had a reason to try and harm her or her mother. At the end of the interview, as her finale, they stepped outside. She took out the videotape and the stove lighter, and burned the tape. On camera. No other way to prove she'd done it. The salacious world, thinking it was a full color video of Senator Buxton having sex, would never get to see him gray-faced, sweating and begging her weary mother for the painkillers he craved to end his misery.

But once she'd told her story, augmenting the version that Morrissey had given earlier, and everyone had gone away to let her rest, she had reverted to her old willful self. She hadn't taken the sleeping pills they'd offered and she didn't close her eyes and try to get that nice rest the nurse had urged. As soon as she was alone, she'd called the hospital in Portland, asked about her mother, and gotten good news.

She spoke with her father, given him an abbreviated version of the story, and promised to appear in the morning. Maybe she'd go sooner, if she could find a ride. Moving hurt like hell but for once she didn't mind. This pain was the price she paid for still possessing the life people had tried to take. Then she'd crawled out of bed, thrown a blanket over her shoulders, and gone to look for Dandy.

She found him off by himself in a darkened room, unconscious or deeply asleep, his face a battered mess of swelling, stitches and bandages, eyes swollen shut. He barely looked human. Having been there, she knew how he felt. This was all her fault. He'd taken this dreadful battering to protect her. In the past week, she'd learned a lot about selfishness and evil and a lot about goodness as well. She tugged a chair over by the bedside and sat down beside him, taking his hand in hers.

"You never were much for praise, Dandy Mason. I know that. It makes you blush and stammer and drop your eyes and try to change the subject, so I'm going to take advantage of your helplessness and say this stuff while you can't stop me. I always thought I had kind of a hard life, you know, not being popular 'cuz I was the smart girl. Not having brothers or sisters. Having parents who always expected so much of me. Having to grow up in a small town where nothing ever happened and there wasn't anything to do. Boy, was I dumb!"

She felt the trickle of a tear down her cheek. "Despite what has happened, I now know I've been about the luckiest girl in the world. I didn't have one brother. I got to have three, and my youngest brother, you, was the best brother a girl could have had. I used to think that an organized mind and the ability to plan were the most useful skills I had, but they were only part of the mix, weren't they? You were part of helping to me learn to be brave and have faith in myself when things got hard, didn't go my way, or when people were mean."

Her tears were flowing freely now, and she had a dreadful lump in her throat, but she went on talking. What did she care if she sounded like she was crying, if she spilled an ocean of grateful tears for Dandy's quiet goodness?

"I'm really, really sorry about your car. I'm sorry that I wrecked it, and that I cursed it, and that I ever wondered how you could like it. It was just a stubborn, cranky, powerful, badass car. You always did have a soft spot for difficult things. Like me. So I should have known."

She rested her head beside his hand, letting the tears drip onto his fingers and down onto his sheets.

His hand moved, fumbled, and tangled itself in her hair. He mumbled something through swollen lips. It might have been "Spit."

"I'm not much for speeches, either, Dandy. You like living outside, or bent over an engine. I like living inside my head. But I don't think people take the time to say 'thank you' like they should. If I did it properly, I'd still be here sometime next week, just beginning to say thanks for all the times you rescued me. Thanks for teaching me to drive. Thanks for teaching me to shoot. Thanks for thinking I was something special when I thought I was great big dork. Thanks for trying to save my life and trying to prevent my death and for just being you, all real and good and genuine and willing to do things for people instead of turning your back and thinking it's not your problem."

She took a shuddering breath. "I wish I were eloquent. I wish I knew some bigger, better words to say what I want to say. I ought to be writing on a billboard thirty feet high: Dandy Mason is a good man. The words "thank you" and "I love and cherish you" seem so smallish and ordinary. Thank you for being there and believing in me when I didn't even believe in myself. Thank you for being on the team that gave me my tools for life. They were good tools, Dandy, and boy have I needed them."

The hand in her hair moved slightly, tightened, and gradually relaxed. His breathing sounded easier. After a while, she untangled it, kissed him gently on the forehead, and went to make a phone call.

It probably wouldn't work. Dandy's wife was stubborn and difficult. But he loved her, and he loved his daughter. She needed to know about this. And she needed to be made to think about what she was giving up.

After that, she lay in bed, miserable and restless, ready now for sleep that wouldn't come, her mind still moving too fast. After he'd given his statement to Marcia Shelton and ushered Jenny into an ambulance, Morrissey had disappeared, probably to talk with the police. A complicated guy, Morrissey. She still wasn't sure she understood what was going on with him. Maybe someday she'd hunt him down and ask about his change of heart. She thought about the past week. About all the people who had helped. She should write thank you notes.

She closed her eyes and composed them in her head.

> *Dear Rose, Charlie, and the Masons,*
>
> *Thanks for wanting to rescue me, and giving me all your cash, debit card, and love. I lost the money and the card, but kept the love, and it sustained me. When Mom comes home, let's all have a big party with tears and hugs. It's been a hard week but thanks to all of you, I'm still on my feet, sore and battered, but grateful.*
>
> *Love, Jenny*

> *Dear Britt and Dr. Sampler,*
>
> *Thanks a million for the ingenuity, the daring rescue, parts one and two, and for doing what I needed without asking a thousand hard questions. Things are fine here. I'm back home, enjoying a restful spring break. Give my love to Dr. Carnevale and tell him he was right about codeine versus Demerol. See you back at school, Britt, and hope, for me, that they will believe the dogs of politics ate my homework.*
>
> *Love, Jenny*

> *Dear Pansy,*
>
> *Don't worry. I'm still alive. Thanks a million for your hospitality, especially the soup and cookies. Sorry I left in such a hurry and that I lost your hat and gloves.*
>
> *Love, Jenny*

Dear Jerry the Truck Driver,
Thanks for brightening up an otherwise gloomy
adventure with the funniest question I've ever been
asked. Am I a hooker? If I can get battered and bashed,
go hungry and sleepless and run miles through the forest
in the rain and cold, and appear in sodden and muddy
clothes and you still think men would pay money for me,
maybe I'm wasting my talents on a college education.
Anyway, thanks for the laugh (in retrospect) and the
rescue. Both rescues. I know you aren't supposed to pick
up hitch-hikers. And I promise I'll tell Adele Mason you
are a stand-up guy.
                         Sincerely, Jenny Cates

There were so many other letters she could write. To Dizzy and Gus. To Gus's Uncle Stephen, who had given her the vest and saved her life. To Tom Morrissey. Who fell on both lists. The thank you list and the no thank you list.

The no thank you list was long, too. But she didn't want to write those letters. She didn't feel like opening the gates and letting out the venom. She didn't want to entertain hatred and anger. Remembering the good felt too good. She knew that over the next few days, beset by pain and recovery and trying to recoup some of the losses, she'd have plenty of time for anger and rage. She pushed back the covers and swung her feet to the floor. She'd been hanging around here long enough.

It was time to go to Portland.

It was time to go back to her family.

A hand drew back the curtain around her bed. She looked over, expecting to see a nurse, but it was Morrissey. "Are you ready?" he asked.

"Ready?"

"To go to Portland."

"If you help me get dressed." She didn't know if she liked him. She wasn't even sure if she trusted him, yet his timing, and his question, seemed entirely reasonable. So did letting him help her dress. They knew each other not at all and they knew each other intimately. Probably that was all they'd ever know of each other.

An hour later, she walked into her mother's room. The bank of monitors still loomed. Data flashed in many colors as things clicked and hissed. Lines dripped and fluids flowed, including Jenny's tears. The TV screen that was on in her mother's room was full of talking heads—the new top story was that both Senator Buxton and Governor Alfonso had suddenly dropped out of the presidential race. Jenny switched it off with the remote. She tenderly kissed her mother's cheek, sank into the chair, and took her mother's hand. "Hi, Mom," she whispered. "I'm home."

ABOUT THE AUTHOR

Maine native **Kate Flora** has long been fascinated by the darker aspects of human nature. Starting her career in the Maine Attorney General's office, she encountered the raw realities of deadbeat dads, child abusers, and workplace discrimination, sparking her curiosity about what drives people to cross the line. An acclaimed author of 24 books, including several award-winning crime novels, Flora's works have been finalists for the Edgar, Agatha, Anthony, and Derringer awards. *Teach Her a Lesson* was published by Encircle in May 2023. Her latest suspense thriller, *Burn the Diaries and Run*, will be released in October 2024.

Flora is a founding member of the New England Crime Bake and the Maine Crime Wave. She divides her time between Massachusetts and Maine, where she indulges in gardening, cooking, and imagining the next dark deed her characters will commit. When she's not writing, she contributes to the blog Maine Crime Writers and occasionally braves the shark-filled waters off the coast of Maine.

If you enjoyed this book,
please consider writing your review
and sharing it with other readers.

Many of our Authors are happy to participate in
Book Club and Reader Group discussions.
For more information, contact us at info@encirclepub.com.

Thank you,
Encircle Publications

For news about more exciting new fiction, join us at:

Facebook: www.facebook.com/encirclepub

Instagram: www.instagram.com/encirclepublications

Sign up for the Encircle Publications newsletter:
eepurl.com/cs8taP